# Flower of Scotland

By S.W. Gunn

For more information contact:
4109 W. Lydia Ln.
Phoenix, AZ 85041
www.swgunn.com/greenwhale

Design by S.W. Gunn
Cover by Oravelle Studio and S.W. Gunn

Print ISBN 979-8-9882511-1-8
Digital ISBN None

FIRST EDITION 2026

For Scotland.

Trigger Warning:

If you're the sort who needs a trigger warning, I recommend you not read this book.

# Prologue

17 April 2023.

Angus paced and shifted nervously as he stood in the large conference room of the Scottish Parliament building. Taking a moment, he scratched his recently grown thick orange-blonde coloured beard. His time building up to this moment for their movement had its moments, but now the actual revolution was about to begin. Glancing around, he looked over at his men and women who aimed to free Scotland from the far-left Marxist ridiculousness that had overcome it. They were all wearing black and armed to the teeth. Silly stupidity like free shit for everyone to imaginary genders had become so bad that a man would be arrested for merely disagreeing with it. At least a half dozen of his friends who were there now had been tossed in jail for words like 'tranny' or 'man in a dress' on social media. It was all political bullying to control people, and really, the most minor of offense compared to what these people had allowed to happen to so many young Scottish women. Importing those animals and letting them violate innocent people was crossing a line. What was about to happen to these politicians was the least of what they deserved.

A voice echoed through the speakers of the parliament building, "We have a long racist history, and we must atone for the crimes of the past."

Angus blanched with anger. These leaders constantly used emotional manipulation about the past actions of long-dead people to control modern Scots. He had enough of that shit, and in Scotland, it was about to come to an end. His only concern was sitting in a large group in this conference room. There was a lot of trust in the security of the parliament who had also joined the cause. It took about six years to branch out to the point that they were at. Angus and the Scottish Republicans had recruited over twenty thousand men and women, most within the military and police forces within Scotland, for this action. Another politician took the podium to babble on about how evil his fellow Scots were. Angus looked at the monitor. It was Collin Ballie, a god damned 'Conservative'. Angus had had enough of hearing their so-called leaders leading them to their demise with this horseshit.

His close friend and brother-in-law, Liam Gillespie, the head of security for the Parliament, came into the conference room and announced, “It's time lads. We’ve got all of security behind us. Let’s deal with these damned traitors and free Scotland.”

Angus’ men all cheered, which caused him to grin widely. He was nervous, but Scotland demanded its freedom from this evil regime. The Brits did nothing but bend their knees to the same leftist shit as the soon-to-be ex-leaders of Scotland did, so they were not going to help. It was up to Angus and his friends to free Scotland. All his men turned to look at him. He was not even sure how he ended up becoming the leader of the movement. Sure, Angus was just as passionate about Scotland as his men were, but somehow, he ended up being the leader of the group. It was incredibly stressful, especially when rumours that someone was trying to infiltrate their ranks early into their movement had reached his ears, but they made it this far. Now it was just a matter of the men who swore to their cause to stand when things started.

Attempting to sound as confident as he could, Angus declared firmly, “For Scotland.”

His men cheered.

Liam then spoke up, “We’ve gone over the security plans several times. The Edinburgh police Divisional Commander works for us, and he has stated that once we make our move, he’ll purge those left within his leadership framework who aren’t loyal and have yet to be removed. Loyalists within the military and police units of every major city in Scotland will act once our actions are broadcast. We’ve marked your positions in the parliament. Angus, you come with me to the guard post by the podium.”

Liam waved at Angus, who stepped forward. Angus had no compunction about what he was about to do, but he had spent weeks working on his well-thought-out speech that he would be giving before they did it.

Turning to the one-time member of the British military named Harry, Angus asked, “Did you confirm our control over STV?”

Harry grinned widely before announcing, “Aye. I got ‘em ready to broadcast the whole thing. They’ll cut over to us right as we take charge of the Parliament.”

Giving Harry a nod, Angus stated firmly, “Let’s go.”

Liam stepped through the conference room door and glanced to his left. He gestured towards Angus with his head to follow. Angus moved behind him and followed as Liam started walking. He gestured at several key points within the building before stating the name of one or another of Angus’ men. Angus realised the strategic importance of each position. It was quite clear that his men would have complete control over the whole Parliament building. Angus had worked to train them to be ready to hold their position without killing random innocent people; he wanted as bloodless a coup as possible. Finally, the last of Angus' men was set in place, and it was only Angus and Liam left. They walked into the entrance of the main Scottish Parliament area. He was quite happy to see that most of the Parliament and the biggest political leaders were there. Sitting in her normal spot was the First Minister of Scotland, Nicola Sturgeon. She was the current leader of the Scottish National Party. Angus grinned widely, knowing what was about to come. Liam slipped through the crowd and then approached the guard standing near the podium. The man there looked at Angus and Liam before cracking a wide grin and moving aside to let Liam take his post. He nodded at Angus before walking away. Angus groaned as he listened to the idiot from the Scottish Conservative Party finish up his speech with a final diatribe about how evil 'white' people were. Damned Americans and their weird ideas about race had infected everywhere. Finally, the Presiding Officer stepped back up. It was time. As the man started to speak, Angus confidently strolled onto the stage and approached the podium. The Presiding Officer looked very confused as Angus approached him. No doubt the handgun strapped to Angus' hip might have scared him. Giving the man a shove, Angus approached the microphone. Once he got to the stand, he looked around and spotted a pair of his men taking over the control room for microphones and lights. It caused him to grin widely. They had trained for this moment like it was the most important event in their lives, and so far, it has been going smoothly.

Clearing his throat, Angus spoke as loudly and confidently as he could, "My fellow Scots."

The voice of the Presiding Officer, in an almost whiny voice, "Security, remove this man!"

Angus chuckled as he noted that not a single member of the security team had moved. They were all loyal to Scotland. Angus turned to the man as he pulled out his handgun.

He brought his handgun to his lips and said, "Shhhh."

That sufficiently cowed the man, and he shuffled back to his seat. Angus placed his handgun back into its holster. There was a hushed mumble in the crowd around him, but it was clear by the lack of security movement that Angus was not going to be removed.

Angus finally spoke into the microphone in a clear voice, "My name is Angus Bruce. I'm a member of Clan Bruce, and I was born and raised as a Scot. I'm proud of my nation, and I'm proud of being a Scot. Under no circumstances should anyone listen to the words of these traitors who besmirch our glorious homeland. The actions of your ancestors are not the responsibility nor burden of any man or woman living to bear. These politicians moralise about long-dead people not out of any real sense of emotional burden but are attempting to manipulate their fellow Scots to cow to their will."

There was a loud murmur in the crowd as the politicians around him clearly did not agree.

Finally, the First Minister herself stood up and stated in a loud voice, "You have no right to talk about us in such a manner!"

The moment when the coup went from being all talk to action had finally come. Angus knew the entire time that it was going to be him who had to push it forward. Swiftly, he drew his handgun, and in a sudden motion, he aimed it at Sturgeon and fired. The single shot struck true and hit her right on the forehead. She fell backwards to the earth and was dead instantly.

Holstering his handgun, Angus turned back to the microphone and announced, "I'm a true Scot and, like those around me, the time of the globalist Marxist horseshit infecting Scotland has come to an end."

There was a large amount of panic and sudden fear. The politicians began to attempt to flee, but security and Angus' men blocked the doors with their rifles, which forced the politicians back into their seats.

"As you can see," Angus declared, "I have full control of the Scottish Government, and at this point, I'm formally dissolving it. All the lands that have long since been known as Scotland are now under our control. We are formally declaring full Scottish Independence from the United Kingdom and its monarch. All lands owned by real Scots will be maintained as theirs. All lands owned by the United Kingdom, the European Union, or any other foreign entity will become the property of the Scottish nation. Once formal recognition of the Scottish nation has been obtained by the United Kingdom, we will be working with the people of Scotland to attempt to construct a government based on the American Constitution that will include free speech and firearm rights."

A female voice from the crowd called out in a panicked tone, "Who do you think you are to dare make such a claim?"

"I represent the Scottish people who tire of leftist oppression. You silence us, arrest us, and worst of all, you invite foreign invaders into our own land to violate us. Your constant Marxist manipulation of our entertainment, media, education, sports, and every other aspect of life will come to an end. To save Scotland from you globalist scum, we'll begin by removing all people within our borders who are not Scots. If you are a foreigner or of foreign descent and not of Scottish descent, you will have 72 hours to leave Scotland. Those who do not leave voluntarily will be forcibly removed or shot. All mosques within the nation of Scotland will be destroyed, and Islam will be banned. Religions that go directly against good Scottish Christian morality must not be allowed to infect our borders."

Another man spoke up, this time clearly an Asian man, "How dare you insult Islam in such a way!"

Before Angus could reply, Liam strode up to him and, with a backhanded motion, struck the man with a violent blow across his head. The man fell to the earth.

Liam declared, "Fuck Islam."

Giving a slight nod, Angus continued, "We've gained control over the majority of military and police functions within the nation. From this point, all COVID rules and restrictions that have been placed upon the nation are removed. Vaccination is to end immediately. No more mask mandates will be allowed. All other laws as they are now will be maintained except for our edict for the removal of non-Scot people and the tomfoolery with these masks. All United Kingdom military and other security personnel have been detained, and once the United Kingdom recognises our independence, they will be released back into the care of the United Kingdom."

Another parliament member called out, "You'll be crushed, you racist fools."

Giving out a hearty laugh, Angus called out in a sarcastic tone, "Aye. Racist fool, just like every other Scot in Scotland, according to you idiots."

The security and Angus' men all laughed loudly.

"Enough!" Angus bellowed out before continuing firmly, "Scotland is now for the Scots."

His men bellowed out loudly in response, "Here! Here!"

"And we'll be defending it from anyone who tries to enslave the Scots. We're meant to be free men. My own kin once fought in the fields of Bannockburn for that freedom, and now, if necessary, I'll give my own blood for that same freedom. Enough Scottish slavery to the Brits. Enough Scottish slavery to the world order. We're free men as God intended us to be."

Angus turned to face the camera that he knew was sharing the whole event with Scotland and the world through STV, and he then announced, "Join us. You've got nothing to lose but these burdensome chains in which our traitorous leaders have placed upon you."

In a loud voice, Angus sang out, "O' Flower of Scotland."

His men and the security forces began to sing the lyrics of the song along with him. Their voices grew in strength, and Angus was surprised to see a few of the Conservative parliamentarians rise from their positions and join in singing along. It brought a small tear to his eyes.

After the song closed, Angus stated, "And we will stand against Proud Edward's Army again, if we must."

The sounds of gunfire echoed through the Parliament building as Angus' men, along with the security there, fired upon the Scottish Parliamentarians who did not sing along.

# Chapter 1

6 June 2016.

"Move, move, move!" Angus bellowed into his headset as he rolled his character to his side and behind a burning car.

His team has been one of the best in the world in Call of Duty III over the whole year, and he would be damned if some group of Hong Kong teenagers were about to take them out here and now. Angus has been playing the game since its release last year, and somehow, he managed to become the squad leader of one of the best CoD teams in the whole world. Angus knew every nook and cranny on every map.

"Liam, take your team left and flank these bastards. We're gonna snuff 'em out."

"Roger." Liam's voice responded with his thick Scottish brogue.

Angus did not know Liam very well, except that he was about the same age as Angus and he worked for some security company. It allowed him plenty of time at work to play. Like Liam, Angus' employer was great for him to have time to play as well. He worked for Northstar Data Reclamation Services in Sterling. Even at work right now, Angus was able to do his work while playing, and he would not have asked for anything else from a job. Even at a young twenty-two years old, Angus was considered a bit of a guru with computers. A prodigy to the point that he was able to go to college for computer programming at seventeen. The second he graduated; the company snatched him up. He was the guy in the company who could fix just about anything. It gave him a lot of freedom and paid well.

Scratching his stubble-covered chin, Angus declared, "Fine shot!"

Liam and his team took down the mainline defence of their opponents, who were suppressing Angus' team from pushing forward and into the objective. It was going to be easy to finish the final push into the object and take the win. Moving forward through the one-time defensive point of their opponents, Angus and his team rolled into the objective of capturing the point. The game banner popped up declaring victory. Angus grinned madly at his success. The members of his squad all cheered.

Liam's thick accent boomed through the headphones, "Hell ya! The R3CK1NG CR3W did it again! Took out a handful of right cunts."

Other voices of the team bellowed out in victory. The squad they just beat was a guild that had been ranked fourth in the world. None too shabby for Angus and his hodgepodge group made up of randos from all over the U.K. It was all about leadership and following orders. Angus' team accepted his leadership and followed him without question. No doubt the R3CK1NG CR3W will end up in the top four after beating them. It put his team on track for a potential bid in the world championships later this year. Only the top four made it, and he was hoping they could pull it off. After some congratulatory babble between the team, Angus logged off team chat and then out of the game. He did have to do some work after all. Thankfully, most of his work was automated due to his own mechanizations. All those classes on programming paid off, and Angus had developed a program that monitored the entire network and all the connected computers for any technical problems. It was such a good program that his company paid him a significant amount of money for the rights to it. They were selling it now, with Angus getting lifetime stipends from its sale. It did not make Angus rich, but it made it so he would not have to worry about money. Its sale helped him buy a small home in Cornton, a village on the northern outskirts of Sterling, while moving out of his parents' home. It also ensured he likely had a job with the company for a long time, assuming he did nothing stupid. Right as Angus moved away from his computer to check out the few notifications his program gave him, his phone buzzed.

Glancing down, Angus saw that it was a text from Liam, 'Oi cunt, you voting in Brexit?'

Angus grunted. Liam was obsessed with Brexit. It was something Angus honestly did not give a shit about. It did not seem smart to leave a massive trade union, and he really did like the ability to just roll on into Europe anytime he wanted. He did not much care for the frogs and krauts, but he did not really mind the rest. Liam, however, had suggested over and over to him that the Krauts were using it as a new way to take over all of Europe. He was adamant that the EU parliament was useless and just rubber-stamped laws that ignored British sovereignty. More shit that Angus did not care about.

Texting back to him, Angus replied, 'Naw'.

His phone immediately buzzed with several replies as to why he should go vote for Brexit, but Angus did not care about it enough to feel motivated to waste a Thursday going to vote. He just replied to Liam that he would think about it, but had to get to work. He then printed off a list of the potential issues that his program was listing. It was a neat program that would list the possible computers on the network that had a technical issue, big or small. Grabbing the printout, he saw only three people: John Sullivan, Afamefuna Adebayo, and Lisette Ferguson. It was going to be an easy day. The printout made it clear that all three of them had their laptops at home and likely just missed the latest software update. Angus remembered when he first started with technical support, he was told never to close out reports with the 'user error' option, but it had been his experience that ninety percent of the time, it was user error. Angus tucked his small administrator laptop into his tool bag.

"Come with me, my friend." Angus said while picking up his tool bag.

The first stop he made as he weaved through cubicle paradise was Lisette Ferguson. Lisette was new to the company while working in the human resources department. Decoration was fully allowed by the company, and Lisette took full advantage of it. She was a lesbian, and it was Pride month. Her cubicle had a huge rainbow flag hanging from it. Angus was cool with her because she was chill.

"Hey, Angus, you here to fix my Outlook?" She asked as soon as he got close.

Her hair was its normal bright pink colour, but this time she streaked a few other colours to form almost a rainbow along the left side of her head. She was wearing a bright green skirt and a short-sleeved green shirt. Around her neck was a rainbow flag muffler.

Giving her a chuckle, Angus replied, "Sure am. What's it doing?"

"It keeps saying that it needs to be started in safe mode, and when I try, it crashes."

"Did you take your laptop home last night?"

Nodding at him, she said, "Yep. I had some resumes to review and respond to."

Angus clicked the Windows button on the keyboard and chose to restart her computer. He then stepped away to let her sit back down.

"We had a patch last night that needed to be downloaded. Once the restart finishes, it will update your laptop, and it should run fine."

"You're a superstar!" Lisette told him joyfully.

"Ya right. I'm not the one working at home to make sure the company keeps on keeping on."

Lisette gave him a quick hug before sitting back down.

Giving her a quick wave, Angus told her, "Off to help others, have a great day!"

She waved back before saying, "Have fun."

Angus chuckled at her before he started walking. This usually made up a good portion of his days. He also got to work on the software he was developing. It was a new program that would allow employees like Lisette to receive these updates while at home. It was a patch over from the network connecting software the company uses, but it adds the update function. It was going to eliminate some of his work, and he had to admit it was one hell of a cool idea. One that would ingratiate upper management by making it easier for teleworking and allow him more free time to mess around with gaming. After a bit of weaving through a few cubicles and a hallway, he found himself at the office of Mr. Sullivan, the office manager. As soon as Angus opened the door, he spotted Mr. Sullivan sitting at his desk with a look of frustration. As Mr. Sullivan looked up at Angus, his facial expression changed from frustration to happiness.

"As if on cue!" Mr. Sullivan said joyfully.

Angus chuckled at him before asking, "My software let me know you were having issues. What's going on, Mr. Sullivan?"

"I can't log onto my computer. When I try it resets to the login screen."

Angus nodded. This had to do with the login credentials of the user not being properly set up on the main server. Mr. Sullivan just got promoted and had moved his office. The system tracks computers based on their location, so the network team probably did not make the easy update in the database.

"I think I can fix it." Angus told him confidently.

"Thank you so much."

Giving him a grin, Angus nodded. Unlike most of the work laptops, his administrator laptop was designed to connect and work anywhere within the building. Angus opened his laptop and set it up. As the laptop started up, he took a moment to note the room number of Mr. Sullivan's office. Once his laptop was ready, he logged into it and then connected to the server. He was right about Mr. Sullivan's issue. The database had his room number 203 instead of room 221. This alone would cause the laptop to not allow Mr. Sullivan to log in. Angus quickly changed the number and saved his change.

"Go ahead and try now, Mr. Sullivan."

"Okay."

Mr. Sullivan logged onto his computer, and it worked perfectly.

"You are the best, Angus." Mr. Sullivan stated quite happily.

"Thanks, Mr. Sullivan. I'm just doing what the company pays me to do."

"I appreciate it."

Giving Mr. Sullivan a wave, Angus strolled out of his office, making sure to close the door behind him. Angus glanced down at his watch. It was almost lunchtime. Normally, he would head off to lunch right away, but he decided he would try to figure out what was wrong with Funa's computer. Funa was one of those engineers who was brilliant in dealing with fabrication, especially with electrical devices, but his knowledge of computers was just enough to cause trouble. Angus had to deal with computer issues that Funa caused several times. It was not so bad that he felt a need to report it, especially since having work to do kept him employed. Funa always seemed to be messing with things he should not be. As was the case with the past two of Angus' visits, Funa reacted immediately to his arrival.

"Angus! You always seem to know when I'm having computer issues."

Standing about six feet tall, Funa was a skinny Nigerian who had moved to Stirling with his family when he was a small child. Angus was impressed with him as Funa scraped and clawed his way from poverty to becoming an extraordinarily successful engineer. He was easily the best at fabrication in the company. Reflecting on it, Angus realised that even if he did complain about the issues Funa was causing with his computer, the upper management likely would not care due to the amount of money that several of Funa's projects had made them. On top of it all, Angus just really liked the man. He was almost a beacon of what hard work and ingenuity could do. Plus, he was funny as hell.

Chuckling, Angus asked, "What did ya do this time?"

Funa's response let him know right away that Funa did something to his poor laptop that was probably either dumb or bold to make something for work. Many times, he played around with the laptops the company gave them to work with, it was to create something unique that the software for fabricating would not normally allow. Funa just laughed heartily.

"Friend, you caught me red-handed. I was trying to make a new microchip for our planned drone line. Damned software wouldn't do it the way I wanted it to, so I was tweaking it a bit."

Clapping Funa firmly on the shoulder, Angus replied, "You're my best customer, Funa. I'd be without a job if you weren't causing so much trouble."

Funa once again chuckled.

"Well, I guess since I'm providing you with work, I'll confess to my crimes. I tweaked the registry to prioritise my fabrication software and give it a bit more computation power for a new chip I'm trying to make."

Angus clucked his tongue at Funa. It might seem like a good idea, but if you change the process order in the registry, it will bog down the computer big time. Angus told him that he took over the laptop and logged in as an administrator. To reset the registry, he would need to do a partial reimage.

As Angus worked, Funa asked, "I don't suppose you could find a way to give more power to my fabrication software."

Turning to look at him, Angus noted that he grinned wickedly at Angus.

"I'll see what I can do."

"You really are the best." Funa told him sincerely.

Once again, Angus chuckled before he got to work. It would take longer to patch the laptop to the server that he maintained to hold all the needed programs to keep the whole network running. Once Angus finally got the laptop updated, he tweaked the registry to try and see if he could help Funa's program run a little bit better. The problem had to do with all the programs that the company's security team insisted each laptop had on it. These programs would tend to bog down a laptop quite a bit. Angus set the security programs to rotate off and disconnect the laptop from the network when Funa was attempting fabrication. This would meet the security requirements and help with Funa's processing issues. After Angus finished up, he told Funa his fix. Funa was quite happy and expressed as much repeatedly. It took Angus a bit to extricate himself from Funa's work area. It was a smidge past lunchtime, so he hurried back to his workstation, which was in a hidden area of the whole building. He was thankful for the privacy, as it allowed him the opportunity to play Call of Duty without drawing attention to himself. Angus quickly submitted complete work orders for the three different jobs. After all, you cannot claim credit for work if you did not log it. Once he finished his task, he decided to go to the canteen to grab lunch. It was already 1 p.m., and he had missed the normal rush, so he knew it would be a quick run. He was about halfway to the canteen when he realised that he had forgotten his phone. Turning back, he grabbed his phone and then headed back to the canteen. Angus made sure to say hello to everyone he saw. One good thing about being the guy who fixes everyone's computer was that he found himself quite popular with his co-workers. Angus strolled joyfully into the canteen and was not surprised to see it was almost empty. It had a few workers cleaning up for those who had left and two or three people finishing their meal. Angus did not see anyone that he wanted to sit down and chat with, especially since the few there were about to finish eating. Strolling through the options that were for sale, Angus decided to go with a classic fish and chips. After getting some water to go with it, he sat down. Dipping his chips in some chippie sauce, Angus savoured lunch. His phone buzzed at him. Glancing down at the text message, he saw it flash that it was from his mother, but it flipped away before he could read it. Opening his phone, he read the message, and his heart dropped.

It said, 'Annis is dead'.

Angus brow furrowed. His fraternal twin, Annis, was dead? He just sat there staring at the message in shock.

# Chapter 2

Angus was startled when someone tapped him on his shoulder. Spinning around, he realised immediately it was his boss, Tomas. Wearing a simple light blue polo shirt and tan slacks, Tomas had a concerned look on his face.

He scratched his scraggly, light blonde beard before he asked, "Are you well?"

Giving a frown, Angus replied, "No. I just found out my twin sister is dead."

Tomas put his hand on Angus' shoulder before attempting to comfort him by saying, "Man, I am so sorry. Is there anything we can do for you?"

He paused for a moment. The shock of the moment threatened to overwhelm his emotions. His sister was one of those bleeding-heart types who did everything she could to help others in need. She was on the front-line helping refugees settle in Scotland and worked regularly with local homeless groups in Edinburgh. She was the best in their family, whereas Angus was just a computer bum. He was great at coding but spent more time playing games than doing anything for the good of his fellow Scots. It really seemed unfair that she would be the one to die. Also, what the hell could have killed her? She was healthy and had no medical issues that he knew of. His mother said nothing else via text outside of the initial message.

Giving out a heavy sigh, Angus said, "I'm going to need some days off."

Tomas rubbed Angus' shoulder before saying kindly to him, "Of course. Greg should be able to cover you for however long you'll need."

Angus gave him a nod before standing up. He had not noticed it, but there were several other people around them, each a concerned look on their faces. Maybe sitting at the lunch table for so long had caught people's attention in a manner that he had not meant, but he was in more than a little shock. Sullenly, he stood up and slowly made his way to his office. After collecting all the things that he would need, he headed out. Angus decided that he would have to go home to see his family, and then he had to find out what the hell happened to his sister. While Angus himself had lived and worked in Sterling, he was born and raised in Gargunnock, which was just west of Sterling. A sleepy little village, but his family had lived there for generations. Angus was left to stew in his thoughts as he took the train home from work to his house. After packing his bags, he loaded them into his clunky ten-year-old Corsa and then headed off. Thankfully, there was limited traffic driving through the city during mid-day travel, and Angus had made his way home. As he pulled up to his family's old home, he spotted several cars parked. There were so many that he was unsure which car belonged to whom. He did see his father's old van and his mother's car parked alongside the house. As he strolled up to the home, he could see a large crowd within the building and overflowing out into the front garden. Angus barely recognised most of the people standing there. Many people offered their condolences as he headed into his parents' home. The moment his mother saw him, she ran into his arms and sobbed heavily. Angus tried to keep his emotions in check, but he could not. He cried along with her.

After a bit of emotional outbursts, his father approached them and said callously, "I don't know if anyone will get our Annis justice. Damned Asians running around attacking people, but the police seem scared to do shit about it."

Angus' aunt calmly replied, "Will now ain't the time for that."

"Right," His father retorted, "When is the time? My daughter fought for these people to come here and live safely from whatever hell they were in. Then they come here to rape and kill her? I'm damned pissed off, and something needs to be done."

Angus could not say a word. His father was mad, but he was right. It was outrageous to think about the gall of people being welcomed in Scotland only to turn on the same people helping them. It was well above anything he could do about it. Their leaders were just trying to help others.

His mother softly said, "Just let him vent, he's mad about Annis."

Angus took solace in his father's anger and hoped it would help push the law to fully deal with those who committed the crime. Right now, he just wanted to be there for his mother. He guided her to their sofa and took a seat next to her.

His father paced from side to side before declaring, "Tomorrow we've gotta go and get your sister's body. We'll pick her up from Edinburgh and take her to Somers & Currid. I'm thinking we'll have the mass next week at Saint Tomas."

Angus just nodded at him. This was all stuff that he really had no idea about. He was quite upset about Annis and could only imagine the horror his parents felt at burying one of their kids.

His mother interrupted Angus' thoughts when she asked, "Angus, will you come to church on Sunday? I know you don't much like it, but I'd appreciate it if you'd come take the sacrament at Saint Mary's?"

Turning to look at his mother, Angus knew immediately that he had to agree, so he nodded at her. She was clearly devastated by his sister's death, and it was his job to be there for her. Angus could hear his father ranting and raving, but he chose to just ignore him since he thought it was probably the only way his father could deal with what happened. The rest of the day whipped by in a blur with more than a few arguments about what happened to his sister. Angus was numb about it. As he was lying about, he got a phone call. It was his friend Liam from Call of Duty.

Answering the phone, Angus coolly said, "Aye?"

"Donce, where are you? We were scheduled to fight some commies from China."

"Ya sorry. I got some bad news about my sister passing away, so I had to go home and deal with all this shit."

"Oh man, I'm so sorry. What the hell happened?"

Angus really was not in the mood for one of Liam's long tirades about Muslims, so he just replied, "I don't really wanna talk about it. I'll hit you guys up once the mass is done next week, okay?"

"Sure man. I'm so sorry. I'll let the boys know."

"Thanks." Angus replied.

"Talk to you later." Liam replied before he ended the call.

Angus set his phone down. As he lay there thinking about what his father was saying, he realised that a lot of it aligned with much of what Liam had been constantly complaining about. Liam was what people would call a 'right-wing extremist'. He talked constantly about how the leadership of Scotland was a bunch of 'leftist cunts' who were selling out Scotland to a group of shadowy global elitists. He never could really name any specific people when Angus asked, as he would just say that Angus was not ready for the 'red pill'. One thing both Liam and his father mentioned was that people like his sister were not the only ones being brutally attacked by Asians. Angus picked up his phone and did a simple Google search. What he found shocked him utterly. In Rotherham, Asians had been abusing girls for almost twenty years, and nothing was done until The Times had a reporter expose the whole thing. Apparently, many of the police at the time were afraid of being called racist or Islamophobic. Angus found a YouTube video of groups of Asians throughout Europe openly assaulting women. It left Angus to wonder what was wrong with people. It really was clear that Liam was a lot more right-wing than he had thought. He wondered how much more Liam was right about. Curious to learn more, Angus searched on YouTube and found a video from a Brit named 'Sargon of Akkad' who talked about the whole situation. He found the man's videos to be fair and well thought out as he went through all the information. Before long, Angus started to become frustrated as he slowly learned more and more. Trying to verify the information that Sargon of Akkad's video represented was a bit more difficult than Angus imagined. The media seemed to either obfuscate or hide details about a lot of what he was talking about, oddly enough, in the same manner that the man claimed they would do. After a lot of frustrated digging, Angus decided to just go to bed. Tomorrow, they were heading off to get his sister's body and see it delivered to the funeral home. He was not particularly looking forward to it.

* * * * *

14 June 2016.

Angus sighed heavily as he woke up. It was the day of his sister's mass, and he was not particularly looking forward to it. It took the funeral home director an extra three days to work with his sister so she would be presentable for the open casket wake. His mother was a devout Catholic, and she was adamant about a full wake for her. Ironically, Annis was pretty much an atheist, but she was just like Angus and very much unwilling to admit it to their mother. This whole time, he was suffering from a mixture of anger and sadness. It was honestly a bit depressing, and he struggled to keep himself from getting drunk, which is where his father had begun spiraling towards. His father's drunken stupor was enough to convince Angus that it was not a good place to be. Oddly enough, his mother seemed to be suddenly at peace with everything. The first day he got back, she was a wreck, but a few days later, she was suddenly calm. After he got ready for the mass, wearing a nice plain suit, he headed downstairs.

As Angus sat down, his mother placed a plate in front of him and cheerily said, "Good morning son."

He was quite puzzled by her pleasant demeanor. His father was still not up, likely sleeping off his drunken stupor from last night. It was quite pleasant to see the breakfast his mother made, which consisted of some eggs, bacon, and a tattie scone. She then placed down a cup of breakfast tea.

Glancing up at his mother, he sincerely told her, "Thank you mum."

Reaching out, she gave his cheek a light pinch before saying, "Of course."

He could not take it anymore, so when she sat down to eat, he asked, "Mum, what's got into you? You were so upset about Annis, but now you seem just fine, even more cheerful than before I last saw you."

She smiled softly before replying, "I had the priest from St. Mary's come over, and we had a long talk about my sweet Annis. I know she's safe in our father's arms now, and that's all a faithful Catholic can ask for."

Angus just replied with a sullen nod. He did not find her belief very reassuring, but he was happy that it gave her some peace. At this point, he found himself much angrier than sad about what happened. From what he read online, what happened to Annis has happened hundreds of times just in the U.K., with the animals doing it getting nothing more than a slap on the wrist. Hell, at this point, the police claimed to have no leads or information about the person who did this to his sister. He still had not reached out to Liam to tell him what had happened, but he could already imagine the vitriol Liam would be spewing when he did find out. It was something that in the past would have irritated Angus, but at this point, he was starting to agree with some of the things that Liam had said beforehand. Angus did savor the breakfast that his mother made. Halfway through the meal, his father came down. He was surprised to see his father dressed and ready to go. Angus was even more surprised to see that his father cut off his long blonde beard.

He must have seen Angus' surprise because his father said, "Aye. I figured I needed a change."

Reaching out to stroke his father's cheek, his mother said, "I love it. Makes you look like the Willy-boy I met so long ago with that baby face and bright blue eyes."

His father just chuckled as he started to eat his breakfast. Angus never really had the best relationship with his father, so he really was not sure how he could broach the subject of his sudden change of demeanor. Maybe he spoke with the priest as well? After eating breakfast, they got into his father's van. He was solemn as hell about the whole thing. When they picked up his sister, he could not bring himself to look at her. It was going to be quite hard to see her at the wake, but there was no way that he could back out. Angus glanced silently out of the window. It was just another standard Tuesday for most of the people in Stirling, and the traffic was light until they got close to the church where the wake was being held. Angus was quite surprised to see the large number of people who were there to attend Annis' wake.

As they pulled up, his mother said, "Angus, I know you've been upset about your sister's death, so I've let Father Crosbie know that you won't be going up to speak. I hope you don't mind."

Angus nodded at her because he was not really in the mood to stand up in front of a bunch of strangers to speak about his sister and was likely to break down emotionally doing so. They parked in a reserved spot in front of the church, which was very much the same as Angus had remembered it from the last time that he had been there with its light brown brick and graceful, wide-open window design that many Catholic churches had. It was the first time that Angus noted to himself that it was a beautiful-looking older building. He never thought about looking at it like that. As they walked into the church, they were greeted kindly by other parishioners, friends, and family. He remained solemn as he followed his parents to the front pew. It was then that he finally saw the open casket holding his sister. Like him, she had red hair and pale white skin. Even with the applied makeup from the funeral director, Angus could easily see that her neck and face were covered in bruises. There was an unusual rough line that cut along the side of her neck and down to the top of her dress. She was wearing a pure white dress that covered everything from her neck down to the closed half of the casket. The funeral director did a fine job of making her look decent based on the way his father had described Annis' condition when they picked her up. Much to Angus' surprise, his mother did not react in an overly emotional manner as she sat down. He sat down next to her as she reached out with a hand to hold his hand. He found himself completely numb, and the whole funeral became a blur. Before long, he was walking out of the church on his way to his parents' home.

# Chapter 3

17 June 2016.

Angus settled down into his gaming chair after finally returning home. The death of his sister still deeply disturbed him as he realised a lot of what the media and their political leaders were telling them was a huge pile of lies. Sure, his knowledge on the subject is just dealing with immigrants who the European Union and the U.K. brought into Scotland, but he suspected it was not the only area of concern. Even after the mass, his father continued his rant about the Asians in Scotland, although thankfully, his mother seemed to have convinced him to lay off the booze. Angus was happy about that at least. He did have a lot of questions, and he fully intended to talk to Liam about it after they played some CoD. As soon as he logged into Discord to talk to his friends, he was greeted with several kind words about his sister. Angus was not really interested in talking about that, so he suggested that they play. Knowing that he would be rusty, Angus talked the crew into running through a few practise runs, and it did not take him long to get back into the groove.

After they finished playing for the night, Angus said over the mic, "Liam, gimme a call in a bit."

"Okay."

After saying goodbye to his other teammates, Angus ripped off his headset. His cellphone rang immediately with Liam's name on the caller I.D.

Picking up his cell phone, Angus answered as he said, "Hey."

"Sup."

Taking a big sigh, Angus took his time to explain to Liam what exactly happened to his sister. Liam responded exactly how Angus had expected he would by reciting his disdain for Asians and the politicians who let them into Scotland. Before what happened to his sister, Angus had just changed the subject of the conversation, but he just let Liam go. The most shocking thing Liam told him about was the New Year's assaults that happened throughout

Germany earlier this year. He did not even hear about it, but apparently, last New Year's Eve, there were somewhere around 1,200 sexual assaults by Asians on women during the festivities. He could only shake his head over it. Liam was furious as he talked about only a small number of them being arrested. After a while venting about Asians, Liam suddenly shifted to talking about the European Union. He blamed them for most of the United Kingdom's problems. Honestly, Angus had nothing but nice things to say about the European Union. He liked to be able to travel freely, and free trade between the different countries was a good thing. As soon as he told Liam his opinion, Liam just laughed at him.

Liam stopped his laughter to say, "Listen Angus. The media's been lying to you and everyone else fucking non-stop. I really am not the best person to explain all this shit to you, but what you need to do is do your own research instead of just hearing me rant. The first place you should go is the Brexit Party website to read all they have to say about the election. They break down the bullshit that is the EU. Red pills are best self-administered than shoved up the arse. We've got an election in a few days, and you need to be ready, so go research."

"Right. I'll look at that website tomorrow."

"Anyways cunt, I'm heading off to bed. I'll talk to you tomorrow."

"Night Liam."

"Out."

Liam ended the call. Angus was left to ponder a lot. He was twenty-three years old, and he really was so focused on computers that he clearly missed out on a lot of other shit. The first thing he looked at was the website of the UKIP Party. They went over many of the grievances that people had with the EU. One focal point was a severe loss of fishing rights, fishing being a once important industry in the UK. Many other blue-collar industries seemed to be supporters of UKIP. They talked somewhat about Asians, but it was only that the UK should control who came into the UK and not the EU. Angus felt the only policy should be to give these people the boot from the UK. What happened to his sister should not happen to a single woman in the UK, especially since it was so preventable by just not importing people who did this sort of thing regularly. He was frustrated as he felt there was a lot more that he needed to read, but it was almost 2 a.m., so he decided to go to bed.

* * * * *

20 June 2016.

Grumbling as he woke up, Angus shuffled into the toilet to clean up for work. He had little doubt that he was going to have a few things piled up from his absence. When he called the boss to let him know he was coming back, he was told that they would not be charging him for holiday time for his time off. That left Angus with a great feeling of appreciation for his boss and the company. He had not shaved in over a week and was now wearing quite a bit of a scruffy looking face. It would not hurt to try a beard once. It looked good on his father, so he decided to give it a go. Strolling down the street to the nearest bus stop, he caught the bus right on time and headed off to work. It was a lovely summer day, and he enjoyed the ride through Stirling to the office. As soon as he stepped into the building, he was greeted with plenty of kind words. Someone had taken the time to put balloons and flowers at his desk, along with a dozen or so cards wishing him condolences. Everything else was exactly where he left it.

As Angus perused the cards, the voice of Tomas echoed into the room, "Angus, I'm glad to see you back. I really am sorry for what happened."

Looking over at him, Angus said with a half-smile, "Thanks. It's been rough, and I just want to say that I really appreciate all that everyone has done for me here. It really has helped a lot."

Giving Angus a pat on the shoulder, Tomas replied, "Of course. We believe in taking care of our employees, especially the ones in critical and irreplaceable positions."

"Thanks boss."

"Of course, Angus. If you need anything else, let us know. I'll let you get back to work. I know sometimes work can be a nice way to forget other issues in our lives."

Angus just nodded at him. He could hear Tomas walking out of the room as Angus started up his computer. He figured that there might be a bit of a workload of different people who needed his technical skills, so once his computer was running, he ran his program to scan the system. Angus was more than a little surprised to see that there was nothing. He knew that Greg was competent, but it appeared that during the ten or so days that he was gone Greg kept everything running smoothly. Maybe Greg would eventually be able to take over things for Angus someday down the road. His phone buzzed, letting him know that he had received a text message. Taking a glance at his phone, Angus saw that it was from Liam.

It said, ‘Oi cunt, how is work?’

Angus chuckled. Liam was a shit-talker of monumental proportions. He remembered meeting him in a match where Angus sniped his sorry arse from 800 metres in Call of Duty. They got along well enough, and it helped that Liam was not some scrub but a skilled player who followed directions in the game quite well. Angus texted back that he was cool. Liam once again asked him if he was going to vote for Brexit. He nodded his head as he texted that he would indeed be voting to leave the European Union. Angus decided to walk around the office to see if anyone might need help before he settled down to play some Call of Duty with his friends. As he walked around, he was surprised to see the amount of Brexit material his coworkers had. It was all unilaterally in favour of Remain. Angus was very surprised. Many of the posters decrying those in favour of leaving the European Union were dehumanizing. Angus was no racist. He certainly was quite upset about what happened to his sister and felt that taking in people who would do such a thing was a fool's errand. Deciding not to say anything, Angus was left to doubt his position initially, but then he remembered Annis' appearance while resting in place during her mass. The man or men who did that to her were monsters, and what really pissed Angus off was the thought that they would likely end up getting away with it. He was told the only witness that was found identified the men as Asians but really seemed useless in anything more than a general description of them. Something niggled at the back of his mind, telling him that likely the witness was likely to fear whoever the people were. While he walked, Liam texted him again to invite him to an election night party for the results. Angus had read all the polls claiming that Remain would easily win, but he figured a night out drinking with some friends might be a good break from his doldrums over his sister's death. He plodded along for the rest of the day.

*****

June 23, 2016

Strolling into the polling station, Angus slid into the long queue. He was quite surprised by the turnout. He had not voted his entire life, but at this point, he knew he had to do what he could to prevent what happened to his sister from happening to any other woman in Scotland. It was completely preventable. As he stood in the queue, a young woman with long hair and blue eyes nodded at him. She was wearing a bright red shirt and a simple red skirt. An elderly man slid into the queue behind Angus.

As they took a step forward, the woman turned to him and asked, "Are you excited to vote?"

Angus just shrugged. He did not think his side would win, but he figured it did not hurt to try.

"I am. I refuse to let a bunch of racists and greedy liars try to ruin our great union." She told him confidently.

Not feeling the desire for an argument, he just gave her a shrug.

The old man behind him interjected in a very grumpy tone, "Right, little miss. The EU is crapping all over us and offloading thousands of third-world primates into the UK. They're a drain on our society while we let the other European countries rob us blind through open trade."

He said the word open very sarcastically.

"Speak of the devil, an old racist just here spewing hate at people." The woman said with venom in her voice.

This was a very uncomfortable situation that Angus suddenly found himself in. He had no clue how to deal with this and wanted to just go and cast his vote. Relief was instant as a poll worker approached and took the old man out of the queue. Angus had no idea what they talked about, but the old man was guided to a booth, and after a bit, he came out with a big grin on his face. It took a bit over thirty minutes for Angus to vote. He had to admit that he was surprised by the simplicity of the ballot. It was just the vote for Brexit and nothing else. After voting for Brexit, he left the polling station and then got on a tram heading home. He was going to have to drive to Falkirk, where Liam lived, since the train did not run as late as he was planning to stay there. After a nice short drive, he made it to Liam's flat. As he walked up Liam's door opened, and Liam appeared. It was the first time that Angus had met the man in person. He appeared to be in his early twenties with short-cropped blonde hair, a neatly trimmed beard, and deep blue eyes. What hit Angus first about him was his size! Liam was about 2 metres tall and probably weighed around 112 or more kilograms. It was not fat either; he was a beast of a man and built like the kind of lad you would run into guarding a popular club.

Liam must have seen the look of shock on Angus' face because he chuckled before saying, "Oi cunt, I told ya I worked security. They didn't hire me because of my good looks, although I got plenty of those too."

He could do nothing but laugh in response to Liam's cheeky words. He shook Liam's hand as he offered it.

As he gestured for them to enter the flat, Liam said solemnly, "It's a shame we're surrounded by dumb cunts, so the chances of winning Brexit aren't that great. Did you get to vote?"

"Ya. It was a much smaller ballot than I expected to be honest."

"Yes or no tends to be."

Angus nodded at him. The flat that Liam lived in was basic, with just a sofa, a large La-Z-Boy chair, and a table with some kitchen chairs in the main area. The smell of various things cooking in the kitchen overwhelmed the flat. The telly was blasting BBC news as they reported on the Brexit election. It was mid-afternoon, and Liam appeared to have invited several of his mates over. He introduced Angus to several of them. Angus missed most of their names, but they clearly were in the same line of business as Liam.

"So, where do you work at?" Angus asked.

"The whole lot of us work as part of the security team for the Scottish Parliament building." Liam replied.

Laughing at his reply, Angus stated, "I wager they won't be too happy to find out that you've voted against all of them."

"Fuck 'em. A bunch of SJW arseholes all pandering to the EU while screwing every damned single one of us?"

"SJW?" Angus asked, confused.

Liam and his friends laughed uproariously, which only confused Angus even more. He had never heard the term 'SJW' before.

One of the guys sitting on the sofa stated to Angus, “It means Social Justice Warrior. It refers to a horde of leftist twats who use ‘muh racism’ and ‘muh sexism’ to manipulate others into doing their bidding. They are pieces of human trash, and our government is stocked full of them, using lies to control us.”

Another one of them asked, “Liam, did ya bring a normie here?”

Liam slapped Angus roughly on the shoulder, which caused him to stutter a bit from the strength of the playful slap.

“Naw. He’s just got the red pill over the fuckin’ muzzies. The rest of it’s been slapping him in the face. He just barely started with Sargon. Won’t be long ‘til he’s black pilled.”

Angus did not say a word.

One of the men slapped the sofa and said, “Well, grab a beer and have a seat man. It’s time to watch as Brexit happens.”

Liam laughed at him before saying, “Jonny, you’re smoking some serious shit if you think the cucks in this damned nation will actually vote the right way.”

“100 pounds say Brexit happens, and any of you other cunts want in, I’ll take all bets. We’re getting Brexit.”

Angus was half tempted to take him up, but he decided not to risk his money on something he still knew little about. Liam and two others did, however, take the bet. Taking a quick count, he noted that there were 6 other men here. They were all a rough sort, wearing various football jerseys, mostly from Stirling Albion FC. Liam was wearing a plain black button-down shirt and black slacks. They were a lively lot. Angus was surprised when a woman appeared out of nowhere and offered a plate of crisps smothered in cheese and diced tomatoes. She set the plate down and then snuggled up against Liam.

“Who’s this?” she asked while pointing at Angus.

# Chapter 4

"That'd be Angus from CoD." Liam replied.

"Oh, from that silly game." she muttered.

Angus chuckled as he reached out a hand while saying, "Nice to meet you."

"Same. I'm Sandy." She replied while shaking his hand.

Angus gave her a polite smile. She was about 1.6 metres tall and thin. Her hair was brown, and she had brown eyes. He really was unsure what to think of Liam's collection of friends. They struck him like a lot of gym rats.

"Look at those numbers. Brexit's already in the lead." The one guy who Angus remembered as Henry stated.

He was a stout man with neatly trimmed blonde hair, blue eyes, and a clean-shaven face. He was wearing a football jersey and tight-fitting jeans. The other men in the room cheered at Henry's news.

Liam interjected, "It's early, and we still must wait for London. It'll take almost all the other areas voting heavy Brexit to make up for those nonces."

Angus nodded to himself. The polling had Remain winning easily, but for some reason, the early results were quite the opposite. Brexit was winning handily, but Angus did think that Liam was right. Once the big cities were counted, it would take a massive majority in the other areas for Brexit to win.

The guy named Henry asked, "Angus, what ya do for a living mate?"

Liam quickly interjected, "He's a computer dork up in Stirling."

Giving a light grunt, Angus answered, "I'm the network administrator and senior program designer for our company. It's my job to keep the network up and to design software to make the use of the systems easier."

"Oi and the cunt spent most of his work time leading our squad to pwning scrubs worldwide in CoD." Liam interjected.

Angus chuckled. He was indeed the team leader, and their team did kick arse.

Trying to talk humbly, Angus replied, "Well, I did create some amazing software that makes my job so easy, my bosses let me do whatever the hell I want."

Liam clapped Angus again on the shoulder before declaring, "And that's probably why he's one hell of a leader. We've beaten pinko commies from China, soft arse Yanks, and more than a Korean team or two."

"Ranked top four in the damned world." Angus said proudly.

"Fuck ya!" Liam said before extending his hand up, clearly looking for a high-five.

Angus responded by giving him a high-five while grinning widely. He was quite proud of his team of misfits. He was having a good time with Liam's friends. They reminded him of the Scottish ideal of the football hooligan, minus any sort of violence. It was close to midnight already, and the lead for Brexit was not only solid, but much of London had been counted already. At this point, Angus was starting to believe that they were going to win the day. As the lads around him imbibed more beer, the night continued with the results rolling in. They also started getting louder. Sandy brought out a few more snacks. Angus took a few crisps as he relished the obvious win of Brexit. He chuckled as he noted that the whole of Scotland voted for Remain. Idiots are clearly brainwashed into thinking whatever the damned media tells them. Based on the map of the UK, it appeared that it was the whole coast of England that was carrying the day.

In a loud, clear, and very proud voice, the lad named Jonny announced, "You clowns owe me 100 each. Brexit is gonna win the damned day."

His bravado only caused Angus to laugh. Today was forming up to be one hell of a day, and it really helped Angus to forget about his anger over his sister's death.

The lad named Henry asked, "I sure hope we get rid of the damned laws getting people arrested for tweets."

"What?" Angus asked, very confused.

The idea that someone would get arrested for a social media post was confounding.

"Liam, this guy is a total normie!" Henry declared before laughing.

Giving a grin, Liam looked at Angus and said, "Let me tell you the tale of the dank one."

"Show him the video first." Jonny said.

Liam pulled out his phone and, after playing with it, for a moment. Eventually, he showed it to Angus with a video already playing. It was a man talking about how his girlfriend loved her dog so much. The man declared he was going to make it the evilest thing that he could think of. Then the video shows the dog acting like a Nazi. Angus could not help but chuckle. It was silly but funny to him. He certainly saw nothing that would warrant someone being arrested, especially since the guy specifically said he was making the video to mess with his girlfriend.

Confused, he asked, "This guy was arrested?"

Liam clapped on Angus' shoulder and said, "Fuckin' insane, eh?"

Giving a sullen nod, Angus mumbled, "Yeah."

As another round of updates came on the telly, several of the guys around Angus cheered. It was about 2 in the morning, and at this point, it was crystal clear that Brexit was going to win the day. The guys around him passed around another round of drinks as they were quite rowdy with their celebration. He really could not blame them; it had been a great night so far. He got to meet a bunch of new friends, and Brexit apparently was going to win by a large enough margin to dissuade any questions about the victory. He could only imagine the salt that Remainers at his work were going to have. Their office will be closed tomorrow because of the election, but on Monday, he will be back at work. Thankfully, for his entertainment purposes, his office was stocked full of Remainers. They were very and unusually committed to the idea of being part of the EU. The United Kingdom has been a nation for centuries without the EU, and it would continue to be one for centuries more afterwards, at least that was Angus' thought process. He just hoped that the UK would stop bringing in those monsters who rape and kill innocent Brits. That alone was reason enough for Angus to vote Leave without a second thought. Suddenly, the doorbell buzzed.

"I'll get it." Sandy declared.

After she opened the door, she called out, "Liam, it's for you."

"Curious." Liam stated as he rose from his chair.

It was very early in the morning, so Angus was confused as to why someone would be at his door this time of day. As Liam approached the door, he began laughing loudly.

He then bellowed out, “Oi lads, come on in.”

Angus was quite surprised to see three police officers enter. Liam hugged one of them.

“Hey Patty, what brings you and the lads to my place?” Liam asked boisterously.

The man who Liam was referring to as Patty replied, “Ya doffs, I got several complaints about noise coming from you.”

“What a bunch o’ cunts.” Liam declared before continuing, “Well, come and see why we’re making a scene. Brexit’s happening.”

“We saw.” Patty replied happily.

Angus was surprised when he saw that all three bobbies were quite happy responding to Liam’s declaration. He had no idea as to why the police would be willing to leave the EU.

“Ya cunts need to quiet down a bit.” Patty announced while giving a wink.

The other two officers chuckled but did not say a word. It was obvious that Liam had it good with the officers in Edinburgh, as they were very jovial with him.

“Want a beer?” Liam asked.

“Naw you mad lad. I can’t roll back into the station smelling of beer. Paintball still on Saturday?”

“Fuck ya. The lads and I are gonna light your lolly arses up.”

Patty laughed as he punched Liam on the shoulder before declaring, “You cunts get lucky a few times, and now you've got it in your heads you are gonna win again. I’ll see you then.”

Liam laughed at him before shaking his hand and replying, “I’ll see you then.”

The other two bobbies gave a nod as they followed Patty out. Angus watched them closely as they left.

He had to ask, so he did, “Liam, you know them?”

“Man, I’m the head of security for the Scottish Parliament, and the lads here all work with me. We know virtually all the police and military leaders throughout Scotland as part of our duties when the bitch and her lackies move about Scotland or go to London.”

“Bitch?”

“Aye, the First Minister. Nicola Sturgeon.”

Angus nodded sullenly. He really did not know much about her, nor Scottish politics at all. It was Call of Duty and programming that occupied all his free time.

Before Angus could say anything, Harry interjected, "She's a right dictator waiting to happen. Everything must be her way or the highway. She used a fake arse sexual harassment investigation to push out Salmond to ensure she was the sole power broker in the SNP. Guarantee if the opportunity comes to grab hold of more power for the SNP, she'll leap at it."

Liam added, "It's why I'm thankful we didn't win independence back in 2014. She'd have pushed Salmond out and ended up being a dictator of Scotland with her touchy-feely arse feminist bullshit."

Angus did not know much about what they were talking about, but it was interesting to hear them go on about it.

Jonny then said, "Aye. I guarantee once Brexit wins, she'll start opening her craw about another independence election. With fucking Theresa May likely to be the next Prime Minister, I bet she'll end up getting her vote."

Giving out a moan, Liam declared, "Guarantee May is gonna screw up Brexit in some manner or another. Can't even trust conservatives to conserve shit."

"We'll find out soon enough." Angus declared.

Giving Angus a nod, Liam stated, "Sure will. It's delicious to see these reporters with their heartbroken facial expressions. Now we just must hope those Americans vote in Trump and we'll have enough salt to mine for ten lifetimes."

"Wait, you guys like Trump?" Angus asked exasperatedly.

Liam and his friends all laughed heartily. Everything Angus had seen or read online about Donald Trump, the guy running for President of the United States, was bad. He was a real estate tycoon turned entertainer who would say whatever the hell he wanted and insult anyone who got in his way. All coverage Angus saw of Trump had been negative. A racist, sexist, and so much more. Liam and his lads seemed nice, so Angus was confused.

Liam leant up next to Angus and whispered, "Everything the media has told you is a lie. Go and search for yourself about Trump. We won't tell you more."

Changing the subject, Liam pointed to the screen to show the reporter for the BBC announcing that Brexit had won the day.

Liam began to sing, "God save our gracious Queen!"

His friends began to sing along. Angus did not sing along, but he was amused. They were clearly very happy about Brexit happening. Angus was pleased, but he was nowhere near as happy about it as they seemed to be.

Once they finished singing the first verse of the song, Liam stood up and announced, "Well, I think we should probably call it a night. Thank God for getting a holiday tomorrow, but it's gonna be one hell of a fun time next Monday. The salt will pour like nothing we've ever seen, and I'm gonna soak in it. I can't wait."

Liam then chuckled. His friends stood up and began to collect their things.

As Angus grabbed his jacket, Sandy asked, "Did you drive here Angus?"

"Ya." He answered.

"Liam, we can't let the lad drive back after drinking. Put him on the sofa."

"Oi cunt, she's right. You sleep on the sofa, and tomorrow you can go home."

Angus nodded as he put his jacket back down.

# Chapter 5

2 August 2016.

Angus rolled out of bed to the sound of his alarm. He grumbled lightly because he was up late helping his team win a set of matches against a few top-ranked teams in CoD, and he was still tired. It was unusual for him to get up early on a Saturday morning. The only reason he was up this early was that Liam conned him into playing paintball in Falkirk with Liam and his friends. Angus had never even shot a paintball gun, let alone actually played a game against other people. Liam had told him to wear clothing that Angus would have no issue tossing, as the paint tended to stain clothing, so Angus picked an old T-shirt and a pair of plain jeans. As he walked downstairs, he made himself a bowl of porridge and then tossed a few fresh berries into it for some extra flavour. Knowing he was going to need a bit of energy, he started up a kettle of water to make himself some builders' tea to give him a morning kick. His phone suddenly rang. Picking it up, Angus noted that it was from Liam.

As he answered the phone, he said, "Ya."

"Good, you're up cunt. Get your arse down to Falkirk, we've got a match against some right good Edinburgh bobbies and I'm planning to give them a whoopin'."

"Ya, I'm getting some breakfast, then I'll head out." Angus told him.

"Okay." Liam replied before hanging up.

Tucking his phone back into his pocket, Angus sat down to eat his porridge. His water kettle was steaming quickly, so he stood to pour hot water into his mug. After putting in some milk and a spoonful of sugar, Angus sat down again. He really enjoyed a good tea, especially when he needed a nice kick to wake up. After eating his porridge and drinking his tea, he set his dishes in the wash basin and headed out the door. The pile in his wash basin was getting a bit high, so he would have to wash the damned dishes once he got home, but he was in a bit of a hurry. Angus checked his phone and saw that traffic was light, so he would be at the paintball place in Falkirk in 30 minutes or so. Angus looked the place up online and saw that it was an indoor paintball centre. There was not much else, but Angus was willing to let Liam talk him into it, and if he was honest, it did sound like a lot of fun. The drive was painless, and Angus was surprised by how full the tiny car park lot was. It took him a few minutes to park his car, and as soon as he walked up to the entrance, he was greeted by Liam.

"There ya are. I wasn't sure if you planned to show." Liam declared.

Angus was puzzled as he never gave any hint that he did not plan to show.

Shrugging at him, Angus stated, "Naw, it sounded like fun."

"Well, we don't play around, so I'm not so sure how much fun it will be for you. My guys aren't so happy about training a new guy, but I've seen you in action on CoD, and you look fit enough."

Angus chuckled. He really had no answer for Liam, but if he ended up not having fun, he just would not come back again. He followed Liam into the building and was pleasantly surprised by what was there. It was a large building with a wide-open space that had been filled with a variety of barriers and camouflage. They approached a group of men, all wearing various bits of plastic armour and holding paintball guns. Angus recognised a few of them from Liam's Brexit party from election night, but the rest were guys that he did not know. They all greeted Angus kindly. Liam knelt and dug through a large bag that was sitting next to the group. Slowly, he pulled out various items and began passing them to Angus. It was clearly protective gear for paintball. Angus fiddled for a bit but eventually figured out how to wear each thing that Liam gave him. Finally, Liam handed Angus a paintball gun. He fiddled with it a little bit; it was the first time Angus had held anything close to a gun in his life.

"Go and buy some paintballs Angus. We use the lime green ones to represent our team." Liam instructed.

Angus nodded sullenly as he slowly walked over to the desk where they sold paintballs in a canister. After paying for the canister, Angus headed back to the group. It was now an even bigger group as another group of men joined them. They were all wearing plastic armour with a badge that appeared to be like the Edinburgh police department. No doubt these were the men that Liam's team would be facing off against. After a brief introduction from everyone, almost none of which Angus remembered when the two teams split up.

Liam approached Angus and said, "We're gonna do a few warm-up runs before we get very serious. It will give you a chance to get used to how to play before we really take it to them."

Angus nodded. He was not sure how good he would be since he had never played in his life. He followed Liam and his friends as they headed to one of the lanes. It was filled with barrels, short walls, and plenty of netting. After playing with his paintball gun for a moment, Angus figured out how to load it, and then he felt ready to go.

Liam reached over and said, "A few things. Don't put your finger on the trigger unless you plan to shoot. Don't ever point it at anyone you aren't planning to shoot. Listen to the tower for instructions and stay with the group. It's just like CoD in that a lone man is a dead man."

Angus nodded at him. The rules seemed simple enough. He imagined it would not take long to figure it out. The men he was with stacked up along a wall that had an opening into the main area where the sides would fight. Angus stacked up behind the guys on his team. He was very nervous since he was new to this. A loud horn sounded, and the men in front of him moved out. It was suddenly all familiar to him as they moved in a slow, stacked formation, just like in CoD! He followed behind and prepared to shoot his paintball gun. Already, he heard sounds of loud pop, which let him know that they were under fire. He spotted a few dark blue-coloured splats of paint hitting the wall around them.

Liam bellowed out, pointing to Angus, "Give us some cover fire."

Angus was surprised by his natural reaction as he raised his gun and fired off some rounds. The weapon fired several rounds with each squeeze of the trigger. Angus continued to fire off rounds as requested. He spotted another man from the opposing team raise his head and aim at Angus. He barely got his head out of the way as paintballs splattered into the wall behind him. Knowing that he needed to move his position before providing more cover, he jogged a few feet to his left and then raised his gun up to start firing again. He purposely aimed where the last man had been and surprised him completely by moving. Several lime green paintballs struck the man in the mask he was wearing on his head. Angus chuckled at his first successful hit. This game seemed like literally the real-life version of CoD, but with paint. He continued to slowly lay down covering fire while his team fought their opponents. It was much harder to see what was going on around him than in the game, but he saw the occasional head bob up and then down from the various barrels and walls that made up the war zone. The same horn that had blared, indicating the start of the battle, echoed once again. The two sides stood up. Angus noticed that several on both sides had splatters of paint covering them.

Liam led his friends back to Angus and announced, "Looks like we won. Good job providing us cover."

One of the other men declared, "Next time let him take point, and we'll see what he can do."

"Aye, and once we finish, then we'll head out for drinks."

The other men laughed at his declaration. Angus had to admit that the whole lot of them seemed like good lads. A bit on the rough side, like most Scots, but very good lads. They swapped out their lime green paintballs for bright red. Apparently, it was to be able to tell who got shot each round, which made sense.

As they stacked up in preparation for the next round, Liam instructed him, "Keep low and close to the barrels or walls as we move. You want to peek quickly around each corner before you head out."

Angus nodded at him without saying a word. He felt a bit of nervousness in his stomach as he waited patiently. The loud horn blared again, and Angus felt the man behind him pushing a hand into his back, a hint that he was to start moving. The sounds of someone from their team providing cover fire echoed into his ears as he turned the first corner. He could not see his enemy in sight, so he continued moving. Remembering from his time playing CoD, Angus knew that he could not sit still long, so he scurried as quickly as he could to the next wall and then turned back into the opening area to provide cover. Suddenly, motion in front of him caught his eye. Right as one of the guys on his team started to move towards Angus, their foes moved into view and began firing their guns. Angus lifted his own weapon and fired back at them. His ally made the gap and then began to help fire. Angus was suddenly hit with an idea. The two sides always just seem to race towards each other and fling paintballs down range. What would happen if someone tried something else? He signaled at the man next to him to take over covering before spinning back around to try and find a way to flank their enemy. He ran into a dead end but decided to see if he could quickly climb over the wall. Slinging his weapon over his back, he scurried over the wall and then pulled his gun back out. He was now along a long wall that seemed to head all the way to the other side of the building. Moving as cautiously as he could, Angus could hear the two sides launching paintballs at each other. Once he finally got past the team of bobbies, he moved to circle them. After a bit of searching, he found the opening where the police had started, so he began sneaking forward. It did not take long for him to find the police firing over barrels and walls at Liam's team. Angus aimed and began shooting them with paintballs. The looks on their faces as they were gunned down from behind were priceless. It did not take Angus long to cut them all down. After a moment of silence, Liam's team began moving in. They were quite surprised to find out that Angus had won the day for them.

"Cheeky cunts trying new shit on us?" One of the police asked.

Liam patted Angus on the shoulder before declaring, "A win is a win. Let's go get drunk!"

The other cheered loudly at his proclamation before packing up and leaving. While at the pub for the rest of the day, Angus made sure to drink as little as he could get away with since he had to work the next morning.

# Chapter 6

27 May 2017.

Angus gritted his teeth as he listened to the inspector who had come to visit his parents talk. The man seemed to be a large mixture of indifference and incompetence as he described the status of the case about his sister's death. It was quite clear that the police either lacked the desire or ability to solve the case. This meant that his sister's death would be unsolved, and they would get no resolution. It was obvious to him that his mother and father realised this, as well as the inspector babbled on and on about the difficulty of the case. His mother looked as though she was about to cry, and his father looked quite solemn.

After the man finished speaking, Angus' father asked, "So basically my daughter's murderer gets away with his crime?"

The inspector shook his head before responding, "No, but the case will end up going into our cold files for our investigators on that team to begin working. The evidence is just too limited to continue using our main investigation force when other crimes could be solved by them."

Angus frowned. That was just word salad to avoid admitting that the police could not, or would not, solve the case. He heard a description of the men who killed his sister, and they were all Asians who had been brought to Scotland as refugees. Angus did not say a word as the inspector left. He was seething, but there was nothing he could do about it. His phone rang. Pulling his phone out of his pocket, he saw that it was Liam.

Tapping the answer icon, he said, "Hey man."

"How's it going?" Liam asked.

"Shit. These cops can't do anything to find out who killed Annis."

"So God damned busy chasing down people on Twitter saying mean shit instead of muzzies who are raping and killing our women. A lot of it is because their bosses are tying their hands. Bastards up top need to go."

Angus did not respond. Liam seemed very much against Muslims in Scotland. Angus had several Muslim friends at work, but the fact that it appeared to be Asian men, who usually were Muslim, that killed his sister was making him change his mind on the matter.

"What can we do?" Angus asked him.

"Jack shite. Come over to the gym in town, man. I find lifting really helps distract my mind. Make sure you bring a nice change of clothes for supper after."

It was Saturday, and he did not have work, so he decided to go ahead and hang out with Liam. Usually, the gym they went to was packed with a whole bunch of police, security, and military men. Oddly, the police who went to this gym tended to just be white Scots, and they were always complaining about the bull shite the government was up to. He had no doubt that a lot of Scots were not happy with their leadership, especially when talking to the lads in the gym.

He responded, "Alright."

"See ya then." Liam stated before hanging up.

Liam had gotten Angus into physical fitness, especially weightlifting, over the last few months. Angus had not really been a fan of exercise before, but he had to admit it was working and made him feel better about himself. It also slowly transformed his body from a bit flabby to overall pretty muscular. He did not want to look huge like Liam, but he was quite happy to be lean and fit.

"Ma, I'm gonna head out."

She hugged him before saying, "Be careful out there, you're my only baby left."

Her words struck his heart. He could only imagine the pain they must have felt burying one of their children. No parent should ever bury a child, and losing his sister really hurts. Angus took a moment to hug his mum.

She squeezed him tightly as he whispered, "Love you mum."

Releasing her from the hug, he headed towards the door.

"See you later Dad." He called out.

"Ok." His dad replied.

Getting into his car, Angus drove off. He took a quick stop at home to change into workout clothes and pack a bag with some nice clothes for dinner before heading off once again. The gym that Liam and his friends went to was called PureGym. It was in Stirling and had tons of great equipment for almost any type of workout someone would want to do. The drive was thankfully brief, and Angus was quickly greeted not only by Liam but also by several of the other lads. It was the usual cheers, insults, shoulder slaps, and general chorus that he was met with by his new friends. He thought to himself that it was funny because he remembered hearing about the types of lads they were, and all he ever heard was bad things, yet these lads treated him like one of their own almost instantly. Their workout went by quickly, even though they were there for over 2 hours. Angus used the gym's shower to clean up and change clothes before heading out. Liam was waiting outside.

Angus asked, "Where are we headed?"

Giving a nod, Liam responded, "My parents. My mum heard about a fellow Catholic losing a family member, and she demanded I bring you over for supper."

Angus was probably the laxest of Catholics ever. The last time he went to church was for his sister's mass, and before that, it had been almost a year.

"Alright." Angus told him as he got into his car to follow Liam.

The drive was almost half an hour long, and they turned off M80 into a small village called Denny. Angus had never been to the village itself but had driven by it plenty of times. It was just outside Falkirk. Liam turned off the main road and onto a rougher road before finally stopping in front of a building that was a very nice, large home with a farm-related building nearby. It was the farm of a well-off family. Angus was quite surprised because Liam struck him as a suburbanite football lad, but instead, it appeared that he was really from a family that appeared to be successful farmers.

As Angus got out of his car, Liam approached him and said in an unusually quiet tone he said, "Oi cunt make sure to not swear and act respectable, eh? My family is a bunch of serious Catholic types, and they'll get quite upset if we go full football hooligan on 'em."

Chuckling, Angus replied, "You're the hooligan, you mook, I'm very respectable."

Liam gave out a guffaw before slapping Angus' shoulder playfully, "Right well, let's go."

He opened the door and gestured his head at Angus to indicate that he should follow. Angus paced right behind him. As they entered the home's entryway, Liam stopped and took off his shoes. Angus followed suit. Several small children screamed out excitedly and called out Liam's name. It was quite surprising to Angus as Liam knelt to hug them. The number of small children also surprised him. There were five children of various ages, who he guessed were from a two-year-old up to a six- or seven-year-old, who were ecstatic to see Liam. Angus realised immediately that they must have been his younger sisters and brothers.

"Dang, Liam, you have a lot of siblings!" Angus announced loudly.

Liam looked up as he ruffled the orange hair of one of the boys before saying, "As I said, we're a Catholic family. There are 10 of us, and I'm the oldest."

Angus' jaw dropped immediately. He could not fathom having that many brothers and sisters.

As he stood up, Liam instructed, "Come on. Mum invited you to supper, so let's go sit down."

Angus followed him into the main family room of the building. After finding out how many siblings Liam had, Angus now understood why the house was so big. The main entertainment room had 3 couches, a pair of coffee tables, and one singular comfy chair. Oddly enough, there was no television. Centred along the main wall where a telly would be set was a massive painting of Jesus Christ. Liam's family was clearly quite religious. Angus took note to make sure to be extra careful to watch his language. He had assumed that the furniture would be as nice as the home itself was, but these couches looked well-worn. As he moved through the living area, he realised that the reason why was these same small children. He spotted a few various coloured marker highlights on one of them. It made him chuckle. They moved into the next room, which was the dining room, and the dining table itself was huge, which made sense due to the number of family members in the home. It was so long that it could seat around 12 to 15 people. It appeared that most of the family was already in the dining room.

A woman, whom Angus guessed was Liam's mum, announced loudly, "Everyone, take a seat, we've got a guest."

Angus took a moment to look at her. She was wearing an old off-white pinny that covered a simple tan blouse and a full-length blue skirt. Her hair was light blonde with several silvered streaks through it. She was wearing it in a tight bun. Taking a scan overall, he spotted an older man who was wearing a nice blue dress shirt and jeans, sitting at the head of the table. Clearly, he was

Liam's father. He had short-cropped blonde hair and a neatly trimmed peppered beard. All the others were various children, most of whom had light blonde hair like Liam and his parents.

Liam's mother raised her voice loud enough to speak over the children chatting, laughing, and giggling to announce, "Everyone, sit down and be quiet."

It was a shock to him that they obediently listened.

She nodded and then announced, "Isla Grace and Mary Catherine, please bring supper for everyone."

Pointing at the chair next to where Liam sat, opposite where she was standing, his mum said, "Liam's friend, please take a seat."

He smiled at her before saying, "Thank you."

Once he was seated, she replied, "You're welcome, young man."

Two young women came out with several trays each. Based on the ages of the two women and Liam, Angus was left to guess that Liam was the oldest and that either of these two was the next two in age. The young woman that he guessed was the next oldest was wearing a pinny over a light blue blouse and a darker blue skirt. She had sharp orange hair that was very close to his own in colour. Oddly, her hair was tied back into a bun like her mother's, and she had a thin chapel veil hung over her bun. His best guess is that she was about 15 years old. The other one appeared to be 12- or 13-years old. She was also wearing a pinny over her blouse, which was pink, and a white skirt. Her hair was blonde and tied back into a ponytail. They both made several trips to bring back tray after tray of food. Angus could only guess that Liam's father was a very successful farmer; all of this would cost a pretty penny. Once the two young women finished bringing the trays, they both took a seat. The one with orange hair sat next to her mother, and the other sat next to her. Everyone at the table turned to look at Liam's father. Angus was curious, so he looked as well.

The man grinned before stating, "First, I would like to thank Liam for coming to break bread with his family and bringing his friend to share this meal with us. Isla Grace, could you kindly offer us grace?"

"Yes father." The redheaded sister of Liam replied before she pressed her hands together, closed her eyes, and then bowed her head.

She then solemnly, in a soft voice, said, “Bless us, O Lord, and these Thy gifts, which we are about to receive from Thy bounty, through Christ our Lord. Amen.”

Angus said, “Amen” once she had finished.

It had probably been six or seven months since he last spoke any words of prayer. The others at the table echoed the same word as he did. They then began to serve themselves food. He waited patiently for Liam to start to serve himself before he moved. It seemed to him as though it would be rude to just start shoveling food on his plate right away. He did, however, take a moment to glance at the meal, which consisted of two large hams, several bowls of mash that had sprinkled with green herbs and butter on them, and two plates with asparagus on them. It smelled quite delicious, but the ham seemed out of place on a Scottish table.

His father looked over at Angus as he was serving his food and asked, “Liam, what’s your friend's name?”

Angus realised that Liam’s father must have been an American! His accent was Scottish, but one that clearly became Scottish after being adopted by an American.

“Father, his name is Angus Bruce.” Liam answered.

Angus was also surprised by the respectful tone in which Liam responded to his father. Much like Liam himself, his father was also quite a large man. Not as muscled as Liam, but still a big guy.

“Ahhh… a Bruce.” His father replied solemnly.

The young woman, who was named Isla, then asked, “Angus… what do you do for a living?”

“I manage all the computer systems for Northstar Data Reclamation up in Stirling.”

Liam’s mother then stated, “Oooo, that sounds like an interesting job.”

Angus shrugged. He did enjoy his job, but he would not exactly call most of it ‘interesting’.

He coolly replied, “It pays the bills and got me a nice little home.”

Isla then interjected by asking, “You have your own house?”

Glancing over at her, he responded, “A small one by Stirling.”

While giving his patchy beard a little scratch, Angus turned to Liam’s father to ask, “Sir, what do you do for a living?”

The man responded with a chuckle, "I'm mostly retired. I used to own a biotech company in Edinburgh, but I sold it when I met the missus to retire up to this farm. Now, I have a manager who runs the farm, and I mostly just dabble in stock trading."

Giving him a brief nod, Angus commented, "Very nice."

Liam's mother then asked, "Did you go to college?"

What Angus thought was a friendly supper with Liam, and his family was starting to feel more like a job interview.

He shrugged it off before replying, "Yes. I got my degree in Software Engineering from the University of Stirling. I was hired almost immediately at Northstar after graduating. I designed several unique pieces of software that provide me with additional income, and I am thinking about going back for a postgraduate degree."

Out of nowhere, Liam's mother reached out a hand and touched Angus' own hand before softly saying, "Liam told me about what happened to your sister, and I wanted to tell you how bad we all feel for your family when we heard about it."

Angus frowned. He was not particularly happy to discuss the death of his sister. It was still something that cut him deeply with both sadness and anger. Annis was his best friend and his twin. He missed her greatly.

He did not wish to offend Liam's mother since she was clearly speaking to him from her heart, so he solemnly replied, "Thank you, Mrs. Gillespie."

"Have you prayed regularly for her?" She then asked.

Angus shifted uncomfortably in his seat. He was never the best of Catholic from the start, and after Annis' death and her Mass, he had not gone back. Thinking about it now made him feel slightly bad.

Glancing downward, he answered, "Honestly, I haven't been able to go back since her mass."

She squeezed his hand before saying, "I'm so sorry, Angus. You should not push away our Heavenly Father when you need him the most; you should race into his arms."

He again nodded at her. It was something his mother did almost instantly when they found out about Annis. He always struggled with his faith.

Before he could respond, she announced, "Sunday, you come with us to St. Alexander's."

Angus appreciated the offer but was not entirely sure he really wanted to go to mass.

"I really appreciate it, Mrs. Gillespie, but I'm not so sure that."

She cut him off by saying, "We'll have none of that. Sometimes people just need a little push back to where they belong."

Angus caved. He saw no reason to argue over something so trivial. It was not like he hated mass; he just was bored there sometimes.

"Alright, I'll come."

She released his hand and then stated, "It starts at 9 a.m."

He gave her a nod and then deftly changed the subject, "It's been a long time since I had ham. It's delicious."

Liam stated, "My father is a bloody Yank. They eat it all the time over there, apparently."

His father laughed before saying, "No, we don't. We usually have it for holidays or other special occasions. I just like a good honey-glazed ham."

Angus chuckled. He was happy to have his suspicions confirmed.

Isla then asked, "Angus, where did you meet my brother?"

He was in the middle of eating a bite of mash, so he finished chewing and then swallowed before answering, "I met him while pwning his rear in Call of Duty."

Liam laughed loudly before boldly proclaiming, "We both know you sucker punched me with that snipe!"

His response was classic Liam. Even though both knew damned well that Angus was the better CoD player, there was no way in God's green Earth that Liam would ever admit it. Probably not even on his deathbed with Saint Mary watching over him would Liam admit it.

Chuckling, Angus retorted, "The stats say otherwise, scrub."

They both laughed loudly. Liam slapped Angus roughly on his shoulder. He looked over at the young woman who asked the question, and she did not seem overly amused by his answer. It was not a surprise since most women did not like CoD.

His mother then asked, "Right in a game, but how did you meet him for real?"

"He invited me over Brexit night to watch the vote. I wasn't doing anything, so I figured it could be fun. We had a great time with his lads watching Brexit take the day. Been hanging out with them all since."

"So, you voted Leave?" Isla asked.

Giving her a nod, Angus replied, "After what happened to my sister, I had no choice."

There was a long moment of silence before Liam changed the subject, "Father, how is the farm doing?"

# Chapter 7

Angus had a fine enough time with Liam's family, and afterwards, they convinced him to stay and play a few board games before finally releasing him.

As he got into his car, he called out to Liam, who was getting into his own car, "Thanks for inviting me, Liam, you've got a nice family."

Liam chuckled before replying, "Ya. Don't think you're off the hook. Tomorrow night 1v1. I'm not gonna let you embarrass me like that in front of my family. No cheap arse sniping either fool."

Making sure none of Liam's family was nearby, Angus retorted, "You better learn to run bitch because when I'm done with you, I'm gonna tea bag every bullet hole I put in your sorry arse."

Liam broke out in heavy laughter before giving a wave and sitting in his car. Angus had a hearty laugh as he started up his car and drove off. As he rode along on the way home, he was half tempted to message Liam with some lame excuse to avoid going to mass tomorrow with Liam and his family, but they seemed so nice that it would have been outright cruel to flake like that. Besides, it was not like going to mass was such a bad thing. Maybe it would help him ease his discomfort over his sister. Once he got home, he set his alarm for 7 a.m. That would give him time to take a shower and clean up before driving to St. Alexander's. Climbing into bed, he closed his eyes and went to sleep.

* * * * *

The sound of Angus' cell phone alarm buzzed in his ears, waking him up. He slid out of bed and hopped to his feet. He was feeling pretty good, so he quickly went to the toilet and then started getting ready for mass. Afterwards, he was going to utterly destroy Liam's sorry arse 1v1, and the best part, he decided to secretly record it and send it off to Liam's family. It was a matter of pride; Angus was the superior man, and he was damned if Liam was going to check him in front of people. He chuckled just thinking about it.

Angus whipped out some breakfast tea to go with a light breakfast. This time, some baked beans, a bit of toasted bread, and finally a few strips of bacon. He was never much of a breakfast guy. Once he finished eating, he cleant up the mess he had made before heading to take a shower. It was only half past seven, so he had plenty of time. Taking a moment to examine himself topless in the mirror, he had to admire the work he had put in. His pecs were solid and his stomach flat.

He looked damned good, so he commented to himself, "Hell ya."

Sadly, his beard was a patchy mess, and honestly, he considered shaving to start over. Maybe later. Also, he noted that his hair could use a trim. No way that he would go with a buzz cut like Liam and his friends, but Angus liked to keep it looking clean. He quickly brushed his teeth, popped a bit of mouthwash, and then took a shower. After drying it off, he dug out his Sunday best and then pressed it. It would not be good to show up to mass dressed like a tramp; that was not how his mother raised him. After finishing, he quickly got dressed and took a moment to peek at his phone. It was slightly past 8. He pulled up Google Maps and checked the drive. It was only about 12 kilometres away, so maybe a 15-minute drive. That gave him time to check his email, his Insta, and message his mother. She had wanted to know that he was doing well, so he tried checking in with her at least once a day. It was only a matter of moments before his mother messaged back asking if he was coming to mass. He replied that he was going to St. Alexander's with his friend Liam and family. The reply was a smiling emoji. He chuckled because there was no doubt his mother was probably very happy to know he was going back to mass. Every Sunday, she had messaged him to try to get him to come. Angus had always made excuses not to go. He shrugged it off and headed out. It was always better to be early than late, so he hopped into his car and drove off. The drive was uneventful, and there was virtually no traffic. Following his satnav on the phone, he found St. Alexander's easily and then parked. He was surprised that it was a bit busier than he expected. Once he got a spot, Angus paused to take in everything. There was a priest in front of the door, greeting people as they entered. Angus had no idea if Liam and his family were already inside. He decided to go and ask.

As he walked up, the priest said to him, "Good morning, my son."

"Thank you, sir. Do you know if the Gillespies have arrived?"

"Of course. They are sitting in the front pew on the left."

Smiling at the man, he said, "Thank you."

"Please go on in my son."

Nodding briefly, Angus stepped into the church. It was full of people, and the church itself was very much like many of the other classic old Scottish churches. He always loved the design of Catholic churches. Glancing around, he saw Liam's family. Liam was not there with them. His mother spotted him entering and waved at him. There would be no escape now. He strolled over and sat down in the open spot at the end of the pew. The person sitting at the end next to the open spot he took was Liam's younger sister with the same hair colour as his own. He had to admit that he had completely forgotten her name. It was one of those Catholic names that was two or more names.

Liam's mother leant forward and declared, "Angus, we're all happy you came."

"Thank you. Is Liam on his way as well?"

The young woman sitting next to him answered, "His girlfriend, Sandra, wanted him to attend mass with her family, so he will not be here."

Giving her a nod, he thought to himself that he was going to make Liam pay for abandoning him with Liam's family. At least they were nice enough.

Liam's sister slid slightly closer to him and then asked, "Did you have a good night's rest?"

"Yes, thank you. My mother was happy to find out that I was attending mass with your family. I'm a bit disappointed in Liam for not being here."

She retorted flatly, "His lazy butt probably just did not want to come. It is rare for him to come to mass anymore."

Angus chuckled. He had to admit that he was not surprised that Liam was likely a very lapsed Catholic. Football lads gonna football lad.

"I am pleased that you joined us today, Angus." She told him.

"Thank you, I'm glad to be here. It's been a while since I came to mass."

She nodded at him and then turned to face forward as the organ began to play. Angus sat patiently through mass and found himself pleased as the sermon was a talk about the embrace of the Holy Spirit in our biggest moments of need. The talk seemed almost as though it was meant specifically for him, and he found himself feeling much better. He partook in the Sacrament, and when Mass ended, he stood up.

Liam's father approached him as he was about to get into his car and said, "Angus, we'd like to invite you to lunch with the family if you aren't busy."

Pulling out his phone, Angus peeked at the time. It was only a bit past 10 in the morning. He saw no real harm in it, plus he thought it would be a fun idea to talk some shite about the limey cunt Liam for not showing up.

"I hope it isn't an inconvenience to have me over."

"Of course not. Liam's a good boy, but I think he needs a more positive influence in his life to get him back on track. Being a security bum isn't a lifelong career."

Now it all started to come together. His family was clearly worried about Liam. They probably felt powerless, so they worked Angus into their home so they could use him to help get Liam back on whatever path they felt he should be on. He could not even blame them; being a security guard, even for the Scottish Parliament, was not exactly a high-end career choice.

"I gotcha, Mr. Gillespie but sure, why not. I had a good time last night, so let's go."

Liam's father nodded and then stated, "Alright, I'll see you there."

Climbing into his car, he started up and followed Liam's family as they drove off. Once they all arrived, he walked in behind them and slipped his dress shoes off. He was finding this more than a little awkward, but now that he knew their motivations as a family that simply loved Liam, he decided it could not hurt to help them out by pushing the cunt. After spending a nice lunch with them, he headed home. Liam's mum got his number so she could keep in touch, and he promised to keep going to mass after a lot of prodding by not just Liam's mum but his sister, whose name he finally remembered her name was Isla. Once he got home and changed into normal clothes, he messaged Liam to let him have it for flaking on mass. Liam replied that he did not go because Sandy did not want to listen to his mother going on about marriage and kids. Then he asked how mass was. Angus replied that it was cool and demanded they settle the matter 1v1 immediately. After Liam agreed, Angus strolled over to his PC and turned it on.

As soon as Angus logged into the game, he started up Discord and announced to everyone in the chat, "Come and watch on my server as I hand Liam his bitch arse 1v1."

The lads in chat all laughed as they logged into the private server Angus set up for the match.

Once Liam arrived, Angus asked in chat, "Fool, which map do you want?

"It doesn't matter cunt. Once I'm done with you, I'm gonna be running the R3CK1NG CR3W."

Angus laughed heartily as he pushed the record on OBS so he could record the whole thing.

"I'm gonna go with Siene River so you can't cry about sniping." Angus announced confidently.

Through the mic, he heard Liam laughing before he declared, "It's your funeral."

Liam's confidence only made Angus laugh. Liam was good, but he was not that good. One of the biggest weaknesses in Liam's game was his overconfidence. He would blindly charge in without thinking or planning. Also, he was easily distracted. Angus decided to use it to cut the sucker down. Liam was a top-tier close-quarters fighter but just needed a cooler head to keep him in check. Angus chuckled. Right as the round began, Angus immediately fired off 4 rounds. He planned to distract and trick Liam.

Liam's voice echoed as he said into the mic, "I'm comin' for ya cunt."

Angus ran to his right and fired three more rounds before cutting back to where he originally was and then turned back around to start slowly moving forward. The plan was to cut Liam off as he went to where the rounds would indicate where Angus was. As Liam moved closer into the trap, he was talking all the shite any man could talk. His voice sounded supremely confident, which was one of the reasons Angus picked the close quarters map of Seine. It would give false confidence that he could take advantage of. It was over quite quickly as Liam never saw Angus coming from behind him, and it only took one clean headshot. Liam suddenly became very quiet.

Chuckling, Angus asked, "Liam… Who is your daddy?"

Liam sounded almost sad as he begrudgingly announced, "You are."

"Who am I?" Angus gleefully asked.

"Angus Bruce, aka my daddy."

Laughing uproariously, Angus stopped recording before he declared, "And don't you forget it bitch."

That got the whole Discord chat wildly laughing along. He could even hear Liam laughing along.

Angus then announced loudly, "Let's go find some scrub Yank losers and get some god damned revenge for 1776!"

Again, the Discord chat cheered in response to his declaration.

# Chapter 8

The next morning Angus' alarm woke him up. It was time to get ready for work, so he got cleant up and then started his breakfast. He decided that he would need to cut out most of the sound on the video so that Liam's family would not hear all the cussing. He did not want to get Liam in trouble so much as just mess with him for cutting out on him yesterday for mass. It was easy enough to cut out everything past the first part, where the match was Angus versus Liam, and then the final part, where Liam calls Angus his daddy. Angus also decided to post the video, unedited, in Discord so that everyone could get a laugh, too. Once he finished the sound edit, he emailed it to himself and then texted the video to Liam's mother with the words 'for your enjoyment' attached. After a few minutes, his mother responded with a laughing emoji. Angus chuckled at his evil deed. No doubt Liam will be contacting him very soon.

The sound of Angus' tea kettle screeched out, so he said, "I'm coming, I'm coming."

Picking up the kettle with a cloth napkin, Angus poured some hot water through a strainer holding the tea and let the fresh tea pour into his cup. It smelled wonderful. He turned off the cooker and then collected some oatmeal, which he sprinkled with a few bananas. After eating breakfast and drinking his tea, Angus collected his bag and headed off to work. Once he arrived, he was greeted by his coworkers. Being the man who fixed people's problems with their computers, Angus was popular. He doubted many of them really knew him too well, but he was fine with that. It was a job. As he got settled in, he began his normal routine. Usually, Mondays were the most relaxing days because few people had time to mess up stuff on their computers that would need his help. He still checked his system. Everything was smooth as silk. His phone rang. Looking at his cell phone, he saw that it was Liam. Angus laughed happily. No doubt Liam's mother sent the video to him. This was going to be sweet.

After letting it ring for a little bit, finally Angus answered, "Hello."

"You limey cunt." Liam stated.

That pushed Angus over the edge, and he broke out laughing once again.

After he was able to recover, he brought the phone back to his ear and asked, "So, how's your day been?"

"You know God damned well how my days been. Sending that video to my mum so she could hear me call you my daddy. It's like you've got a death wish."

Once again, Angus laughed loudly. He did not doubt that Liam would never live this one down with his family, the team, and likely anyone else who heard about it. Angus decided right then he would ask the lads if they knew who Liam's daddy was.

"Ya got me good cunt. Secretly recording your knee-scraping escape from me in battle."

"More like you were the one on your knees." Angus quickly smacked back.

"But seriously man, thanks for at least editing out our bull shite talk between. My mother would have gone insane if she heard how we were talking."

"Naw man, your family seems nice. I don't mind putting the screws to your bitch arse, but I wouldn't do them dirty."

"Ya, ummm, speaking of my family. I know this is gonna sound weird, but I was wondering if you could do me a huge favour."

Angus felt like he was slowly going to end up becoming Liam's replacement if he kept sending Angus to fill in for family events. He paused quietly to wait and see what Liam was thinking.

"But seriously…. I am not sure how to say this."

"Well, spit it out."

"I was wondering if you could take my sister out on a date."

"Wait, what?" Angus asked, very confused, before continuing, "Are you talking about the 15-year-old girl?"

"Naw man."

Angus let out a sigh of relief; he was not down with dating kids.

"She's 18."

"No way. You're talking about your redheaded sister, Isla, who sat next to me in Mass, right?

"Isla Grace, but ya man. She turned 18 and graduated this year. She starts at Uni this fall."

"But she looks hella young, man."

"I know. She's always looked a bit younger than she is. Doesn't help that she takes after our grandmum and is kinda short too."

"So, wait… you're serious?"

"I guess she told my mum after you left yesterday that she wanted to go out with you, so my mum called me and asked me to see if you would at least go once. I'd totally understand if you don't wanna go, she's super religious and honestly, I think a smidge on the 'tism scale."

"I noticed the religious part but not the 'tism."

"Well, she hasn't been diagnosed or anything like that, but she's one of those socially weird kinda people. Just says what's on her mind and doesn't seem to give two shits about what anyone thinks of her. Plus, she isn't emotional at all."

Angus shook his head. This was not quite what he was expecting when Liam called him.

"I don't know man." He told Liam on the phone.

"Bro, can you please do me a solid. She's a nice girl, but just a little unusual."

"I didn't see it."

"Ever heard of an old arse telly show from America called The Addams Family?"

It took Angus a moment, but he remembered it. Some kind of Halloween-themed family show from America.

"I kinda do."

"My sister is like if you took the little girl Wednesday on that show and then made her super Catholic and good instead of evil."

"This seems kinda off man. Taking your sister on a date and all."

"Naw its fine. Take her out one time and do something all goodie goodie like bowling or some shite."

"Just once?" Angus asked cautiously.

"Of course. I won't ask you again, I promise."

Sighing heavily, Angus caved and said, "Okay. I'll go."

"Awesome man. I'll let mum know this Friday after work, you'll pick her up."

That seemed fast to him, but Liam hung up the phone before Angus could lodge any sort of protest. Angus sat down in stunned silence. He tried to picture Liam's sister in his mind, and he was struggling to remember precisely what she looked like. He remembered her hair colour, her plain clothing, and the chapel veil. It was something that did strike him as odd; very few Catholic women wore a chapel veil outside of church events. Shrugging it off, he decided to take a moment to find something that he would like to do so that he could take her to. Suddenly, it hit him, he loved going on roller coaster rides. There was a pretty good park near Glasgow called M&D's. They had rides, animals, and even bowling. It was wholesome fun that he was sure any good Catholic girl would like. He was a bit surprised that Liam suckered him into this. His phone buzzed, and he saw that it was a message from Liam. It said that everything was set up.

He then sent a second message that read, 'Keep your cunt hands to yourself while out there or I'll beat your arse like a drum'.

Angus chuckled. He had no ill intentions since it was Liam's idea in the first place.

There was a knock on the door, which Angus replied to by saying, "Yes?"

Slowly, the door opened, and he saw that it was his boss, Tomas.

"Hey Angus, I just wanted to check up on you and make sure you're doing okay."

Giving a wide grin, Angus replied, "I'm doing much better. Thank you for both asking and being patient with everything."

"Of course. I was wondering if you could come check up on my computer. My Outlook stopped updating, and I really need to be able to get in my email."

Giving out a little chuckle, Angus replied, "Of course. Let me get my stuff, and I'll meet you up in your office."

Tomas gave a nod before turning and leaving the IT room. While he had to admit his job was not difficult, it was rewarding when he could help others. He collected his tools and his admin laptop before heading out.

As soon as he stepped into Tomas' office, Tomas said, "Thanks again. It also seems my computer is a bit slow today. I don't suppose you could fix that, too."

"I'll take a look while I am at it." Angus replied.

He plugged his admin laptop through a USB cord into Tomas' laptop and started it up. It did not take long to see what was wrong with his Outlook: just a file misplaced. After fixing that, he let the admin laptop run a performance check.

"Angus, a couple of the folks in the office were going to have a big party this Friday, and they suggested that I invite you."

At first, Angus was going to say yes, but then he remembered he promised Liam that he would take his sister on a date.

"Oh man, I'd have come, but I have a date this Friday."

Tomas got an unusual look on his face before saying, "I understand."

Angus gave a nod before getting back to work.

# Chapter 9

2 June 2017.

Somehow, Liam convinced Angus to take Friday off work so he could take Liam's sister out during the day. He was unsure why the hell he agreed with it, but it was far too late to back out now. He probably should have taken up Tomas' offer to hang out with his coworkers, but there was nothing to be done about it. He selected a simple pair of slacks and a nice green dress shirt that matched his eyes nicely. It was his mother's favourite dress shirt. His phone rang, and he saw that it was Liam. Angus was confident that Liam was much more nervous than he was. Hell, Angus had only planned to do this one time just as a favour. Hopefully, Liam could find a way to let his sister down easily afterwards.

"Sup?" Angus asked as he answered the phone.

"How ya doing, man?"

"I'm good. Just about to head over and pick your sister up."

"Where ya going with her?"

"M&D's. Good, clean, and safe fun."

"Oh cool. My mother reminded me to tell you that Isla Grace's favourite flowers are pure white lilies. Make sure to bring some k? Also, shave that scraggly arse excuse for a beard off your face."

Angus chuckled. This 'date' was slowly getting more involved. It was not like he could not afford it, but he really was not that serious about her.

"I'll see what I can do."

"Thanks man. Have fun." Liam stated before hanging up his phone.

He had thought about shaving, so he figured now was as good a time as any. After he draped a small towel over his shirt, he got his electric trimmer to trim down his beard and then his electric shaver to finish the job. He dusted off any loose hair before he splashed a bit of cologne on his neck, and then he grabbed his keys. There was a flower shop on the way, so he stopped to get a dozen flowers. He had to remember it was white lilies, so he said it a few times as he drove. Thankfully, the local florist had them, so he slapped them on the passenger chair and headed to Liam's family home. He was still surprised that Liam conned him into this. As he pulled up to their home, he saw the same cars that were there when he last visited. Liam was not there. Angus was starting to think there must have been a reason he did not visit his family much. He stepped out of his car and made sure to bring the flowers with him. Tapping the buzzer, he waited.

The door opened to Liam's father, who then said, "Angus, it is good to see you, and on time as well."

Mr. Gillespie turned backwards and called out, "Isla Grace, Angus is here, hurry up and don't keep him waiting."

Looking back at Angus, he then said, "Thank you for taking her out. We usually have a hard time getting her to socialise with people, so when she said that she wanted to go out with you, we were quite surprised."

Chuckling, Angus commented, "I was surprised too."

Mr. Gillespie then leant closer and, in a slightly softer voice, said, "Just be patient with her, she's a good girl but a bit awkward."

All Angus could do was raise an eyebrow in response. This was now two members of her family saying something unusual about her, and they both seemed happy to have Angus take her out on a date. There was no proper response that he could give to Mr. Gillespie.

In a hushed tone, he could hear Liam's mum say softly to someone, "Maybe you should leave the chapel veil behind?"

He could not hear a response, but after a moment, Isla appeared at the door. Since she was still wearing a light lace chapel veil over her tightly formed bun on the back of her head, he was left to assume that she ignored her mother's advice.

Before he, or anyone else, could say something, she said, "Hello Angus. Thank you for accepting my invitation. I trust that my brother was not too awkward in his request."

Chuckling, Angus replied, "No, it's fine. I was just a little bit surprised."

Her head tilted slightly as she looked at him before commenting, "It appears that you brought my favourite flowers. I can only assume that either my mother or Liam informed you of the best selection."

"Liam."

She gave a slight nod before taking the flowers from Angus and saying, "Thank you."

Turning back to her left, she passed the flowers to someone and asked, "Mother, could you kindly place these in a vase, then set them in my room?"

Angus was entirely unsure whether she was happy to receive the flowers or not. She was quite stoic.

She then turned back to Angus before stating, "I am ready to go when you are."

Angus gestured towards his car before asking, "Shall we?"

Turning back to her father, she then said, "I will be back later, Father."

He hugged her and then released her. She seemingly did not respond at all to the hug before turning and walking towards Angus' car. He followed her, and then once she stopped in front of his passenger door, he circled before getting into the car on the driver's side. She was still just standing outside the door, unmoving. It took him a moment to realise that she must have wanted him to open the door and assist her in the car. He quickly got out of the car and scurried over to her side before opening the car door. Offering his free hand, she took it before sitting down, and then she tucked the loose part of her skirt underneath her leg. After she finished, he shut the door and strolled over to his side and got in. As he started the car, he took a moment to look at her. She was wearing a light blue full-length skirt and a white lace blouse that had a collar that started in the middle of her neck and full-length lace sleeves. He could not see any skin below the point where her neck met the collar. Her skirt was belted by a white leather belt with her blouse tucked into it. It was an appropriate outfit for a proper Catholic woman. She was young-looking to him, but he did think that she was attractive.

As he pulled away from her house, she said, "Your selection of dress shirt was a good choice, it seems to match your eyes perfectly."

It was a compliment. The first thing that he thought of was how Liam said she was like a good Wednesday Addams. He had gone online that day to watch more videos about the character for shits and was now surprised to see that Liam was right. He thought that her mannerisms were almost robotic.

"Thank you, Isla. It is my mother's favourite shirt for me." He replied.

"Isla Grace." She stated.

"Huh?"

"My name is Isla Grace."

"Oh, sorry about that."

"It is fine. I think it is best that we start by being honest with each other."

"That seems like a good idea to me."

"I only date to find someone to marry. I am not playing games, nor am I looking for fun like today's horrible modern woman."

"Okay." He replied.

"What about you?" She asked.

It was slightly odd to him that she kept a flat face and only stared straight ahead.

Taking a moment to construct his answer carefully to not offend, he responded, "I really have not put a lot of thought into it. I haven't been going on a lot of dates recently."

"What about when you did?" She pressed.

"Just to hang out mostly."

"Fair enough. I just wanted to make sure that you understand where I stand."

"Understood."

"When was the last time that you had a girlfriend?"

Angus chuckled because she was really pressing all the information out.

"Did I ask something amusing?" She then asked.

"No," He replied, but then continued, "I just find your forthrightness interesting."

"I have always been direct, which I have been told many people do not appreciate."

"Ahh… but to answer your question, it has been over a year."

"Why so long?"

He scratched his now clean-shaven face before answering, "Honestly, I've just been more focused on my work and wrecking your brother's face in CoD."

She then stated, "I saw the video where you defeated my brother handily and then got him to call you his daddy. I assume that it was a male bonding ritual where the winner gets to embarrass the loser in some form or another?"

Angus was finding her extremely entertaining, so he laughed heartily before replying, "I bonded his rear end into the earth."

She finally turned to look at him before raising an eyebrow, then stating, "I assume that is another metaphor for defeating him."

"It is."

"Angus, can I ask you another question?"

Giving a light chuckle, he replied, "You didn't seem to mind before, so why ask now?"

"Fair point. Do you find me attractive?"

It was a slightly surprising question, although he had to admit, based on their short interaction, not one that he should have been surprised by. He looked over at her. She then turned to face him. Her expression was flat and even. Her porcelain white skin was smooth and soft with several light tan freckles. Her eyes were a light blue colour, and her face was delicate and slightly curved, betraying her youth. The best he could do was describe her as simple and pretty. He did indeed think that she was attractive.

"Yes." He told her to face forward.

"What about me would you say is my most attractive feature?"

"I would say your eyes." He told her.

He was being honest; she did have very pretty eyes. He was a fan of women with red hair like his. She did not say anything.

Deciding to turn the tables on her, he asked, "And me?"

"You?"

"Do you find me attractive?"

"I do."

"And what would you say is my most attractive feature?" He asked.

He was surprised how quickly she answered, "I appreciate your muscular form. You are clearly very fit but not built like a man who spends all his time in the gym."

"So not like your brother?" He asked.

"Indeed. My brother is entirely too big. I was quite surprised when he brought you home, as most of his friends are big lunkheads with the intellect of a year-old potato."

Angus could not help but laugh. There was a sense of humour under all that stoicism.

Once he finished laughing, he told her, "I appreciate the kind words."

"Sticking with honesty, however, I must let you know I also appreciate the fact that you have a nice job, a car, a home, and most importantly, are a fellow Catholic."

"A woman with very specific requirements, I see."

"Yes. I am a high-quality woman who deserves a man who is on equal standing to me."

"High quality?" Angus asked.

"Yes," She answered before continuing, "I will make a superb wife and mother who is loyal, faithful, and of fine Catholic virtues. I demand a man of the same cut of cloth."

Angus nodded.

"Are you one of those types of men?"

He really did admire her complete honesty. She seemed to be unafraid to ask anything.

"Honestly… I'm not sure. I'd like to think that I'm nice, and I feel as though I'm doing a good job in my life. Really, it's not if I think that I'm a high-quality man. That'll be up to you to decide."

"Fair enough. You did an excellent job of turning that question back on me."

He chuckled. She was much sharper than Liam on multiple levels.

"I suppose I should ask where you are taking me. I trust you have planned something appropriate for the current level of our relationship."

She was surprisingly bold as well.

"To an amusement park called M&D's Scotland's Theme Park."

"I have heard of it. It has roller coasters, carousels, bowling, food, and animals, correct?"

"Yes. I hope you'll find it to your liking."

"I believe it is an appropriate destination for a first date."

"Have you been there?"

"I have not. Outside of playing your game, what other interests or hobbies do you have?"

She was unrelenting, for sure, he thought to himself before answering, "I do computer programming not only as part of my job but for fun."

"Do you play any musical instruments?"

"I tried learning how to play a guitar when I was younger, but I just could not figure it out. You?"

"I played the clarinet in band and plan to continue playing it in university."

"Will that be your major?"

"No, I am going for a degree in Data Science. I was thinking that if I could not find a proper husband, a career in artificial intelligence would be an excellent use of my skillset."

She was clearly highly intelligent, maybe even more so than he was, and Angus considered himself to be pretty smart.

"What other hobbies do you have?" He pressed.

"I have recently taken up painting and have a deep love of classical Italian operas."

"Opera, eh?"

"Indeed. What is your preferred musical style?"

"Classic 70's rock."

"An interesting choice. At least you are not a fan of Robbie Williams."

Angus laughed because he knew that Liam was a huge Robbie fan. He realised right there that she was looking for someone who was very much the opposite of her brother in virtually every way possible.

He then stated, "Most definitely not."

She suddenly reached up and adjusted his rear-view mirror so she could see behind them.

"As I suspected." She stated before shifting the mirror back.

"What?" He asked.

"It would appear that my cousin Geoffrey is following us."

"Really?"

"Indeed. Look carefully, and you can see a light blue Toyota seven cars back. He is attempting to follow in a stealthy manner. My mother is anything but predictable."

Angus spotted the car. He could not see the man sitting behind the wheel very well.

"Signal and then pull over please." she commanded.

It was on the M73, and usually people did not pull over, but he followed her direction. He was quite surprised to see the blue Toyota pull over far behind them. He turned on his flashers.

"I assume he pulled over as well."

"Yes."

"Well, I suppose if he is going to follow us, we should at least give him something worth reporting back to my mother. Place the car in park and take my hand."

He had no idea where she was going with this. He turned his car off and then shifted to look at her while taking her extended hand.

"Perfect, now give me a kiss."

Angus was very shocked.

"Umm."

She firmly stated as she leant closer to him, "I would like you to give me a kiss."

He shrugged mentally and then gently kissed her on the lips.

# Chapter 10

After she broke off their kiss, she said, "Thank you."

He flushed lightly before leaning back into his seat. It was quite a pleasant kiss, and it helped him realise that he was indeed attracted to her.

After a bit of thinking, he replied, "You're welcome."

"Let us continue driving. I believe my cousin now has something worthwhile to tell my mother."

"Do you have a problem with your mother?" Angus asked.

"She is possessive, controlling, and many times overbearing. Really, she is the perfect Catholic mother."

Angus was not sure if she was joking or not, but he gave out a slight chuckle. He turned off the flashers and pulled back out onto the M73.

"You seem to find many of the things that I state humourous."

"I appreciate dry humour."

"Did you appreciate our kiss?"

He blushed in response to the question. It was going to take quite a bit to adjust to her uniquely bold directness.

Before he could answer, she stated, "You did. I am happy to hear it. I, too, enjoyed our kiss. Can I tell you something, Angus?"

"Of course." He answered.

"I knew from the moment you talked about your feelings over what happened to your sister that I wanted to date you. It is rare to find a man who can be honest with his emotions around others and yet maintain his aura of masculine energy."

"Thank you. I won't lie that it had taken me some time to be able to discuss it and maintain my… masculine energy. My sister was the one person I was closest to."

"Understandable. I, too, would be upset if something happened to one of my siblings."

"One of your many siblings." Angus replied with a chuckle.

"Yes. My mother performed her duties of bringing my father many children. I am hoping to someday match or surpass her."

"So, you want to have kids?"

"Of course. It is the greatest way that we can honour God by bringing as many of his spirits into our lives. Do you wish to have children?"

"Honestly, the subject has not really been high in my list of priorities."

She quickly replied, "I am under the impression that many young men feel that way until they find a woman worthy of bearing their children."

Looking to change the subject, he pointed out the Ferris wheel in the distance before stating, "There it is."

He took the ramp toward the park, and after a brief bit of driving, he found a nice spot to park. It was quite smart of Liam to suggest an early start time; the park had barely any visitors when they got there. Once he turned off the car, he got out. Isla Grace was still patiently sitting in the car. It was clearly a clue that she wanted him to open the door. He gave a chuckle to himself as he thought that she was very good at getting others to do what she wanted. After opening her door, he extended a hand to help her get out. After she got out, he released her hand and closed the door.

"Shall we?" he asked as he gestured towards the park.

Giving him a nod, she stated, "I believe it is customary for dates to hold hands while out together."

He could not help but grin at her. She had a unique way about her, and he found it fascinating. Tenderly, he extended his right hand and took her hand. Her hand was very small and soft. He glanced at her and swore that he thought that her mouth shifted into what he would describe as a very slight, almost unnoticeable upturn at the corners. He thought that perhaps she was not emotionless, just very reserved. Looking forward, he guided her to the entrance. M&B's was different from most parks. Instead of bleeding you for cash to enter, they got it one ride at a time. Angus paid for a good number of ride tickets so they could go anywhere they wanted.

Right as they entered, Isla Grace pointed with her free hand and then stated, "I wish to ride on the Ferris wheel first."

"Alright." He responded as he began walking her to it.

There was no line, and they were able to board immediately. As he sat down next to her, she shifted so that she was pressed into his side. She moved her arm so that her open hand was facing upwards. He could not help but grin because she was very subtle in letting him know what she had wanted from him without demanding it. He reached out and held her free hand.

She gave him a slight nod before stating, "This is my first date. How do you think it is going?"

"I'm having a good time." He honestly stated.

"As am I. Can I ask you what your honest opinion of me is?"

If any other person had asked him that question, Angus would have been shocked. Just in their brief time together, he expected it.

"Since I know you appreciate honesty, I'll be honest and tell you that originally, I didn't want to come. I only came because your brother insisted. However, I'm finding you quite charming in what I can only describe as unusual."

"How so?"

"You seem brazenly open and direct, as though you don't seem to care what anyone thinks. It's refreshing, and while I'm not sure if it is intentional or not, I like what I'm perceiving as an extremely dry sense of humour."

"Very few people seem to understand or appreciate any of those qualities about me. I must admit that I am quite relieved that you do."

He turned to look at her while giving her a big grin. Once again, the almost imperceptible slight upturn of the corners of her mouth happened as she slightly tilted her chin upwards towards him. He recognised an invitation for a kiss when he spotted one, so he leant towards her and tenderly kissed her lips. He was slightly surprised when she kissed him back with quite a bit of passion. Outside of the very tiny smiles, it was the only emotional reaction that she had given him this whole date. He had little doubt there was plenty of hidden emotion beneath the surface, likely waiting for the right person to see it.

She broke their kiss again to turn back forwards and then say, "The view from here is quite nice."

He was still looking at her when he told her, "I agree."

It was not a surprise to him that she did not react emotionally. He could not see her face well enough to know if that tiny little smile appeared or not.

“Do you regret being convinced by my brother to take this date?”

“Not anymore.” He replied sincerely.

“I was thinking that for our next date, I should pick what we do. Would that be acceptable to you?”

Once again, he grinned. She was bold and presumptuous.

He liked her enough to want to see her again, so he responded, “That would be fine with me.”

After the Ferris wheel stopped, he guided her out, and they started walking again. They bounced around the park, and finally, he took her to the biggest roller coaster in the park.

“I love roller coaster rides. Would you like to ride this one with me?” He asked.

“I have never been on one, but I will try it.”

The park had picked up a little, so they had to wait for a while in line. As they moved through the line, he looked at her and saw her little chapel veil on her bun. He realised that it would be a bad idea for her to wear it on the ride.

“Isla Grace, I think you should remove your chapel veil.”

“Why?”

“The ride moves very fast, and you could lose it.”

Her face shifted to a thoughtful look for a moment before she declared, “Very well, as you are the man of this relationship, I shall acquiesce to your wisdom.”

She let go of his hand and then began fiddling with her veil. It appears that she used quite a few pins to hold it in place. Once she was done, she folded it neatly before extending her hand, holding it out to him.

“Could you place my veil in your pocket, please? I do not have anywhere to place it.”

“Sure.” He replied as he took it from her hands and slipped it into his right pocket.

She reached out and held his hand once he took it out of his pocket. He could not tell because of the veil, but her bun was very large, which meant her hair was likely quite long.

He commented, “I bet your hair is probably beautiful out of the bun.”

“It is.” She stated before continuing, “Perhaps the next time you come over to our house for supper, I will not wear a bun so you can see it.”

“I would like that. Do you always wear a veil?”

"Whenever I am outside the house or if we have guests."

He nodded. She was indeed quite religious.

"This is the first time I have been outside without it on since I was a small child."

"I hope you're not upset. I'd just hate to see you lose it."

"Of course not. I appreciate that you are considerate enough to think of protecting my property from loss."

It was now their turn to board the ride. They got the 2nd from the front seat.

Once the bars locked down, she stated, "I have to admit to you that I am feeling very apprehensive about this ride."

Angus chuckled. She was scared, but her own stoicism prevented her from showing it. He reached out and took her hand, which he then squeezed to reassure her. She squeezed her hand softly back, a show of appreciation. As soon as the ride started, her squeeze on his hand became quite a bit firmer. He looked over at her and saw what he would describe as an expression of determination. Looking forward, he yelled out in joy as they hit the first drop. She made what he thought sounded like a grunt. He laughed uproariously. This was a story he could not wait to tell Liam. Once the ride was finished, he got out and then helped her exit.

"That was a most unusual experience." She stated.

He chuckled before asking, "Would you like to go again?"

"I would not." She replied.

Her response made him laugh even harder.

"I feel as though you are laughing at my expense."

Giving her an evil grin, he replied, "I was."

Raising an eyebrow at him, she asked, "A little wicked streak?"

Even with her stoic behaviour he could sense that she was playing along so he answered, "Perhaps."

He saw the telltale very slight upturn at the corners of her mouth, which he was confident meant a smile.

She then stated, "Many women believe that men are wild creatures that must be trained to become a proper husband."

"Is that so?" He asked.

He was quite curious about what she was suggesting.

She then answered, "I believe they may be right, and I am looking forward to the challenge."

Angus could not help but laugh. There were many more layers to this girl than he had thought. Reaching into his pocket, he pulled out her veil and handed it to her.

"Thank you." She said.

"Of course."

He stood patiently as she slowly pinned her veil back in place.

Once she was done, she declared, "I believe it is time for lunch."

"Sounds good. There are plenty of food options here at the park."

She pointed off to her right and said, "That family restaurant looks fine."

He gave her a nod and led her in. He ordered the fish and chips, and she got the tuna mayonnaise baguette. After they finished eating lunch, they continued to walk in the park. They stopped at the various animal exhibits and even bowled a few games. He assumed that she would not like him to let her win, so he crushed her. Back when he was a kid, his family used to bowl a lot, so he was pretty good. His best game was 223. After they were done in the park, he brought her back to his car, and they headed back to Denny.

"Angus, I know it is soon, but I would very much like it if you could accompany me tomorrow to a play in the park at a park in Glasgow. Originally, I had planned to go with my family, but I feel as though I would enjoy it more with you."

He thought for a moment, trying to make sure he had nothing else planned. Most likely just CoD, but if he were honest, he felt like spending more time with her would be nice.

"That sounds good."

"I was hoping you would agree. Do you think Liam will be upset when he finds out that we will continue seeing each other?"

Angus laughed heartily before declaring, "He'll probably be confused since he had to push me into coming."

"What about when he finds out that we kissed?"

"Oh boy. He's probably going to blow a gasket since he told me to keep my hands off you or he'd break my arm."

"Good."

He was slightly appalled as he asked, "You want him to break my arm?"

"Of course not. To be honest, we do not have the best relationship, and it is pleasant to know that he cares at least a little bit."

"He does, but his attempts to convince me to come were a lot less caring."

"How so?"

Angus realised that he had made a mistake. She might not appreciate being called a 'good' Wednesday Addams.

She interrupted his thoughts by saying, "He probably claimed that I was a 'spaz' or a Catholic Wednesday Addams."

He gave out a light chuckle before stating, "Yes and no. He did say you were a super Catholic and good Wednesday Addams, but then he said you had the 'tism."

"And what do you think?" She asked as she turned to look at him.

"Well," He started to say before pausing to speak carefully, "I can't lie, I do see the Wednesday Addams comparison, but I don't think you have the 'tism. You're just a very blunt person."

"My parents took me to several psychologists, and they all believe that I may have schizotypal personality disorder, which they claim means that I am a person who does not socially interact in the same way others do, but otherwise they believe that nothing was wrong with me."

He nodded thoughtfully but did not say a word.

"Is that a problem for you?" She asked.

Taking a moment to think about it again, he answered, "I don't think so. I find you delightful. You're definitely different from anyone I've met before, but I'm starting to be able to pick up on your physical clues of emotion."

"Such as?"

"When you are happy, you get a very tiny upturn of the corners of your mouth for a brief moment, and when you are scared, your face shifts to a look of focused determination."

"I think that you already understand me better than my own family does after a single date. I am truly impressed."

He recognised high praise from her, so he replied, "Thank you, Isla Grace."

It was around 4 p.m. when they arrived at her family's home. Angus got out of the car and circled to let her out. She took his open hand and held it as he closed the car door and guided her to the front door of her home.

"Angus, I had an enjoyable time with you today."

"Thank you, I had a lot of fun as well."

"Can you pick me up tomorrow at noon? The play starts at 1:30 p.m. and I always like to be in the front row."

"I'll be here at noon sharp."

She did not say another word as she tilted her chin upwards slightly towards him. A clue for a goodbye kiss. He leant forward and kissed her lips. She, once again, responded with a good amount of passion.

After she broke their kiss, she stated, "Have fun demolishing my brother in your game tonight."

He laughed as he watched her walk into her home. She turned around to close the door, and he could see a small smile on her face as she closed the door.

# Chapter 11

As Angus stepped back into his home, he said to himself, "That… was the most unusual date of my life."

He started up his supper after changing clothes. He decided to fry up a steak and some mash with a beer to go along with it.

His phone buzzed, so he read the message, which was from Isla Grace's mother, 'Thank you for taking her. She stated that she had a nice time and that you're going with her to the play tomorrow.'

He texted back to her that he was indeed going and that he had a great time. He also messaged her that he thought Isla Grace was a kind young woman. Her mother texted back thanks and then wished him a good night. After finishing supper, he started up his computer before logging into Discord. He was immediately greeted with cheers as more than a few of the guys called him "Liam's daddy". It was something Angus would hold over Liam's head for years. His phone rang.

Picking it up, he saw it was Liam, so he answered by saying, "What's up, mate?"

Liam's voice sounded more than a little bit upset as he answered, "I told ya not to put your hands on her, and my mum said you were kissing her in the car and then right there on the front porch of my parents' house. Have ya gone batshit insane?"

"The car one was her idea. I guess she was right when she said your cousin was following us."

"Well, it was her first date, of course, a Catholic mother is gonna have her daughter followed, but that doesn't explain what my father called 'very passionate kissing' on the porch."

Deciding to be an evil bastard, Angus coolly declared, "What can I say, I'm not only your daddy but also a smooth arse pimp that all the ladies love."

"Har dee har cunt. You're about as smooth as the cast that I'm gonna be putting your dumb arse in."

"Seriously though Liam, I really liked her."

"HOW?" Liam almost yelled.

Being honest, he stated, “Sure, she is without a doubt the Catholic and good version of Wednesday Addams, but I found her delightful with a very, VERY dry sense of humour. We got along swimmingly.”

Deciding to screw around with Liam, Angus stated, “I was also very surprised to find out that your parents clearly gave her all the intellect and left you dumb as a rock.”

“Oi ya cunt, I’m gonna beat your arse like a drum.”

Giving out a laugh, Angus replied, “Is that any way to talk to both your daddy and your sister’s beau?”

That must have done the trick because Liam finally laughed before he eventually stated, “I can’t believe you liked her. She’s almost like a wooden plank emotionally.”

Angus could not resist messing about, so he replied, “She doesn’t kiss like a wooden plank.”

Liam laughed at his joke and then said, “When I told Sandy you kissed Isla Grace, she almost fell out her damned chair. So, you're gonna see her again tomorrow?”

“Ya, she wants to go see a play.”

“Sounds boring as shit.”

“It’s fine. I enjoy her forthrightness. She came right out and said she found me attractive and straight up asked me to kiss her when she saw your cousin behind us.”

“Fuck, Geoffrey can’t even be sneaky.”

“She knew we were being followed before he was caught. She’s very sharp. Also, what’s up between her and your mum? She almost acts like they are adversaries.”

“Catholic women shit, not really sure. I’m still sitting here in shock that you liked her. Sometimes I swear she’s either a robot or a lizard person.”

“She isn’t. Just a sweet girl with a unique personality.”

Liam gave another chuckle before saying, “Very unique is one way to put it. Rules still apply, except now if you keep seeing her, you’re on your own if you decide to break it off. Also, if you break her heart, I’m gonna have to beat your arse.”

“So, you do care?”

“She’s still my little sister. Just keep your shite in your trousers.”

“It’s not like that man, plus she made it crystal clear that she only dates for marriage.”

“You planning to join the family?”

He wickedly replied, "You've abandoned me to them so many times that I might as well."

Laughing along with Liam Angus finally stated, "I don't really know mate, but I'll gladly admit I'm intrigued by her, and I think she's quite pretty."

"Alright ya cunt, that's enough talk about my sister, let's go kill some bitch arses."

*****

Angus woke up the next morning with no alarm. He was up late with the team playing CoD, and it was now about 1030. He slipped out of bed and got ready for the day. Since he was attending a play with Isla Grace, he decided to dress up a bit more than jeans and a T-shirt. This time he went with a pair of black slacks and a light brown short-sleeved dress shirt. As he pulled up to her family's house, he was surprised to see Liam's car outside. He was 20 minutes early, but he figured no one would mind. Strolling up to the door, he pressed the buzzer. The door opened to her father, Mr. Gillespie.

"Angus, welcome back."

"Thank you, sir."

He looked back into his house before stepping outside and closing the door behind him.

"Angus, may I have a private moment with you?"

"Of course, sir."

The man nodded and then asked, "As her father, I must ask what your intentions are with my daughter."

He felt it was a reasonable question to ask.

"Sir. Nothing but honourable. I greatly enjoyed our time at the amusement park. Isla Grace is a charming but intriguing woman. She also seems to like me, which I appreciate."

"I must admit, I didn't like her odds of finding a nice Catholic boy, but I'm very happy. Let's go inside."

Giving a nod at the man, Angus followed him into their home. As he walked in, he saw Liam sitting with Sandy on one of the couches. Isla Grace was not there. Sandy smiled brightly at him, but Liam looked a bit more serious. Angus could not tell if he was being serious for show or if he was actually serious.

Mr. Gillespie called out, "Isla Grace, Angus is here to see you."

There was a bit of an uncomfortable wait before he could hear footsteps coming down from the main stairwell. He looked up and was in complete shock when he saw Isla Grace appear. She was wearing a simple green blouse and a darker green skirt, but what threw him off was her hair. It was no longer in a bun but instead loosely flowing around her. It was very long, reaching all the way down to her elbows, and he absolutely loved it. Her hair was beautiful. She still had her chapel veil on, which was pinned on the top back half of her head and dropped down to her shoulders. She looked quite lovely to him.

The first person to speak was Liam's mum, who asked, "Where's your bun?"

She replied, "Angus wanted to see my hair down, so I thought that I would wear it like this, hoping that he would like it. Based on his facial expression, I am led to believe that he does."

Angus flushed with embarrassment. Her bluntness was something that he was still adjusting to. Liam laughed in response.

Instead of taking the embarrassment lying down, he boldly stated, "It looks wonderful, Isla Grace. I still find it hard to believe someone so beautiful is related to an ugly lunk like Liam."

His words worked perfectly as almost everyone in the room laughed. Isla Grace even responded with that tiny little smile of hers.

She then stated, "Thank you for the kind words." Before walking up to him and slightly lifting her chin upwards.

He recognised it as her, letting him know that she wanted him to kiss her. He was not sure that he wanted to kiss her in front of her family, especially with Liam there. She continued to stand there unmoving. It dawned on him that she was not going to move until she got her way. Even as stoic as she was, she was clearly still a stubborn Scottish woman. Caving in, he leant closer and then kissed her on the lips. She responded with a soft kiss but did not kiss him aggressively as she did on the porch.

After she broke their kiss, she stated, "Let us go. I have not seen Hamlet live before."

"Me either."

Before any of her family could say anything about the kiss, he briskly walked her out of their home and to his car. Opening the passenger door, he helped her in and then circled to start up his car.

As they pulled away, he told her, "Your hair is quite lovely."

"Thank you. I believe, based on your facial expression when you saw my hair, it is fair to declare you openly as my boyfriend. You are clearly more attracted to me than someone I would be merely dating."

Angus was surprised by her open declaration. He had thought that they were just dating.

Before he could answer, she asked, "Does this seem reasonable to you?"

He turned to look at her. With her hair down, she really was beautiful to him, and he found her unusual personality interesting.

After taking an extra moment to ponder, he decided that he would like that very much like that, so he told her, "Yes."

She gave one of her small smiles as she stated, "I am very pleased to hear that you agree. I was wondering if you could help me acquire a cellular phone so that I may keep in closer contact with you. I would ask my parents, but I suspect that my mother would take to her duties as a proper Catholic mother and spy on me."

He was more than a little surprised, so he asked, "You don't have a cellie?"

"I find those sorts of electronic devices can be distracting from proper spiritual growth, but to answer your next likely question, I would prefer to have one to communicate with you without intermediaries."

"That's fair. I would very much like to be able to talk to you as well. After the play, we can swing by a shop and pick one up. Since you probably won't use it very much, I'd say we get a pay-as-you-go plan."

"Whatever you think is best, Angus. We are both adults and do not need my parents for our communication."

He nodded in agreement.

"I was also wondering if it would be possible to meet your parents after we pick up the cellular phone?"

"Hrmm. I can't guarantee they'll be home, although usually they are, but we can go and see."

"Where do they live?"

"Just outside Stirling, not far from my home."

"I would also like to see your house as well. Obviously, keep in mind when I am saying this, I am not suggesting anything unbecoming of a proper Catholic lady."

"Of course not. I would be happy to show you my home."

"Before you get a chance to alter it for my arrival. I want to see your natural living environment. I feel as though it would give me a better understanding of you as a person."

He chuckled. She really did just say whatever the heck was on her mind. Since he always kept his house clean, he had no problems showing it to her. His mother was on his arse when he was a kid to make sure that he kept things clean.

"Today it is." He declared confidently.

"You are not concerned that I may be unimpressed with the condition of your home? Most single males struggle with home maintenance."

Giving out a laugh, he commented, "You're not the only one with a Catholic mother."

"Which is why I felt it important to meet her before we go any further with our relationship. It is highly important to me that I receive her blessing."

He was confident that his mother might be initially confused by Isla Grace's distinct personality, but she would appreciate her for both her appearance and her religious fervor. His mother had wanted to arrange a date with this girl or that one from the church many times. Usually, they were not really his type. Although he was starting to think he had no clue what his 'type' really was. Taking a glance over at Isla Grace, she was staring straight ahead with a blank face. Reading her emotions was challenging. He was just glad that she seemed to just openly tell him what she was thinking most of the time; it made her much easier to deal with than the women he had dated in the past. Usually, it was a wild guessing game.

"I would suggest you concentrate on the road. While I watch the play, you are welcome to stare at me all you want."

He chuckled before turning back to continue driving. The rest of the drive was silent, and once they arrived at the park, he bought the two tickets they would need to enter. He imagined that she was pleased to get a seat up front, but she said nothing as they sat.

Suddenly, she stated, "I am predicting that one or more members of my family will be arriving to keep an eye on us."

"Speaking of your family, why did you want me to kiss you in front of them?"

"It is important for a daughter to declare her independence from her parents boldly. Even more so as a Catholic woman. I was trying to transfer control over me from my parents to you by having you take a kiss in front of my whole family."

"I don't really consider myself controlling you."

"I am speaking more in a figurative than literal way."

Giving a light chuckle, he commented more to himself than her, "I doubt I could control you if I wanted to."

"I believe that you underestimate how strongly your masculine energy influences my thought processes."

He was intrigued, so he asked, "How so?"

"Since meeting you, I have found myself distracted by thoughts about you and unable to concentrate on other tasks."

Deciding to be a wise arse, he used her own words and stated, "I believe, based on your comments, it's fair to declare you openly as my girlfriend. You're clearly more attracted to me than someone I'd be merely dating."

Turning to look at him, she raised one of her eyebrows before stating, "It would appear you are also a smarty pants as well."

"Guilty, however… I'm under the belief that you are as well."

Once again, her very slight smile showed itself before she replied, "I do not know what you are talking about."

He broke out laughing heartily. Her outward appearance may have been calm and stoic, but he had no doubt there was so much more about her. He enjoyed it greatly. A man strolled on stage, and the play began.

As soon as the play ended, Isla Grace asked, "Did you enjoy it?"

"It was good." He answered.

"I concur. Shall we head off to the cellular phone shop?"

Giving her a nod, he stood up and took her hand. As they walked away, he casually scanned the crowd. He noticed a young man watching them unusually too much but did not recognise him. It was likely one of her cousins keeping tabs on them. He chuckled to himself, thinking about the cousin's reaction when he brought her to his family's house and then his own later today. He took her to the shop to pick up the phone and made sure to put his number into her phone and her number into his. Once they were done, he shot off a text to his mother to make sure she was home. She replied they were home, so he took Isla Grace back to the car, and they headed off.

As they were driving, Isla Grace stated, "I am feeling slightly apprehensive about meeting your mother."

"Why?"

"I am hoping that she likes me, but my life experiences lead me to believe that most people do not like me."

He realised that she probably suffered a lot of mistreatment from others who did not understand her. Probably, it was particularly rough in high school for her. Teenagers can be brutal.

Reaching out to grab her hand, he stated, "I really like you."

"Thank you. I cannot express how much our relationship means to me."

"Yes, you can. You did so on your family's porch." He replied with a very wicked laugh.

He glanced over at her and could have sworn her face shifted to a slight red hue of embarrassment.

Taking a moment to let her recover, he then stated, "I'm certain once my mum gets to know you, she'll love you. Most likely, the fact that you're pretty and so pious will help. She has wanted me to date a Catholic girl for a while."

"You flatter me, but I hope that you are right."

"Can I ask you a question?" He asked her.

"You are my boyfriend, so you can ask anything you wish to know."

"What's up between you and your mum?"

She paused for a while before finally answering, "We have what I can only describe as a complex relationship. I believe since I am her oldest daughter, she was expecting a specific type of daughter, and I am most definitely not what anyone would have in mind."

He chewed on what she was saying. What he could guess was that her mum was disappointed because of Isla Grace's unique personality.

She interrupted his thoughts by saying, "I suspect she probably also did not believe that I would ever find a potential husband. Which, if I am honest, I did once agree with her."

"And now you don't?"

"No. It is my belief that you would make an excellent choice for my husband. You have a very mellow and patient personality that seems to blend nicely with my personality. As well as the fact that you meet my personal requirements that I laid out yesterday."

"I suppose I do."

"There is a concern about your status as someone who has been lax in their duties as a servant of God. I will work to inspire you in that manner as I am confident you will assist me in my own shortcomings."

He commented, "As any couple would."

"Yes. If I am honest, I anticipate our wedding night greatly so that I will no longer have plan trips to the confessional."

Angus pondered on what she was saying for a moment before he realised that she was talking about sex. He gave out a chuckle. In all their time together, he had not once thought about it. Now it was probably going to stick in his brain. It did not help that her skin was soft and almost the colour of porcelain. The more he thought about it, the more physically attractive she was becoming.

He spotted his parents' house down the road, so he pointed it out and stated, "There is my parents' home."

# Chapter 12

As they pulled up to the driveway, he spotted both of his parents' cars. He had to admit to himself that he was not entirely sure about how they would react to Isla Grace's unique personality, but he was sure that everything would be fine. Once he got out, he walked around the car and helped her get out.

She commented, "Your parents have a nice home."

"Not quite as grandiose as yours."

"Perhaps, but our home size is based more on need than financial status. Also, it is quite a bit out of the way of most everything."

He gave a nod at her before tapping on the door of his parents' house and then opening it. He made the mistake of just walking in on them one time, and it was a permanently life-scaring event that he would never repeat again.

As he took his first step in, he bellowed out, "Mum, I'm home, and I brought someone I want you to meet."

"We're in the living room, dear."

As they walked into his parents' living room, his mother's face shifted to surprise. His father did not even look up from the paper he was reading.

Mum said, "Will."

His father did not look up.

"Will!"

"Huh? What?" He responded, looking up before noticing Isla Grace and then commenting, "Oh, Angus is back, and he appears to have brought a young lady with him."

"Mum and dad this is my girlfriend, Isla Grace."

His mum responded, "Honey, you didn't tell me you were dating anyone."

Before he could answer, Isla Grace responded by saying, "We have recently started to date and quickly came to an immediate understanding that we were an excellent pairing."

His mum looked more than a bit confused as she echoed Isla Grace's last words, "An excellent pairing?"

"Indeed. His mellow and charming personality is an excellent contrast to my own. It greatly helps that he is a fellow Catholic, is well employed, and owns both a car and a home."

His father chuckled before asking, "Did he also tell you that he loves to play video games with most of his free time?"

She responded, "He plays it with my older brother and has proven to be superior in the game by sharing a video of him defeating my brother and getting him to declare Angus 'his daddy'. I found it amusing as my brother is 50% ego and 50% muscle."

The look on his mum's face was one of a mixture of bemusement and confusion. No doubt she was very unsure of the unique way Isla Grace talked. It made Angus chuckle.

Her face quickly shifted back to normal before she stated, "Your name is quite lovely, dear."

Isla Grace replied, "Thank you, Mrs. Bruce."

"Of course. Why don't both of you have a seat?" His mum instructed as she pointed towards the love seat in their living room.

Angus guided her to the seat, and once she was sitting, he took a seat next to her. She slightly shifted so that she was sitting closely next to him.

"So how did you two meet?" His father asked.

Isla Grace replied, "My brother told my mother about what happened to your daughter, for which I wish to offer my sincerest condolences, and she insisted that Angus come over for supper. I found myself immediately attracted to him, and when I told my mother, she arranged for us to go on a date."

His mum reached out a hand to take Isla Grace's hand as she said, "Thank you. My poor Annis was a sweet girl. I prayed to Heavenly Father that he would help our family, and now here you are with my little Angus. He works in mysterious ways."

Isla Grace replied, "Yes, he does. It makes me quite happy to know that Angus was raised by a strong Catholic woman. Outside of his fit physique, it was one of the biggest reasons I was attracted to him."

His mum turned to him and asked, "Are you going to marry this one, honey?"

Before he could reply, Isla Grace answered, "That is very likely the direction that our relationship is headed; however, it is still too early for either of us to make that commitment."

His father interjected, "She's quite direct."

That made Angus chuckle. Calling her 'direct' was probably only half of it.

"I was diagnosed with schizotypal personality disorder, which I was told means that I do not socially interact in the same way others do."

His mum's eyes bugged out slightly at Isla Grace's statement. It was probably not the right time to tell his parents that, but at this point, he had expected her to say just about anything that crossed her mind.

Isla Grace then continued, "Mrs. Bruce, based on your facial expression, I suspect you may be concerned; however, I can promise you that, outside of my forthrightness, limited physical reactions that expresses itself in what would appear to be emotionlessness, and my bad timing in providing constant honest commentary, I am a perfectly normal Catholic woman."

His father guffawed before stating, "If Angus likes you its good enough for me."

Giving a smile, his mum then said, "Of course. I was just surprised. Really, I'm just glad he found a Catholic girl. I was worried he was going to end up with some hussy from college or that cesspool he calls work."

Angus peered over at her. He had not known her opinion on his coworkers.

Isla Grace raised an eyebrow before asking. "Cesspool?"

He was quite embarrassed when his mother answered, "Most of the people working there are homosexuals and foreigners. It's not a Godly place, and I worry that they might eventually influence my son."

Before he could express outrage at her comments, Isla Grace replied, "I can assure you that your son is a Godly man. He has been nothing but completely honourable to me, even though I did express to him that I was very physically attracted to him. A man who was not Godly would not behave as your son has. He worked there long before he met me, so I have no concerns about his coworkers."

Angus was impressed with Isla Grace's kindness. While his mother was technically right about his coworkers from a Catholic and Scottish point of view, they seemed like nice people to him.

"Of course, you're right, Isla. I'm just worried for my son."

He corrected his mum, "Isla Grace."

Right as he said it, he noticed that tiny little smile appear on Isla Grace's face. He realised immediately that making people say her full name correctly was one of her many crafty ways of managing others around her.

"Oh yes. Sorry." His mother replied before continuing, "But I'm much less concerned now that I know he is with a proper Catholic girl."

Isla Grace then said, "I am quite relieved to hear that. I was telling Angus on the way here that receiving your blessing for our relationship was of the utmost importance to me."

"As any proper Catholic girl would want." His mum interjected before continuing, "You have it, dear. I want to say that your hair is beautiful."

He was quite pleased that his mum and Isla Grace were getting along so well. He was more than certain that the fact that she was Catholic played a key role, but it worked for him.

His father then asked, "So how long 'til we get some grandbabies?"

Isla Grace was much faster in responding again when she answered, "If our relationship blossoms into a marriage, I promise that we will not only have children immediately, but we will have many."

He was slightly uncomfortable with the speed at which everyone around them seemed to want to rush their relationship. After all, they still met just a few days ago.

His father chuckled before saying, "Looks like we're making the boy uncomfortable with all this marriage and kids talk."

Flushing lightly, Angus replied, "It's fine. I just don't wanna rush."

"I concur with Angus. I was very relieved when we began dating, and it was immediately apparent to both of us that we connected, but we must make sure the match is right before moving forward." Isla Grace stated.

His mum grinned before saying. "You have an interesting way of saying things."

Interrupting them, his father stated, "Brutally honest and direct. I like it."

Angus chuckled. His father was always great at getting a bead on people. It was probably one of his greatest strengths. He could read a crowd and then find a way to escape it as soon as possible.

"One psychologist stated that the way I communicate was a compunction and that no amount of training or sessions would alter it."

"Do you want to?" His father asked.

"Honestly, I do not. I was made by God as I am, and even if there were a drug or something that could change it, I would not. I trust our Heavenly Father's plan. I am as he intended me to be."

Angus was confident that her answer was probably the best answer that anyone could give to gain favour with his mum, although he was sure it was not Isla Grace's intent, but her honest answer.

His mother grinned widely before stating, "I can see why my boy likes you. I love your honesty, and your hair is just gorgeous. Can I ask you a question, Isla Grace?"

"Thank you for the kind words, of course you can."

"How old are you?"

"I turned 18 on January 7th. I completed High School almost a half year earlier than most."

Chuckling, his father commented, "I guess the boy likes 'em young looking."

It caused him to blush. Initially, her age was a concern to him because she did appear to be younger than she was.

Isla Grace then stated, "Most men prefer their wives to be younger. Youth and beauty are traits of healthy women who can provide offspring, so men are attracted to them without even realizing it. My brother stated on his phone call after confirming our first date that he was greatly amused when Angus thought that I was only 15 years old. I have always appeared younger than I am, and I am short because of my grandmother. I can provide proof through my identification if you need me to."

His father laughed before stating, "That won't be necessary."

"Isla Grace, it's about an hour before supper, and I was wondering if you could join us this evening?"

"Mrs. Bruce, I greatly appreciate the offer, but I was planning to cook supper for Angus at his house before he takes me back to my parents' home. I want to start early by showing him my many skills that he would appreciate having in a future wife. You need not worry; we will, of course, behave as proper Catholics."

His mother chuckled before stating, "I believe you, Isla Grace, and the thought of anything else never crossed my mind."

Suddenly, his father pulled on his shoulder and said, "Boy, you might wanna speed up the engagement period. Behaving properly gets old quickly."

Angus looked over, and his father gave him a little wink. He flushed lightly in response. Discussing his personal life with his parents was a very new experience, one he did not wish to repeat in the future out of embarrassment. His father just laughed in response. The small, little upturned smile that Isla Grace would occasionally have appeared on her face.

She then stated, "I am hoping that if we decide to be engaged, it will be brief as well. I imagine the priest will tire of my weekly confessionals talking about my feelings over Angus."

His jaw hit the floor. While he thought he was getting used to her openness, her outright admitting that she wanted to have sex with him to his parents was more than he was expecting. His father lost control of himself in laughter.

Reaching her hand out to softly touch Isla Grace's hand, his mum said, "We're all imperfect humans. If you don't act on such thoughts and confess your flaws, you'll be fine, dear."

"Thank you, Mrs. Bruce. I would never act in such a way out of marriage, but I will not lie about my feelings. Your son is very fit, and I am pleased that he has the same hair colour as I do. I suspect most of our children will be redheads."

"His grandmum would be happy about that, Isla Grace. She's a redhead as well." His father commented.

"Where does she live?"

Angus answered, "Up north in Dunblane."

Isla Grace nodded.

Deciding that he had enough talking about his future potential sex life with his parents, he stood up and announced, "Well, it's time for us to head out. Isla Grace wanted to meet you both, so I brought her over right away."

Angus helped her to stand up, and as soon as she was standing, his mum hugged her. She responded in the same manner to the hug as she did when her father hugged her. He wondered why she acted so cold to people physically, but when he kissed her, she almost exploded in passion.

Figuring it was just her way, he hugged his mother before saying, "I'll see you both later."

Isla Grace announced, “It was a pleasure meeting both of you. I was thinking that maybe soon you both could come meet my parents.”

“I would love that.” His mum stated.

After saying their goodbyes, Angus took her back to his car, and they headed off. His home was not far away so they arrived there quickly. It was a simple 3-bedroom and 2-toilet home that was painted tan. He was quite proud of himself when he bought it. Very few fresh college graduates during the first year of their new job could afford one. He sold the rights to some of his software to Northstar and used that money to pay for most of it.

As he turned to park in front of it, Isla Grace asked, “Is this it?”

“Yes.”

“I believe that it will work perfectly for a new family.”

“Probably. Lemme give you a tour.”

He then unlocked his door to let her enter. She walked right past him and entered his home as though she had been living there for years. He flipped on the main hallway light that led into his living room. He had a small dining room that was connected directly to the kitchen and next to the living room. There were two smaller bedrooms that he did not even use. Sitting in the master bedroom, he had his computer desk and gaming chair on one side and his bed with a nightstand on the other. Most of his clothing was folded and stored neatly in the shelved wardrobe that was built into a wall. His mother came over one time and was quite happy to see that her years of training paid off. He had organised it because he was just used to it, and it almost hurt him to keep his home a mess.

“Your confidence seems to have paid off. I am impressed with how well-maintained your house is. Your wash basin is empty of dishes, and it appears that your floors are regularly mopped and clean.”

She strolled into his kitchen and ran her fingers along the edge of the refrigerator. When she lifted them, she glanced at her index finger before noting, “Some improvements could be made.”

He chuckled because it felt like he was under some sort of inspection. She began opening and examining his food stores. Usually, he kept a good amount of food, although since it was just him living there, it was nowhere near the amount a family would need. She simply nodded as she moved from cabinet to cabinet. Once she finished, she moved into his living room. He had a large screen telly connected to cable; he loved to watch Stirling Albion F.C. and national team games when they were on, but otherwise, he never used it.

She rubbed the top of the telly before commenting, "You do not use this much, do you?"

Chuckling, he answered, "Only some football games."

"You are a football hooligan like my brother?"

"Naw, I just like watching the occasional match at home."

Giving a very slight nod, she continued to his sofa, where she pushed down on the seat cushions before picking one up.

Immediately, she commented, "You appear to have missed a few spots."

He glanced at the barren sofa and spotted several small pieces of rubbish. He could only chuckle at her inspection. Normally, he would take personal offense, but after all he had seen from her, he realised it was all her way. Maybe she was even trying to prove to him her value, which was something he felt she did not need to do. She was quite valuable to him already.

"It is quite sparse. I think we need to at least get you a cross to hang on one of the walls and maybe a picture of the Saviour."

"Okay. I have only lived here for a few months."

"You do not need to justify yourself to me, Angus. I am duly impressed. When you first said you owned a house, I was expecting a mess. This is a very well-maintained house."

"Thank you."

She spun and headed towards the 2nd toilet that he never used. He walked behind her and watched from the door as she examined his toilet. She said nothing as she passed by him and then headed through each of the empty rooms.

As she left the last of the empty rooms, she commented, "Hopefully someday we can put someone in these rooms."

He chuckled because he knew what she was talking about. She entered the master bedroom, and he immediately followed behind her.

She commented to him, "Not the best job, but your bed is made. I am not surprised to find that you keep your computer here. It will have to eventually be moved to the living room once we are married. We will need a bigger bed and a few other pieces of furniture."

Turning towards the cabinets, she examined the folded clothing before commenting, "I think for one of our future dates, I am going to have to come here and refold all your clothing. It will save you about twice the space."

Deciding that he had had enough of this game, he walked up behind her and then wrapped both of his arms around her to hold her closely next to him. He expected her to stand still as she had done for both her father and his mum, so he was quite surprised when she leant her head into his chest before reaching her hands up to clasp onto his forearm. It was at this point that he was able to really grasp how petite she was. He found that he greatly enjoyed holding her this close; it also helped that she seemed to smell like a light vanilla scent. It was pleasant.

She announced, "I assume this means you are calling an end to my inspection?"

He chuckled before answering, "Kinda. I have just wanted to hold you for some time."

"Do you find it pleasant?"

"Yes, although I am surprised. When your father and my mum hugged you, you did not respond."

"I do not like making physical contact with people."

Giving a sneaky smile, he commented, "And yet here you are snuggled against me."

"As I have stated, your masculine energy has an unusual hold over me. I have hoped for you to finally adjust to my distinct personality traits before taking charge of me in a masculine manner."

"I hope it is living up to expectations."

"Surpassing. You smell pleasant, and I am enjoying the feeling of your firm muscles against me. Of course, you know that we will not be engaging in any inappropriate behaviour."

As soon as he spoke, he was embarrassed to realise that he was quoting his mother when he stated, "A fruit that is allowed to fully ripen is much sweeter."

She shifted away from him before stating, "I am greatly relieved to hear you say that."

He reached out tenderly to touch her chin with his right index finger before softly tilting her chin upwards and then bent slightly to kiss her.

# Chapter 13

Angus was quite pleased when he woke up the next morning for work. His relationship with Isla Grace was going great, and it helped him feel motivated to get back to programming new software. If they were to get married, he figured that he would need much more money, and new software programmes were the way to go. This one was going to be an automated system that would work to resolve many issues his coworkers were having without needing him to deal with them. The idea being he could sell it on the open market for a significant amount of money. He had records at work of a massive number of issues that he had commonly dealt with throughout his career. Most of which he would program his new software to deal with automatically once a report was submitted. It was going to be a brilliant piece of software, maybe worth a shit-ton of money. Since he did not want his work to claim even partial ownership, he decided to write it exclusively at home. Last night, before going to bed, he texted Isla Grace to tell her about it, and she was very encouraging, even stating that she felt that he was brilliant. Something about having her in his corner gave him much more confidence. He got ready and went to work. The day was spent bouncing about joyfully, helping everyone in need. During his lunch break, he sent himself a generalised log of all the most common problems people had, along with how he fixed them. This was going to serve as the basis for his software. Once the day was over, he headed home and shot off a text to Isla Grace asking how her day went. Apparently, she had been working on applications for a potential scholarship at Uni. After cooking himself a light supper, he got back to work on his new software programme.

His phone buzzed with a message from Liam that said, 'Oi cunt log into Discord.'

Chuckling to himself, he started up Discord. He could probably work on his software while chatting with Liam. The second he logged in, Liam invited him to a private chat.

The second he clicked 'JOIN', Liam spoke, "It's time to invite you into our personal group for the lads. Now that you're virtually my brother, you belong."

"Well," Angus said with a pause before continuing, "Let's not rush anything just yet."

Liam laughed riotously for a moment before saying, "If you saw your facial expression when Isla Grace came down the stairs with her hair loose, you'd know you're already done for. Might as well just get married now instead of waiting months to finally get laid."

"I don't know what you mean."

"Cunt, you were freakin' staring at her like she was Madonna come down from heaven. My whole family fucking saw it."

He was flustered and unsure how to respond.

"Also, what the fuck was up with the staring contest between the two of you before you kissed her?"

Angus chuckled before saying, "It was a battle of wills."

Liam laughed once again before declaring, "And you got your arse wrecked by a tiny little 45 kilos barely 1.5 metres tall girl."

Begrudgingly, he chuckled before he solemnly replied, "Ya."

It only made Liam laugh once again, and once he calmed down, he stated, "Pussy sure has a way of controlling us."

Angus did not say anything in response. He was still struggling in dealing with Liam's declarations about him and Isla Grace.

"But anyways, ya cunt, join our Discord. Keep in mind that you cannot tell anyone about it, ever."

"Oh sure." Angus said before disconnecting the chat,

Liam sent the link to it, and Angus noted it was titled 'Stirling Albion FC Club'. He was confused as to why Liam would claim a Discord about a Football Club would be secret. As soon as he entered Discord and began reading the posts, he immediately realised why. Liam and his lads appeared to be members of a Scottish Nationalist movement. He estimated that there were maybe 40 or 50 members, and they clearly deeply disliked the various immigrants, refugees, the LGBT community, communists, and literally every political party in the UK. There was particularly strong vitriol for the SNP.

After reading much of it, he reconnected the chat with Liam, "That was an interesting read."

"And?"

"Honestly, it feels like a lot of bitching with no plan or action."

"And what do ya think we can do?"

Angus frowned, pondering Liam's question before stating, "Maybe come up with a plan and how you'd execute it. It's kinda like a programming issue. You need to decide your end-state and then work out how you'll get there."

"If the lads and I were to propose an end-state, as you call it, do you think you could come up with a plan?"

Angus scratched the light stubble on his chin. Part of being a great programmer was the ability to design plans. He probably could design a plan, although after reading all the stuff those guys talked about in their Discord, he felt they probably wanted to do something he was not so sure about.

"I could, but I'm not even sure what the hell you guys are up to."

"We're sick and tired of the Brits, the EU, and even our own politicians poisoning our society as they turn men into pussies and women into unfuckable bitches. Scotland was always meant to be the home of the Scots, not a bunch of third-world monkeys. It makes me sick when I hear politicians spewing a bunch of virtue signalling bull shite while in the background, they rape our nation. Right now, it's just us talking about it. When I met you at first, you were a flabby goofball with the confidence of a clamshell. After only 4 months of working out with the lads and being around us, you could probably have pulled the hottest bitches left in this place with your job and 6-pack abs. Instead, you did what all Scots should do: you reached out for God, and now you're gonna marry probably the most religious woman in the nation. It's what all Scots should strive for, a pure Godly Scotland. No degenerate arseholes walking around in parades with their fucking dicks out. No hordes of Asian bastards or other foreigners soiling Scottish lands, and lastly, no god damned sell-out politicians holding back Scottish pride and raping our wallets. Fuck every one of them."

Angus was impressed with Liam's passion, and he suddenly realised maybe Liam was not as lax a Catholic as he thought.

All he could say, however, was, "Oh."

Liam chuckled into the mic before stating, "I get it. You're still a normie, not seeing the world for what it is. You've barely tasted the red pill, and since you're probably months away from happily marrying my sister, you probably won't get the black pill for a while."

"The black pill?" Angus inquired.

Liam answered, "Yes. The red pill is when people start to realise something is wrong with our world. Much of it is a lie, constructed by the powers that be to manipulate and control us. Once that realization sets in, people get the black pill. That is when everything feels hopeless because the powers in charge are so strong and the sheep normies around us would fight to the death to protect their precious false reality. Finally, it's the white pill when hope returns, and you start to decide to fight, in whatever way you can."

"And where are you?" Angus asked.

"I'm at the white pill, but I'm struggling with finding a way to fight back. Scotland is a beautiful land filled with plenty of noble men and women. They have been deceived, and somehow, I need to find a way to save my home."

He could do nothing but nod. Liam's passion was undeniable.

"What do you think cunt?" Liam then asked.

"I'm not sure. I agree with much of what you said, and what happened to my sister should never have happened, and now that it has, must be stopped from ever happening again. I just don't know what a bunch of cunts from Stirling can do about it. It isn't like we can barge into Parliament with guns and simply remove the Scottish government."

There was a moment of silence before Liam stated, "Perhaps. For now, I want you to think about it. I'll talk with the lads, and we'll see about your end-state. I'm expecting complete silence on this. Don't even tell Isla Grace."

"I can't lie to her."

"Of course not. If you don't mention it, she won't know. You're essentially my brother. I expect you to act that way."

He was more than a little miffed. The idea that he would betray trust was more than a little insulting to him.

However, he did understand Liam's concerns. After all, the douchebag government was literally arresting people for saying that mentally ill men in dresses were men online, so he said, "Of course ya big lunk."

"Alright, I'll talk to you later." Liam stated before ending the call.

Angus scrolled through some more pictures, comments, and links to various articles. Much of what the lads in Discord were claiming had evidence, evidence that he had never seen before. It was apparently part of the red pill to realise that everything the media, which was controlled by people trying to control everyone, was a lie. He had remembered hearing about the Asian rape gangs running rampant throughout the UK, terrorizing young British girls. It was nauseating and a disgrace. He was still confused, so he decided to call Isla Grace.

She answered the phone after one ring and said, "Hello Angus."

"Hey, Isla Grace."

There was a moment of silence before she said, "Your voice sounds upset. Is there something wrong?"

Making sure not to mention Liam or his friends, he went over all the major claims about Scotland that their Discord made.

She listened patiently the whole time before saying. "My father has spoken of these issues many times at home. I find all of it quite concerning, as Scots are an amazing and resilient people. It does indeed seem as though our own leaders have abandoned us to the wolves of the world. It is one of the major reasons that my sisters are never alone without a male relative in public. My father has stated that he felt our politicians should be removed from office and Scotland should be free, but he said the SNP would just grovel over to the European Union right away. He and my mother celebrated when Brexit won."

Angus nodded. It was obvious that Liam was cut from the same cloth as his father.

He asked her, "What do you think?"

"I concur with my father. Scotland is on a path of ruin. Eventually, the only people left will be victims of Asians, degenerate homosexuals, Asians, and the corrupt political body controlling it all. I, however, cannot do anything about it except attempt to bring as many Godly Scots into the world to aid in stemming the tide."

Angus nodded. He had a lot to chew on.

She then asked, "What has inspired this conversation?"

Something about his relationship with her made him unable to lie, so he asked, "Can I trust you to neither tell anyone what I am about to tell you nor act on it?"

"You could trust me with your life, Angus. I would sooner die than betray you."

"And what of Liam?"

"Liam?"

"Yes. Do you feel the same?"

"Not only is he my brother, but he brought you to me. I would not betray him. I can assume however, that he is the one who brought this information to your mind."

"He did."

"I must concur with my brother, who clearly concurs with my father. Now my question is, what is about to happen?"

Giving a deep sigh, Angus answered, "I don't know. Liam wants to do something to save Scotland, and he wants me to help by making him a plan."

"A plan?" she asked.

"I'm really good at planning and organizing. It's part of what makes me a great programmer."

"Are you going to do it?" She asked with the same calm voice that she would use to order some fish and chips.

"I don't know. I do agree Scotland is in dire trouble, but if they are found out, everyone could get in trouble."

"True, and as a man on the cusp of having a lot to lose, it is probably a scary thing to think about."

He nodded to no one in particular as he answered, "It is."

"Angus, my feelings for you are great. I would even say love. I will not tell you which path to take, but I will say that it is the boldest of men who leap when there is the most to lose."

"If you were me, Isla Grace, what would you do?"

"I would plan." She told him before continuing, "It is time for me to sleep for the night. Let me know tomorrow what you decide; either way, I will always support your decision."

"Okay. Good night, Isla Grace."

"Angus."

"Yes?"

"I believe that this is the part of the communication where you are supposed to declare your love for me."

He chuckled. She really had a way about her.

"I do love you, Isla Grace."

"As do I, good night."

She hung up the phone. Spinning his phone in his hand, he turned back to the computer screen. The next article in the Discord messages was a video of several Asian men in Germany dragging a German woman into a tunnel as she screamed for help, while the large crowd around her just watched it all happen.

He opened his text messages and texted Liam with the message, 'I'm in.'

# Chapter 14

14 October 2017.

Angus strolled around the shopping centre in High Street, Stirling, trying to find a jewellery shop. He was really lost. While Isla Grace had not said to him what type of ring she would want for the engagement, he was quite confident that it would have to be simple and elegant. His only problem was that he had no idea what that was. There were a few jewellery stores, but as he wandered through each one, he found himself unable to decide. Everything was shiny and golden with diamonds all over the place. This was a battle that he was not going to win, so he decided to call his mum.

"Hello?" His mum said as she answered.

"Hey mum, I need you to help me."

"Okay, what do you need?"

"I'm trying to find a ring and" He started to say, but was cut off by his mum when she cheerily asked, "You're already going to pop the question?"

"Ya mum. I love her and really don't see a point in waiting anymore."

His mum snickered before responding, "More likely the girl just told you to go out and buy her a ring already."

Giving a little chuckle, he replied, "Actually, I'm out on my own right now. Could you come high street to The Thistles and help me pick one?"

"I'm on my way honey."

"Thanks mum." He said before he ended the call.

He was quite relieved when his mum showed up quickly. She had on a pair of jeans, a jumper, and a beanie. It was quite chilly outside after all. She pointed over at a bench, a hint for them to sit down. As she sat, he sat down next to her.

"So, tell me what you think she wants in her ring."

"I'm sure she wants something simple and elegant."

"And how much do you have to spend?"

"Hrmm… I mean, I can easily drop 10 or 15 thousand pounds."

Her jaw dropped as she paused before finally saying, "How the heck do you have so much to toss into an engagement ring?"

"Huh? Oh, I didn't tell you guys, I recently sold a programme to Microsoft. It automatically detects the most common network and software problems that large networks of employees have before they become significant, and fixes most of them. They paid me a lot of money."

"I am very proud of you, honey. What are you going to do with all that money?"

"Most of it I put into investment funds, but I'm thinking about buying another house."

His mum giggled at him before saying, "You'll probably need it if that girl has her way."

He nodded. Of all the things he was most worried about, being a father was highest on the list. It dawned on him early on, when Isla Grace kept talking about having children, that it was a serious problem for him. He figured that between his father and Mr. Gillespie, he would have enough help.

"Well," His mum said as she paused before continuing, "I believe you are right, something simple. So, we can look for rings with only a single diamond. With so much to spend, we can get her a platinum band. Also, might as well pick up a platinum wedding band as well."

"Okay."

"Well, let's go take a look."

They spent three hours bouncing between several jewellery stores before finally settling on a simple platinum ring. His mother convinced him to select a ring that also had a series of much smaller diamonds set into what looked almost like two petals forming a two-dimensional flower stacked along the band from the side of the ring and stopping with a large, but not massive, circular-shaped diamond. He had to admit that it was simple and elegant, just like he thought Isla Grace would like.

Before they parted ways, his mum asked, "So when are you gonna ask?"

"I figured since you and dad are gonna be at her parents' house tomorrow for supper after mass, I thought it would be a perfect time."

"Sounds perfect. Love you, honey."

Angus hugged her and watched for a moment as she walked away. He popped open the little box holding the ring. It was probably perfect, but he had to admit he was quite nervous about the whole thing. Shrugging, he closed the box and then headed back home. After getting home, he tucked the box away on the top shelf of one of the cabinets holding some dishes. Since Isla Grace was coming over to cook supper tonight, he needed to put it somewhere she could not find it. He chuckled, thinking about the dozens of times she had come over and needed him to get items off the top shelves or cabinets throughout his home. He then sat down at his desk to play around with another programme he was designing. At the rate he was going, he would be able to quit his job and programme full-time. Microsoft cut a deal with a small annual stipend, dependent on sales, and then offered him a job. He did not want to move to America, so he passed on the offer. He especially liked this new programme, it served as a patching system to allow computers on the network to shift on and off security measures based on the processor needs of other programs running. It would allow the admins to prioritise appropriately based on user needs. Because of the complexity of the programme, he figured it would take a lot longer to complete. He had been so focused on the programming that he had barely been playing CoD. In fact, a new version of CoD was about to come out, but he did not even pre-order it. This was much more important to him now. The buzzer for his door rang. He glanced at his phone and saw that it was only 3 p.m. He had no idea who was ringing him. Standing up he strolled over and opened the door to be surprised to see Isla Grace standing there.

"Hey!" He said happily.

"I hope you do not mind me arriving on my own and early. I was bored sitting at home, so I asked my father if he could drop me off here."

Taking her hand to help her walk in, he responded, "Of course not. I was just working on my latest programme."

"You told me about it. I am quite proud of your work efforts. At the rate you are working, our family will never have to be concerned about financial considerations."

Chuckling, he commented, "That's the plan."

As the door closed, Isla Grace wrapped her arms around his midsection to hug him. She was still very emotionless in general, but she became much more physically warm with him, mostly he noted when they were alone. He held her close and took a moment to inhale whatever lovely perfume she was wearing. Her hair was back in its bun, which she had told him she did because it made managing her hair while doing chores much easier. He felt one of her hands rub against his chest. He had no doubt their engagement would not be a long one. Suddenly, he felt an overwhelming urge to just get the ring and do it right away. It might be a better idea than in front of their families, since she was so reserved. Their families would love to see him do it, but he realised that they would be happy either way, and Isla Grace would be much happier if he did it in private. She avoided attention like the plague. He decided to do what she would prefer, so he released her.

Lifting a small bag of groceries, she announced, "I had my father purchase the items so that I could make us some Cullen Skink tonight for supper."

Nodding, he told her, "That sounds good."

As she turned away to put the bag that she had brought onto the counter, he quickly snatched the box holding the ring and tucked it into his palm.

As she turned around, he immediately dropped to a knee and then said, "We both know that we belong together, and I'm tired of waiting, so I'm just going to ask. Isla Grace Maria Gillespie, will you marry me?"

Her expression did not change initially, but when he opened the small box to offer the ring, her mouth cracked slightly open in an expression of shock. She clearly liked the ring that he picked. She stood there saying nothing.

"Isla Grace?"

"Oh, sorry. I accept your proposal."

She extended her left hand outwards, open towards him. Angus took the ring out of the box and then slid it on her ring finger. The deed was done, and he was happy about it. While he was still kneeling, she stepped close and then kissed him quite passionately. After they broke off their kiss, she pulled on one of his hands to help him stand.

"I hope you like the ring." He stated.

She glanced at her new ring and then commented, "It is quite lovely. The sides appear to look almost like a side view of a lily repeated along the band, and I am guessing this is made of platinum. You paid a lot for it. You did not need to do so, but I appreciate it."

"I feel as though you're worth it."

"You are most kind."

He gave her a grin, and as he was about to kiss her, she said, "Go sit on the sofa and relax. I will prepare supper."

"Do you need help?"

"No. You do your work now, let me do mine."

"I've already learned better than to argue with you." He retorted with a chuckle.

"You are an intelligent man who learns quickly. I suspect it was our second date when I came down the stairs, and you stubbornly refused at first to give me a kiss. However, I want you to know that you are the man; if you decide on a path we must take, I will accede to your wishes. By becoming your wife, I offer myself unto you and trust your wisdom to guide me and lead me."

Angus nodded before heading into the living room. He could hear her working in the kitchen. After the first time she cooked for him, he had to move most of the items down to lower shelves so she could reach them. He also moved his computer into the living room as well. Instead of sitting on the sofa, he started tweaking the programme he was working on. This one was quite complex and very different from most he had written, so it was giving him some trouble. He was so busy that time flew by, and before he knew it, Isla Grace called him to come sit down at the dining room table. As he took a seat, he could smell supper. He was not a huge fan of seafood, but so far everything she had cooked for him was very good. Her mother taught her to be an excellent cook.

She took a seat across from him and then said, "Now that we are formally engaged, we should probably go through a few things."

Chuckling, he stated, "Probably pick a date and go from there."

"I wish to marry, complete our honeymoon, and lastly get settled in with you here before Lent begins."

Angus almost gagged on his soup. That was only 4 months away! He did think of having a brief engagement, but they would likely have to wed at the latest in the first or second week of January.

"Is this too quick for you?" She asked.

"Well," He said before pausing to gather his thoughts and then continuing, "It isn't that it is too fast. We could marry tomorrow, but I feel as though we should have a proper wedding, and everything takes time to plan."

"Indeed. Therefore, we are going to pick the date right now, and then I will start to work on executing the wedding. Both of our mothers have offered to assist, and I plan to take them up on the offer so all tasks can be delegated and executed with efficiency." He was quite surprised. The relationship between Isla Grace and her mother seemed tense at times, so unless something had changed, he thought it was odd that she would so willingly accept help from her mother. Maybe his arrival in their lives had shifted the relationship; he did not know and could not think of a way to broach the subject.

"My birthday is January 7th, and most of the time before my birthday is occupied by holidays. Perhaps January 13th. We can leave for our honeymoon for a week and then return with plenty of time to set up our home and prepare for Lent. What do you think?"

"Works for me. Where did you want to go for our honeymoon?"

"I have an idea, but I was curious if you had any possible locations you wished to see."

"Somewhere nice and warm would be great, but I'm open to anything. What is your idea?"

She answered very quickly, "The Vatican City."

Giving out a light chuckle, he had to admit that her choice was not a surprise. A Catholic girl wanting to go to the capital of the religion was almost predictable.

"Sounds good. We can go to see Rome and maybe even visit a beach."

"Excellent. If you are comfortable with it, we can have my father and maybe Liam help move all my things into your house while we are gone."

"Our home." He corrected her.

One of her tiny little smiles appeared as she corrected herself by saying, "Our home. I greatly look forward to our wedding, honeymoon, and living together. I did have a question for you, however."

"Which is?"

"Has my brother contacted you about the issues he was concerned about with his claimed end-state?"

"Not yet. I think he's still decided what his goal is."

She nodded solemnly before saying, "I am sure it will come up sooner or later. For now, we should probably concentrate on the task at hand. By Monday, I will probably need access to funding for our wedding and honeymoon so I can get started."

"Oh, of course. I can take you to the bank and have you added to the accounts."

"I will also need you to explain your budget and planning, so I do not accidentally make a mistake and ruin your financing."

Angus suddenly realised that merging two people into a single couple was a lot more work than Isla Grace simply moving into his home.

He gave her a nod before saying, "Of course. Most of my money is tied up in stocks and other investments, but that software I recently sold has set things very nicely. We've got plenty to ensure we can do the wedding however we want."

"That is good. I am not planning to do anything too extravagant. My gown will be simple and modest."

"Of course. I just need a nice tux, and I was thinking that Liam would be my best man. After all, without him we wouldn't be here."

"As I predicted. Let me clean up after supper, and we can go over more details."

# Chapter 15

7 November 2017.

Angus was quite surprised by how quickly and efficiently Isla Grace had organised and set up everything for their wedding. The date was firmed up with St. Alexander's as the site, and Angus took charge of planning the honeymoon. They were going to have an afternoon wedding and then fly to Rome for the honeymoon with Sunday mass at the Vatican the next day. It was perfect. He was now at work, still grinding for money by making sure everything continued as planned. It was a pretty light day since he kept on with all the computer issues as they came up. His performance review was yesterday, and his supervisor gave him the highest scores with a special mark noting his work effort overall had gone up. He had not been playing CoD at work either because of his focus on the future. While he did not want to work on his personal programmes at work, he did upgrade the old programme he had installed at work. After work, he headed home and decided to take a little break from non-stop work and buy the most recent CoD. This one was a World War II version that was released just last Friday. After the game was downloaded, he started it up. It was going to take a while to learn all the maps, weapons, and sneaky tricks available. Angus decided that he was not going to grind hard like the last game to become a top team, but instead, he would play it for fun while taking care of his soon-to-be arriving family. While he had not considered Isla Grace a sexual being when he first met her, it was clear to him that she was as much a woman as any other. It took all his strength, more than a few times, to stop himself from having sex with her. She was just as guilty as he was, but they held their ground in the end. Soon they will be married, and then they can finally just do it.

His phone rang, and seeing it was Liam, Angus answered, "Hey."

"Oi cunt, you got the new CoD yet? I know my sister's got your balls in a sling, but are you sure you finally got it right?"

Angus laughed before answering, "Just downloading it now. I needed a break from the grind. I'm not gonna be able to grind like before, but I'm still gonna have fun shooting some bitches."

"Ya me too. I can't wait to gun down some fucking Nazis and Commies. It's like Christmas early."

Angus commented, "As long as you remember who your daddy is, everything will be just fine."

"Cunt don't make me gun your arse down right away."

Chuckling, Angus replied, "I've gotta learn the game first. I hope this 5-day lead has allowed you the opportunity to not be a scrub."

Liam laughed before responding, "Maybe. I mostly hit you up about something we talked about a while back."

Angus paused. Maybe Liam finally decided to come up with their end-state. He had considered changing his mind and backing out of planning for them, but he was a man of his word.

Liam continued, "Remember when you said it isn't like we couldn't just charge in and do something?"

Giving it a thought, he did remember saying that it was not like they could just charge into Parliament and shoot them all.

With hesitation, he answered, "Yes."

"That's the end-state. I want you to come up with a plan."

He signed heavily before saying, "Okay."

"I'm gonna head out. I'll talk to you later cunt."

"Okay."

Liam hung up the phone. Angus' head was spinning with Liam's declaration that he wanted to revolt violently against the Scottish leadership. The only way it could even be possible is if the British decided to mind their business, which Angus highly doubted, or they would have to be prepared to not only remove the Scottish government but also be ready to fight a Civil War against the British. It would be a monumental undertaking and require a lot of very secretive planning. Angus decided he would need to talk to Isla Grace first, so he picked up his phone and dialed her number.

"Hello." Her stoic voice came through as she answered.

"Liam called and told me his end-state that he wants me to plan for."

"And?"

"They want it all. Removal and replacement of everyone."

"That is likely the only way that it could be done to save everything. Are you going to go through with it?"

"I feel as though I must. These people won't stop, and I don't want to raise my children in this Scotland when I could do so in a better one."

"I support your decision. I only recommend a high level of security as you go."

"I will. Thank you for your support, Isla Grace."

"Always. I must meet with the priest about some details, so I will talk to you later."

"Okay, I love you."

"I love you too."

As he hung up the phone, he chuckled. Her voice was so monotone and stoic that he thought if anyone else stated that they loved him in such a monotone voice, he would not have believed them. He felt her passion alone on his sofa, so he knew it was true. Turning back to his computer, he decided to ignore CoD and turned on his VPN. The first step in any project is research, so he decided to take time to research successful attempts to see how they did it.

*****

2 December 2017.

Angus was quite surprised when Liam recommended a meeting after Angus had told him that he had come up with a plan. They had been exclusively meeting through Discord, but Liam said he was concerned about keeping things quiet. Liam chose a pub with several private rooms that could be rented out for parties. It was in the southern part of Stirling. The oddest part was Liam telling Angus not to bring his cell phone or any other electronic devices. It left Angus with a larger level of respect for Liam's intellect. Maybe he was not just a mindless meathead gym rat? After he got to the pub, he was surprised by the number of men who were there; it had to be easily 50 or so men. Perhaps the full membership of the Discord chat they had for their "fan club". Maybe some of them were wearing jerseys as well. He was greeted rowdily as he entered the small private area set aside for their 'fan club' meeting. Liam was standing in the front of the room by himself; he waved at Angus to have him come up front.

As soon as Angus walked up, Liam called out in a loud voice, "Oi cunts sit down, it's time to start."

The room became silent. Angus nodded as he was impressed by Liam's leadership. He rarely got to see Liam outside of the family and CoD, so he really did not know him as well as he could.

Liam continued, "Everyone knows what we're here for."

One of the men in the back, "To save this God damned place."

Others around them cheered. It was obvious to Angus that he was with friends and loyal Scotsmen.

Waving at the crowd to be quiet, Liam said, "Right cunts, now shut the hell up. Lemme introduce you to Angus Bruce."

"A Bruce!" One of the men called out before continuing, "Just like the first time. We can't lose."

"Right, right, right, simmer down. Angus, here is the man with the plan. Shut up and let him tell everyone what's up."

Angus was more than a little nervous. He really did not know any of these men that well. Swallowing down his nerves, he stepped forward.

The crowd was watching him patiently as he spoke, "We all know what our final goal is... Freedom."

Before he could continue speaking, the men around him cheered out, "Huzzah!"

Liam called out again, "Ya cunts let the man talk."

Once they stopped talking, Angus continued, "I did extensive research on previous attempts that were successful to identify the key requirements to ensure success."

From the crowds, someone asked, "Where'd ya find the nerd Liam?"

The others in the group laughed uproariously. Angus had never considered himself a nerd, but he probably was one.

Liam spoke once they stopped the ruckus to say, "How the hell are we gonna pull this off if we don't have a brain to tell us what's what, ya dumb arse?"

No one else said a word, so Angus took the opportunity to continue, "Now, as I was saying before being interrupted. You must understand what you're doing before you can do it. I have taken all the best parts of successful attempts from the past and melded them into a cohesive plan. First, we must co-ordinate and expand our network. We need to somehow recruit a huge number of police, military, and other control groups, like firemen or media, that can lock in our power base. Once they're on board, we then need to recruit raw numbers. On average, most successful attempts required at least 4 to 5 thousand raw fighting forces just for the first step of our end-step."

Liam asked, "First step?"

"Removal," Angus answered before explaining more, "What do you think will happen once we remove them? The British are about 75% likely to refuse our declaration and start a military conflict. Once that happens, our numbers will need to be at about twenty thousand fighting men in what will probably have to be a guerrilla campaign to draw out the enemy and sap their fighting will. There are more than 30 military facilities for the United Kingdom throughout Scotland. We'll need to neutralise or control each one of those. I estimate that by doing so, we'll probably eliminate 35% of the entire British available fighting force since our arse leaders constantly keep sending men overseas for shit that isn't even our business. That alone will give us a fighting chance. To make this happen, we need to infiltrate and recruit as many personnel as possible for all these garrisons. Once we have those recruits, we'll then need to find a way to gain control of STV so we can have our own media organization. After that, we will need to train, not only for the primary action but for the potential fallout. Scotland is full of cucks and beta males, but there are plenty of honourable Scottish men who will likely rise and fill our ranks if the British decide to invade. Assuming we get through all of that and defeat the British, then my question is, what's next?"

Angus could have dropped a pin in the room and heard it fall; it was dead silent.

Finally, Liam announced, "Simple. We'll institute laws removing all non-Scots from our lands, we'll ban all commie bullshit, and lastly, we'll implement a Constitution like the American one but with more protections to keep arseholes from corrupting our shit. Term limits, no corporate money, and that sort of shit."

One man in the crowd yelled out, "Ban the fuck outta Islam."

Liam nodded, "Of course. We've gotta get those bastards out of Scotland. Now, lads, this is where all of you come in. If we don't keep this secret, it'll be all our heads. These bastards would love to catch us in the act and parade us in the streets. Each of you is a founding fucking father of a new free Scotland. We've already got a shit-ton of lads here in the military and the police, but now we need to pump those numbers up and spread everywhere. We'll meet in a week, and all of you will come up with names and locations of how you plan to recruit. Anyone got a question?"

A man in the crowd asked, "Are we really doing this?"

Liam nodded, "Yes. You can back out now, but if anyone betrays us, it'll be their head."

There was utter silence for a bit before Angus spoke, "We must do what we must do. All of us. Each of us is highly important to the success of this. One mistake will cost all of us our lives. I'm about to marry and have children, but I'm here. We all love Scotland, and we all have a lot to lose. This is not for us; it's for our children's children, so each of you keep this in mind and move cautiously to find others to join us. I put an unmarked list of every military base in Scotland on the Discord. Use that to help find recruits. All those garrisons must be under our sway before we can do anything else."

Again, there was silence as Angus realised those around him were finally starting to figure out just exactly what they were doing, a coup and possibly then a Civil War. It was daunting. The crowd around them began to break away as they slowly shuffled out of the room.

Angus began walking away, and he was stopped by Liam, who asked, "Do you think we can actually do this?"

"We're in it now. We have no choice but to do it. I'm thinking we need to find allies, but the only people who could ally with us outside of Scotland are scum. Iran, China, and the lot. It sickens me to think of having to use help from any of them."

"For now, we go it alone." Liam announced firmly.

# Chapter 16

15 December 2017.

Angus grinned as he hung up the phone. He just spent the last hour going over the details of the wedding with Isla Grace. She and both of their mothers had put everything together, and the wedding was a go. She informed him that her dress had been selected, along with everything else for the wedding and the reception. The wedding itself was going to be at 11 a.m., and then the reception started at a banquet hall in High Street, Stirling. Their flight to Rome was at 5 p.m. He was quite excited about it all. The Stirling Albion FC group had another meeting where each member came up and discussed who they knew and how they would get them to join the cause. Angus was quite surprised to find out that not only did every man return, but they came back with a few dozen more men. Their cause was already headed in the right direction. Liam seemed to be letting Angus take more of a lead in things to the point that Angus was pretty much running most of the show. It was not long before Angus knew most of the lads at the meeting. Like him, many had a family and a lot to lose. They all knew it had to be done to save Scotland. Today, he was going to have a meeting with Liam and a small group for something special. Liam would not say what. It was after dinner, and Liam told him to meet them by himself with no cell phone and alone. He called Isla Grace and wished her a good night before heading out. It rained a little earlier in the day, but it was just a smidge cold outside. He wrapped himself in a jacket and hopped into his car. The drive was quick, and it was not long before he had got to the pub. Liam messaged him where specifically to go. While they had been quite secretive about most everything, Liam had not been this quiet about this stuff before. As Angus approached the booth, he saw Liam, and he spotted three other men with him. All three were large lads with neatly cropped short hair and clean-shaven faces. All three of them looked older. Angus guessed they were easily in their early to mid-forties. He was not the best at guessing ages. Immediately, he thought that they were military men.

"Have a seat." Liam instructed Angus as he approached them.

The pub was quite busy, which was not a surprise since Scots loved to drink when the weather turned to shit.

Sliding into the booth next to Liam, Angus said, "Thanks."

"So, this is the guy with the plan?" One of the men stated.

Liam then answered, "He's our leader. I've already given ya the plan, but I wanted you to smash brains with Angus so we can develop more."

Angus began to open his mouth to object to being called the 'leader', but he felt Liam's foot nudge into him as a hint to be quiet, so he said nothing.

The man who asked the question spoke first, "Nice to meet you, Angus. I'm David Rutherford."

He then pointed to the man sitting next to him and said, "This is Markus Keith, and this is Harry Agnew."

Giving them a grim half-smile, Angus nodded before saying, "Angus Bruce. It's nice to meet all of you."

The man named Markus looked mildly surprised as he commented, "A Bruce, eh?"

"It's like I said," Liam stated before continuing, "Angus is the man with the plan. We just need real muscle. Muscle, you lads can provide."

"Who are you guys?" Angus asked.

The man who seemed to be the leader of the three declared, "I'm Colonel David Rutherford, the current Commander of the Black Watch, and once we start, I'll be serving as your Commanding officer in freeing Scotland."

Angus was shocked by his boldness. He glanced around them to make sure no one was close enough to hear or even pay attention to them. All the Scots around them seemed to be enjoying their drinking and not paying much heed to Angus and his associates.

The man named Harry then said, "We're all sick of the SNP, the Brits, and the EU. Every damned one of them seems to not give a shite about Scotland or Scots. There had been rumours in the ranks about our own men sick of the shite going on. I guess one of our men heard the three of us talking about how we were sick of it, so he approached us to tell us in secret about your group. We leapt at the chance to join."

The other man, named Markus, interjected, "To save Scotland."

Angus nodded. If these men were serious, which they seemed to be, they could be the beginning of a real tide in their favour.

"Now… Liam told us about the plan to institute a Yankee-style Constitution, and we're all in agreement on that. He also mentioned adding more measures to prevent cunts from being corrupt as well. Obviously, our services will not be free. Each of us is expecting high positions once this is all over, but we all want to serve honourably in greater roles that the British military limits us from doing. We aren't looking for money or power, just greater duties and the honour that comes with it."

Angus leant closer to them before saying. "If we do it, we'll all be hated by most of the world."

The one named Markus chortled before saying, "So what. Scottish men shouldn't give a fuck what others think of 'em."

Angus nodded at him before stating, "Likely we'll be hated here for a while as well. Once we free Scotland, we plan to make it so the nation can never fall under the sway of a foreign force ever again. Then… maybe… We'll be heroes. If we win, there will be a period of disorganization that likely will require a man with a firm hand to lead. That man will probably need to have men like you to work with him."

Liam interjected, "We've already got that man."

Angus looked over at Liam before saying, "I don't want to run anything."

David then leant towards him before declaring, "That's why you are gonna lead us all."

"No, I'm just a planner."

All three men around them chuckled before Markus stated, "That's usually the guy who ends up in charge and should be the one there. The fact you don't want it makes me want it to be you even more."

"Anyone of you could be the man" Angus started to protest before he was interrupted.

"No, it's you." David stated firmly before continuing, "Not only do you have the plans, but you also got the name. Imagine the reaction of the people when they find out a Bruce is the one leading us."

The others nodded. Angus sighed. He realised they were not going to be talked out of it. He understood their logic. The last time Scotland won its freedom was when Robert the Bruce, his ancestor, led them on the fields of Bannockburn. All Scots knew it, so he guessed that having a Bruce leading them again could inspire others.

"Alright, but I'll be leaning on all of you. I'm no fighter. I'm a computer programmer."

Harry commented, "You look right fit for a computer nerd."

That got the others chuckling, and once they finished laughing, Liam stated, "After I met the cunt, I've been dragging him to the gym. My mistake because the cunt took the first chance that he could seduce my little sister, and he's about to marry her."

"Ahhh. So at least we know he's got as much to risk as everyone else." David stated before standing.

The others stood with him. Liam and Angus stood as well.

"We'll keep in touch. The three of us will begin recruiting carefully and co-ordinate with you. I understand the plan is to begin proper training once we have the numbers. We'll co-ordinate that as well."

Giving the man a nod, Angus reached out a hand.
David took his hand and shook it before declaring, "For Scotland."

Angus did not know what spurred him to say it, but he replied, "For Scotland."

Each man shook his hand, and then they left Liam alone with Angus. As Liam sat down, Angus sat as well.

Before Liam could say anything, Angus said, "I don't know about me being in charge of the whole thing."

"Naw Angus," Liam replied before giving a big grin and then saying, "It isn't just about the fact you're a Bruce. People respond to you when you take charge. Don't hesitate or question yourself again. A man's gotta be strong and confident. Your lead will inspire the rest of them. I don't have the brains to run this show, and many men would falter when their honour is pushed. You're the only one I trust."

Giving him a nod, Angus did not say a word. This whole thing was now past the point of no return, and he was more than neck-deep in it. He knew that he would have to talk to Isla Grace about it all.

"I'll agree to it, but once it's done, I'm out. Someone else will have to take charge. I'm no politician."

Liam laughed before telling him, "I'll be out too. I just wanna be rid of these corrupt evil bastards and let Scots be free. Once everything is settled, it'll be an election for whoever the Scots pick."

"Alright. I'm gonna head home, I've got work tomorrow."

"Right cunt, I'll see you later."

Angus got up and headed out. He was not overly happy about being pegged as the man in charge. He got into his car and started driving. On the radio, the reporter talked about Brexit, babbling on and on about how everything was in a complex gridlock with no end in sight. He sighed. Liam was right when he said Teresa May was gonna screw everything up. It would probably take even more time to finally get their release from the EU. Angus felt the urge to speak to Isla Grace. She might have been stoic and monotone on the phone, but she always seemed to know just the right thing to say to help him see things clearly.

After taking his jacket off, he called her, and she quickly answered by saying, "Hello Angus. I am pleasantly surprised to receive your call even after you had already wished me a good night."

"Ya. I had an interesting meeting with Liam and three other lads."

"Did it go well?"

"In the sense that they've decided for some reason that I should be the leader of the whole thing." He sullenly answered.

"Clearly the best choice." she replied coolly.

He was quite surprised. He knew that she supported him, but he could not see how she would think that he should be the person to lead a large military coup, followed by what could possibly be a Civil War.

"I don't think so." He replied.

She gave what could only be described as a half chuckle, which surprised him since she never so much as fully smiled around him, before saying, "You are a highly intelligent, honourable, fit man, and you have the name Bruce. Nothing screams 'Scottish leader' to other men. I imagine the other men seemed unwavering when you protested."

He gave a light grunt before claiming, "They insisted."

"You have got unlimited potential, Angus. I fully support them in calling you, their leader. Scotland must have a man of Christ who is honourable and loyal leading it out of this mess that much lesser men have placed us in."

"I suppose. I'm just worried the amount of risk we're taking will lead to our downfall."

"Either go all in Angus, or do not go at all." She replied firmly.

He was starting to think that she was as committed to this coup as Liam and the lads were. His heart steeled as he decided that he would no longer question it. It seemed as though he needed to learn more about warfare so he could lead the men if it came to that.

"You're right, Isla Grace. I'm gonna go and start researching more. I need to know how to lead, and I need to know fast."

"I am glad to hear you have accepted your role. I cannot wait until I can sit down shoulder to shoulder with you in our home and help you."

"Me too, although you're already making me better."

"Thank you for the kind words, my soon-to-be husband. I have a meeting with the florist tomorrow to select arrangements, so I should go to sleep. Good night."

"Night. I love you."

"I love you as well." She replied before hanging up the phone.

Angus pulled up his browser to find books on warfare, leadership, and anything else he could think of to help.

# Chapter 17

13 January 2018.

Angus rolled out of bed and quickly got ready to go. Today was finally the day of his wedding, and he was about as ready for it as he had been for anything in his life. Isla Grace picked out a beautiful all-white tuxedo with a black tie for him to wear. She had wanted him to wear a kilt, but he just did not like the red and green of his Clan's tartan. Instead, she bought him a pin for the middle of the tie that was his clan's crest. The colour that was chosen for the bridesmaids was the same red as the red in his clan's tartan. Liam accepted the offer to be the best man, so everything was set. Angus took a shower and then got ready to go. After slipping on his tuxedo rental, he headed off to St. Alexander's in Denny. They must have practised the actual wedding a dozen times or more. Angus could probably recite the whole thing in his sleep at this point. Isla Grace did not surprise him when she told him they were doing a nuptial mass wedding ceremony. She was as much a Catholic as any person he had ever met, so a proper Catholic wedding was what he knew their wedding would be. It was quite lengthy with a lot of blessings and prayers within it. Kneeling before the altar and staying there for what amounted to about an hour was not something he looked forward to. Giving himself a chuckle, he headed off. Once he got to the church, he was greeted by his parents, her parents, and the rest of their families. Reflecting on it, he was quite sad that Annis was not there to see him get married. He was certain that she would be very amused by Isla Grace's distinct personality.

Stepping out of his car, he was greeted by Liam, who said, "Hey man. I hope you're happy. Sandra got one look at Isla Grace's dress, and now she's squawking about us getting married."

Angus laughed before shaking his hand and replying, "It's time that you stop messing about and get married, ya lout."

Liam gave what was an obvious mock frown before declaring, "You too?"

Slapping Liam on the shoulder, Angus answered, "Yep. Let's go."

The whole ceremony went as smoothly as silk. Angus had not seen her wedding dress, so he greatly enjoyed it. The whole thing was a full-length lace affair that covered every inch of her skin below her neck, where the collar started. She had on a light white lace veil that covered her head and her whole face. They knelt there in front of the altar and stayed there the whole time through each rite, and he was quite happy when the priest finally declared them husband and wife. After they solemnly left the church, they were rowdily greeted by the crowd waiting for them outside. He could not help but grin madly at the response to their marriage. It was not just his family and her family, but he spotted many of the Stirling Albion FC club members, as well as a huge number of strangers. He glanced at Isla Grace. Her face was stoic as usual. Now, her veil was flipped over, and he could see that somehow her family convinced her to apply a little makeup. It was the first time he saw her wearing it, and it did a fine job of accentuating her features without being caked on. He waved out to the crowd as they walked towards their rented limousine. He booked it to take them to the reception and then the airport. They were going to change into travel clothing once the reception ended. Their first night together would be at the hotel in Rome. He helped her climb into the limousine before sliding in next to her. The door closed as he took her hand.

She rested her second hand on his before saying, "I am so proud to have you as my husband and join your Clan."

He looked at her. She gave him one of her almost microscopic smiles, so he grinned back at her. The limousine began moving to the reception, which was booked in the whole dining area of The Allen Park, a very nice pub and restaurant, in Stirling. His mum was the one who co-ordinated everything,

"I'm proud to be married to you as well, Isla Grace."

She then told him, "I wish we could have skipped the reception for some time at our home before our flight, but my mother and your mother were quite adamant that the reception must occur immediately after our wedding."

He knew exactly what she was suggesting, and he had to admit that he was excited for that moment.

While he would not have complained, he understood why they had receptions, so he told her, "Well, these sorts of events are as much about the two families celebrating together as they are for the bride and groom. We'll have plenty of time together tonight.

Mass at St. Peter's Basilica is repeated throughout the day on Sunday, so we can pick and choose whichever time we want to attend. I'm thinking of either half past 10 or half past 11. Everything is closed in Vatican City on Sunday, so we can tour nearby and the next day we'll go to tour Vatican City. The rest of the week, we'll explore Rome and pay a visit to the coast for some time at the beach."

"I have never worn a swimsuit nor gone swimming. I am also very uncomfortable wearing such a thing in public."

"You don't have to, but I really would love for you to come swimming with me. I'll be with you the whole time."

"I, of course, will attend to our events in the manner you choose."

Chuckling, Angus stated, "Well, generally I'd never want to make you do something you don't want to, but I've been daydreaming about seeing you in a swimsuit for about 4 months now."

"Very well, I will make your dream come true as it is my duty as your wife to please you as best I can."

Giving a light chuckle, he asked, "And you?"

"Me?"

"Do you have any of… those kinda dreams?" he asked with more than a little bit of embarrassment.

"I do not have any sort of sexual fantasies if that is what you are referring to. I just anticipate being held closely in your arms, undisturbed and without fear of sinning."

"Well," He commented while giving out a laugh, "That fear has gone to the wayside now that we're husband and wife."

"Indeed. I know that you are wary of having children, but we will go through it together and raise righteous Christ-like Catholics."

The limousine stopped, likely indicating that they had arrived at the reception.

He told her, "I know, but for now… let's go have fun."

She raised an eyebrow at him before stating, "I doubt being the centre of attention for hours on end as people praise you and then expect you to dance about will be 'fun'."

He laughed once again. Maybe it was her mother's revenge to foist an event that she knew Isla Grace would not enjoy, or maybe her mother was excited that a daughter she thought would never marry ended up getting married right away. He probably would never know because he doubted there was a way that he could broach the subject with either woman. He did like the fact that his mum and Isla Grace's mother seemed to have become fast friends. They were spending time shopping and even went to see a film together. He had heard so many times that mothers-in-law would become enemies, but it was the opposite in this case. The door of the limousine opened. Angus stepped out and then turned back to offer a hand to Isla Grace. She took his hand and then slipped out of the limousine.

As they walked towards the restaurant, he commented, "You look stunning."

She replied in her usual monotonic voice, "Thank you. I think white suits you as well."

Giving a light chuckle, he responded, "Thanks."

When they entered the restaurant, they were greeted by one of the many hostesses. A young blonde-haired woman wearing a simple red and black shirt, black trousers, and a white pinny.

She gestured towards them and announced, "Please follow me."

Angus led Isla Grace behind the hostess as she took them to a central table along a back wall of the main restaurant area. There was a wide-open space in the middle of the room that Angus guessed was going to be the dancing area. Surrounding that were a few dozen tables with chairs surrounding them. There was a spot where the band was already set up and ready to play. Guests of the bride and groom had begun to filter in. Angus could not see any of their family yet, but he suspected most of them would arrive soon enough. He guided Isla Grace to her seat at the main table and then sat down next to her.

Once he was seated, she commented, "I anticipate the end of this event more than anything I have ever anticipated in my entire life. It will feel like three hours of torture by being forced to listen to Robbie Williams sing 'Angels' on repeat as I am strapped to a chair watching grown men chase a ball around on a field of grass."

Angus laughed uproariously at her comment. She had a way with words that, for some reason, just tickled him in the right spot.

Turning to face him, she raised an eyebrow before asking, "My suffering brings you joy?"

"No, but your specific descriptions of how you'll be suffering are funny. I'm looking forward to our first dance together as husband and wife."

"I suppose that there are some benefits to this… ritual." She stated before pointing off to her right and then saying, "It appears that our wedding cake has arrived. It looks beautiful."

He glanced over and saw it. The cake was a three-tiered affair with white frosting and seemed to have what looked like pearls lining it. On top of it was a bride and groom. It was nice enough. Angus was not much of a cake person. Finally, their family began to arrive. Angus was not dreading the reception like she was, but he was more excited about going to Italy with her. He had not yet left the U.K., so he was very excited to see Europe.

Liam sat down next to him and sullenly declared, "So ya… I'm completely doomed, and it's all your fault."

Giving a little chuckle, Angus asked, "How so?"

Letting out a heavy sigh, Liam answered, "Sandy told me that I've got a month to propose, or she'll leave."

He was surprised when Isla Grace interrupted, "Good. You have strung that girl along long enough, and you are getting too old to be playing around as some football hooligan security guard. It is time to grow up and become a responsible adult."

The delivery of her words was the same as everything else she ever said, but the words must have cut Liam deeply because he softly replied, "I know."

She then continued, "Excellent. When Angus and I return from our honeymoon, we are expecting to hear that you are finally engaged. If you are not engaged by the time we return, I shall use my feminine wiles to convince my husband to not only have you removed from your video game team but hunt you down every time you play and brutally kill you."

Angus broke out laughing. For some reason, the factual and straight way that she said it made it seem as though she was about to order a hit on Liam like a mob boss.

Once he finished laughing, Liam somberly responded by saying, "I will."

His jaw almost hit the floor in response. Liam had talked more than once about marriage being for suckers. Maybe he was about to grow up on that front. They sat in silence waiting.

Once all the guests arrived, Liam stood up and raised his wine glass before declaring, "A toast to the bride and groom!"

The guests called out, "Here! Here!"

Liam then spoke, "When I met Angus Edward Bruce, we were both playing a video game called 'Call of Duty'. I was wrecking his face left and right, so he had begged me to stop."

A portion of the audience, who all knew better, laughed at Liam's claims. Angus decided right then, and there he would get revenge when Liam's wedding came.

Liam continued, "After we bonded as friends not only over the game but our love of leaving the EU, Stirling Albion FC, and the church."

More cheering from his words, and once they stopped again, Liam spoke, "When my sister, Isla Grace, asked to be taken on a date by Angus, I knew that trouble was afoot."

The crowd again laughed.

"They took to each other like fish to water, and now, less than a year later, they're married. I can think of no man I'd wish to marry my sister than Angus, and I can think of no woman who could give my friend Angus the love he deserves than my beautiful sister Isla Grace. I say this toast to both; may the Almighty bless this union not only with happiness but with many children. To the bride and groom!"

Cheers echoed out into the crowd. Angus took a sip of the champagne in his glass. It was crisp. He glanced over at Isla Grace to watch her hesitantly take a tiny sip. He suspected she had never tasted alcohol before because there was a tiny furrowing of her brow that let him know she did not like it. It was a movement so slight that only those who knew her would have spotted it.

As they set the glasses down, Isla Grace said, "Thank you brother, that was a fine toast. I must confess that I was relieved to find out that you were going to break Angus' arm in my honour."

Angus could not help but chuckle.

Liam then said to her, "Of course. I love you sis."

"I love you too brother. I wish that I could show my affection to you and all our family better, but I do love all of you."

Liam replied, "We know Isla Grace."

She simply made a little nod. The rest of the reception went well. For Angus, the biggest struggle was going to keep himself from the time-honoured tradition of giving the first bite of the cake to his bride by 'accidentally' smushing it on her. He decided in the end that she would not appreciate the humour so he fed her a piece normally. Isla Grace danced with her father, who seemed quite proud, and he danced with his mum. She was crying the whole time. Finally, they had one last dance with him and Isla Grace. She was a surprisingly good dancer for someone who claimed to detest it. After the reception, they quickly changed their clothing and headed off to Edinburgh airport. His family was kind enough to clean up and take care of all the closing concerns after the reception. Their flight lasted about 3 hours, and before long, they were checked into their hotel, Residenza Paolo VI. He chose it because it had a view of St. Peter's Square.

As they stepped off the lift, Isla Grace stopped walking before declaring, "I believe it is a time-honoured tradition during a honeymoon for the groom to carry the bride into their bedroom on the first night."

He was not sure if he would ever tire of her blunt and yet very direct humour. He gave a chuckle before scooping her up into his arms and then marching her to the door. Sadly, holding her made it much harder to open the door, but he got it open and stepped into the room.

Giving her a sly smile, he declared, "I believe it's now time for the next time-honoured tradition during the honeymoon."

He used his left foot to kick the door behind him closed.

# Chapter 18

Angus awoke the next morning, resting on his back to see Isla Grace resting half on top of him, looking at him. She had her right index finger slowly tracing his eyebrow. It felt nice to him.

"Good morning husband." She said in her usual manner.

"Good morning to you too."

"It is quite a relief to no longer have that burden in my life. Shall we get dressed and head off to mass? I wish we could tour the Holy See today."

He chuckled before asking, "Is there something very specific you wish to see?"

"No. I wish to see everything that we are allowed to visit."

"Sadly, most of it is closed today, but I promise tomorrow we'll visit every nook they'll let us into."

After they got out of bed, they showered together and then dressed. She once again was wearing her bun and veil with her simple blue blouse and a black full-length skirt. He went in a nice dress shirt, slacks, and a formal coat. As they stepped out, he was a bit surprised that it was a lot chillier than he expected it to be. It would seem as though the beach trip was not going to happen.

She commented, "It appears to be a little colder than I expected."

Giving her a nod, he replied, "Let's go grab you a coat."

After turning back, they grabbed her a jacket and then headed back out. They had plenty of time to walk from the hotel to St. Peter's Basilica. It was sunny and there were a good number of people walking back and forth.

"This is my first time leaving Scotland." Isla Grace stated.

"I've been to London twice, but otherwise my first time leaving too."

"It is quite exciting. I would love to visit Paris and see the Eiffel Tower and Mona Lisa."

Nodding at her, he responded, "We could do that for a holiday sometime soon. I'd very much like to see Iceland."

"Why Iceland?"

"I took a history course as an elective in my first year of Uni, and the professor talked about how the Norse named it to trick people from coming, so I've always wanted to go."

Isla Grace pointed at a huge wall that was part of Vatican City before saying, "I cannot believe how close our hotel is. You made the right selection."

There were a lot of choices for hotels in Rome, but Angus felt that being so close to Vatican City, they could stroll right in. It just seemed like a great option. It was a very brief walk before they found themselves in a large crowd waiting for Mass. He wanted to get as close to where the Pope would be, but the crowd got so dense that he had to settle for a spot about halfway between the obelisk and the building where mass would be conducted. Isla Grace held tight onto his arm as they had to stand through the whole mass, and once it was done, she gestured towards a sign written in Italian.

"We should come when they first open and at 9 a.m. tomorrow." She commented.

"We'll see. I figure on our honeymoon; we should just wake up whenever and then go. It's not like they're gonna close things down if we show up an hour later than they open."

"I always rise early."

Giving a little chuckle, Angus commented, "We'll see how early you get up with me keeping you up late every night."

"Are you suggesting that I am unable to function with only a few hours of sleep?"

With a sly look on his face, he answered, "Well… not after I'm done with you."

"We shall see. Where are we headed now?"

Pointing to the east and away from St. Peter's Square, he answered, "There's a really cool castle down here and the Leonardo Da Vinci Museum. After that, I found a few other museums not too far away. We can just stop at any restaurant on the way for lunch."

"An excellent plan. Please lead on."

They bounced about, slowly walking through a few museums. He was quite surprised to find out that Isla Grace was a fluent Italian speaker, which made sense since she stated early in their relationship that she loved classic Italian Opera. After their walk, he took her back to the hotel for a shower and a change of clothes. In preparation for the honeymoon, Angus sent a message to her mother so she would slip an elegant gown into Isla Grace's bag. It was going to be part of his surprise. Being in Rome was the perfect opportunity for them to catch a live Italian opera. She was very confused about how it got into her bags, but after he insisted that she wear it, he dragged out a suit that he brought along. After she put the gown on, he took a moment to admire it. Isla Grace was quite slender, but she had all the curves a woman should have, and he felt as though she was simply stunning looking. The gown was snug and a light blue colour that matched her eyes. It covered her almost as much as any of her other outfits, except that instead of long sleeves, it had short sleeves, and the rest of her arms were covered by long gloves. Only a tiny gap where her pale skin peeked out between the sleeves and gloves.

He told her, "You look magnificent."

"I feel like a sausage stuffed into a velvet slip, and I do not like it."

Giving a light chuckle at her description, he stated, "This might be one of those kinds of events where you have to leave the chapel veil behind."

"Which is?" She asked.

Clucking his tongue at her, he answered, "A surprise."

Her eyebrow raised slightly as she responded by saying, "I have never been a fan of being surprised."

He retorted, "We don't always get what we want, but, in this case, I'm willing to bet that you'll love this surprise."

"Very well… I will trust your judgement on this matter, Mr. Bruce."

Chuckling lightly, he replied, "Thank you, Mrs. Bruce."

She took a minute to slowly unpin her chapel veil and then loosen her hair out of the tight bun that she had been wearing. He simply adored her hair when she let it free from the bun. Reaching out a hand, he slowly ran his fingers from along the side of her temple all the way down and through her hair. He was able to spot her tiny smile as he did it.

After they were both ready to go, he extended an elbow before asking, "Shall we?"

In his research, he found a 19th Century Opera House called the Teatro dell'Opera di Roma. He struggled mightily to say the name since he took 2 semesters of Russian, most of which he had long since forgot. There were a bunch of options in Rome, but he chose this one because he thought that the interior looked cool. To keep the surprise, he scribbled the name on a slip of paper to hand to the taxi. He was going to take her to see a live opera. He had no idea if the one he picked was any good, but he figured she would appreciate the experience.

After they got in the taxi, she asked, "So you really are not going to tell me where we are going?"

"Nope."

He could not see any change in her facial expression to let him know how she was feeling. The taxi started, and he enjoyed the sunset in the distance as they drove through the thick traffic of Rome. The website he bought the tickets from had the opera at about 3 hours in length. It was a long time, but he had little doubt that most of them were that long, so he would just tough it out for her.

As the taxi pulled up to the opera house, Isla Grace immediately realised where they were headed because she stated, "An opera house. You are taking me to see an opera. An excellent choice that shows you pay attention when I talk."

"I do. Hopefully you'll enjoy it."

The taxi stopped, so he hopped out and then gave his hand for her to come out. Once he paid for the taxi ride, they headed into the opera house. He used his phone to display the ticket, and an usher gestured to show them to their seats.

As they entered the building, she stated, "Tosca. Puccini took a play that he liked and attempted to convert it into an opera. It was both successful and unsuccessful. I watched a rendition of it on a website called YouTube. It was pleasant enough, although it felt rushed at times."

Laughing, Angus retorted, "A 3-hour opera is rushed?"

"Converting a long play into an opera at times has issues."

They continued walking through the building, following an usher.

As they settled into their seats, she commented, "I had tried many times to attend the opera in Edinburgh, but sadly, my family was always busy when it was available. This is going to be my first time watching an opera live. I am anticipating it greatly."

The view from their booth was quite nice. He made sure to select one that had a perfect front-facing and centred view of the main stage. The crowd around them was slowly beginning to fill in their seats, and the orchestra that sat near the stage had already been seated. They were making a wide variety of noises as they seemed to be tuning or warming up. His musical knowledge was severely lacking.

"Angus."

He turned to look at her. She extended a gloved hand for him to hold. As he took her hand, he noted that the material of the glove was very soft and slick. It was unusual to hold her hand while wearing a glove, but he was happy to be here with her.

She shifted her head to look at him before saying, "Thank you for taking me to this. I still do not like this dress as it is far too revealing for a proper Catholic woman, but you are right that it is appropriate for the event at hand. I am just thankful that I am at least fully covered."

"I understand, but you look amazing. If we didn't have an event to attend to, I would have made love to you right as you walked out with it on."

"Thank you. I know physicality is not as important as spirituality, but it is pleasing to know that you appreciate my appearance as much as I appreciate yours. Every time you dress formally, I find you exceedingly handsome."

"It's kind of you to say so, Mrs. Bruce."

"However, I think we might need to cancel your plans to attend the beach. The weather is more than a little chilly. I hope that you are not too disappointed."

Angus chuckled. He would have loved to see her in a 2-piece bikini; it was always one of his weaknesses. She was right, though; it was entirely too cold for them to go to the beach. Pretending as though he was sad, he solemnly replied, "I'll survive."

"I am sorry that you are disappointed. I would have done it, but to be honest, I am quite relieved to avoid it. I am not comfortable exposing my body in public."

"Of course, although I hope it's more out of religious obligation than shame. You have an amazing body."

"Once again, thank you. I must confess that it is probably a mixture of both. I have always felt as though my frame and youthful appearance made me appear less womanly than others. Based on how you keep staring at me while in this gown, I assume that I was incorrect."

"Yes."

He was about to continue to praise her figure when the opera began. He was quite thankful that the opera house must have been quite used to having tourists because there was a screen with translations of Italian into English. As the music echoed throughout the building, he admired the acoustics. This building was clearly designed to have music played regularly in it. He was impressed. The opera itself was about a man who was painting a woman during a rebellion or a war. As it continued, he could not understand what the hell was even going on. They sang beautifully, but since he had to watch a screen to know what they were saying, he got lost quickly. It did not take him long to just give up and watch the opera. Midway through the second act, he peeked over at Isla Grace. Her face still had the same stoic expression as she was watching; however, he was completely stunned to see tears slowly rolling down her cheek. She was crying! In all his time knowing her, there had been so little emotion that he was somewhat stunned in shock. After taking a moment to recover, he pulled the kerchief out of the front pocket of his jacket and then gently dabbed away the tears.

She did not look at him at all, but her mouth cracked open slightly, and he could barely hear her say, “It is beautiful.”

After the opera ended, he took her hand to help her rise to her feet. Her eyes were still slightly reddened from when she had cried, but otherwise her expression was the same as it normally had been. Once they exited the opera house, he flagged down a taxi with instructions to take them to their hotel.

As it began to drive, she said, “I apologise for my emotional outburst.”

Outside of crying, he had not seen an outburst from her, so he responded, “Huh?”

“From the moment that I had told my mother that I wanted to go on a date with you all the way up until the moment of our wedding, I had expected you to call it off. I dreaded it deeply, and now instead we are here. I guess that my emotions from seeing such beautiful performers and the relief of knowing that we are together had finally overwhelmed my normal senses.”

He leant into her a little bit before taking his index finger to turn her to face him, before telling her, “I never wavered. I didn’t know it until Liam told me later, but the moment you walked down the stairs with your hair loose, I was all in. I love you dearly, Isla Grace.”

“And I love you.” She replied.

He kissed her. After breaking off their passionate kiss, they rode for the rest of the taxi ride in silence. Once it pulled up to their hotel, he paid the driver and then took Isla Grace back into the hotel and up to their room. As they entered, she excused herself to go to the toilet. Angus sat down on the bed and pulled out his phone. After connecting to the hotel Wi-Fi, he started to message his mother to let her know that they were safe and everything was going great. Next, he sent a message to Liam and told him how Isla Grace shed tears during the opera. Liam expressed shock. He told Angus how, even as a baby, Isla Grace did not cry like normal babies. He heard the door of the toilet crack open, but he responded to Liam that he was not shocked.

As he continued typing, Isla Grace said, “Early on in preparation for our wedding, your mother took me shopping. She told me that I had to find something visually appealing to wear during the honeymoon. After we bought it, I admitted to her that I had no idea when the most appropriate time would be to wear it. She told me that I would just know. I hope you like it.”

He glanced up and was very pleasantly surprised to see that she was wearing a matching light blue lace and silk bra and knickers with a similar coloured garter belt that was attached to a pair of light blue stockings.

“Based on your facial expression, you very much like it.”

“I do.” He responded as he tenderly grabbed her by the hips and pulled her into him.

# Chapter 19

23 February 2018

Angus grumbled to himself as he finished work. It had been a long day as the whole network decided to crash down all around them. He ran around like a chicken with its head cut off, trying to fix everything. It took him all day, but he was finally able to recover the system without losing data. It was well past 6 p.m., and he was ready to go home. Right when the network went down, he texted Isla Grace to let her know that he was going to be very late. It could have been worse, but he got hold of the issue.

There was a knock on the IT door, so he called out, "Yes?"

When the door opened, he spotted Tomas, who immediately said, "Great job recovering the system, Angus. You're a hero. I personally let the CEO know what you did to save our biscuits."

Giving a grin, Angus replied, "Thanks, boss. I was just doing my job."

"You and your new bride have a great weekend. Thank you."

Nodding at him, Angus said, "I will."

After Tomas left, he packed his gear and then headed home. He had found he really enjoyed having a wife waiting when he got home. Isla Grace seemed to have taken quite a bit of pride in ensuring that their home was immaculate, and supper was ready when he got home. In what was the most direct way he had ever seen, she made him replace all the furniture in their home. He had to buy new dishes, pots, pans, and cutlery as well. As he was driving home, he chuckled to himself, thinking about how his home was almost unrecognizable from just before the wedding. One would have thought the last tenant moved out and a new family moved in. She also hung a massive cross along the back wall of the living room, and every room in the home with furniture had a small portrait of Jesus somewhere. As he pulled up into the driveway, he saw the door open, and Isla Grace appeared. She was wearing a white pinny over her red blouse and a brown skirt. Her hair was tied back into its usual bun with the chapel veil over it.

Once he got out of the car, she walked up to him and said, "I am happy that you have returned."

Bending over slightly, he kissed her. As she started to kiss him, he wrapped his free arm around her and lifted her. He was finding being married a wonderful experience. It was also the most sex of his life, and many times he would come home to a nice back massage after a wonderful meal. Setting her down, he gave her a big grin.

She said, "I am sorry that you had difficulties at work. I have prepared supper, and once you finish eating, I propose a nice joint bath to wash away your worries."

"I'm not sure I deserve a wife like you."

"Of course you do, let us go."

Taking her hand, they walked into their home. The smell of cooking fish wafted into his nose.

"Normally, I would not cook any sort of meat during lent but after you told me about your day, I decided we could follow the church's guidance that allows fish. It is important after a rough day of work to eat a full meal to restore the body."

"Alright. Things got a little messy, but I was able to get it all back on track."

She moved to serve supper while pointing towards the dining room table. It was a clue for him to have a seat. He set his work bag on the small hook that she had him install on the wall before slipping off his shoes and having a seat. It had only been a month of living together, and she already had domesticated him. Supper for tonight was some salmon, mash, and steamed asparagus.

Giving her his best smile, he said, "It smells wonderful."

"Thank you, my mother was an excellent teacher."

He chuckled before declaring, "I'll say grace."

She sat down and then pressed her hands together.

Closing his eyes, he recited the prayer, "Bless us, O Lord, and these Thy gifts, which we are about to receive from Thy bounty, through Christ our Lord. Amen."

"Amen." She responded to his prayer.

As he took a fork to cut off a piece of the salmon, she said, "I was wondering if you could acquire a vehicle for me to run errands. I already have a driving licence and believe it to be unfair to expect you to work all day and then drive me all over town."

He nodded as he responded, "We can go look tomorrow."

"Thank you. Could we possibly see about attending an opera in Edinburgh in a fortnight?"

"As long as it isn't during work, I'd be delighted to take you."

"It is not during work hours. However, to state outright that I will not be wearing the same dress, it is a much more casual affair."

Giving a little chuckle, he responded, "We can save the gown for more private events at home."

Raising her eyebrow at him, she commented, "You are quite incorrigible."

Laughing loudly, he replied, "Do you not like it?"

He spotted her small smile creep on the corners of her mouth before she answered, "I spend much of my time alone daydreaming about being in your arms. Until I met you the idea of sexual intercourse had very little appeal outside of procreation. Now, I want you. The burden of concern about sin is long gone and replaced with wanton lust."

He laughed once again. For some reason, she still tickled him in just the right spot with her words.

"Is my desire for you amusing?"

Shaking his head, he answered, "Of course not. I just love how you describe things. We've got a bathtub that will be a lot of fun after supper, I'm thinking."

She took a bite of her food, and after chewing, she said, "I have some bubble bath soap that I picked up while out shopping last week with your mother. It has therapeutic properties that help muscles relax and is perfect after a long, hard day of work. I think I will use it in our bath."

"I like it."

The buzzer for their door rang. He was quite surprised since no one had planned to come visit them.

She asked, "Were we expecting guests?"

"No." He answered while standing up.

As he moved towards the door, he heard her following behind him. Peeking out of the window, he saw an East Asian man standing at his door. He was wearing a light blue jumper, a beanie, and a pair of black slacks. Angus was quite confused, especially since the man looked vaguely familiar to him.

Opening his front door, he said, "Hello?"

The man replied, “Hello Angus Bruce, right?”

“Yes. What can I do for you?”

“I’m Deng Li. I work at Northstar.”

“Okay…”

“I need to speak to you privately. May I come in?”

Angus was quite confused. Now that the man said he worked at Northstar, Angus recognised him. He was a new accountant who Angus had done a few tweaks to his laptop when he started working there about a fortnight ago.

“Umm… I guess so.” He answered the man before gesturing to allow the man to enter.

As he stepped in, Isla Grace stated, “Please remove your shoes in our entryway.”

Bending down, the man slipped off his shoes before saying, “Of course.”

Closing the door, Angus gestured towards the man as he said, “Isla Grace, this is Deng Li. He works at Northstar in accounting. Deng, this is my new wife, Isla Grace.”

“It’s a pleasure to meet you, Mrs. Bruce.” The man said.

“Thank you, Mr. Li.”

Curious as to why the man was in his home, Angus asked, “So what can I do for you?”

“I believe we should sit for this.”

Frowning at him, Angus just nodded before heading into his living room. The man followed behind him, and Isla Grace was not far behind.

Gesturing towards their new sofa, Angus took a seat in their love seat. The man sat down on the sofa. Isla Grace sat down next to him and then looped her arm around his before holding his hand.

“I believe this conversation should be between the two of us.” Deng stated.

Shaking his head, Angus stated, “My wife can hear anything I can hear. Now, please tell me what brings you to my house during supper?”

Nodding his head, Deng answered, “I know what you’re doing with your football club.”

A nervous pit hit his stomach. Could this man really know, or was he probing? Even so, how did he even know anything to the point of knowing it existed?

Trying to remain cool, he responded, “I’m listening.”

"So, then we shall ignore the pretense of pretending both of us do not know what's going on with your friend and wife's brother Liam Gillespie and get right to the matter at hand."

"Okay. Tell me what the matter at hand is."

"My name is not actually Deng Li, and I work for the People's Republic of China. I've been sent to help you by providing you with a warning."

Angus was in complete and utter shock. He was talking with a damned Chinese spy who somehow found out about their group.

Deciding to move cautiously, he asked, "A warning?"

"Yes. People have found out about your movement."

Isla Grace interjected, "Perhaps you could explain to us how you found out, then we can move from there."

Nodding at her, the man responded, "We've got people in other agencies, and when we heard about you, we muffled that information from spreading within those agencies in order to protect your movement."

He raised an eyebrow before asking, "Why would you wish to protect us?"

Shifting to lean a bit closer to them, he answered in an almost conspiratorial tone, "Because the people of China want to see the people of Scotland finally freed from the oppressive United Kingdom."

"You realise that our movement is in direct conflict with your nation?"

"Perhaps so, but our leaders believe that your people should at least have the right to have a choice, don't you agree?"

Pausing to think for a moment, he answered, "I do. Our lands have very little that could interest yours."

Isla Grace then interrupted, "The embarrassment of the British and her allies alone in losing control of Scotland would likely please the Chinese government."

Giving her a grin, the man stated, "She's as intelligent as she is beautiful."

"She is." Angus stated before continuing, "Now that we both have an understanding of the situation, how did these agencies you mentioned discover our movement?"

"One of your own men has betrayed you."

He frowned deeply. If one of them had betrayed their own cause, it would have made success impossible.

"I see your concern, Mr. Bruce, and I understand it. I do have some good news."

"Which is?"

"We've muffled the agency in question by having the case transferred to our own man and then making it all disappear. You probably have a few months to discover who your spy is. If you succeed in removing the spy on your own, my people can assume enough competence to further our assistance to your cause."

Not wanting to be indebted to the Chinese, Angus quickly retorted, "If you help know that we won't be indebted to you, nor should you expect any benefits or favours."

"We've examined the information provided about your movement and have come to a full understanding. We, however, would ask that you at least consider opening trade between our nations on an equal playing field. Also, I've been empowered to let you know that if you succeed in your first phase, our government will immediately and openly declare recognition of your cause on the world's stage while pushing to give you a platform with the same standing as any other nation."

He was puzzled. Sure, embarrassing the Brits would be great, but it seemed as though the Chinese were willing to step out on a limb for the Scottish cause.

"I understand your confusion, Mr. Bruce, and I suspect you must realise that anytime a foe of our nation is weakened, it benefits us. Even without us aiding you, if you succeed, it benefits us, even if slightly. Our leaders see no reason why we should not aid you in the process. Of course, if you come forward claiming we did so, we'll deny it fully."

"Of course." Angus replied with a nod.

He had much to think about, especially since they had a spy in their group that must be found as soon as possible.

The man stood up and announced, "I must leave. You'll not hear from me again, but be aware that we've got people watching your progress, and if we see an opportunity to aid you, we will."

Angus stood up as well.

The man walked towards their door before stating, "I shall see myself out. Mr. and Mrs. Bruce, I wish you a good night and good luck."

Angus followed the man as he slipped on his shoes before walking through the door of their home. He then climbed into a waiting car. The car drove off.

Closing the door behind him, Angus turned to Isla Grace and then said, “Looks like we’ve got some work to do.”

Angus called Liam immediately after closing the door and demanded that he come to his home immediately. He did not feel comfortable telling him all that the Chinese man had told him over the phone. They had a code word they would utilise to indicate that things were an emergency, so he made sure to let Liam know. After Liam arrived, Angus turned on the telly and set the volume to high before telling him everything that the Chinese man had told him. Liam was quite upset, and they both agreed to go through the Discord logs to see if anyone was saving or accessing information to utilise. Liam left saying that he would not talk about anyone until he could confirm who he could trust, even the closest of lads in their group. Everyone was a suspect but the two of them. After Liam left, they finished their supper and took a nice bubble bath. Initially, Angus was not overly enthused about the idea of making love in that tub after the news that he just heard, but as soon as she climbed into the tub naked, that went away immediately.

# Chapter 20

27 February 2018

Angus cleared through a fine day of work with few issues. He was glad to be able to spend his free time with his personal laptop and hotspot to research every microscopic inch of the Discord. After doing so, he had identified about 20 people who seemed to be utilising the files unusually. It was going to be difficult to figure out which one of them was the bastard who was betraying them. While he was confused why the Chinese would care enough to help, embarrassing the Brits did not seem like the main reason, he was glad for it. He made it crystal clear to the Chinese man that they would not be bending knees to the Chinese any more than to the British. He did wonder what other nations would be quite pleased to see the Scots give the Brits a firm kick in the arse out the door. It really did not matter; the Brits and their globalist lackeys in the Scottish government needed to go. They were ruining the nation and the Scots themselves with their evil. Heck, maybe what Angus and his friends were going to do would inspire others to do so as well. A nationalist uprising was the only thing that could save Western nations from ruin. After he finished work, he hopped into his car and drove home. As he pulled up to his driveway, he was surprised to see Liam's and two other cars that he did not recognise parked there. Pulling in, he got out of his car and strolled up to his home.

The door opened to Isla Grace, who immediately said, "Welcome home. I have prepared supper for both you and our guests."

Bending slightly, he kissed her on the lips, and once he broke the kiss, he told her, "I missed you."

"I missed you as well. I ran all my errands this morning, and while I was out, I bought you a gift. I hope you do not mind my spending money in such a manner. I saw it and immediately thought of you."

He chuckled lightly before replying, "It's as much your money as mine. I appreciate the sentiment."

"After our guests leave, I shall present it to you."

"Okay." He said before slipping off his shoes and hanging his bag on the wall.

As he fully entered the main hallway, he spotted Liam and could hear him talking to someone else. Once he entered his living room, he spotted who it was. It was the three men who were part of the British military and joined their cause. Taking a moment to think about it, he remembered their names as David Rutherford, Markus Keith, and Harry Agnew.

The first one to speak was David, who said, "Angus, it's a pleasure to see you again, although the circumstances are a bit concerning."

He took a moment to look at Liam, who nodded confidently. Angus knew right away that Liam must have told them about the Chinese man and the spy in their midst. He shook each man's hand before sitting down on the love seat.

Isla Grace announced, "Supper for everyone will be ready in 30 minutes. I wish to remind each of you that this is a Godly home, so I ask that you kindly watch your language. Men are known to use inappropriate language when gaggled together."

Giving a light chuckle, he pulled her hand to bring her close and then gave her another kiss.

As she walked away, Liam announced, "We'll watch our language, Isla Grace."

David watched her closely, and once she was out of sight, he turned to Angus before asking, "What exactly happened with the oriental man?"

Angus went over everything that happened and what the man had told him when he came to visit the other night. It was all very concerning, and Angus racked his brain over who it could be. He had felt they were doing a fine job recruiting loyal men.

Harry brought his train of thought as he asked, "Have we any idea who it is? Each man here has the most to risk, and even if we betrayed the cause, we'd be ruined. Leadership is always the first to be strung up."

Giving a little nod, Angus answered, "I've been crunching the Discord for unusual activity. I assumed that whoever it is would need to have some kinda evidence to provide to even be believed."

David then asked, "And?"

"I've got a list of 20 names of people who have been downloading or moving data in unusual ways that are outside the normal parametres of the server's daily functions."

Markus chuckled as he commented, "It's a good thing we got the nerd on our side. Christ."

Isla Grace's voice called out loudly from the kitchen, "That includes using the Lord's name in vain."

Flushing lightly, Markus called out, "Sorry!"

"Do not do it again." She ordered.

David gave out a light laugh before saying, "Can you write down the names? I know people who might be able to get us some very quiet information about each that might help identify the culprit."

Standing up, Angus strolled over to the notepad that Isla Grace used to write her shopping lists. He picked up her pencil and scribbled down all 20 names. He had to admit that he personally only knew about 4 or 5 of the men on the list. Tearing out the page, he set the pencil down and then gave the list to David before taking back his seat. He read the list slowly before passing it to Markus.

"Captain Keith, I believe you can work your magic with your lad over in MI6 to enlighten us on these men."

"Aye. It'll be four or five days, but we'll know which one it is."

It was slightly relieving to know that their group had such powerful men helping their cause. He was initially concerned with bringing them in, but he had to admit, they would have been damned if found out and yet here they were. Their numbers had recently broken one thousand men. It was a daunting task for sure, but they broke off into small cells that allowed a few men to know a huge amount about the whole group. Somehow, they even managed to gain a large foothold in several military garrisons surrounding Edinburgh. Until the Chinese man had spoken about a spy in their group, Angus was quite happy with how things were progressing. It was crystal clear to him that many more people in Scotland were very unhappy with the direction their politicians were taking them.

David continued talking, "We've got to route our information from this Discord server to something more secure that we have control over. Angus, do you think you could make us a private server?

He chuckled before stating, "I'll have something this Saturday and then move everything over to the new server. I can make a hidden program under a cloud server that will move around from different providers in countries that don't like letting anyone access private information."

Liam then commented, "Maybe instead of dumping the Discord server, we could leave it as is to pretend we're still doing stuff there, but then have Angus' new server for our real work?"

He was mildly surprised by Liam. That was a sharp idea that they could use to keep recruiting people while hiding the real purpose of the group. Angus simply nodded at him.

Isla Grace called out, "Supper is ready. Please wash your hands and then come sit at the table."

Angus stood up and went into the kitchen to wash his hands. Once he was done, he took a seat. Isla Grace had brought an extra chair to the table, so everyone had a seat. Once all the men were there, Isla Grace began bringing plates to everyone. She was serving some sort of vegetable pasta with slices of buttered bread. He was not a fan of vegetarian meals, but during lent there were few choices, and Isla Grace would not budge on following the church policies during Lent.

Markus announced, "It smells great Mrs. Bruce."

"Thank you." She responded as she brought the last plates.

Angus announced, "Liam, could you say grace?"

Nodding at him, Liam closed his eyes and then said, "Bless us, O Lord, and these Thy gifts, which we are about to receive from Thy bounty, through Christ our Lord. Amen."

Those around the table responded at the end of the prayer with 'Amen.' They ate supper silently and once finished, each man thanked Isla Grace for the meal before leaving. Liam left with them as well.

Once they left, Isla Grace asked, "Do you think that they will be successful in finding out who our traitor is?"

"I do. They've got resources we don't. I wouldn't be surprised if we find out who it is right away."

"And then?" she asked.

"Huh?"

"Let us say these men find out who the traitor is. What action do we take in dealing with them? They have not just betrayed a movement, but by doing so, they have put the lives of every member in extreme danger."

He frowned. That was a major problem he had not realised was about to come their way. It was not as though he or anyone else in the group had some sort of punishment mechanism available to them.

Pulling on his hand, she said, "Let us not worry about it. It is time for me to present you with the gift that I had purchased for you."

"That sounds nice." He told her as he followed her into their bedroom.

He was hoping that whatever gift she had got was some sort of complex lingerie or maybe something made of silk. She stopped in front of their bed. Sitting on the bed was a medium-sized box. It was wrapped in green paper. He looked at her, and she gestured for him to take it. He picked it up and shook it briefly. It barely made a sound. Slowly, he unwrapped the box. Once he got the wrapping off, he took off the lid. It was a dark green T-shirt with the words 'I'm your Daddy' written in white letters in the middle of it. He laughed at it. It would be quite funny to wear it next time he saw Liam. As he took the shirt out of the box, he spotted a rectangular piece of white plastic fall out of it and then dropped onto the floor next to his bed. He set the shirt and box down on the bed as he slowly bent down to pick up the piece of plastic. Once he rose, holding it in his hand, he was surprised to realise immediately what it was. It was one of those little pregnancy tests you can buy in the pharmacy. He spun it over to see that it was showing two pink lines. Written next to the circle was an indicator that said two pink lines meant that it was a positive result. A sudden and very intense realisation hit him that Isla Grace had taken this test, and she was pregnant.

As he looked over at her, she stated, "I scheduled our honeymoon during my ovulation period and when my normal menstruation cycle had passed, I decided to buy the test. I am pregnant with our first child."

He grabbed her tenderly by her arms and pulled him into a hug before saying, "That's wonderful news. I know our parents will be very happy."

She then asked as he felt her arms wrap around his mid-section, "Are you happy as well?"

He broke up their hug before softly placing his right hand on the side of her face as he answered, "Very much so."

Leaning a little closer to her, he gave her a kiss.

After they broke off their kiss, he smarmily commented, "It really isn't a surprise you're pregnant. You couldn't keep your hands off me!"

The corners of her mouth crept upwards as she replied, "Husband, I fully acknowledge my role in the creation of our forthcoming child; however, I distinctly remember you being not only a willing but eager participant in our sexual relations."

He laughed loudly at her reply. There was little doubt in his mind that even when he made old age, he would be quite amused by her sense of humour.

"Guilty as charged." He declared before kissing her once again.

# Chapter 21

9 March 2018

After finishing his work for the day, Angus was to meet Liam and a small handful of men up in Cauldhame. He had no idea why Liam called this meeting, but Angus guessed that it was either a planning meeting or to discover who the traitor was. Even stranger to him was picking Cauldhame, which was just a bunch of hiking trails and a few houses. Not much else was out there, and from what Angus remembered, few people ever went up there. He hopped in his car and headed home. The meeting was later in the evening, so he had time to go grab supper with Isla Grace beforehand. After a long conversation about her pregnancy, they decided to wait for a month or two to be sure everything was safe before they would announce it to their family. She already had names picked for both a boy and a girl. Robert William Bruce for a boy and Abigail Christine Bruce. He really had no idea what to think about naming a child, so he decided to just let her have at it. As he pulled up to his home, the door opened, and Isla Grace appeared. He chuckled, noting that she was wearing her favourite pinny again. Underneath it was a plain green blouse and a dark brown skirt.

After he kissed her, she said, "Welcome home."

"Thank you. Did you get the tickets for the Opera tomorrow in Edinburgh?"

Taking his hand, she guided him back into the house, and once he was taking his shoes off, she answered, "I did. I am certain that opera is not your favourite thing to attend to, but I appreciate the fact that you share in my hobbies. I had considered sharing in your hobby of shooting people through your computer, but then I realised I would rather be tied to a wall and forced to listen to my brother brag about his sporting accomplishments for hours on end."

As usual, her descriptive take on her suffering amused him greatly. She was truly a Catholic with the idea of suffering always somewhere in her mind. He laughed again.

"Maybe I should insist then?" he asked with a wicked grin.

"I am starting to think your claims of liking my descriptions are a ruse where you mask your pleasure at my suffering."

Angus began laughing uproariously. She tugged on his hand, leading him towards their table. He could smell the supper that she had cooked for him. Since it was Friday during Lent, she had been avoiding meat. It was a chilli dish, but he knew that instead of beef in it, it probably had pumpkin. It smelled nice.

As he sat down, he turned towards her while he said, "Thank you very much, Isla Grace."

Slowly, she brought his hand up to her lips and then gave it a tender kiss before saying, "You are welcome. It brings me great joy to provide for you as best I can."

Giving a grin, he told her, "Just make sure you eat plenty, you're already eating for two."

"The weight gain from pregnancy is one of my biggest concerns. I have already found several fitness programs to help me maintain proper health both during and after my pregnancy. My mother always said that it was of utmost importance for a wife to maintain her attractiveness if she possibly can."

While he shook his head, he told her, "Don't be silly."

"I know that you love me either way, Angus, but I also really like looking fit."

"It's nice for certain."

After saying grace, they ate supper. There was still some time before he had to leave to meet Liam, so Angus sat down on the sofa with Isla Grace. Since he found out that she was pregnant, he loved slowly running his hand along her bare stomach. It was hard to believe that soon her perfectly smooth and flat stomach would start to expand as a new life grew in it.

"I love it when you rub my stomach like that. I have never had someone do so, and it feels marvellous."

"And I love to rub your stomach. It's so flat and soft. Your skin is just the best. Sometimes at work, I daydream about slowly kissing every little freckle all over your body."

She turned towards him and stated, "Perhaps once you finish your meeting, you should come back here. I will gladly remove all my clothing and let you try. However, I am certain that you have noticed that I have a lot of freckles. It might take hours."

Slowly moving his lips closer to hers, he commented, "I'll have all night."

They kissed passionately, and once he broke their kiss, he grumpily stated, "I guess I should head off. I'll try to be as fast as I possibly can."

"I anticipate your return. I know that we agreed to wait, but I was wondering if you would object to telling our families about our forthcoming child?"

"If you feel comfortable sharing the news, Isla Grace, then go for it."

"Thank you."

He gave her a quick kiss before slipping his shoes back on and leaving. He had to load up the map on his phone to guide him to the spot where they were meeting. The sun had set, so he had to drive carefully. It was lightly snowing outside. The fact that they were meeting in the middle of nowhere north of Stirling, had him confused. Since he trusted Liam, he was not concerned. It was only a quarter-hour drive, and he found the spot. Several cars were already parked outside the small building. One of them was Liam's, and he recognised a few others as some that had once parked in front of his own home. He parked and headed into the building. Once he entered, he saw everyone there. It was Liam, the three military men who came to his home, and Henry. Angus did not know Henry very well, but he was one of Liam's lads whom he met back on Brexit night. Henry was part of the paintball team and one of the original lads who joined the Stirling Albion FC club. He seemed like a nice enough lad.

Liam spoke immediately, "Oi cunt. It's nice of you to show up."

Angus nodded before responding, "Isla Grace refused to let me leave without filling my belly first."

Chuckling, Henry stated, "I still can't believe you married her. She seemed like a robot or something."

Giving a nod, Angus responded, "She's amazing, but you've gotta get to know her. Anyways, what's going on that has brought us out here?"

David then answered, "If you remember our conversation last week."

"I do."

"Captain Keith, could you give us your report?"

"Of course. I took all the data from the list you gave me and extrapolated it with a combination of cell phone data and my contacts at the mentioned location came back one name."

Angus realised immediately that Markus was suggesting that Henry was the traitor. He was stunned. Henry had been with them since the start. He was one of the Parliament security guards and was friends with Liam for a long time. Liam looked mad. He must have realised it as well. Henry must have figured out that he was caught as he started to step back. Suddenly, David and Harry grabbed his arms.

David then announced, "We've got our man."

Henry angrily denied the suggestion as he wriggled from the grasp of the two men, "I don't know what you're talking about."

Markus then stated, "I looked at the records Angus pulled, and you're the only one drawing huge amounts of specific data about the members of the group. I reviewed the phone records from all our targets, and you're the only one with calls to Scotland Yard and MI6 offices."

Liam lashed out with a punch into Henry's gut before yelling, "You're fucking all of us, you bastard. If you didn't want in, just walk away, you cunt."

Henry coughed, roughly bent over before he said, "I didn't do it."

"Why the fuck did you call Scotland Yard? MI6? It's obvious. Guess what, we got our own spies, and they've been ratting you out." Markus stated.

Henry stood up straight before saying, "It isn't like you're gonna do shit."

He pulled his arms out of the hands of the two men and then stormed out the door of the building. Suddenly, a loud explosive bang echoed into Angus' ears. It sounded like a firecracker or even something from CoD. Henry fell to the floor, and he was unmoving.

Liam yelled out, "What the fuck!"

Angus could say nothing through the shock. He glanced at the men with him and saw David lowering a pistol.

Markus confidently stated, "Either we're all in on this shit, or we're not."

Harry added, "Fucker got what he deserved. He forced our hand."

Angus could say nothing. They shot fucking Henry dead right in front of them. He had never seen anything like it and was just unable to say a word.

"But you killed him." Liam stated angrily.

It was likely that Liam was upset that they killed his friend, whom he had known well.

David tucked his pistol away before stating firmly, "And what the hell do you think would happen to you if this bastard got his way? He'd have sold all of you right into prison for life. The Brits would drag all of us out every fucking chance they could to lock down power even more."

Angus was upset, but he realised that David was right, so he stated, "It was either him or us, Liam. He stabbed us in the back."

Liam turned to Angus angrily as he asked, "Fuck… you too man?"

Angus grabbed Liam by his arms as he responded, "You put me in charge of this shit. You're number 2. What the fuck do you think happens to you? If the Brits find out, they'll hang both of us. Henry was your lad; I get it, but he betrayed you. If it weren't for the damned Chinese spy, he would have succeeded, too. We'd probably already be lined up for a shooting squad."

His words must have worked because Liam took a deep breath before finally saying very solemnly, "I know, but fuck man, I went to primary with him."

David nodded, "And even after being lads with you, watching footy, and likely millions of other memories, he stabbed you in the back. If you boys can't let your balls drop, we're fucked."

Markus then grabbed Angus by the collar and stated, "People are gonna die. You two boys need to decide. Will it be fucking us or people who stand to stop us?"

Angus stepped back and gritted his teeth before saying, "Them. What the fuck are we gonna do with this cunt's body?"

David instructed, "Nothing. Harry, take his wallet and keys. Make them fucking disappear far away. It'll look like a robbery, and the cops will piss off about it real quick. Fuckers can't even catch gang rapists in plain sight, so they'll shuffle this case off right quick. You two boys go home and get your shit together."

Liam began sullenly shuffling out the door as Angus stepped up to David before declaring, "My shits together. I don't give a fuck if it's you or any other cunt that must get it, but this movement's happening."

He then turned to Markus and declared, "You let your MI6 guys know to keep an eye out. We're gonna need more men, and I'll be damned if they betray us."

"Keep me up to date on everything." Angus ordered before strolling out of the building.

As he walked out, he heard Harry comment to the other men, "We've got the right one."

As Liam shuffled past Henry's body, he sullenly looked down at him.

Angus slapped him on the shoulder before declaring, "Fuck that cunt. He had his chance to leave peacefully, and he tried to screw all of us. We're gonna have to accept what we started and finish the job. Go home to Sandy."

Angus climbed into his car and drove off. His head was spinning from what had just happened. Those military men were not fucking around, and they got Angus realising he would have to either be like them or he was doomed. He drove as quickly as he could back home. The snow they were in had long since stopped. Once he pulled into his driveway, he got out and headed into his home.

Isla Grace must have known something was wrong because she immediately asked when she saw him, "What happened?"

After taking his shoes off, he sat down on their love seat before he told her everything that had happened. Her facial expression did not move whatsoever, even when he got to the part where David shot Liam's friend.

Once he finished, she stated, "This is not a good thing."

"I know, but Harry forced our hand. We walked down this path, and there is no going back."

"Of course, Angus, it is also not as though we can go to the confessional and tell the priests. They will have no choice but to report it."

Giving out a heavy sigh, Angus said, "I know. I could have backed down, and at first everything was all rosy as we talked about a free Scotland, but how many of us even knew where we were headed? We didn't, and as we pushed forward, we forced this. Henry might have walked through the door that caused it, but we opened it. It's all on me, and I've got to harden myself to what will need to be done."

“What will need to be done?” She asked.

“More of what happened tonight. It’s us or them.”

She shifted her head away from him to look out towards the nearby window. He was very unsure what she was thinking, but he imagined that she was probably upset.

“You are right Angus. I pushed you down this path, and I will walk with you down it. I had not thought about it fully, but those military men are right. Times are hard, and we need hard men to save Scotland.”

He reached out and softly turned her chin towards him before stating, “And hard men need soft women to tend to them. Thank you for being mine.”

The corners of her mouth crept up slightly to indicate the tiniest of smiles as she stated, “Someone has to rein in you men in, or you would prank each other off a cliff.”

Angus could do nothing but laugh in response to her clear joke.

He stood up and reached out a hand before saying, “Let’s go to bed, and you can work on making sure I stay far away from cliffs.”

# Chapter 22

11 August 2018

The beeping sound of Angus' alarm echoed in his ears. He reached over and grabbed his phone to turn off the alarm. It was a lot earlier than they would normally wake up, but Liam and the others had called a meeting for the main parts of the leadership group for their Stirling Albion FC club.

Isla Grace's groggy voice said, "Good morning."

He turned to look at her. She was resting on her side with her back to him. Since she started to show, she began shifting and moving a lot more in bed. He loved touching her belly as it grew. Something so common in the world just seemed miraculous to him.

"Good morning." He replied.

She shifted towards him and onto her back. He took the opportunity to gently place his hand on her belly. She set both of her hands on his hand resting on her belly. He was hoping that the baby would be moving again, but it did not move this time. The first time he felt it moving was amazing. Isla Grace insisted that they not find out the gender of their child until they were born, so he had no idea if it was a boy or a girl.

She sat up and then declared, "Let me make you breakfast before you head off for your meeting."

Shimming on the bed, he slid next to her, slipped his right hand alongside her neck, before leaning into her, kissing her.

She broke off their kiss and then stated, "You will be late if you continue attempting to seduce me."

"I don't mind."

"I do. You have a reputation to uphold as the leader. Let us go." She responded before climbing out of their bed.

Angus chuckled. She had quickly become the glue that held his life together in a matter of a few months. He got out of bed and then ran to the toilet. Once he finished there, he got ready to go. It was still another hour before he had to leave, so he took a shower before eating breakfast. He made sure to give Isla Grace a long hug. She seemed to really appreciate his physical affection towards her, even though she would not change her facial expression or tone of voice the whole time. Really, the only way he knew was the fact that she would cuddle closely up to him and almost be molesting him with her hands every time he got near her. After he finished hugging and kissing her, he climbed into his car and then drove off. Liam seemed to love having these meetings far away from civilisation. They all bought fishing gear to appear to anyone who saw them that they were just a bunch of lads out fishing. He hated fishing and would cast his line out, but never do anything with it. This time, they were meeting at a river south of Gurnnock. He found a spot in the village shop car park, and after buying a bottle of water and a small snack, he headed for a walk down to the spot they selected. Once he found the spot in question, he was the first one there. He set up his fishing pole and then cast a line. After about 5 minutes, he heard people walking towards him. The first man he spotted was the military man who joined them, named Markus. Right as Angus was about to say something, the man gestured with his finger to be quiet. The man then walked over to a tree and put down an unusual device. He fiddled with it for a bit and then walked over to Angus.

"Hello Angus." He said.

"What was that thing?" Angus asked.

"It emits a set of subsonic waves that prevents people from listening to us while we converse.

He was impressed because he had never heard of a device like that. It was something that would probably be quite handy.

Markus then asked, "How is your wife?"

Giving a grin, Angus answered, "She's expanding rapidly but otherwise doing well."

Markus clapped Angus on the shoulder before chuckling and then asking, "A boy or a girl?"

"Isla Grace wanted to wait to be surprised."

"Ahhh, traditional."

Liam's voice cut into the conversation, "Probably the best word one could use to describe my sister."

Angus turned to look at Liam. He spotted Liam and about 10 other men. Their main leadership had grown significantly as they needed to build a trusted group to manage their growing group. It was the rural areas where they expanded the most. The Highlands were filled with men who wished to change Scotland's current path. He was quite surprised when he found out how many military men had joined the cause. In fact, all the new men were hand-selected by David and seemed to fit in nicely. He was initially nervous about adding them, but he found them good lads who loved Scotland as much as any other. There was one man who was new to the group, and Angus was curious who he was.

Once everyone had cast a line and the general conversation had died, Angus asked, "So… How long til that useless May is out of the office, and who's gonna replace her?"

Harry answered first, "Probably in a few months. My money's on Boris."

Liam laughed. Angus knew that Liam used to love Boris, but over time, he changed his opinion to think that Boris was a buffoon. Angus liked him, but he had no trust in him or any other supposed conservative. After a bit of chatter, there was silence again.

David then announced, "I suppose it's time to introduce the new man."

Angus nodded at him. He was curious. The man had peppered grey hair and a clean-shaven face. His eyes were brown and if Liam guessed, he was probably in his early 50's. He was wearing a brown T-shirt, a red flannel, and a pair of blue jeans.

"This is Michael Kerr."

Angus nodded. He guessed the man was probably retired military or maybe working in a large company or another.

The man named Michael declared, "I'm a member from Scottish Parliament with the Scottish Conservative and Unionist Party."

Angus was utterly surprised, somehow, they recruited a member of the Scottish Parliament! Maybe, just maybe, they had a real chance.

Liam interrupted his thoughts by asking in a stern tone, "Why the hell would you be here with us?"

Michael turned to Liam to answer, "The EU has completely destroyed my family's legacy by allowing fucking frogs to fish in their ancestral waters. Our towns are slowly being infested by Asians who hate us. My granddaughter can't even walk in the streets of a village that our family has been living in before the god damned Roman Empire showed up to build a wall. It must stop. When Harry told me secretly about your plans, I decided if you lads can step up, then I should too."

Angus interrupted, "You know what'll happen if we're caught and you understand our plans fully?"

The man looked at Angus before responding, "I do. It'll be the head of all of us."

He pushed further, "And what'll you provide to us? I get it, if we're successful, you'll be important to us in forming a new government, but what about now or over the next two years?"

The man turned to David and asked in a slightly huffy tone, "Who is this man to question me?"

Angrily reaching out to grab the man by the top of his shirt, Angus said, "I'm the man whose head is gonna be hung on the fucking London Bridge if we're caught. Either answer my questions or I'll have these men end your arse."

His firm tone must have impressed the military men, who nodded.

Michael looked quite shaken, and after taking a moment to recover, he answered, "So you're the leader."

"Yes, and this isn't a fucking Democracy. My word is law until we win out and save Scotland."

Liam grinned.

"Fine. I'm starting to understand. I'm a senior Parliamentarian on the Criminal Justice committee. I've got access to a lot of people who feel as we do. I can expand the whole movement."

Clapping the man on the shoulder, Angus responded, "Excellent. I apologise for being aggressive. It's important not only to see how you react but that you understand the stakes."

"Since you're our leader, then perhaps I can get a name?"

"Angus Bruce." He answered as he extended a hand.

Then the man shook his hand before responding, "I see why you lads picked this one. I'm in. We are looking at 2 years to act?"

"Depends on how far we get along in my plan." Angus replied.

"I know a lot of loyal men who feel as we do. It'll take time, but I'll have more than a fair share to aid us. I know the police chief of Edinburgh personally, and I'm sure he'll be in once I approach him."

Angus nodded. The whole plan was slowly creeping along. David and his men had started planning for training, which made sense. They would all need to know how to fight to remove the bastards in the Parliament, but also if the British decided to attack. It was something they argued about in depth when it came to dealing with the British. Angus had presented several ideas based on successful revolutions. It would take a mixture of standard military warfare and an intense guerrilla campaign. The goal would be to draw the British thin through Scotland and then weaken the will of the British public to want to fight. The largest conflict they had was whether they should attack British soil itself. Angus did not want to harm civilians, if possible, but he knew some casualties would occur. In the end, they decided to follow Angus' plan to keep fighting as much as possible in the Lowlands. The rest of their meeting was spent discussing the various goals and plans to divide and control more Scottish territory once they moved into action. After all the men left, Angus was left alone with Liam, David, and Markus.

David turned to Angus and stated, "Fine work. It's good that we let these people, as important as that politician, understand the stakes. He thought we'd just roll over and put him in charge of something."

Markus chuckled, "That's probably the first time he's had someone get physical with him in his life."

Angus shrugged before commenting, "We can't screw around anymore. We're past the point of no return."

David clapped his shoulder as he told Angus, "Yes, we are. I want to sit down with a few of the brains of our group and put together a plan of how we'll set up our government."

"I've been assembling a few ideas to weed out the flaws of the American Constitution and specific blocks to prevent future leaders from doing some insane shite like trying to join the EU."

"Of course you did." David retorted with a grin.

Liam interrupted, "He's as much of a compulsive weirdo as my sister. I'm convinced he's got the 'tism."

The other men laughed. Angus had never looked at it nor thought of himself as anything but another normal lad. He did enjoy organising and research, but that was not some social anomaly. He just shrugged at them. David nodded at Markus, who then turned and began fiddling with the device he had brought.

"We'll contact you for that meeting." David announced before turning his head to Markus.

Both men walked away, leaving Angus and Liam alone. Liam gestured with his head for Angus to walk with him.

As they started walking, Liam said, "That was some savage shit posting Henry's news article in the Discord."

Nodding solemnly, Angus stated, "A way to let men know what happens when you mess with the club without admission."

"You've changed Angus."

"I had to."

Liam grunted. They walked back to the village in silence. Liam waved at him as Angus split off to go to his car. He folded his fishing pole up and put it in the boot of his car. After getting in his car, he drove home. The drive was a little busier than he would have liked, but it was a Saturday afternoon, so he was not surprised. As soon as he pulled up to his home, the door opened, and Isla Grace appeared. He gave her a soft kiss and a hug as soon as he got out of the car.

"I am pleased that you have returned." She stated that once they broke their kiss.

"Me too."

"I have made you lunch. A nice mutton butty with crisps."

"Sounds wonderful. In case I haven't said it today, thank you for being my wife."

She wrapped her arm around his arm to walk with him as they entered their home.

"You are welcome. Thank you for providing so much. You have proven to be everything I knew you could be as a husband. I pray daily to Heavenly Father, thanking him for providing you to me."

"As so I. You've helped me reconnect with God and make myself better."

"Sit down." She instructed as she let go of his arm.

He sat down as she walked into the kitchen. In a moment, she returned with a butty, some fresh crisps with tomato sauce, and a cup of juice.

As she set them down, she asked, "So how did it go?"

"We've got a politician who knows the chief of police in the capital to join the FC club."

"Impressive."

Chuckling, Angus commented, "I also scared the piss outta him."

Raising an eyebrow, she asked, "How?"

"A little bit of physicality and a few ungodly words when he challenged me."

"I do not like it when you use curse words Angus."

"Sometimes I've gotta let these lads know I'm the boss or they'll ruin us all."

"I understand; I just do not like it."

He then commented, "I used to swear like a sailor on weekend pass 'til I met you."

She placed her hand on the back of his neck and then leant closer before saying, "I will get it all out of you eventually."

"Probably."

Suddenly, she pulled her hand away from him and set it on her belly.

"The baby is moving."

He took his hand out and placed it on her belly, which she responded to by grabbing his hand and placing it on the spot where he could feel their baby move. He grinned widely when the little rascal kicked roughly.

"That was a good kick." Isla Grace commented before continuing, "I imagine this child will probably be a troublesome rascal like you were when I met you."

"Were?"

The corners of her mouth moved before she declared, "I domesticated you."

He laughed heartily, knowing full well she was right.

# Chapter 23

23 October 2018

With Isla Grace ready to give birth, Angus took leave from work so he would be ready. She was a bit overdue, so the doctors scheduled an appointment for today to induce labour. He loved to watch her walk around like a penguin as she waddled from side to side everywhere she went. She had done a fine job of not gaining large amounts of weight outside of the baby and a bit of fat, but at her height, it unbalanced her. He was impressed with her toughness; she never complained, although she had asked for regular foot and lower back rubs. It was still early enough in the morning that they spent time packing a bag for her. The doctors stated that everything looked great on the sonograms, but they usually held the mother and baby for a few days at the hospital. He was nervous as all hell, but Isla Grace maintained her usual calm demeanour. First, he took out her bag and then guided her into the car.

As he sat down, she declared, "I am well past ready to get this child out of me."

He laughed before stating, "No doubt. They've been free riding for long enough, time to get outta there and get put to work."

She tilted her head slightly as she raised her eyebrow at him before saying, "I believe that you may be confused. I aided my mother in raising many of my younger siblings, and children tend to not only be useless but also an actual detriment to any required work we could have for them."

Grinning at her, he said, "I know."

"Ahhh. I am afraid my usual ability to detect your humour is a bit off due to my condition. Once we have returned from the hospital with our little charge in hand, I am certain I will be back to my usual self."

"No worries." He quickly told her while backing out to drive them to the hospital.

"I have studied everything I could find on childbirth and have spoken with both of our mothers. There may be moments during the process where I am unable to control my emotional state as normal, so please remain calm, as I want to assure you that I will be perfectly fine once the pregnancy is concluded."

He chuckled. She was trying to reassure him about giving birth. If anything, he should be the one reassuring her since she was the one about squeezing out something the size of a small watermelon. He just had to sit there and try to comfort her.

"Aye, I'll be fine, Isla Grace. It's you who needs to be assured."

"I am fulfilling God's plan for me by him letting me become a mother. I do not need assurance as I have faith in our Heavenly Father."

Reaching over, he grabbed one of her hands before saying, "Perhaps, but you're still squeezing a baby out."

"Admittedly, there is a level of nervousness from the whole process, but I retain my faith overall."

"I'll be there the whole time." Angus told her firmly as he leant a little closer to her and then applied a soft kiss on the back of her hand that he was holding.

"Which is greatly assuring to me."

It was still something he was surprised by with her. If any other person had said they were assured by his words in such a monotonic manner, he would think they were lying their faces off. He knew her well enough to know that she was telling him the truth. As they pulled up to the hospital, he parked in one of the special spots for pregnant mothers. Once he helped her out of the car, both his and her parents arrived. Many of Isla Grace's younger siblings were there for the occasion. Usually, her parents would take them everywhere they went. It was a madhouse a few weeks ago when they came over to the home with all the kids. They ran free like wild animals. He chuckled, thinking that someday he would end up being at his own home with his own kids. They went into the hospital and checked Isla Grace into the maternity ward. He was thankful that most of the family would have to wait in the waiting area for the family. He, along with her mother and his mother, was able to go into the main delivery room after the doctors began preparation. It was only after he filled out a massive pile of paperwork that they would even start. The doctor explained that they would give her medicine that would induce labour, and once she dilated to a certain point, she would go into labour automatically. After he finished all the paperwork, he walked into the delivery room with all the protective stuff they put on everyone. A nurse walked up to him and gestured for him to follow her out into the hallway.

As they left the room, the nurse asked, "Is something wrong with your wife?"

Very puzzled by what she was asking, he asked, "What do you mean?"

"She doesn't seem to be responding emotionally to anything we're doing."

He chuckled before answering, "She's pretty stoic, but she's fine."

"Okay." The nurse responded before heading back into the room.

He sat next to Isla Grace and grabbed her hand.

She looked at him and then stated, "This is an unusual experience. The reading on it really does not describe the physiological effects that I am feeling."

"You're okay?" He asked just a little bit too nervously.

"Of course. Having people poking and prodding at me down there is not overly pleasant, but I understand the reasoning. I cannot wait to hold our child."

Giving her a big grin, he told her, "Me too."

One of the nurses announced, "Mrs. Bruce, you have dilated to 10 cm. Pretty soon you should fully go into labour."

Isla Grace nodded. He held her hand throughout the whole thing, and it was not long until the doctor running the whole thing announced that he could see the baby's head. As she pushed, Isla Grace's facial expression shifted from her normal stoic expression to concentration mixed with pain. It was probably one of the rare moments that he saw a significant emotional reaction on her face outside of their home. There were beads of sweat moving down the sides of her face. He reached out to take a kerchief to wipe her sweat away. She grunted and groaned while squeezing his hand as hard as she could. He was quite thankful to have such a petite wife because she did not have the physical strength to hurt his hand while squeezing it. Finally, he heard his child scream and began to tear up.

"It's a boy!" The Doctor announced.

Looking into Isla Grace's eyes, he swore that she, too, had some tears, but it was hard to tell because his own vision was slightly blurred. Taking his free hand, he pinched between his eyes to rub away the tears. If she had cried, he could not see it anymore.

Her face was glistening from sweat, and she was paler than usual, which he suspected was probably normal for childbirth. After a few moments of waiting, the nurse brought a small baby wrapped in a blanket, which she then placed in Isla Grace's arms. Angus was surprised when she cracked an actual smile after she first took the infant into her arms. The little boy had telltale signs of being a redhead with his very light orangish coloured eyebrows. His eyes were closed as he wailed away, crying so Angus could not see his eye colour.

Isla Grace's smile disappeared, and she announced, "Robert William Bruce."

Angus nodded. It was the name that she had selected beforehand, and since he just wanted to avoid the insane names so many people in Western nations seemed to be giving their kids, he was pleased with the choice. He knew a coworker who freaking named his oldest son Optimus Prime after the damned Transformer! Angus watched as the nurse was instructing Isla Grace on proper breastfeeding. Little Robert took to it immediately and quite greedily. After a minute or so of feeding, he suddenly dozed right off to sleep and lost his grip on her.

She covered herself up before turning to him and asking, "Would you like to hold him?"

Giving a wide grin, he answered, "I would."

The nurse helped Isla Grace pass him over to Angus carefully. She then showed him how to hold the baby properly, which Angus already knew because Isla Grace told him a month ago, but he politely listened before taking hold of Robert. He was sound asleep, and Angus could hear him breathing softly. Reaching out his free hand, he gently touched the boy's cheek. It was as soft as anything he had ever touched. His skin was very pale, and he thought that he could spot a few tiny freckles. There was no doubt in Angus' mind that Robert would be a redhead like his parents.

Angus held the baby for some time before a nurse announced, "We need to take the little guy for tests."

He placed Robert into her open hands. As the nurse walked away with him, Angus turned to Isla Grace. She reached her hand out for him to hold.

When he took her hand, she stated, "He is a handsome boy, just like his father."

"He's got our hair colour, but I couldn't see his eyes."

"I think they were blue, but it was hard to tell in this lighting, especially since he was letting us know that he was hungry."

Angus nodded before he stated, "Can't wait to take him home. Nurses said a few days since everyone appears to be healthy."

"I agree with you; I think that decorating his room will be a pleasant experience as well."

He shrugged. Home décor was not really a top priority in his life.

She pulled his arm to bring him closer next to her before she whispered, "The wait here without being in your arms will be more painful than what I just went through."

Chuckling, he stood up and bent down to hug her.

# Chapter 24

10 August 2019

The sound of Robert's crying woke Angus from a deep sleep. Since he had come home with them, Isla Grace would cuddle him closely next to her every night. He glanced over at her and saw that she was awake, although very sleepy-looking. She pulled Robert into him and then began to feed him. It was part of their daily routine, little sleep, and lots of crying. He glanced out the nearby window and could see that the sun was barely beginning to peek through. It was early morning, but he decided to just get up. Today, they were planning to take Robert to King's Park. Isla Grace's family wanted to meet them for a nice sunny day before the weather really began to drop. Little Robert was barely starting to stumble around as he learned to walk, and Angus found it quite amusing to watch him learn new things. As he headed to the toilet, he checked his phone.

There was a text message from Liam that read, 'We'll have a visitor in the park.'

Angus was curious, so he replied, 'Who?'

'You'll see.' Liam replied.

It was likely someone or something about the FC club. Over the last year, their club has grown from a thousand to well over ten thousand strong. Scottish men from the British military had begun to flock into their club's open arms. Men were sick and tired of the bullshite. Harry, one of the first military men, was removed from the military when he commented about the ridiculous idea that the military was pretending that men who claimed to be women were women and should be treated as though they were women. Their whole nation was sick. It was not just the transgender nonsense. The whole Asian rape gang thing was a complete shame on the United Kingdom. Police were afraid to even arrest them without worrying about being called 'racist'. He could only hope that they would at least be able to save Scotland; the UK was likely doomed.

Isla Grace's voice called out, "Could you get me a drink of water, please?"

"Okay."

He filled a glass of water for her, and then, after she drank it, he put the glass in the wash basin. She was still cuddling little Robert, so he decided to pack a few things for their trip to the park. The plan was to arrive just before lunch and then have a nice picnic. Angus knew in the back of his mind that Isla Grace wanted to have a lot of children, but he was still surprised when she declared that she intended to get pregnant again. Before Robert was born, he might have protested some, but the boy was so much fun to him that the idea of having more was a positive one now. As he was packing, Isla Grace came out carrying Robert, who was awake.

"Could you hold Robert while I prepare breakfast?" she asked.

He took Robert from her. He giggled as Angus tickled him on his belly. The boy was very ticklish and seemed to love being tickled at any opportunity that he got. He had Isla Grace's blue eyes, and his hair was growing a bright orange colour, much like his own. Once she finished making breakfast, Angus put Robert into a highchair and then sat down. He had been "eating" real food for a little over a month, although most of it seemed to be wearing it or tossing it around rather than eating it. Today they were having a bowl of oatmeal, some sliced fruit, and a cup of orange juice. She always made simple breakfasts after their first week of living together when she discovered he always ate light first thing in the morning. She made a buffet, and he barely ate anything.

As they were eating, Isla Grace asked, "Do you have any idea when you plan to move onto the next phase?"

"We have enough for the first part, but we don't have enough for when the Brits act. I just don't see them rolling over and letting us take charge."

"That seems like a sensible approach. How long until you think that it will be ready to move forward?"

He shrugged before answering, "Recruiting has been moving exponentially, and I'm guessing summer next year."

She said nothing else. Once they were done, they took Robert to clean him off. He succeeded in wearing half the oatmeal and spilling the other half all over the floor. They still had some time until they had to leave, so Angus took Robert into the living room and helped him practise walking. He had to hold both the little guy's hands as he stumbled about.

As they walked around the living room, Isla Grace commented, "Pretty soon, he will be trashing the whole house as he runs around."

He chuckled. Throughout his life, he had never spent much time with small children. It was just him and his sister, so they never had little ones. Robert was a lot of fun, but he was loud, smelly, and generally demanding. Isla Grace seemed to handle him with little issue; he guessed an advantage of having so many younger siblings. There was absolutely no way that Angus could have handled Robert without her. Once Isla Grace had finished packing and was ready to go, she scooped up the little guy, and they headed off to the park. As they drove, he realised that they were about to need a new car very soon, maybe an SUV for more space. The weather was 25° Celsius, so it was a nice day for some time at the park. Once they got to the park, he was able to find a spot, and after a brief walk, they found the spot where her family was at. Her parents, siblings, and Liam with Sandy were there. Angus was quite pleased with Liam when they returned from their honeymoon to find that he had popped the question. Their marriage was not going to be as fast as he was, but early next year, they planned to get married. Everyone around them seemed quite happy when they announced it. As soon as Isla Grace set Robert down, he was immediately scooped up by her mother. Liam nudged his head off to the right, a hint that he wanted Angus to walk with him.

Once they got a good distance, Liam announced, "We've got an interesting guest who wanted to take a moment to talk to you, but far away from our normal spots."

"Who is it?"

Looking to his left and right, Liam answered, "He works for the same company as your late-night guest before you got married."

Thinking for a moment, Angus realised Liam was talking about the Chinese spy who came to his own to warn him about the traitor in their midst. Angus remembered how the man had told him that if they were successful in finding the traitor, they would be in communication with him again. As they walked, he spotted an East Asian man sitting on a bench.

Liam stopped walking and then whispered, "Sit on the other end of the bench and look out into the woods like you're enjoying the weather."

As Angus walked over to the bench and sat down, he spotted Liam heading back towards their family. Sitting down, he shifted his eyes to look towards the nearby golf course through the woods.

The Chinese man spoke, "We're quite impressed with your surprise resources in how quickly you dealt with your problem. We've been working on our end to ensure that no one in the British or American services has any idea you or your movement exists. We've reviewed your plan and find it satisfactory."

Making sure to continue looking straight ahead, Angus responded, "Thank you."

"Our estimates, based on your recruiting, are that you'll be ready in either mid- or late-summer next year."

Angus nodded lightly.

"Our leadership has decided that we'll be pushing our support to the next level. Once you have the numbers, you'll need equipment for both phases.

Interrupting him, Angus firmly stated, "We'll not take this if there is any sort of demand or requirement."

Lightly chuckling, the man responded, "Our people will be friends and nothing more. Friends help each other in times of need. There is no other demand or requirement."

He found that reasonable. The embarrassment of losing Scotland would indeed be significant, especially when the world someday discovers the Chinese helped. Scotland would need allies who would be willing to trade with it once it cut itself free from the U.K. He suspected most of Western Europe, Australia, and the Americans would not be pleased with Scotland's sudden, and likely violent, independence. Angus knew that too many Scots and the huge swaths of third-world scum would never vote for what he wanted. He and his men would have to force it.

The man then said, "There is a village with a harbour in Scotland that was the birthplace of a man who saved Bermudan lilies. That'll be the place where we'll be making this donation. Once your recruitment gets you control over their harbor then we'll begin donating to the cause."

Standing up, the man said, "We'll be keeping an eye on you and the club."

As he walked away, Angus rubbed his chin. The Chinese were going to end up being instrumental in the success in the freedom of Scotland. One of their biggest concerns was weapons, ammunition, and body armour. He originally planned to steal it from British military garrisons, but this was a better route for ensuring they would not be caught by some random nerd accountant by accident. They would just need to take over whatever town the man mentioned. He pulled out his phone and began doing research. The first thing he did was start up a VPN to help mask his search. Once his phone was ready, he found out the name of the man really fast, Lawrence Ogilvie. He was a plant pathologist who was born in the village of Rosehearty. It was a small village in the northern part of Scotland with an ageing population. He felt confident that the club would be able to take over the village easily since it had a strong conservative Council area. Angus nodded to himself. This was very good news. He stood up and began walking back to the family. Halfway there, he spotted Liam, who immediately strode over to him.

"And?"

"They want to help us with gear."

"Really?"

"Yes, and they've already picked the meet-up point for the exchange."

"Where?"

"Not here. We'll talk about it at the next meeting. In the very near future, there will be a fishing village that our club is going to be expanding into and then fully. They've offered to give us everything we'll need."

"And what do they want in exchange?"

"Friendship."

Liam scoffed before declaring, "Fucking commies probably want to take over."

"Well, my thought process is, if we succeed, we're gonna be enemy number one with most of the world, so it'll be important we have strong allies. Few are stronger."

Begrudgingly, Liam said, "Ya… I just don't like the idea of being beholden to them."

"I made it crystal clear to him that we'll take nothing before being controlled by anyone. He said that they knew it, but they know we'll need allies, and we're welcome to become one."

“Having them on our side is better than having no one.” Liam then commented.

“Truth.”

They then headed back to their family. Once he got close enough to see her face, Isla Grace looked right at him and raised an eyebrow. He grinned at her. The fact that they had the Chinese as allies who could help make everything possible was very reassuring to him. He sat down next to Isla Grace.

She slid closely next to him and then leant closer before whispering, “I must assume by your facial expression that you received some good news from your meeting.”

He responded with a slight nod, “Our visitor from a while back is now an ally who wishes to provide us with help.”

“That is good news indeed. I cannot wait to hear all about it once we get home.”

Robert crawled over to him, so he scooped him into his arms. The little guy squealed in joy. He likely expected Angus to give him a nice tickle attack, so Angus obliged him by setting Robert down and assaulting his sides with both hands in a tickling assault. Robert responded by laughing uproariously. Being tickled was the boy’s favourite thing to do, and Angus was confident that he was the only one consistently providing the tickle barrage that he wanted. Isla Grace acted more like the bossy mother figure, and Angus’ role was as the fun father figure. He wondered how their relationships would change as more children came along. Although he was hoping that Robert would not turn into a version of their family that Liam was for Isla Grace's. The rest of the picnic was quite pleasant with the food they brought along.

# Chapter 25

2 February 2020

Angus' alarm buzzed to wake them up for church. It was a very chilly Sunday morning, but that would not stop them from attending. Isla Grace rolled over to wrap her arm around him after he had reached out to silence his alarm. She was already pregnant again with his second child. He knew that she wanted a lot of children, but he was surprised by her desire to leap right into their second one, with Robert being barely a year old.

"Hello." He told her.

"Good morning."

He leant over to give her a little kiss before sliding out of their bed. He was quite happy that Robert was moved into his own bedroom so they could have at least some private time. The little boy had begun running at full speed, and he was a pure barrel of energy that would leave a mess in his wake as he moved. After getting up and helping Isla Grace to rein in and then dress Robert, they headed off to church. When they first got married, they attended St. Alexander's in Denny, but they eventually went to St. Mary's since it was so much closer to their home. He had to be very careful, strapping Robert into his car seat because several times the rascal had somehow managed to escape, laughing madly as he climbed all over the back seat. Once they got to church, they sat down. Isla Grace spent as much time attempting to keep Robert from running around as she listened to the sermon. He could only imagine what they would be dealing with when they had more children. Angus shifted the god-forsaken mask on his face. Somehow, a disease of some kind had been released in a city called Wuhan, and it was spreading across the world like wildfire. Everyone started wearing those blue surgeon masks, and there was talk that they might order a nationwide lockdown. Angus was quite concerned because this sort of thing would shift their plans. They had finally got their first shipment of weapons from the Chinese, and he was stunned by what they sent. He had only assumed it would be rifles and ammunition, but the Chinese sent rocket launchers, mortars, mines, and more. They sent a message that included information on another traitor in their midst. Angus ordered David to deal with the man, and Angus heard it was taken care of without knowing the man's name. He did want to push forward with the coup, but after a talk with the leaders, they decided to wait and see what was going on with this disease. Once Mass ended, Angus took his family to visit his parents. Usually, they spent time after Mass visiting Isla Grace's family, but she wanted to let his mother spend a little time with Robert. His once cool relationship with his father had warmed greatly after Robert was born. Heck, even his mother said that his father stopped drinking as much.

As they sped away, Isla Grace asked, "I wonder how long we will be wearing these masks. From what I understand, COVID-19 is a virus, and these masks cannot block it from passing through. The virus is too small to be obstructed, so it would take something more than a piece of cloth or a surgeon's mask. I doubt they could help people around sneezing or coughing either."

Angus shrugged as he took the damned thing off. He had tried to grow a beard again, but the mask made it a miserable experience, so he shaved his face clean. They continued driving, and he could hear Robert in his car seat tinkering around with a toy trolley. It was his favourite toy. The drive was pretty smooth, and before long, Angus was parked in front of his parents' home. He still made sure to knock and announce their arrival before entering. As soon as Isla Grace let go of Robert's hand at the doorway, he dashed off into the living room.

"Robby!" He heard his father say happily.

Angus grinned because they adored his son. As he walked into the living room, he saw that his mum was on the phone. Her expression shifted from happiness to grim. It was not good news and caused him to frown.

After she was done talking and hung up, she announced, "My mum has COVID."

It was not the news he was expecting, and it was not good news at all. The way the media and politicians talked about the disease, it was deadly and highly contagious. He strolled over to his mum and hugged her. She hugged back but did not seem as upset as he thought that she would be.

As she moved away to sit down in her chair, she stated, "She is refusing the treatments that are being offered."

His father chuckled before declaring, "She always has been as stubborn as a mule."

"I spoke to the doctor at the residence we placed her in when she got too old to take care of herself, and they said she is only showing symptoms of the flu."

"Odd," Angus stated before taking a pause and then continuing, "Reporters on the BBC claim it's deadly."

"Well honey, we'll see how she does in a few days, but they claim she's fine."

"That is good news at least." Isla Grace said.

His father then stated as he was wrestling with Robert, "There's nothing we can do now but pray so I suggest we eat supper and then do so."

*****

17 February 2020

Angus got permission from work to take the day off to visit his grandmum. She was staying at a home for the elderly in Edinburgh after his grandfather died a few years ago. Unlike his grandmum on his father's side, his mum's mum was frail and much older, so she was unable to take care of herself. He was still deeply surprised when his mum called to let him know that she had fully recovered. The BBC and politicians were treating this like a disease that could kill anyone. How could his elderly and frail grandmum have survived something that, according to the BBC, could kill a strong, healthy man like him? It was very confusing. Because of Robert's age, the doctors at the home asked Angus not to bring him right away, at least until they made sure everything was safe. He dropped him off with Isla Grace's family since there were so many other kids for him to play with while he and Isla Grace went to see his grandmum.

As they entered the freeway, Isla Grace asked, "What do you think of the government's proposal to lock down the whole nation?"

He shook his head before answering, "I don't know. The disease sounds horrible, but I'm still confused how my sickly grandmum could survive it. Mum said she claimed it was nothing worse than the flu."

“I have been reading articles about it on your computer while you were at work, and I have seen nothing to indicate it is something so simple.”

Nothing aligned, and it caused him to furrow his brow. She reached out with her hand and gently rubbed his shoulder. The drive took a bit over an hour due to traffic. Angus hated driving in Edinburgh, but they finally arrived. The home had all sorts of rules in dealing with people who had caught COVID, and part of that required an N95 facemask and a plastic shield while wearing scrubs. Once both were dressed up, they were escorted to his grandmum. She looked almost the same to him. Her once blonde hair had long since silvered, and her light skin was still quite wrinkly. She was close to 80 years old. He was glad to see that her light blue eyes were still sharp as ever.

As soon as she saw him enter, she happily said, “It’s about time my grandson brought his bride to visit me.”

He blushed as he responded, “Sorry gran, I was super busy since our wedding.”

She cackled before stating, “Based on her condition, making me a horde of great grandbabies.”

He laughed because his grandmum was probably the only person he knew who could compete with Isla Grace for directness.

“It is nice to meet you finally, grandmother.”

“Oooo, she’s so formal. Just call me gran dearie.”

“Very well, gran it is.”

His grandmum took a bit of Isla Grace’s long hair into her hands before declaring, “And she’s a lovely one too. I love your hair, young lady.”

“Thank you.”

Angus interrupted them to ask, “Gran, are you okay?”

She guffawed as she answered, “Thankfully, I just ignored these clowns. COVID this and COVID that. It was just the damned flu. I’ll take more than a little cough and high temperature to take this old hag out. The only frustrating part is that these goofballs won’t let me go anywhere. Keeping me locked up like some kinda experiential test dummy.”

“I’m sorry gran.”

She chuckled once again before declaring, “I’ve been through the Krauts bombing us as a small lass; this is just a nuisance.”

He nodded and then sat silently, thinking, and his grandmum and Isla Grace chatted. While at first Isla Grace did not like her cell phone, she used it more to take pictures of Robert than to call people. She took her phone out to show those pictures to his grandmum. He thought about this disease. It was clearly just the flu, maybe more contagious, but still the flu. There were rumours that the Chinese made it, and on top of it, that the Americans were somehow involved. It was clearly a real disease; his grandmum would not fake something like that. He had heard about several elderly and other sick people dying, but nothing from the club about anyone healthy dying from it. Suddenly, it hit him. The government and media were overinflating the disease to gain more control as part of their globalist schemes. The government talked about a full national lockdown to save lives, but if his grandmum could survive it, why would they need a lockdown? After spending an hour or so with his grandmum, they excused themselves to head home. Angus made sure to hug her, even in the silly gear they put on him.

Once they got into the car, Isla Grace said, "I can tell that you are thinking about something seriously. What is going on?"

He backed the car out, and as they started moving, he answered, "They're clearly lying on the BBC about this disease."

"For what purposes?"

"Control. These evil clowns want to control all of us and likely are planning to take the opportunity to use COVID as a new wrinkle to add to their power."

"And what are you thinking of doing about it?"

"Well, I would say go forward with the coup, but I suspect we would lose a lot of momentum we'll need to deal with COVID. The logical thing to do would be to wait and see what happens and then to act."

"That does seem like a prudent plan. Most likely, many people will not easily ally with our cause if they think they could die from a disease."

"Yup. I suppose the only advantage of waiting will allow us time to recruit even more people. We're not quite where I'd like us to be. Once we get back, I'll have to contact the leaders of each cell and let them know we're gonna be waiting 'til after this COVID crap ends. But it is a bit tangentially related to all that. I think we've got enough finances so that I should quit my job and focus full-time on the club. Our investments have finally gotten to the point where they can easily cover our bills."

"About that Angus, I was wondering if you had considered moving our family to a larger house."

"Of course. I was looking at the numbers, and I think if we can start searching after I quit the job and then I am planning to rent out the house we're in for a little more passive income."

"Very wise."

"How many rooms did you think we'd need?" He asked.

She paused for a moment before answering, "Maybe 6."

"We'll probably end up having to live a bit away from Stirling to be able to afford one that big while maintaining our finances."

"I understand and will move wherever you take us."

He grinned at her and then stated, "I might just copy your father and buy a farmhouse. It'll also make a nice base of operations for the club as well."

"That could certainly serve as a secondary purpose. I am intending to keep having children while I am in my youth."

"I've noticed." He commented with a light chuckle.

"Do you approve?"

"Of course. I just want you to be happy, and I've found myself really liking Robert. I bet the others will be just as much fun."

"He is a delight. I love the fact that he does not seem to notice or judge my lack of emotions, but loves me unconditionally. I also cannot express my pleasure that he did not have the same condition. It is my greatest concern about having many children in that it is possibly heritable."

"If we do have one who is like you, we'll love them the same. Probably having you as a mother will help our child understand themselves better."

She nodded and had a slightly thoughtful look as she stated, "I had not thought about that. I suspect that if I had someone who understood my unique personality and concerns better in my youth, perhaps things would have been easier."

He nodded. There was not really anything that he could think of saying to her. After they picked up Robert, they went home, and he made sure to log into their secret server to let everyone know he was thinking about the whole issue with the coup and COVID. He asked them to respond with feedback. He claimed earlier that he was the final word, but he always wanted input from others, especially since many minds made for a better selection of ideas to make things work. After setting up the inquiry, he went to eat supper with his family, and once they had eaten, he took some time to play with Robert. Quitting his job had been something he considered for the last year. He no longer liked being around his coworkers. They seemed to be degenerate in their behaviour, and many of them seemed to outright hate Scotland. Being married to Isla Grace and absorbing the scriptures more made him realise that negative influences like that only bring trouble. Not only for a man but for a nation. He logged back into the server and was pleased with the overall concurrence with his suggestion. The men wanted to make sure everything was going to be okay with the whole COVID thing before making their move.

# Chapter 26

12 June 2020

Sunlight shimmered down on Angus as he worked on chopping wood. After buying the ranch house, he found out that he greatly enjoyed physical labour much more than he used to. Something about being alone and not having to think about anything but chopping wood was very relaxing. The new house that they bought was a bit further out from Denny than her parents' home. It was a tiny bit smaller than theirs, but instead of a farm, it was a ranch home designed for raising cattle. He mixed the land that came with it to be split between Highland cattle, sheep, and goats. After hiring a few ranch hands, it turned quickly into a profitable business, which allowed him to copy his father-in-law and hire a manager. It ran itself without him after he hired an accountant to manage the money. He just got to live on the big ranch and enjoy the lovely and open Scottish environment. Isla Grace, who was never a fan of groups of people, was quite happy to move out of Stirling. He suspected that their new home was more like her childhood home. His son Robert loved running free in the wide-open spaces and even playing with their several herd dogs. As he was about to heft his axe, his phone buzzed. He glanced and saw it was Liam.

Answering his phone, he said, "Hey, ya cunt."

"Oi. I'm getting damned tired of these COVID lockdowns. They keep promising to let us do shit like go out for dinner, but then it's 'stay 1 metre away'. I really hate that bitch, Sturgeon."

Angus nodded as he replied, "I hear you. It's been freaking great for our recruitment, though. People like you are sick of it all. I'm no economics expert, but mass printing money to keep the country afloat is just gonna make the pound useless. Once we can finally get free of these lockdowns, we can get to proper training, and before we know it, we can make our move."

"It's hard to believe we're really gonna do it, but honestly, this COVID crap clearly is way overblown."

"They wanna control us. Get used to being locked down before they start in on the commie bullshit controls."

Liam then said, "Well, I guess I should get back at it. They keep us security types busy, but the rules, the masks, and all the other bullshit they themselves ignore. It's like rules for us peons, but they think they're royalty. Sturgeon and a bunch of 'em had a special party where they all were there maskless while the servants and security had to wear masks. How bad is the disease if they aren't scared of it?"

"Not at all. Talk to you later Liam."

"Okay." He replied before hanging up.

Angus set his phone down and then finished chopping his wood. At night and in winter, they would use wood to keep the house warm. He had been slowly working on his stock for the long term and then storing it in a rack along the back wall of their home. The growth of their club was quite impressive. Scots think themselves free men, and so when the government starts dictating insane rules, they get upset. He was able to use this to push the club over 100,000 members. They now had people in all but three military garrisons and in the police forces of every major city in Scotland. Rosehearty was their largest percentage of control. They had well over 800 members in that village. Angus personally visited the village about four months ago, and he met many loyal and fine Scots there. They received him reverently as their leader or a mythical figure rather than just another man. The Chinese have been slowly rolling equipment out, and Angus had it spread out under the control of each cell. They had one or two men leak information, but David was able to use his MI6 and Scotland Yard contacts to muffle the traitors before making them vanish. He did not like the idea of ordering the deaths of these men, but they betrayed the club, so at this point, he rarely gave it a second thought. He strolled into his house and saw Isla Grace hard at work in the kitchen. Lunch was due soon, and she was always at it. She was now 5 months along with their second child, and he was quite excited to see if they had another boy or a girl this time.

Wrapping his arms around her to put his hands on her belly, he said, "Hello beautiful lady."

"Thank you for your kind words, but could you go wash your hands and collect Robert from his room so we can have lunch?"

Pecking a kiss on her cheek, he answered, "I'm on it."

Releasing her, he walked down the hallway to Robert's room.

The boy was playing with several lorries, and when he saw Angus, he said, "Pop!"

He then dropped his lorries and then ran up to hug Angus. Angus chuckled at him.

"Robby, it's lunch time. Let's go wash our hands and then eat."

After they washed up, they ate lunch together. Once they were done, Angus said his goodbyes and headed off. He had another meeting with several cell leaders. They had begun to start getting antsy to make a move. He understood their frustrations, but he still wanted to be patient. It was his view that if they did a coup now, it would give them the unneeded headache of COVID rules to deal with once they took charge. He felt it was more important to focus on the coup and then the Brits before finally leaping right into building a new government. The next meeting place was in a village called Aberfeldy. Angus was convinced that Liam liked long drives because he always picked the most out of the way villages deeper into the Scottish countryside than the last. Angus chuckled, thinking about where their meetings would end up in a few months. He had to admit Liam did have a flair for finding places; this one was located at an old Black Watch memorial on the outskirts of the village. He suspected that David and the other men would appreciate it. The drive was over an hour long, but it did remind him how beautiful Scotland was. Upon arriving in Aberfeldy, he drove to the memorial and parked. Several men were already milling about. Once Angus arrived, they formed up as a group near the memorial. Their numbers for the whole club had grown so big that they were forced to expand the leadership circle from the original 10 to 30 men strong. He walked into the group and shook hands with each man as they all greeted each other.

Since he was the leader of the group, he announced, "Welcome everyone. We've made massive progress in membership thanks to the Wu-Flu. The Chinese have been helping our cause in more ways than gear. Scots are getting sick of being locked up like prisoners."

The men around him chuckled.

He continued speaking, "I know that each man here wishes to charge into Parliament tomorrow morning, but I'd like to consider that we maintain prudence. I aim to lessen the stacks of problems we'll be dealing with on top of the fucking Brits trying to kill us."

Some of the men nodded, and others looked disappointed. The reading he had done on leadership expressed that looking for conflicting opinions and consensus was critical to success.

"I'd like to hear your thoughts and recommendations." He stated.

One of the men from their second phase of recruitment commented, "I'd have loved to put an end to the commies ruining Scotland immediately if I could."

Angus nodded at the man. He completely agreed.

David then responded, "I can see why moving immediately to ensure we don't eventually get caught. We've had more than our fair share of close calls. Many of our friends have stopped incidents from sprouting up, and the longer we wait, the more likely we'll be caught."

Angus could see the logic behind his point.

Markus then interjected, "I've got to concur with Angus, but the reasoning isn't the same."

Raising his eyebrow, Angus asked, "I'd like to hear them."

"Easy." Markus stated before pointing around them and continuing, "No one is here because they're all scared the piss out of by the fucking flu of all things. Even our military has been routed home. If we made our move now, there would be many more men from the Brits coming at us initially than we originally planned for. We'd need to double our numbers just to have a chance to form a proper revolution."

It made sense. It would take another government fraud war in some foreign shithole to get those men far away from Scotland. Markus' wisdom seemed to work as the others around them nodded.

Liam then commented, "Good idea. We've gotta keep an eye on when the best change to make a move."

One of the other men, who was a bit older than most of the group, asked, "Maybe we should set a hard deadline by which we'll forgo worry about COVID lockdowns and make our move?"

David answered, "A wise idea."

"We need to shift from making our move to proper military training. We will have to examine how training is going and when we feel battle-ready before leaping right into Parliament. Few common men have proper military training and will need to know techniques on guerrilla military warfare." Angus firmly stated.

One of the other men chuckled before asking, "Do you have a plan?"

Before Angus could respond, Harry answered, "Do you think birds fly? Of course, he's got a plan."

The other men laughed uproariously in response. Angus' reputation as a man with layers of plans had become well-known. He spent all his free time, when not with his family, working on different plans and scenarios that could be executed. The guerrilla warfare was probably his most detailed plan. The first part, removal of the Scottish Parliament, would be easy. They controlled most of the key points of Scotland already. He was not sure how nations outside of the Brits would react. If the Americans decided to get involved, things would get very difficult. He had no contacts outside the U.K., and the Chinese themselves have stated they had little influence outside of the obvious ownership of much of the American political class. Those cunts were the only ones he could think of that were more corrupt than the U.K. politicians. Trump was probably the only one he liked.

Once the men stopped laughing, he answered, "I've extensively studied the most successful guerrilla warfare campaigns and have put together a complex strategy that utilises the pro-offered Chinese equipment from mines to rocket launchers. My estimates have it that anywhere from one to two years of constant effort will put the British on a path of willingness to give up on Scotland."

"Dang." One man stated.

Nodding, Angus said, "The reason it's so short is the amount of planning and time we're taking to execute. Most terrorists fail because they fuck around and leap too soon."

Once Angus said 'terrorists', he saw several men blanch. It was a tough term to accept, but that was about to be the reality they would have to fight to win, however they could. Unless they got a few million men to join their cause, they would never be able to defeat the British in direct combat. It would have to be small hit-and-run strikes and terror attacks against British targets to wear the British public down to the point they would demand peace.

He continued speaking, "Once the COVID lockdown shit ends, I was thinking we would move into a leadership training mission where I could give the details of my plans for each phase, and then we'd move into a mass training phase. I have spent a good amount of my own money buying warehouses for storage and several forested areas up north to use as a training ground."

"You're a rich cunt?" Another man asked.

Liam interjected, "One of those self-made ones. He was a computer nerd 'til he took charge of our little ragtag effort."

Angus chuckled at the comment 'took charge'. It was foisted on him. He, however, was glad Liam stepped in there. Most ordinary Scots, himself included, had a deep-seated distrust of men who inherited money. They felt less trustworthy and obsessed with power than a normal man should be. Angus nodded in confirmation.

"I sold a few computer programs. Now I'm a rancher and family man. Back to the plan, I'm estimating it could take a year or more just to execute the training, and then after that we'll have to move our equipment south to the villages of Langholm and Gretna."

"Why those two towns?" David asked.

"The Brits are so cocky they'll come right up the A7 and A74 looking to capture both Edinburgh and Glasgow right away. It'll be the bulk of their forces, and if we can hit their first major thrust hard, they'll have to seriously reconsider their whole plan. Once we have equipment in those two villages, we move out to villages covering the A68, A697, and A1. They may try to hit us there instead, but we'll set up scouts at the villages just south of the border to let us know when they're coming so we can adjust accordingly."

David looked impressed by the plan, but he pressed Angus by asking, "What if they decide to go with air attacks?"

"Initially, they'll avoid it due to the civilian population, but eventually they'll have no choice. The moment we take Parliament; we'll take possession of any anti-aircraft weapons on military garrisons throughout Scotland and then move them south into the Lowlands. Our goals are to trick them into attacking those weapons with their aircraft since they'll have satellites telling them where they are. We can use their own love of technology to hinder them with trickery. I've spent the last year selling my last program, designing viruses to disable or interfere with their computer military systems. Several lads in the club have given me keys that allow me to increase my success rate. We're gonna run a full-scale multi-front operation on the British military the second the bastards refuse our declaration of independence."

The men around them looked quite impressed. Angus' research into military warfare led him to believe that the Americans had planned the same sort of attack against Russia or China if they ever went to war. It made him laugh when he saw the American military leadership openly posting papers talking about 5th-generation warfare.

Another lad then asked, "We're gonna win with this cunt on our side, aren't we?"

David answered, "We are. Every one of us will someday be referred to as the founding fathers of a new free Scotland. We just gotta do our part, and I don't know about you lads, but I'm really liking Angus' plan."

Harry then added, "Just be prepared for a hard slog before we get there. Many of us won't live to see that free Scotland."

"I'll die for that cause." Markus stated boldly.

The others cheered. Angus could not help but cheer along. He did not want to die more than anyone else did, but a free Scotland would be worth the cause. He wanted his kids to be able to go to school and not worry about some faggot leftist teacher trying to brainwash them. Education in Scotland had become indoctrination. Fucking commies did not breed since they murdered their babies left and right, but they reproduced by brainwashing normal kids into being commies. Banning communism would be one of the first major pieces of the new Constitution. Communism was evil incarnate.

After the men calmed down, Angus asked, "So we agree? We wait until the COVID restrictions loosen to avoid attention and then start grinding out training."

Several men nodded, but no one objected.

"For Scotland." Angus declared before turning around and walking away.

He heard the others call out 'For Scotland'. It had become their calling card. He walked over to his car and got in. It was a long drive home, and he hoped to make it for supper.

# Chapter 27

18 December 2020

News about a new vaccine had hit Scotland, and Angus was very unsure about it. Many times, the government had lied or tricked them. Shit, it had been over a year, and they still had to deal with damned lockdowns, and it was stressing his patience. He was itching to start training. Angus had been working on his next idea, a virus he wanted to push into the satellite system of the Brits. It could, in theory, block them from being able to easily use that technological advantage. He had several members of the group give him access to the security keys so Angus could interrupt it all. Early disruption of the Brits would be key to making them question the idea of invading Scotland. Demoralise to overcome their bad odds. It was early in the morning. He found himself getting up much earlier than he used to since he bought the ranch. Taking care of the animals took a lot of work and needed an early start. He got used to it after having to do much of the work himself initially, so he continued to wake early. Even with hired help, he would still help on the ranch. There was a lot of pride in raising fine animals. After cleaning up from work, he made himself a cup of tea and then had a seat. His doorbell rang, so Angus stood up and went to answer it. It was Liam and David.

"Hello gentlemen." Angus said as he opened the door.

The two men stepped in, and Angus closed the door. They removed their boots and then followed Angus as he led them into the living room.

Once they all sat down, Liam asked, "How is Isla Grace?"

"Very pregnant."

"Can't keep your hands off her?"

Angus laughed before smartly answering, "The other way around. She knows a pimp when she sees one. Either of you boys want a cup of tea?"

They both agreed, so he took a moment to make each one a cup of tea and then sat back down after serving it.

David chuckled before asking, "You know the new vaccine that they've started pushing on people?"

"Ya."

"Our health service contacts are spamming heavy warnings on the private server." David stated.

Liam then interjected, "Some scientific shit. They said whatever the cost, avoid the fuck outta it."

Angus sighed. At this point, he had no trust whatsoever in the government. It would not have surprised him at all that something was up with it. He watched a long video from Alex Jones talking about how the vaccines would ruin your immune system. It was concerning since Alex Jones was considered a 'conspiracy theorist', but he was awfully right too many times.

"Okay Liam. I'll spread the word, telling folks to keep their family off it."

"What if the government forces people?" David asked.

The idea that the government would force people to take an experimental vaccine was initially shocking, but then Angus realised it would likely be a control mechanism. It was obvious they would do it.

After thinking for a bit, Angus then stated, "Let's find out if we can find a way around it. My gran had it, and she recovered in a week. She still has no other problems, and I believe it's just the flu. Maybe they're forcing it to shift more government funds into Big Pharma's pockets?"

"All I know is the people in our group were saying Alex Jones was right about the vaccine." Liam stated.

Angus chuckled. There was a meme about an 'Alex Jones was right' jar.

"Liam, I'll go and see what they think and see if anyone has a plan to make sure our people avoid it. If we can find a way to dodge that vaccine, it might even turn into another recruiting point."

"Good idea. We've gotta run Angus, but we wanted to bring this to your attention." David stated.

"Thanks. I'll get to work right away."

After both men left, Isla Grace walked out. She was holding their newest family member, Abigail. He was quite pleased when their daughter was born. Robert was still sleeping.

"Another issue?" She asked.

"Apparently, our sources in the NHS claim the vaccine the government is about to push on all of us is bad. I haven't had a chance to read the claims, but Liam and David felt so concerned they stopped by to let me know."

"That is disconcerting. My parents have stated they plan to take it once they can."

His parents had said they would as well. Most people fell hook, line, and sinker for this whole COVID scam the government was foisting on them. Many did not and ended up being part of the club.

She passed Abigail to him and then said, "I'll prepare some breakfast."

He took the little girl in his arms. It was quite a surprise when she was born to discover that she had blonde hair. He felt that all their children would have orange hair as they did, but she came out blonde like her grandparents on Isla Grace's side. Taking her over to his computer, he sat down. Using one hand, he started up the laptop before logging into his private server. It was indeed surprising to read the notes from their NHS people. All of them claimed outright that the vaccine was bad and that no one should take it. Blood clotting, heart damage, and other issues were being stated happened. Many mentioned the fact it was not a real vaccine but something else entirely that was very untested. He took time to write a post asking people what they could do to dodge taking it without anyone knowing that they did not take it. The aim was to blend into the crowd. He suspected that if the government pushed hard, the last thing that his men needed to do was to stand out on this issue. One man, a significant administrator at the NHS in Edinburgh, replied that they could set up a fake vaccination program that would allow all their men to seem as though they were vaccinated with it without actually being jabbed. He liked it. It would be a great way to recruit others if they pushed hard enough. The biggest concern would be trusting people with a list of everyone's name. Maybe they could secretly spread this fake vaccination programme outside of just this one administrator? The wheels in his head began to turn. Of all their contacts, the health services were probably the weakest. His focus had been on recruiting in the military, political, and policing infrastructures. It was time to shift a little bit. He submitted a post in the forum calling for his men to begin recruiting medical personnel. After he logged out, he stood up and put his sleeping infant into the nearby bassinet. He then sat down with Isla Grace to eat breakfast.

Once she sat down, he told her, "Under no circumstances should anyone take that vaccine. It looks like some kind of drug that alters your RNA to force your own body to make proteins that interfere with the disease."

"That sounds like something other than a vaccine if I remember my biology classes correctly."

"Our guys say that it messes up your blood and heart because it wasn't fully tested. Even the doctor who theorised about making it was opposed to it being used for a vaccine."

"I will let my parents know to avoid it."

"I'm working on a plan to get our guys in health services to get us fake vaccinations in the system. I'll try to get our parents into the system if they want us to."

She nodded lightly before replying, "If gran can survive it easily, I do not understand why a vaccine is even needed."

"Only really sick people are dying from it, just like the flu would do them in. Our guys have questioned the numbers; the hospitals are just tagging everyone who dies as having died of COVID."

"More government lies?"

"As usual. The new Scotland will have to prevent this stuff from tricking Scots. Distrust of the government should be the status quo for every man. Even my own."

She simply gave him a light nod. Angus had grown to distrust governments and politicians. Even the ones that were supposedly 'democratic' turned out to be run by ultra-rich oligarchs who want to manipulate and control everyone.

Angus then stated, "We should probably invite both of our parents over to tell 'em what's going on, so they won't be tricked into this dang drug."

"I would appreciate that. To change the subject, I was thinking about possibly redecorating our bedroom."

"Of course, you can. Why the sudden desire to change it?"

"Frankly, this lockdown is draining. I do enjoy spending time alone, but I miss events like the many times you have taken me to the opera or a ballet."

"I understand, Isla Grace. This lockdown has been horrible for everyone. Our politicians don't care about us. All locked down for the flu. But back to your question, we can go tomorrow to pick up whatever you need."

"I appreciate it. Do you have any arranged meetings today?"

"I have to do some stuff with the ranch manager and then later speak to the accountant, but that is later today."

The little smile she got when she was about to cause trouble appeared as she asked, "I do not suppose that if I were to place little Abigail into the bascinet, you would be interested in following me to our bedroom?"

He laughed heartily at her before standing up and declaring, "I would."

*****

Angus still had some time before he had to go meet with the ranch manager, so he logged back into the club server to see if anyone had come up with ideas. The responses were quite enlightening. One man recommended that they hack the database to add vaccine information for their members. It was a hard trick to pull off since hacking government systems without inside help would be very difficult. Another guy said they should get to the guy entering the data and have him change the information. That was the right call, but Angus wanted to see about getting well over a hundred men to do this to lessen the risk for the club as a whole. They could also consider adding some sort of COVID card system to help them have access to proving it in person. He started posting suggestions on the chat to get people to start working on it. They would not be caught up in any problems and would stay far away from that vaccine.

# Chapter 28

17 April 2021

Poking a nearby cow with a stick, Angus helped move the herd towards the next field. He had his land set up to rotate the herds to allow the land to recover from the herd trampling it. Everything was set up in five sections, with one for the Highland cows, one for the goats, one for the sheep, and the last two set aside to rotate through over time. He was hoping that once they got finished with this coup business and someone was installed as the new President of Scotland, he could get back to his ranch. Robert was a bright little boy and a lot of fun for him to play with. Abigail had just started crawling about, and Isla Grace was pregnant again. He found that bringing up his family was a great point of pride. The club had begun the first phases of leadership training, where Angus was able to start in-person and hold training events at his own home. He felt it was important that the men who would lead the whole thing fully understood exactly how to execute his plans and then how to adjust to problems that would occur. Mike Tyson once said that everyone had a plan until they got punched in the face. He wanted them to be ready for when that punch comes with a counterpunch. After he helped the men move all three of his herds, he headed back into his home and cleant up for breakfast.

As he entered the house, he heard Isla Grace call out, "Robert! Come and eat breakfast."

Chuckling, he went to take a shower, and then once he was done, he got dressed and joined his family in the dining room.

"Good morning, Angus. I see that you were out early working with the herds."

"Morning, Isla Grace. We had to rotate the fields, and I thought the men could use a hand. It's a great opportunity to inspect my herds."

"And how was it?"

"Smooth as silk. They looked healthy and strong. We're on the path to a very profitable year with the herds."

She walked up closer to him before stating, “Working on this ranch has greatly improved your masculine energy.”

He gave her a wicked grin, knowing her intentions. A small smile appeared at the corners of her mouth. Suddenly, Abigail let out a loud squeal. Looking at her, Angus laughed loudly in response. She had managed to somehow get a hold of her whole bowl of porridge and tilt it over her own head! She was covered in warm porridge.

Isla Grace said in a sterner-than-normal tone, “Abigail!” as she stood up and extracted the girl from her highchair.

Robert laughed uproariously at it all, which only caused Angus to laugh along with him. He watched as Isla Grace carried her away. He took the highchair out into the front lawn quickly to hose it off and wash away the porridge on it. As he brought it back in, he sat down in his chair. It was a matter of a few minutes before Isla Grace returned with a now clean and changed Abigail. The little girl had frequently spilled, poured, and purposely dumped her food on anyone nearby, the floor, or herself. She seemed to laugh every time with that giggling little squeal. Isla Grace brought more porridge, but this time fed her one spoonful at a time.

As she fed Abigail, Isla Grace said, “My father was wondering if you have had a chance to add our available family members to the vaccine database.”

Angus nodded. He had to argue with his mum to get her to realise that she needed to avoid the vaccine. She watched the news regularly and had fallen into their brainwashing scheme. Once he showed her the research that the club was able to get, showing the ‘vaccine’ did not work even a fraction as much as they claimed. There was also missing data about the negative effects of the research that the NHS has carried out, but he was able to get hold of other information online. He was surprised by the brazen effort that websites like Twitter and Facebook seemed to silence anyone who disagreed with the vaccine. It turned out to be very wise to make sure everyone in the club knew to keep a low profile about the vaccine or COVID to not draw attention. The men were surprisingly loyal to his orders, and it was nice. A smoothly running machine was important to success.

“We put in everyone over 16 and got them set up for COVID passes. The system is digital, and you can get physical copies. I got everyone a physical pass and set it up for digital if they want to access it through an app on their phone. Our passes are sitting on my desk, and I've already got passes sent to our parents and siblings."

"That is good to know. It sounds like you have covered all the basics."

Grinning at her, he replied, "I just managed it, Isla Grace, we've got people in the NHS taking care of us."

"What are your plans today?"

"Well, I have several men coming over today to brief on the COVID passes, and then I'm free."

"And that would be the boxes you have stored in our garage?"

"Yes. I didn't want anyone taking such a risk with so much, so when the lads come over, I'll send them off with each group so they can distribute them out to their men."

Nodding solemnly, she asked, "How many men do we have?"

Wickedly, he answered, "A bit over fifteen thousand. People have become very upset about the COVID regulations."

"That is good news. I was wondering if you wished to add input to the selection of our next child's name."

He pondered thinking about it for a moment. Names for children were never an issue, but he did think it would be nice to name one of his sons after his father.

"I think my father would like it if we named a boy after him."

"William Thomas Bruce. And for a girl?"

Rubbing his chin, he answered, "I've got no clue there."

"I was thinking to go with Elizabeth Maria."

He nodded. Catholics loved having some variant of Mary in their daughters' names. Mary, Marie, or Maria was quite common. It was a nice enough name.

"I am glad that you approve. I find that as we continue to have children, selecting names has got increasingly more difficult. Once we catch up with my mother, we might end up having start getting a lot more creative."

He laughed. She had told him before they got married that she intended to have more than 10 children. She was well on pace since she was pregnant with their third and was only 21 years old. After having the first two, he had completely changed his mind about children. He found his children to be delightful. When he finished eating, he helped her clean up a little bit before stepping outside. He was going to check up on the ranch before the lads started showing up. It was another lovely Scottish summer day, and he loved to walk around in the open fields. The air was crisp, and there was a light breeze. His hired help had everything under control, so he just took a bit of a walk. It was not long until the first car pulled up to his home. He had purposely opened a part of the field near his home to allow a good number of cars to park. The car he spotted was Markus'. He had got to know the vehicles of all their leadership.

As he walked up to Markus, he called out, "How have you been?"

Markus grinned as he replied, "Good Angus. Been busy trying to keep busy doing my job and working on recruiting people."

"And the wife and kids?"

"They're doing well. My oldest just started high school."

"Seems like time cruises by fast." Angus commented.

Markus nodded. Several other cars arrived and then parked. He recognised every man who arrived. After twenty or so more minutes, the last few arrived, and they all followed Angus into his home. Isla Grace had chased the kids out of the living room and into their own rooms to give them privacy. She also set up a dozen chairs and a whole buffet of snacks for them to enjoy while they talked.

David commented, "Your wife really takes care of you, eh?"

Grinning Angus stated, "She's the best."

He gestured for the men around him to take a seat. As they sat down, Angus asked them to give him an update on each man's cell. They had grown so big that their cell leaders now have 3 layers of men below them spread out, so the reports took a bit of time.

Once they finished, Angus announced, "We've had complete success with our poison avoidance plan. I've got about a hundred boxes with physical copies of the vaccine pass for each man and the names of their family members that they requested. Each man must understand the level of importance to never reveal or expand past their direct family these passes. Our secrecy is the most important thing they can protect. Remind them what happens to men who betray the club."

The men around him did not say a word, but their facial expressions spoke clearly. They understood the importance of this issue. If they were caught with fake vaccine passes, it would ruin everything they had planned. He felt it was worth the risk to ensure his men avoided the myriad of medical issues the vaccine was going to cause. Rumours of people having heart attacks or passing out once they took it were simmering below the surface of the highly regulated social media. The old Angus would have been surprised by the silencing of the opposition to the vaccine on social media a few years ago. Now, he expected it and knew it was coming when he first heard about the vaccine being bad. All the big talk about how oppressive the Chinese government was, and yet these nations like the U.K. and America were fucking oppressing the shit out of their own people while ruining their country. He thought that at least the Chinese were honest about who they were. That is what he was going to aim for with Scotland. A country for the actual people of that country, not foreigners forced on them by the globalists.

"Let's go load up the passes. "I've then sorted and labelled by cell number, so we'll just have to load the boxes for each of you. Make sure you're driving slowly on the roads 'til you get them secured." He stated.

All the lads followed him out into his garage, and then he guided them on loading them into each car. Once they finished, Angus made sure to greet each man and see how he was doing in his life. He read a few leadership books stating that many people appreciated a leader who cared about their lives. Angus attempted to apply this to those men he interacted with. It was a hard thing to do because, in his heart, he was an introverted computer nerd, but he felt it was hard to do what it took to succeed. Most of the men left, and only three were left. David, Markus, and Liam.

David was the first to speak, "The leadership lessons you've been giving the lads have been good. I was wondering if it would be possible for me to give a series on overall military command."

Angus was more than happy to learn new things, especially in areas he knew little about, so he answered, "I'd like that. I've read a lot of books on the subject, but having someone who is an expert in the field giving insight would be great."

Chuckling at him, David responded, "I'm not sure I'm an expert, but I know a few things."

Markus then stated, "After that, we should investigate military tactics, especially the ones we'll need to use against the Brits. Our first phase should be a simple hit and run."

David nodded before stating, "I know some lads who have been involved in a few civil war actions in Africa. They'll do the trick. I do have a question for you Angus."

"What's that?"

"When we barge into the Parliament, who takes the first shot?"

He scratched his stubble-covered chin. Taking in David's question, he realised that since he was the leader, there was a very high likelihood that he would be the one who might have to shoot someone to start things off.

It took him some time to respond before he finally answered, "I'd guess there is a good chance that it'll have to be me."

"Do you think you can do it?" Markus interrupted to ask.

He nodded. At this point, he was all in and fully understood that they would have to become violent to save Scotland.

Liam stated, "He's not a bad shot in paintball, but he'll probably need to practise with a real gun. It's a totally different beast."

Pointing out into the woods, David stated, "We've got plenty of open fields to practise. I'll bring some handguns and let you pick one out to play around with. You've got to become excellent at it."

Liam interjected, "We can't have the lead cunt being a piss poor shot. I'll make sure to ride his arse to make sure that he's a marksman."

Angus chuckled. He had never fired a real gun in his life. He understood what David was saying. If he's the leader, he might need to be at least good at everything needed for the coup.

"Sounds good to me." He told them.

Clapping Angus' shoulder, David stated, "Excellent, I'll be back tomorrow with plenty of options. The key is to find a handgun that you're comfortable with and can shoot smoothly."

Angus saw David and Markus off. Liam went into his home and sat down. Robert came running into the living room.

He bellowed out, "Unca Liam!"

Liam scooped him up and immediately started spinning him in a circle mid-air. Robert cackled with glee. The boy was quite a fan of physical roughhousing. Angus had to play fight with him regularly.

Isla Grace strolled out with Abigail in hand. She set the little girl down and then hugged Angus. Almost every time she hugged him, her hands would explore his chest just a little bit before she released him.

"Hello Liam. It is a pleasure to see you. I hope Sandra and Tommy are doing well."

"Hey sis. They're good. Tommy is now walking around and making a mess."

Angus chuckled. Liam had grown into a family man quickly enough. Tommy was Liam and Sandra's first child. They came over plenty of times. Robert and Tommy had quickly become best friends. Liam set Robert down, and the little rapscallion took off, no doubt making a mess somewhere.

# Chapter 29

8 September 2021

The last two herds from his ranch were highly successful, and that allowed him to buy a very significant piece of land in the southern part of the Highlands. It included sections of forest and rough land. The idea was to be able to train in multiple environments. He bought a little more land around his own home to allow him to set up a range that would allow him to fire a gun and not be heard. He was slowly getting better at firing his chosen handgun, a Beretta M9. It seemed light enough to carry and use, but it fired effectively. David and Markus both seemed quite amused by the selection, but they never told Angus why. He found himself both appreciated by the men and, at times, a point of amusement. He patiently aimed his handgun downrange and calmly exhaled before squeezing the trigger. The kick on it felt just right as he hit the target. Once he finished his practise time, he headed back to his house. Isla Grace was already preparing supper. She was heavily pregnant, and her due date was in 2 weeks. As he walked in, he stored away his handgun in a secret safe he had built in the floor by the entryway for safe and quick access. He could not let Robert accidentally find it.

"Angus, go clean up so I can serve supper."

Kissing her, he responded, "Okay. It smells great."

"Thank you."

Quickly, he got cleant up and then headed into the dining room. Isla Grace cooked up a nice meal with some lamb chops, mash, and green beans. Sitting down again, he took the opportunity to say grace for the meal.

Taking a bite of mash, he commented, "They just announced that we'll finally have a lot freer movement."

"So, it's finally time to start training?"

"It is. We're going to be spending every Friday night and Saturday on training trips up in the Highlands. I'll have to be up there for that, so I won't be home while we get ready. We plan to start off slow, but eventually we'll really get deep into combat training."

"When do you plan to start?" She asked.

"This Friday." He answered, waiting to see her response.

Angus suspected that she would not be happy to have him disappear to train the men on the weekend, but he knew it was the only time most of them would be free.

She gave him a slight nod before stating, "As the leader, it is important that you can lead through your presence. A day and a half out of the week is more than satisfactory. Hopefully, our next child will oblige your plans as I would very much like you to be present for their birth."

"I wouldn't miss it for the world." He replied confidently.

"That is reassuring."

He was not sure if she was being sarcastic, as she did not have an emotional reaction. Giving her a grin, he chuckled.

She announced, "After supper, I was wondering if we could go visit my parents. I have not seen them in a while and thought they would love seeing all of us."

"Of course." He responded.

*****

10 September 2021

Angus was quite excited as the clown in charge of Scotland finally started to release many of the restrictions on Scotland over the COVID fraud. He made sure to kiss Isla Grace before taking off early morning. The land he bought for their training was located north of Laggan. It was about 2 hours away and so far away from the nearest person that they would be able to have a literal war. They had spent the last few years training all the leadership from the main command team down to squad leadership. He had expected these men to train their own, but he could not trust them without seeing it on his own. The rough estimates from this date were about a year before they would be trained and then ready to start the deployment in preparation. He wanted his men to be ready to fight the second the Brits crossed the border. He enjoyed the nice ride up and was met by his leadership. David was standing with Markus and Liam near the car park. Angus parked in a spot and strolled up to them.

"Hey ya cunt. I'm surprised my sister let you out." Liam called out with a grin.

Angus chuckled as he shook each man's hand. The weather was a little chilly, but it was still lovely the same.

He then asked, "How are the men?"

David answered, "Good so far. Most of them are not here, but our cell leaders have been keeping us up to date. Once everyone is here, we'll start on basic movement drills and then move on to more complex battle drills. It's quite exciting to finally be on the ground and in action."

He nodded before asking, "How many will be arriving today?"

"Maybe a few thousand or so." David replied.

He was still surprised by how big their movement had become. Until now, they were just names on a secret server, and yet now the numbers were becoming a reality in front of him.

Markus then said, "Let's go walk around and meet the men."

He followed Markus and David as they walked around chatting with the various men. Angus was surprised to see they were made up with a wide variety man of all ages. From young men that he guessed were barely adults to old men who had long since retired from work. Scots who detested what Scotland was becoming and were willing to fight for Scotland to save it. It made him quite proud. They all looked ready for action, and as Angus began walking towards the group, they moved into one large group.

Liam whispered, "You should probably say something inspiring."

Angus paused for a moment. He was unsure what to say, but decided it would be wise to try and at least say something since they were his men. There was a murmur of the crowd around him as they chatted.

Calling out in a loud voice, he said, "Men."

It was more than a little surprising when the whole crowd stopped talking. It was well over one thousand men there, and he could now hear a needle drop on the earth.

"I wish to thank you for coming to stand forward in defence of our beautiful Scotland. Our foes have tilted her on the edge of squalor by importing thousands of third-world animals to pillage her women and attack her men. They've stolen our waters for the filthy French and others. They rob the coffers for their own gain as we suffer. All of that comes to an end soon enough. Like my ancestor Robert the Bruce, I stand here to offer you all only an opportunity at freedom. It'll be up to you to seize it, and today is the day we begin. For Scotland!"

He yelled the last part loudly for emphasis. The men around him rowdily cheered his words, with many calling out 'For Scotland' as well. After about four or five minutes of rowdy cheering, the men around him seemed to calm down enough for others to talk.

David then spoke in a commanding voice, "Cell leaders, take charge and begin our first training."

In a quiet and efficient manner, the men around them started to form off and wander out into the fields in small groups. It was quite impressive to watch them move. He stood back as the cell leaders began individual instruction.

Liam asked, "You bring some supplies for an overnight stay?"

He nodded. Angus had bought himself a nice sleeping bag and a little tent to stay in. David wanted everyone, leaders on down, to live in the same condition to let the men know they were all in it together. It made sense to Angus, and honestly, it had been a good 15 years since he last went camping with his father.

As the men moved further away to continue training, David stated, "We've got a squad of men who'll be serving as your personal bodyguard. Today they're going to be training with you on command and staff movements with them."

"I'm not really sure that a bodyguard is necessary." Angus protested.

"And then the Brits invade and kill you. Do you know how foolish we'd look? Nope, you get a bodyguard."

He realised it was not really a point in arguing, so he just shrugged. David introduced Angus to ten men whom he assigned to serve as a bodyguard. The lead man was a middle-aged, military-looking man.

David introduced him, "Angus, this is Lieutenant Greg Napier. He's one of my best men, and I've put him in charge of your personal squad. Whenever there's direct military conflict that you're involved in, he's in charge."

The man extended a hand, which Angus shook.

"It's nice to meet you sir." Greg said.

"Just call me Angus."

"Alright. Colonel Rutherford briefed us on the plan and gave us a series of combat training exercises that we need to include you in. Tonight, and tomorrow, we'll go over a bunch of things that we'll practise several times until they are perfect."

Angus nodded. He was there to learn and was willing to take it all in.

"Follow me, Angus." The Lieutenant instructed.

He followed the man to a rough field with trees sprinkled throughout it.

Gesturing towards one of the trees, he stated, "We aim to keep you out of combat whenever possible, and if you find yourself engaged, we'll always look to withdraw. You're the brains of the operation, and keeping you safe will be our highest priority. Today we'll be instructing on tactical withdrawals, and tomorrow we'll work on squad-level combat for the times we can't force a withdrawal."

Angus nodded. He followed the man and his squad through an hour of basic instruction before they began running and dodging through the field. He was a little winded when they finished later in the evening. It was a good thing that he took daily runs and worked out every morning back on the ranch. He had originally kept doing it to keep his fit form, but it really paid off during all this training. Once everyone finished training, the field was sprinkled with dozens of campfires as each group formed up for the night to relax. He could hear laughing and joking as those around him enjoyed the pleasant weather and camaraderie of their goal. Part of packing for this was to bring a small stool to sit on while out, and he was happy for it. Many people had to sit on the earth directly.

Liam clapped Angus on the shoulder and then said, "Oi cunt. It's going pretty well so far. They've got me in a defensive group assigned to strike anyone coming up to Edinburgh."

"Nice. You're learning a lot, eh?"

"Hell ya. I'll be a squad leader, and we're working on some crazy third-world-style combat shit."

Angus nodded his head. Guerrilla warfare was going to be their main strategy. Sneak attacks, ambushes, and then improvised explosives. The Chinese had provided quite a bit already, and they promised that once the Scottish leadership was removed, they would bring a very large supply of weapons. He suspected that once they removed the Scottish Parliament, the Chinese would openly declare an allegiance with Angus' new Scottish government. At first, he was very hesitant when the Chinese offered to form an open alliance, but after stewing on it, he figured that if they were going to be hated by the Western countries, he might as well go all-in. Hell, the Chinese also promised to bring in other nations as well. The whole leadership team was in a jam over it. He wished that Trump had won a second term. Trump was a notorious fan of the Scots, and Angus felt that there was a very slim chance that the Americans might have either fully stayed out of things or pushed for a separation. This clown Biden was clearly a puppet being pulled by some other power. No doubt his masters would not be fans of Scottish embarrassing the Brits so there was a good chance that they might just join the cause against Angus and his men.

"Angus." David said as he stood up.

"Yes?"

"Let's give the men a good pep talk about our upcoming plans as we get closer to executing our goals."

Angus nodded as he stood up. He watched David flag down the different groups. Slowly, the men around them began to form into a large group. There were several thousand men, and he knew that he would have to speak up loudly so they could hear him. Once everyone was silent, he stood up on his stool so he could be heard over the crowd.

"Gentlemen!" He began to speak and was met by a bunch of hoots and howls.

After they calmed down, he continued, "We all know why we're here."

Someone in the crowd yelled out, "To free Scotland from commie bastards!"

Angus chuckled as the group around him began to cheer loudly. They were just as ready as he was to get rid of the damned SNP and their lackies.

It took a bit for them to stop before he spoke again, "Yes. Each of you knows our goals. We've had some setbacks due to a flu being pushed as the next Black Death. We've overcome that fraud, and our moment of truth is about a year away."

His declaration of a timeline got the men excited again. They cheered and whistled. Grinning at them, he waved to the crowd to silence so he could continue.

"I'm confident in our success, but I'll warn each of you, the path we're on isn't going to be easy. Every man here understands the risks and the rewards. We all know the meme about hard times and soft men. We've collected hard men here in this field for the purpose of ending the hard times. I'd like to recite my own Clan's motto, Fiumus, or we have been. It makes me think of the freedom Scots once had and inspires me to think that freedom will once again be ours. We just must take it… For Scotland!"

Angus made sure to yell out their motto as loudly as he could. The men around him exploded in joy at his words. He had known that eventually, during this event, he would be asked to give some sort of speech, so he had thought about some words that he felt would inspire their cause. He was pleased with the results, and clearly the men around him were pleased too.

David gave him a fist tap on the shoulder as he stepped off his stool before saying, "Let's get some rest, tomorrow's a busy day of hard training."

# Chapter 30

15 June 2022

Elizabeth started crying again. It was the middle of the day, and she was likely either hungry or needed a nappy change. Isla Grace was bathing Abigail, so he scooped Elizabeth up, and almost instantly, he smelled the telltale sign of a nappy change. The little girl had filled her nappy with poop. He laid her down on a small mat and then collected up a spare nappy, some wipes, and a bottle of powder. After a quick change of her nappy, Elizabeth cooed and fiddled with a small rattle. She was like her parents and brothers with bright orange hair. He was quite pleased to discover that she had his green eyes. Their other children had blue eyes, and it was a minor point of pride to have a child match his eye colour. His phone began buzzing.

Angus picked it up and answered, "Hello."

He heard David's voice speak, "You need to read what our dear leader just said today."

"Okay."

David hung up. Angus picked up Elizabeth and strolled over to his computer. After logging in, he read the first article he could find. Sturgeon announced a plan to have another Scottish independence election in 2023. It was rebuffed by Boris, but it was concerning Angus. Sooner or later, they would be able to get the Brits to agree to the election. He reflected on their training. Things were going well, but they could have been doing better with their training. It was difficult with everyone's complex timetable that limited full training. It slowed them down, and now he felt they would have to wait until the end of the year. It got very cold in Scotland, so he was unsure if the end of the year was the best time to start a war. He decided to post a commentary on the private server to see what everyone thought. They could not wait any longer than they had to remove the current government before they could force Scotland into the EU. He posted a recommendation that they set a date in the spring of 2023. It seemed wise to avoid the heavy winter. They had so few people that the last thing they needed was to deal with winter injuries. They were not the Russian army after all. He logged off and stood up. Isla Grace came out with a freshly bathed Abigail walking behind her.

"Angus, I would like to go for a picnic out in the field. We have such a nice garden that it seems a waste to not use it."

Grinning at her, he responded, "Sounds good to me. I'll collect up a picnic rug and the umbrella for us."

She told him, "I will prepare lunch. Could you also bring a small bascinet for Elizabeth?"

"Of course. I'll take it all outside and set it up."

"Thank you."

He gently set Elizabeth down in her bascinet before he started to set up their picnic. He loved the warm sunny summer day. He had to walk a good distance away from the house to find a spot far enough away from the animal fields to get a spot that did not smell like shite. After setting up the large picnic rug and umbrella, he collected the bascinet holding Elizabeth and then guided the whole family out to the location he picked.

Isla Grace commented, "It was a good choice to have a picnic today."

"Yup." He replied.

Once they settled and Isla Grace set up the lunch, she asked, "How are things going with the club?"

He rubbed his stubbled face while answering, "Our First Minister announced that she'd like to vote once again for Scottish Independence."

"Is that not what you want?"

"Yes, but not with her running the show. She'll continue doing what she's doing now in Scotland and likely leap right back into the EU the first chance she gets. She's one of the biggest problems facing Scotland and needs to go."

Isla Grace looked thoughtful for a moment before asking, "When will you do it?"

"I just posted in the server asking just that. I'm thinking that we're not ready yet, and by the time we'll be ready, it'll be winter."

"It is probably not the best idea to leap into war during Scottish winters."

Nodding at her, he said, "I'm thinking spring. I looked at the Parliament timetable, and my best guess would be to do it right after a break, so most of these clowns would be there. I'm thinking right after the April break for Easter."

"That sounds like a good selection. Are you ready to do this? I was thinking that you might have to do more than a few things that are not very Christ-like."

"I've come to terms with that. Sometimes, to stop even worse evil, you must act in ways you'd normally not wanna act."

She nodded again, this time not saying a word. He could tell she was thinking about it all. He had spent many hours struggling with the idea of having to shoot people. It was not ideal, but really, it was likely the only way to free Scotland. A huge part of him hoped that the Brits would just cave in and let the Scots go, but deep down inside, he knew there was almost no chance of that. They had held Scotland captive too long to just give them up. He was just glad that the Russians invaded Ukraine. It was a huge distraction that allowed the club to grow as the Brits tossed money like it was on fire in the war. After they finished eating lunch, Isla Grace took two older children, and he brought Elizabeth back home before coming back to clean up. He sat down to log back into the server and was pleased to see that the men had responded. It was all agreed that the time to act was going to be spring. There were a lot of different dates offered, but Angus' suggestion of the 17th of April seemed to be the most popular.

He logged out again and then announced to Isla Grace, "April 17th. We're going to do it. I'm gonna go out and practise shooting. I need to be as good as I can be."

She walked up to him and wrapped her arms around his midsection.

While hugging him, she said, "I'm concerned for you, Angus, but I have faith our Saviour will protect you during all of this."

"I'm concerned too, but I've got no choice. Scotland needs saving."

# Interlude

17 April 2023.

A loud buzzing from Angus' alarm echoed into his ears. He hopped out of bed instantly. He was so nervous about what they were about to do. It was the day that they would finally be rid of the communist influence in Scotland. The nerves were so strong that he struggled to sleep, but the excitement of what they were about to do had him full of energy. He looked over at Isla Grace and saw that she was awake. Once again, she was pregnant, and he was surprised by how quickly she kept leaping right back into having another child. She slowly climbed out of their bed and then circled it to hug him tightly.

"I shall pray for your success today." She told him.

"Thank you, Isla Grace. I'm hoping that we pull this off safely. I know you don't watch telly, but you can probably see the whole thing online."

"I will watch you."

He gave her a passionate kiss before releasing her and heading off. Taking time to give each of his children a quick kiss, he grabbed his bag and headed off. The plan was to meet up with Liam and then drive south to Edinburgh. Liam and his security team were going to sneak Angus, his bodyguards, and the rest of their single strike force into the parliament. The bulk of his forces were ready in their positions throughout Scotland. David was serving as the military manager of the whole thing, and he was staying at a bunker on Angus' land up north with his own personal force. He grabbed the pack that he had set up with his gun, some ammo, and a few other things that he thought he would need. The last week or so, he was thinking about the speech he would be giving when he took over Scotland. It was probably going to be the most important thing he had ever done in his life. As he stepped out of his home, he spotted Liam's car waiting.

Climbing in, Liam asked, "You ready for this cunt?"

"Yes. I've issued orders to everyone to limit civilian casualties. We're gonna give every non-Scot and the leftist pussies afraid of a free Scotland 72 hours to get the hell out before we start getting rough with ‘em.”

“Shoot ‘em”

“I was thinking we’d just drag ‘em to the border and toss ‘em out. I’m sure the Brits will take ‘em.”

Liam nodded. They spent most of the ride in silence. As they parked in the parliament car park for employees, Liam said, “Let’s free Scotland.”

# Chapter 31

The light for the camera went off, and Angus nodded. They had done it. The SNP was no more, and Scotland had been formally declared a free state.

Glancing at all the bodies of the previous members of Parliament, Angus ordered, “Get the lads to clear this scum out of here. We’ve got a lot of work, and our administrative folks are moving in soon enough.”

His phone rang, and Angus picked up to see that it was David.

“Hello.” Angus said while answering.

“Phase one complete. The internet is a buzz with what you just did. Most of it's quite mad.”

“Fuck ‘em.” Angus replied.

“Agreed. I’m going to maintain control from here. We’ve taken all the Brits’ military garrisons in Scotland but 2.”

“What happened there?”

“Just not enough lads. We took the opportunity to sabotage their gear right when you took over, before our lads there cut ties and split. At this point, they’ve been mostly neutralised.”

“Great news. Everything else seems to have gone off without a hitch. We’ve got men in every major city rounding up the criminal politicians who’ve been running everything into the ground.”

“What’s the plan with them?”

Angus chuckled before he answered, “I told each cell to lock ‘em up in cells, but if they resist, just end ‘em right there. We’ve got men contacting the civilian bureaucrats, letting them know the new chain of command and report to us.”

“You’ve thought of everything.”

“I tried. I’m sure we’ll discover stuff we’ve missed or miscalculations that I’ve made; we’ll have to learn as we go.”

David then interjected, “Agreed. I’ve got some calls. I’ll talk to you later.”

“Alright.”

Angus quickly took a moment to call Isla Grace.

She answered immediately, “Hello.”

"First phase complete." He told her happily.

"My prayers were with you. There is much work to be done, Mr. Bruce."

"Yes, there is. Thank you for the prayers, Mrs. Bruce."

"Of course. I will continue to pray for you. Go about your work. I love you."

"I love you too." He answered before hanging up the phone.

Liam walked up to him and announced, "We've attracted a huge crowd of reporters outside who likely want to know what the hell's going on. Should we chase 'em off?"

Angus paused to think about it for a moment. No doubt if he went out there and talked with them, they would have some less-than-nice things to say. Shrugging it off, he decided to continue their momentum by giving a little more detail to the public. He had nothing to hide.

"I'll talk to them in a moment. We need to clean up a bit and prepare for a new government. I've already got men selected who joined us, and they should be sliding into the building soon."

"Speaking of which," Liam said as he lifted his phone, showing a new message before continuing, "They've arrived."

"Bring 'em to the conference room that we started in."

"Yes Mr. President." Liam sarcastically replied.

Angus chuckled as he walked with his bodyguards towards the conference room. He took a seat at the head of the table and waited. The wait was not long before his Secretary of State, Michael Kerr, walked in. He had with him several of the conservatives who had stood when Angus' men shot the parliamentarians and other men who joined their cause. As the men walked in, Angus stood up and shook Michael's hand.

Michael then said, "Congratulations, Mr. President. We've got a lot of work to do, but the first phase has been completed."

Nodding at the man before sitting back down, Angus responded, "Indeed. I'll be relying on every one of you to help me in transitioning to our new government. Our forward-facing government until Scotland is stabilised will appear to be a dictatorship with me as the man to take the stones thrown at our movement. I will appear to settle everything with a firm hand, but the reality is that everyone in this room will be working together. We all know the vision that we've got for Scotland, and it'll be our job to make it happen. If there is contention over how to complete something, I'll step in to make any final decisions. Things are about to get very hard for everyone here, but I've got faith in each man here to do the right thing."

The men around him nodded at his words. It was part of their planning steps to assign each man to a position that was important in keeping things running smoothly. He expected many people from the old government to come forward to volunteer for the new government. Most people worked just to survive when they could. Although he expected they would probably wait to see what happened to the Brits.

He paused for a moment before asking, "Does anyone have a question?"

None of the men responded, so Angus then stated, "Very well. Each of you has a lot of work to do so I'll let you get to it. We've got to get our government up and running before the Brits decide what they're gonna do about us."

Each man looked grim as they likely knew what he did; the Brits would not take this lying still.

Angus rose from his seat before declaring, "For Scotland."

The men in the room called out. "For Scotland!" And then began walking out. His bodyguard followed him. He decided to meet with the press outside before heading off to the makeshift headquarters they were planning to use initially. Normally, the First Minister would stay in a building called the Bute House. The plan was not to stay in something so obvious, but they had set up multiple flats throughout Edinburgh and its suburbs for Angus to run Scotland from until they knew the final decision of the British. He had a computer setup in several of them to allow him to access the internet and do his own work. For each one, there was a shell company that the Chinese helped him set up so he could mask that he was involved with each location. The Chinese had been vital in assisting each phase of this, and he did not doubt that Scotland would treat them as allies once everything was done. His bodyguards pressed closely by him as he stepped outside the front of the Parliament building. While he expected there to be a press gathering, he was shocked by the large crowd there. They saw him and immediately began screaming out questions. Angus stopped in front of them and then raised his hands to silence them. They immediately stopped talking.

"I'll answer your questions, but I'll be picking out who asks 'em." He stated before pointing at a nearby man.

"Yes. Firstly, we must know who gives you the authority to murder duly elected officials. The people are outraged."

Chuckling, Angus pulled out his handgun and then responded coolly, "I asked my friend Annis here, and she told me I've got the authority."

The crowd around him began calling out angrily with various names and insults towards him. It was fully expected as he heard names like 'fascist', dictator', and 'warlord' spat at him. He slipped his handgun into its holster and then raised his hands once again. The crowd was silent immediately.

"As you now know, I'm in charge of Scotland now."

A female reporter asked, "And what do you plan to do?"

Giving a grin, Angus answered, "Free it. Once the Brits acknowledge our independence, we'll set up a proper government free of any outside interference."

One of the men in the crowd then asked, "No Scots will follow a fascist like you."

Stepping down away from his bodyguards, Angus reached out to grab the man by the back of his collar. He then swiftly pulled out his handgun and brought it up to the man's face. The man shrank in fear and tried to move away, but Angus pulled him closer.

Glowering at the man, he spoke in a serious tone, "Scots respect power."

He moved his handgun closer to the man's face before he continued speaking, "It's why they originally fell to British rule so long ago. It's why I've taken Parliament so easily. Our government has become weak and pathetic. Look at you. I offer you freedom, and you call me a fascist."

Taking his firearm away, he scratched his own chin with the barrel before pointing it back at the man as he spoke, "Perhaps you're right. Maybe I'm an evil fascist dictator, as you've said. I've got a question for you. If I'm the fascist you say, who's gonna stop me from splattering your brains all over this pavement?"

The man was shaking in his boots and did not answer the question.

Keeping his voice calm, Angus asked, "Well?"

The man's voice trembled as he answered, "No one."

Angus laughed heartily before he stated, "Exactly. I'm in charge of Scotland, and my men will follow my orders to ensure Scotland's freedom from the Brits. Mr. Reporter man, you live today."

He let the man go.

A woman reporter nearby asked, "You're not going to stop us from reporting."

Laughing heartily, Angus answered, "Yes and no."

Several of them looked confused, so he continued, "From henceforth it will be the charge of every Scottish reporter here to speak the truth. You'll report what you see without your idiotic opinions or the opinions of the West. None of you are smart enough to have the right to imprint your opinions on the public, so I'm declaring a law that reporters in Scotland are only authorised to tell the truth. For example, everyone here damned well knows that men cannot be women and no amount of 'feelings' will change that. I'm expecting you to be honest. If something happens, it'll be your job to report it. No feelings, no rumours, and no reporting Twitter bull-shite. Just the truth. If you don't report the truth, then permission for you to report will be… terminated."

He said the last part as a threat. Glancing over the crowd, he could see they fully understood.

Another woman then firmly stated, "We won't lie for you."

Angus then turned to one of his bodyguards and asked, "Did I say to lie for me?"

The bodyguard answered with a chuckle, "No, Mr. President."

He then looked back at the reporter and stated, "I said to tell the truth. You'll report on the activities of the Asian gangs. You'll report how the previous government was forcing men into women's spaces. You'll report how my men violently removed the previous government. You'll report the British response. You're to report the unfettered truth."

The reporters around him seemed to be confused by his statements. He suspected that they probably thought they would be forced to be mouthpieces for his government. That was never his intention.

"What do you plan to do when the British decline to let your government maintain control of Scotland?"

Angus grinned as he answered, "Fight. I've got a lot of work ahead of me, and we'll have a spokesman assigned to co-ordinate communication with you soon enough."

Spinning on his heel, Angus strode away from the squawking reporters behind him with his bodyguards in tow. He climbed into a nearby waiting van and sped off. The police provided him with an escort for a while before cutting off to help him disguise where he was headed. It was part of their plan to trick anyone from tracking where Angus was headed. Once they made it to the first safe house, the vehicles were moved away to mask his arrival. He had a few men waiting, and once they entered the building, they locked the building behind them to secure it. Angus rushed over to his computer to log in and check up on the server for the latest updates. Everything was going according to plan as they secured control over Scotland. There was an incident with a few security guards and their politician charges that forced his men to kill a few dozen people who were part of the mayor's staff. One of the junior men who worked with the club was able to get his men access, and while many of them were killed, Angus now had control over Glasgow. He grinned as he checked Twitter. The whole world was watching what happened. Almost every nation in the West claimed to be outraged by Angus' actions. Oddly enough, the Irish seemed to be completely silent on the matter. He chuckled because he knew that the Irish hated the Brits as much as his men did.

His phone rang, and while he did not recognise the number, he answered it, "Hello."

"Mr. Bruce. My name is Zheng Zeguang. I'm the Ambassador from China to the United Kingdom."

"Okay." He responded hesitantly.

"I'm transferring you to the General Secretary."

"Alright."

The phone crackled as the telltale sound of a transfer had occurred.

In stilted English, a man spoke, "Congratulations, President Bruce. It is an honour that our friends in Scotland have succeeded in declaring their independence from the British with our help."

"Thank you, General Secretary." Angus replied.

"We have an understanding and I'm hoping our friendship will continue on the world stage after your nation receives its full independence."

"We do, and I'm privileged to state that our friendship will continue. The Scottish people consider the people of China to be one of our closest allies."

"Thank you, President Bruce. I know you're busy, so I'll not take much of your time. A declaration of recognition of your nation will be forthcoming from the people of China. Good luck."

“Thank you, sir.” Angus stated.

The phone clicked, letting Angus know that the call was terminated. He scrolled over to Twitter to examine the response, and within a few moments, he discovered that the Chinese government had formally recognised Scottish independence. They called on other nations to do so as well. He was quite pleased. Everything in the first phase had gone almost perfectly. Taking a moment, he texted Isla Grace to let her know what was happening and that he loved her. She responded that she loved him too. His phone rang again, and he saw that it was David.

“Hello.”

“The Chinese followed through. They’re all in with us now. I suspect the Russians and others won’t be far behind.”

“Things are going well for now, but we’ve got to be ready. I imagine by tomorrow we’ll have the British response. I’m prepared for the worst but hoping for the best.”

“Same here. I am calling to give you an update. We’ve taken control of Glasgow, Edinburgh, Aberdeen, and Dundee. In Glasgow, some were protesting from a bunch of dumbass college kids.”

“What happened with that?” Angus asked.

“We let ‘em be until they tried getting rough with the police. Then they got a proper spanking, like their fucking parents should have been giving them all along.”

“Unfortunate, but since we’re putting on the mask of a fascist state for now, we’ve got no choice.”

“Yup. The two garrisons we couldn’t control were close to the border, and I’m happy to report that the Brits there withdrew south into England.”

“And our men on the border?”

“The trap is set, and when the Brits try to roll in, we’ll spring it.”

“Speaking of which.” Angus interrupted before saying, “Let me deal with their satellites so the game is on a fair footing for a good while. I’ll talk to you later.”

“Yes Mr. President.” David replied before hanging up.

It was going to take him a bit to get used to the new title. He planned to rid himself of it as soon as he possibly could. He then turned his attention to his computer. Angus designed a program to not just interfere with the British satellites but to scramble the computer systems running it so that it would take months to fix it for even the best computer programmers. He also set it to remove all key-codes and block any British I.P. from being able to access it. It was his finest computer program, and he was sad that it would have to disappear once they won. Utilising the key-codes that his men gave him; he uploaded the virus. Once it began its work, he logged off.  Without their satellites, the Brits would have to fight blindly, and their Air Force would struggle. Men were already moving the anti-aircraft into position in open fields near the border to distract the Brits. Taking another look at Twitter, he was amused to find a large group arguing for Angus' actions. They claimed it was just another independence movement like any other for a group of people. He also found that his name was smeared as every name in the book. He chuckled because it did not matter. Scotland was now free. Now they just needed to hold it.

# Chapter 32

Angus rolled over in his cot as his alarm buzzed. He felt odd being by himself, but he had work to do that was dangerous, so he had to stay far away from his family until things were resolved. Glancing at his phone, he noted that it was 7 a.m. No doubt the Brits would be announcing soon their reaction to what Angus and his men did. He perused the messages that he had been receiving from various cells, and everything so far was going well. There was a small protest in Edinburgh, but his men just ignored them, and they got bored quickly. For all the talk of him being some evil fascist dictator, he found that he had a lot more people supporting their cause than he hoped. Many of the 'MAGA' American types seemed to support him. He had to move positions to keep his location a secret, so after a light breakfast, they headed off to the next spot. Once he arrived, he took time to send Isla Grace a message to let her know that he was okay before loading up on the next computer. The news gave reports about satellite issues, but the British government denied that there were any issues. He knew they were lying when he reviewed the connection; it was dead. It would be months before they could get their own satellites up; the Brits would have to rely on the Yanks help on that front. The news announced that the Prime Minister, Rishi Sunak, would be giving a press briefing very soon. Angus was on the edge of his seat, waiting. He messaged David to confirm that they were ready to respond instantly. Watching the reporters talk about the briefing, they all speculated that it was about Angus and Scotland. He had to agree. There were a few more urgent issues at this point, which is why they chose to make their move when they did. After a bit of a wait, Sunak appeared and walked behind a podium. Angus watched intently at the screen.

He started speaking through the microphone, "Good morning. As I am sure you are all aware, there is a situation in Scotland where the First Minister and the entire Scottish Parliament were just assassinated by a group of terrorists."

Angus chuckled. This was going to be war and the words that Sunak used made it clear.

"As it is well known, the people of the United Kingdom do not negotiate with terrorists. My government intends to see that these men and their accomplices are arrested for their crimes."

Angus messaged David to tell him to begin the defensive plan and to ask for the status of the anti-aircraft. David replied that everything was in place and that their men were ready.

Sunak continued speaking, "We have co-ordinated with our allies and have received full support in dealing with what is nothing more than an internal issue. I will answer a few questions."

A reporter then asked, "What do you think about the Chinese formally acknowledging Scottish claims of independence?"

Angus was very curious, so he listened intently.

"We reject their claims and the claims of the Chinese entirely. Scotland has been part of the United Kingdom since 1707 and will continue to be so."

"What about the United Nations refusing to comment or provide support to either side?"

Sunak coolly answered, "The mechanizations of the Chinese and their allies. Most of the world concurs with us."

"Do you have any idea of their numbers or claims of control over most of Scotland?" Another reporter asked."

"No. That is all the questions I have time for. Have a good day and God save the King."

Sunak strolled away as reporters continued to shout questions at him. War it was going to be, and Angus was sure that the Brits had no clue just how many men Angus had working for him. It was well over twenty-five thousand, and since they took down the Parliament reports came in that more joined eagerly. The Brits were going to be in for a very hard time. Angus hoped that a solid and hard punch in the face of the British forces when they crossed into Scottish territory would be enough to re-examine the claim that Angus was more than a mere terrorist. He chuckled because he knew he was about to become a fucking damned good terrorist. The Chinese brought in a few men from Iraq and Afghanistan who were part of the terrorist groups there to teach their men how to make improvised devices and masking techniques to use against an arrogant Western force. It was a tricky process, but they had a nice stockpile of these kinds of weapons ready to go. His men would bleed the Brits slowly. His phone rang, and he saw that it was Isla Grace.

"Hello." He answered.

"I saw the Prime Minister's comments. He called you a terrorist. It is most unfortunate to be labelled in such a way."

Angus chuckled, "I'm not one yet, I'm about to become one. How is the baby doing?"

"It is flattering that you are concerned about my baby when you have so much more going on than a common pregnancy."

"I don't want you to worry yourself about this and focus on taking care of our next child. Have you selected names yet?"

She had a brief pause before answering, "I decided to stick with William if it is a boy and if it is a girl, we can name her Christina Joy."

"I like them both."

"I assumed that you would. I was curious how you can have a phone and not worry about the British tracking you."

He chuckled. David thought of a lot of things that Angus missed when they started moving this plan forward.

"I canceled my old service and moved on to one with a fake name. This phone and yours have been set to block anyone from tracking them. We've covered a lot of tracks to try and keep the Brits from knowing where I'm hiding."

"You did mention your plans to hide your location by moving regularly. I am relieved to hear that you are trying to take as many precautions as you can."

"Yes. How are the kids?"

"I have not informed any of them about the situation; they all believe that you are on a business trip and that you may be gone for some time."

"That's good. I've got some meetings I need to attend. I'll talk to you later."

"Very well. My prayers are with you, Angus."

"Thank you. I love you."

"I love you as well."

Angus hung up his phone and sat down. He had to get a briefing from Michael about the status of their new government. It was quite relieving to have actual politicians who helped set up and manage the bureaucratic part of the coup. He was not ready to add that task to his current plate. He was a figurehead so that the political and military aspects of their coup could deal with their business unharassed. Logging out of the computer, he stood up. The meeting with the bureaucrats was going to take place at a private meeting hall they had reserved months ago. He climbed into the van that rolled up, and they headed off. As they drove along, he was quite pleased to note that traffic was at its normal pace, and the people of Edinburgh seemed to be living their lives as normal. It was likely to change once the Brits invaded, but it was a good start. His van pulled up to a dance hall that they rented for this event. As he stepped out, he noted that security had already taken over the whole building. Angus strolled inside and was led through the building to a conference room. Michael Kerr and the others were already waiting.

Angus shook each man's hand before sitting down and saying, "Thank you for seeing me. As you are all likely aware, the Brits have decided to decline our declaration of independence. I've purposely kept the lot of you out of our battle plans, but rest assured, we've got some off-putting surprises for the Brits when they enter Scotland."

Michael asked, "I've heard the Brits lost their satellites. That your doing?"

He grinned before responding, "Yup. I'm a computer programmer, and I've taken down their whole system. It'll be years before they can get it working again. But I asked you all here for an update. I've noticed that Edinburgh seems to be running as normal."

"Yes Mr. President. This is Gerald Boyd. He's my man on the front of dealing with the mayors."

Gerald was an older man wearing a dark brown suit with a red tie. His nicely cut hair was peppered with grey, and he had light blue eyes. He was clean-shaven.

"Nice to meet you, Gerald."

"Thank you, Mr. President. May I?"

Angus nodded.

"I've co-ordinated with the mayors of each city with a population higher than 25,000 people. I've let them know that the provisional Scottish government, led by you, is expecting them to continue running business as normal within their cities. They expressed concern, with most declaring outrage over our actions. I informed them that their opinions were noted, but if they wished to remain in their posts, they would not cause trouble and mind their business. After a stern warning, they decided to continue business as normal. Unfortunately, we had to remove most of the leadership in Glasgow and Paisley as they were vehemently against us."

"And?" Angus asked.

The man answered, "We've replaced them with men more agreeable to our interests. We've decided not to call for elections of a new Parliament until after issues with the British are resolved."

Angus shook his head before stating, "There won't be elections until we fully write a new Constitution that is based on the American one. I wish to ban any political party in Scotland and let each man run on his merits alone. The Americans have two parties, and most of the world has a bunch of them. Clearly, neither system works, so we're going to dump it entirely. I want full freedom of speech, gun rights, and as many civil protections as we can get to ensure freedom for all men within Scotland. We're also going to set up a judicial system like the American one. I also want term limits for all political and bureaucratic positions."

The men around him simply nodded. Angus felt that the American system needed great improvements and he intended to make them to the Scottish system.

"A wise decision." Michael stated.

"How about our emergency services?" Angus asked.

Another man stood and said, "My name is Edward Duncan. I've been coordinating with the police, fire, and other emergency services. They're currently all green status as we have maintained control over the police forces of the biggest cities and towns. We've had a few that we didn't have control over, contact us. All were amicable to be left alone to maintain services within their own city or town. I informed each one that if they did not push back on our new federal government, they would be left alone."

"Fine work Edward. I'm curious if anyone has heard from an envoy from any other nation? We've got regular communication with our Chinese friends, but I've not heard from any other nation."

Michael answered, "Nothing yet Mr. President. If any of us hear from a third party, we'll report it immediately for you to deal with."

Angus then asked, "Do we have a status on the non-Scots who have been ordered to leave Scotland?"

Michael again answered by saying, "A very significant number of them have begun fleeing south into England."

"And those who have not left?"

"They've got 48 hours, and if any are found by the police, I've had Edward inform them that they're to be secured and then transferred to our men for transfer south and into England. We've expressed to everyone working for us that physical removal can be utilised, but it is not preferred. Our goal is to shed as little blood as possible, freeing Scotland from globalist mechanisation."

"Thank you. I hope to avoid shedding blood unnecessarily, but at the deadline, I want every mosque in Scotland emptied of anyone in them and then bulldozed to the earth. That stain must be removed from Scottish soil immediately. Understood?"

The men around him all nodded at his words.

Angus then continued speaking, "I just want to take a moment to thank each of you for your fine work. I couldn't do this without each man here. Continue to mask your actions under the guise that it was placed as an order from me. Do any of you have any questions?"

No one spoke, so Angus declared, "For Scotland."

The men around him responded with 'For Scotland." He stood up and shook each man's hand before he headed out of the building and back into another waiting van. The plan was to return to his spot for today, and then tomorrow morning, he would move on to another position. The club co-ordinated with him about thirty different locations around Edinburgh for him to bounce between. He looked to rotate between them as much as possible to keep anyone trying to track him guessing. Splitting tasks throughout the club was a tactic to make it hard for the Brits to simply eliminate one person and end things. Once they pulled into the new location, he was dropped off with his bodyguards and quickly entered. If the people living around them noticed, they seemed to limit their responses. He went into the small kitchen and put together a light lunch. A nice butty and some crisps hit the spot nicely. Thinking about it, there was a high likelihood that it would take the Brits several days to assemble any sort of military plan or force to head into Scotland. He hoped that it would be ramshackle and allow time for his own plan to be executed. Checking in on their private server, he noted plenty of positive comments from their men. They were happy with the first phase of success, and there was plenty of bragging about what they planned to do if the Brits crossed into Scotland. He made sure to post a reminder that everyone makes sure to follow the orders given. It was all part of the plan, and each man was needed to free Scotland. After he linked to another secret server that he set up for updates from David when possible. Everything appeared in order, and they were ready as they could be for the Brits to come.

# Chapter 33

21 April 2023

Angus could not believe the arrogance of the British. They were not only ready to move into Scotland, but they were letting it all be televised as they formed up just outside Newcastle and clearly planned to push straight up into Edinburgh to deal with Angus. The number of men was impressive, and it would be a significant blow to the Brits when his forces hit them moving up into Scotland. Today, Angus was moving up north to meet David in the Highlands on his land. They were likely to shift the plans to bring enough weapons and forces to Lamberton to strike the huge force the Brits were planning to bring up. Based on what he saw on the news, the Brits were bringing at least a thousand men with plenty of weapons and gear. It would be a nice blow to the British if his men pulled off this attack right. He ate his breakfast and then headed out. The drive was more than a few hours away, and he was planning to meet with Isla Grace in Kinross on the way there. He had her check into Travelodge using cash and facing away from the view. The drive to Kinross took about 50 minutes, and it was not long until he pulled up to the hotel. He spotted Isla Grace's SUV parked in the back. She opened the door when his van and the other vehicles holding his bodyguards arrived. As the van stopped, he got out.

Isla Grace hugged him tightly as she said, "I have missed you greatly, Angus."

Grinning, he told her, "I missed you as well."

She released him and stated, "Come inside."

He was slightly surprised to see that her eyes were a little reddened. She must have cried a little while holding him. As she turned and headed into the small hotel room, he followed behind her, holding her hand.

"Daddy!" Robert yelled out before running into Angus' leg to grab hold of him.

Abigail squealed, "Daddy!"

He knelt and hugged both tightly. There was a nearby basket that he spotted Elizabeth lying in. Isla Grace closed the hotel room door before sitting down on the bed.

"Angus."

"Yes?"

"Do you have any idea how long all of this will drag on for?"

He shook his head. The hope was that they could resolve things with the British in a few months, but he suspected it could take years. It was all a matter of the will of the British people to watch as their military was getting beaten up from guerilla and other hit-and-run strikes.

"I'm hoping that we can finish things quickly so I can just come back home to you guys and the ranch."

Standing up, he knelt in front of her and then placed his hands on her belly. It was just barely poking out from their newest addition. Isla Grace tilted her chin upwards, her favourite clue for him to kiss her. He stood up and then tenderly kissed her on the lips. He realised how much he missed her over these last few days. After he finished kissing her, he helped her to stand up and hugged her again.

"I assume that you have to leave soon." She stated.

"I do. I'm meeting with David to discuss and look at our plan in action. After the Brits make their move, I'll be heading back down to Edinburgh."

"Any idea when they plan to attack?"

He laughed before answering, "They're so arrogant they've openly announced that tomorrow morning they'll push into Scotland."

"What are the odds you will win the day?"

"I'm very confident. Their own arrogance and our huge surprise will shake their confidence. Maybe they'll realise we're not messing around and simply just recognise our independence."

"I have my doubts." Isla Grace stated.

"Agreed. I like to keep a positive outlook. We'll see what happens."

"Fair enough. I will continue to pray for your safety and the success of your mission."

"What did your parents say about everything?"

A little grin peeked up on Isla Grace's face as she answered, "They were quite surprised, especially when they found out that Liam was involved as well. My father was particularly pleased. Neither liked seeing you shoot that woman in the face, but I believe they understood."

"I didn't want to gun down Sturgeon like that, but it was really important to boldly take control."

"Of course. Once this is all done, I am afraid you will be spending a significant amount of time in the confessional booth."

He knew a joke when he heard one from her, so he laughed. She still had just the right sense of humour to tickle him just so. His phone buzzed. He glanced at it and saw a message from the head of his bodyguards letting him know that it was time to go.

"You must leave now." Isla Grace stated.

"Yes." He told her as he wrapped her in his arms once again.

As he held her, he stated, "We've booked another hotel for us to meet when I head back. This time I'll stay with you there for a day before heading back to Edinburgh."

"That is good news."

He hugged her once again before giving her another kiss. It was going to be a painful few days until he could see his family again. He then gave each of his children a hug and gave a sleeping Elizabeth a little smooch.

"I love you." He told her sincerely.

"I love you too." She said.

He exited the hotel and then scurried into his waiting van. Isla Grace was standing at the door of the hotel room with Robert and Abigail watching. He waved at them. As his van pulled away, he saw them waving back. He took a deep breath and then sighed heavily. It was going to be a rough few years, if they won, before he could settle down properly with his family. A small part of him regretted the whole thing, but he realised he was doing what must be done. If he did not act, who would? Scotland would eventually fall to the globalist agenda as Scots would slowly be replaced or outright removed over time. Major figures openly stating that they wanted to use vaccines to lower the human population, with no one doing anything about it, was scary. The drive up north was a long one, and Angus kept an eye on his phone to see if any significant updates had occurred. Nothing really had changed, so he had little to do. Once they arrived, he hurried into the bunker that David had built on the hillside on Angus' land. It was a piece of land that Angus bought using a shell corporation to disguise his ownership.

David had a wall of monitors showing a variety of cameras that he had set up near every border of Scotland. It allowed him to watch the borders closely. It was an impressive setup, and he had not seen it before. David was sitting at a table with a few dozen men.

Once David spotted Angus, he rose from his table and said, "Hello Mr. President."

Shaking David's hand as he offered it, Angus replied, "Hello. It's nice to see you again."

"Same Mr. President. I have a brief to give you about our plans with the Brits showing their starting gambit so openly."

Nodding at him, Angus replied, "I was shocked by their brazen build-up. I'm suspecting that they might be trying something else outside of this move."

"My first guess was they planned some sort of air or naval assault over Edinburgh, but I think that they guessed our numbers are much smaller than they are. I've put our forces in Edinburgh on high alert just in case."

David pointed at one of the news channels and said, "Looks like we're live. The media is showing that the Brits have started moving out. They're heading north according to the reports."

Angus quickly looked over all the other cameras. There was nothing out of the ordinary there. He wondered if anyone heard something in Edinburgh. One of the screens was a live update of their leadership server online. It had nothing new on it. If the Brits were up to something underhanded, it was very well masked. Most likely, they simply plan to push right into Scotland to arrest Angus and his men.

David commented, "This is going to be ugly for them. The entire U.K. military is maybe 110 thousand men with reserves. They've got a few thousand overseas, and we've captured around two thousand men. If we can hit them hard enough, they might just cave in right away."

"Or they'll call on their reserves and get some help from the Yanks or the Krauts?"

David nodded as he scratched his chin.

He then announced, "For now, we'll just stick with what's in front of us. The Brits are slowly working their way north. Thanks to the press, we know where they are, and right now, they're about an hour and a half at their pace from hitting Lamberton. We've got our men set up in some fields and wooded area just north of Lamberton, and once the Brits line up, we'll spring the trap."

Angus sat nervously watching the two screens side by side. One with the camera watching the spot where his men were set up for their attack, and the other from the news cast showing the Brits' military slowly driving up the A1. It was the fastest route without any turnoffs available. He had men on A68, but at this point, it was the A1. The wait was nerve-wracking as the media showed the caravan of military vehicles heading along the road. There were around 50 to 60 heavy vehicles and a lot of smaller ones. He chuckled when the media was speculating on why the Brits did not use any aircraft. Not having satellites was a problem for military aircraft. The British convoy slowly crossed over the border.

David picked up his phone and said, "Let the first few overtake you, and then hit them hard."

Angus watched intently at the cameras. The media talking head was bragging about how the Brits easily entered Scotland. The camera David had installed where the men were stationed started to show the convoy.

The first few overtook them, and then David called out on the phone, "Now!"

He knew it was about to happen, but when the first rocket launched from the forest impacted one of the larger armoured vehicles as it exploded violently, Angus flinched. A barrage of rockets was launched into the sides of the vehicles, before it was followed up by heavy gunfire. Angus' men were relentless in their assault. The first lead vehicles stopped, and he spotted British soldiers getting out to advance on the position from which his men were firing. David must have known this was going to happen because men came out from behind them, where there was a railway track opposite the wooded area, and started to gun down the Brits. It went from a big fancy convoy heading into Scotland to a sudden and overwhelming defeat filled with rubble and dead bodies everywhere. A good amount of the British forces was destroyed, but the rear half of the whole formation was able to withdraw from Scotland and back to Newcastle. He was surprised that the media was allowed to watch the whole thing. It made him grin. David was still on the phone; he was ordering his men to sweep the remains of the British forces for weapons and any possible prisoners. Angus could see his men walking through the damaged and destroyed British vehicles that remained.

David ordered on the phone, "Don't kill injured, take them prisoner."

Watching the screen, he saw some survivors being pulled out of the combat area and then brought to vans. David must have known this would happen and was clearly prepared. The men also seemed to be collecting up weaponry and body armour from the corpses. It was more than a little grizzly, but if the Scots were going to win, they would need to gain any advantage that they could get. Once they finished their work, they took whatever they could to recover and withdraw.

"They'll be back." David declared.

"And we'll need to find another point at which to hit them again. I bet they won't fall into the same trap again."

"Of course. I'm thinking that we'll need to go right away to hit and run attacks. Probably guerrilla-style bombings. No suicide bombings or terror attacks on civilian targets."

"I've been thinking about the terror attacks on civilian targets. I really don't want to do that sort of thing, but I'm thinking we shouldn't pull it off the table on English land. Our goal is to tire the civilian population in England of war with us to the point that they would force their scummy politicians to sue for peace."

David looked thoughtful for a moment. He looked as unhappy about the idea of killing innocents in England as Angus was.

"Okay. It'll be our weapon of last resort if the Brits don't cave in."

Angus looked over at the screen showing the BBC newscast. They were replaying the attack and critiquing the Scots for fighting instead of just bending over to the Brits. He was not surprised at all. They were merely propagandists.

David clapped Angus on the shoulder as he stood up. He had a large grin on his face.

"Mr. President, we've won the day, and while it might be a night of celebration, we've got to be ready for them to quickly recover. I've been looking at various points throughout Scotland where we could strike the Brits. Their next move will be much more cautious and less open."

"And?"

David clicked on the screen of his computer to load up a map of Scotland. On the map was a series of about 30 different red dots.

"On the map are the key points I've identified that the Brits could move along the roads or even flat land that they could try to sneak through. I plan to have small strike groups near each point to drop hit and run fights where they are to fire on the Brits to soften them and retreat."

"No open engagements?" Angus asked.

"It's best to avoid that. We want to put it to them without taking too many losses if possible."

He turned back to the talking heads. They openly declared that Britain might be in a lot more trouble than they originally planned. It was an obvious statement for anyone who just watched the Scots lay waste to the initial British thrust into Scotland. There was no doubt that it was a great day for his movement, but there would likely be bad days coming, at least that is what he was prepared for. It was late enough in the night that Angus decided to get some sleep. Tomorrow, he would spend the day with his family, and then it would be back to Edinburgh for him.

# Chapter 34

24 April 2023

Angus rolled out of bed and made sure to kiss his family goodbye before heading down to Edinburgh. It was a pleasant day off, but he had to get back to work. David let him know that the next phase of surprise attacks was ready, but he suspected that the Brits would eventually make it to Edinburgh. The plan was to shift their headquarters to Stirling if that happened. He suspected sooner or later the Brits would find traction in Scotland pretty quickly, and moving to Stirling would happen eventually. The next city they looked at was much further north in Inverness. Angus would not have been surprised if he eventually ended up in Inverness. The fight against the Brits would be a slog since the bulk of his forces were police and civilian forces that had been put in place to control the cities and towns. They were not a fighting force; that number was about ten thousand men who were available to fight. It was a much smaller force than what the Brits had, but they were highly trained and well-motivated for the task at hand. While sitting in his seat in the van, his phone buzzed. He did not recognise the number.

Answering the phone, he said, "Hello?"

He immediately recognised the voice but was unsure who it was, "Hello Mr. President. I'm calling to congratulate you on a stirring victory."

After a moment, he recognised that the voice was from the Chinese man who visited his home to warn him about the traitor in their midst early on. He initially stated his name was Deng Li, but then later admitted that it was not his real name.

"Thank you."

"The General Secretary himself was impressed with your success. He wanted me to relay that he felt as though our investment in your cause has paid off nicely."

Angus grinned as he replied, "Please thank him for me. We're not done yet, but I'll ask patience as I suspect the Brits aren't finished with us yet, and we'll have bad days as well as good ones."

"We fully understand that Mr. President. Our men in the British Secret Service were impressed with something they called a revolutionary cyber-attack on the United Kingdom satellite system."

Angus chuckled. It was probably going to be the one thing that gave the Scots a chance by attacking the technological crutch the Brits had.

Deng continued speaking, "We guessed that you were involved in that attack."

"Guilty."

"The General Secretary asked that we inquire about the software used and wanted to remind you of all of the assistance that the people of China have given the people of Scotland."

Angus thought about it. He had forgotten to delete the program, and it was just sitting on his laptop. Originally, he did not want to share it with anyone, but based on the response of the Western nations, he wondered what loyalty he had to them. The answer was none.

"I wrote the program. It requires access to the system itself but serves as a worm that erases the data and then locks out access entirely."

"It sounds brilliant. The General Secretary stated that if the people of Scotland were to share this program, the people of China would see this as a generous gift, making us feel even more validated in our support of the people of Scotland."

He chuckled to himself. A clear request that was layered in hints of debt. He decided that he saw no reason not to share with the Chinese since they have been insanely generous with his movement. Plus, a rebalancing of their relationship was important to ensure Scottish independence later down the road.

"I'd be more than willing to share it with the people of China." He firmly responded.

"I can tell you that the General Secretary and the people of China would be very pleased by this. Even to the point that we feel as though balance has been restored in our relationship."

"Of course. How would you like it delivered?"

"We'll send you server information on delivery. We know that you're busy, so we don't expect you to drop everything you're doing to take care of it. Of note, we'll be increasing deliveries and were wondering if you'd be willing to accept assistance in the form of personnel?"

"Personnel?"

"Yes. The Americans are notorious for interfering in other nations' affairs, usually utilising their special forces to serve as a training and limited initial contact missions. We've trained several units of our own men for these types of affairs, and we want to get them valuable first-hand experience in Scotland."

He thought for a moment. It was a risk to have third-party personnel in Scotland, as it might draw other nations in. If the Chinese were willing to take the risk, he saw no reason to reject the help.

"As long as they know it's our operation, we'd welcome all the help that we can get. It's us against the whole west."

"The whole corrupt west." Deng corrected him.

A few years ago, Angus would have disagreed, but the reality was that the West was a rotten, corrupt egg. God has been lost, degenerate behaviour tolerated, men who hated the people of the West allowed to invade and violate the people, and, of course, politicians who were openly corrupted ran everything. It felt like a lost cause. The conservatives of the United Kingdom could not conserve their own socks, let alone a nation worth protecting. The liberals were openly evil piles of excrement who deserved to be shot in the face. He knew at this point that what he and his men did was the only way to save Scotland.

"Indeed." He firmly told Deng.

Deng then continued, "I'll let you go about your work. We'll be in touch with the co-ordination of the issues we've discussed."

"I'll talk to you later." Angus replied.

The man hung up the phone. Angus set his phone aside and looked out the window. They had arrived on the outskirts of Edinburgh. His phone buzzed with a message. It was from Michael telling him he had a visitor. Angus replied that he would be there soon. He asked the driver to take him to the Parliament building. The driver stopped at the entrance and guided Angus through the building to the conference room he regularly used. He was surprised to see Michael and many members of his staff with a well-dressed British man. He had neatly cut salt and peppered hair, light blue eyes and was clean-shaven.

"Mr. Bruce." The man started to say before he was interrupted.

"President Bruce." Michael said firmly.

"Sorry, I stand corrected. President Bruce." The man stated.

"And you are?" Angus asked.

"Yes, my name is Ian Burton from the Home Office."

Smoothly, Angus stepped away from the man and took a seat in the chair he usually sat at when there.

Gesturing to a nearby seat, he ordered, "Take a seat."

The man took the seat that Angus gestured at before he said, "I've come from the Home Office, and I've been despatched to find a peaceful resolution."

Grinning at the man, Angus responded, "Ahh… so you're here to acknowledge our new government."

The men around him laughed. They, like him, knew that the Brits would not be so easily defeated. It would cause a lot more damage for the Brits to move on.

"I'm afraid not quite. I've been empowered to offer clemency for your men if you surrender this foolishness and let the United Kingdom regain control of the Scottish government."

Michael interjected, "His men, eh? Seems like he's not included in your generous offer."

Angus noted that as well and appreciated Michael's sarcasm when he said the word 'generous'.

"I'm afraid the Home Office insists that someone must be held accountable for your actions here."

Angus interrupted, "And of course, me being the face of Scottish Independence must be treated exactly how you Brits treated William Wallace."

The man looked put off by the insinuation before he answered, "Of course not. We're not barbarians. The Scots are part of the United Kingdom and will remain as such."

Raising an eyebrow, Angus asked, "Confident of it, eh? I'd expect a lot more humility after getting your arses handed to you a few days ago."

"Well," The man said with a long pause before continuing, "That was unfortunate to see your men so willing to attack their fellow Britons."

Angus suddenly rose from his chair, which caused the man to flinch. The man was afraid of him. He swiftly pulled out his handgun and set it on the table in front of him. Slowly, he ran his right index finger along the length of his weapon.

"We reject that label." He firmly replied as he took a moment to slowly spin the weapon on the table with his finger.

"Perhaps, but the United Kingdom does not." The man stated in a smooth tone.

Angus noted that the man seemed to recover quickly from his moment of fear. He took a moment to slowly spin his weapon round and round with his finger. It was as much about taking time to think about the man's words as it was to distract the man in an unusual situation. After soaking in the moment of power, he collected his handgun and then gently placed it into its holster.

"I'm afraid I'm going to have to decline your kind offer and offer my own. The Home Office should, instead of demanding the complete surrender of the Scottish people, suggest to the Prime Minister a full acknowledgement of Scottish independence and the installation of my government. We won't be surrendering anytime soon, and we'll make the British pay a heavy toll in their attempt to force their will on us."

The man paused for a moment before stating, "That's an unfortunate response."

Raising an eyebrow at the man, Angus asked, "Did you really think we'd just bend over and surrender just because you showed up at our door?"

"Of course not. I was sent here to lay out the Home Office's offer."

"And what did you think would happen?"

"Exactly what happened." The man answered.

Giving a nod, Angus continued speaking, "We've had enough Mr. Burton. The Brits have ruled over Scotland for hundreds of years longer than they were ever welcome. That rule had been fruitful for both parties, but over the last 10 years our so-called leaders seem to have decided that they don't give a shite about Scots. You've turned our education system into a Marxist brainwashing centre filled with faggots and trannies that trick our children into becoming disgusting degenerates like they are. You let men and women lead us who are open thieves. You import thousands of third-world scum that rape and murder our women while assaulting our men. And on top of it all, you made us the ones guilty by degrading us for voicing these concerns. We've had enough of it, so we're doing something about it. We'll not surrender, we'll not let you weak-willed frauds rule Scotland anymore. If you want Scotland back, be prepared to bleed for it."

The man did not say a word. He was clearly thinking about everything Angus had said. It felt good to let the Brits know his motivations directly. He doubted that it would matter to the man since he saw British politicians as weak and pathetic.

Angus declared, "Well, we now know where each other stands. The next time I expect to hear from you will be when the British decide to acknowledge Scottish independence."

The man stood up before he stated, "I doubt that day will come, sir."

Chuckling, Angus stated, "Perhaps. You should consider using your satellites to send me your next message."

The man's face, which generally remained calm, shifted to curiosity before going back to the same calm expression he had the whole time they spoke. He had not known that it was Angus' group that had knocked out their satellites.

The man offered a hand before saying. "Indeed. I'll let the Home Office know your reply."

Raising a hand, Angus replied, "Sorry, I'm not shaking hands with strangers for now. I don't know if you've noticed, but I'm not exactly the most popular world leader right now."

Giving a brief nod, the man told him, "I understand. Have a good day."

Angus watched as a pair of security guards escorted the man away. Once he was long gone, Angus turned towards Michael to see his response to the meeting.

Michael must have known that Angus wanted his opinion because he spoke immediately, "That was interesting, but honestly unsurprising."

Angus just nodded.

"The Brits have not lost their arrogance. We initiate a war with them, and they march in here immediately demanding our surrender when we utterly put it to them in the field." Michael stated.

Chuckling, Angus said, "I'm clearly unpopular with them."

"Putting it mildly. They'd give clemency to the whole lot of us if only to be able to parade your head on a stick."

"I'm certain that's why I was picked for the role. A figurehead of sorts."

"For a figurehead, you've handled everything quite deftly. When you stood up quickly, I was convinced the man was about to shite his drawers. Publicly putting a round in the head of Sturgeon on the telly will give people the impression that you're a dangerous man."

"As was my intent. I was even toying around with my handgun to give the man the idea I was a bit unhinged. I figured it'd make them think they could take advantage of me being emotional or something. Maybe they'll make a mistake by misunderstanding us."

"Very crafty Mr. President. It's also clear they've got no clue just how many men we've got available. Maybe they'll make some mistakes there."

"Possible. For now, we'll assume no mistakes on their part and execute our plans as needed. Do you have our secondary and third government positions prepared in case they make it to Edinburgh?"

Michael answered, "Yes, we do. I'm predicting we might have to use multiple sites until we can get the Brits to finally acquiesce to our demands."

"Probably. Let's get to work getting prepared for when they come back. It'll take all of us to finally defeat them, and blood will be shed."

# Chapter 35

2 May 2023

Angus watched the reports intently. The Brits took a week to reestablish themselves, likely to get their reserves and any other men they could acquire. Now, the actual war was about to begin, and the Brits took the Scots seriously. He got reports showing build-ups near every major road and some of the minor ones crossing from England into Scotland. The Brits were going for a multi-pronged attack. He spoke extensively with David, and they deduced that the plan was probably have these splintered groups form up as they entered Glasgow and Edinburgh. No doubt the Brits felt that once they took the two biggest cities, his movement would be crippled. That would not be the case. There were cells in both cities planning extensive terror campaigns for every single Brit who dared stay in either city. He was sitting with David in the bunker and was surprised by how many more cameras David had access to. He had found a way to tap into the city street cameras in Edinburgh and Glasgow.

David pointed at a few of the border cameras he had set up and announced, “They’re moving out. It looks like we’ve got them crossing in almost every point they can fit in.”

Angus gestured at one of the cameras and stated, “Helicopters, too. I guess they figured they could manage without satellites for them.”

“Makes sense. They can use radar more easily and more slowly. Notice how slowly they’re crossing? They’re scanning for another sneak attack.”

Giving a light chuckle, Angus stated, “Well, I can’t blame them after what we did.”

“True. I think they’re likely be surprised again.” David stated before pointing again at the camera showing the helicopters and continuing, “Watch that one.”

He was quite curious about what David had in mind, so he stared intently at the screen. It showed a group of about 10 helicopters. In a wide formation passing over the camera and then continuing deeper into Scotland. Suddenly, a barrage of rockets came into view as they smashed into several of the helicopters. Angus was surprised as most of them exploded violently. The remaining four helicopters spun away quickly and began heading away from the direction from which the rockets came.

David pumped a fist as he called out, “Six of ten! Not too damned bad.”

Angus pointed at several other screens, stating, “They’ve stopped moving.”

“Hesitation. We just shot down several hundred million pounds in British property. This will drag out for a while.”

Angus nodded as he continued to watch. The Brits started moving again. This time, something exploded on the side of a narrow road, taking out one of the lead British vehicles. There were a few survivors in the vehicle who managed to escape and flee back into the rest of the group. They withdrew from the road. Most of the convoys seemed to be moving along the road unharassed. He was confused because he thought that David planned attacks for them all.

David must have seen his facial expression because he stated, “We spread out our points and types of attacks to confuse them. Some are even fake smoke bombs or confusing items that look like I.E.D. on the side of the road. We’re gonna hit and run them tons of times.”

Finally, another screen had action as heavy gunfire seemed to come from a nearby building onto passing British military vehicles. None of them stopped moving and passed through with what did not seem to Angus to be any damage. Several other screens showed different timed attacks. In many cases, the Brits immediately turned around; in others, they pushed on. He was impressed with the heartiness of the British military when several of these attacks would take out men, but the others kept moving forward.

“We’ve had a few casualties, but it appears as though it has been limited.” David stated.

“I’m sorry to hear that.”

Giving a nodded David told Angus, “We all knew the risks. No matter what that British clown told you a week ago, every man who’s joined our cause is not going to walk free. You fucking put a bullet in the skull of their lapdog Sturgeon in front of the whole world. We've backed you, and so we're all done for if we don't win."

He nodded solemnly. They all had everything at risk. It was all in or at the end of them.

David pointed at one of the screens and then said, "The Brits are too thin to take Edinburgh, and they must know it. The lead caravans have stopped and are going off path."

Angus turned to look at what David was showing him. The Brits seemed to have turned off and were heading off the wrong way to go to either Glasgow or Edinburgh. David raced over, pulled a map of Scotland off the wall and then tossed it onto the main table. He pulled a marker out and dotted several points. Angus had no idea what he was doing. He drew several lines from the dots and then crossed them together.

Tossing the marker aside, he declared, "Hawick."

"Huh?"

"They're headed to Hawick. My guess is to set up a base to regroup and then relaunch their attack."

"Ahh. A foothold in Scotland."

"And of course, we're gonna make them pay for it."

David picked up his phone and started texting. Angus had no idea what he was saying, but a grin started to cross his face as he continued typing furiously on his phone.

As he placed his phone down, he stated, "We'll send them a few surprises to help them enjoy their stay in lovely Scotland."

"Sounds like a plan."

"We're restocking and rotating our border defences and having men move into position at Hawick now. Some will be there before the Brits, but we're gonna let them set up and then send some Chinese artillery to them."

David clicked on his mouse for the computer that ran everything there. One of the screens moved over to a BBC report. The reporter was going over a timeline of what they guessed was the entire Scottish independence movement, dating all the way back to the Scottish Wars of Independence involving William Wallace and Robert the Bruce. Angus grinned when they mentioned his name with those great Scots. He did not feel particularly on their level, but no matter what happened, his name was going to live on in history books. Hopefully, he will be able to retire to his ranch soon and give Isla Grace all the children that she desired. The reporter finally got to Angus and his movement. They were not kind in their opinion of Angus, which he knew would be the case for some time. If they did win the day, he knew history would favour him and his men in the long run. Their cause was just, and he knew it. Included in their story were several interviews with people that Angus used to work with back at Northstar. They all claimed to be surprised by his actions, with some even claiming he was 'inclusive' to them. Angus hated leftist bullshite talking points like 'inclusive' or 'equity'. It was newspeak, like from the novel 1984, meant to control people into doing the bidding of these leftist bastards.

"Brainwashed clowns." David stated.

"I was, too, when I worked there." Angus stated and then paused for a moment before continuing, "It took the death of my sister to even start to open my eyes. Asians raped and murdered her, and the police didn't do shite to find out how it happened. I felt lost and frustrated. My father fell into a bit of a depression about it. I ended up meeting Liam and his lads, and then everything about what was really going on came to me."

"We've all got a story. For me, it was when the military started making up rules that weakened our military force. First, they started trying to let women do all sorts of crazy shite without admitting that some things women just can't do. Then, they started to let the trannies in while paying for all their shite. Sensitivity training overwhelmed our actual mission. Finally, they started to use all these rules to let weak asses use the system to ruin good men."

"A slow grind to the red pill."

David chuckled, "You millennials and your silly terms."

"It's from the film The Matrix."

Waving his hand dismissively, David replied, "No shite. Everyone's seen it. First one was great, but the rest were stupid."

Angus chuckled. David was a stodgy older man, but he was clearly very good at what he did, which was all that Angus asked for. Turning back to the screen, he watched as the reporter went on talking about Angus' family, barely covering the death of his sister, which included a not very flattering commentary about Isla Grace. It made him quite angry. There was no reason to mock Isla Grace as she was not involved in the fight.

"Bastards." David stated with an upset tone.

He felt his jaw clenching as he watched until the end of the report. He did not mind them tossing mud at him, but throwing mud at Isla Grace made him quite upset. It was tempting to have his men pay that reporter a little visit, but he decided it was best to just let it go. Murdering random idiot propagandists would not help their cause. He would probably need to save that energy for tomorrow. It was going to be his first interview with a reporter in Edinburgh. He suspected that it would likely be done from the usual far-left crying and random buzzwords. Also, there were likely to be quite a few aggressive questions about Angus' government. There would be no ally in there. He did not care and already planned to record the whole interview to keep them from cutting it up to try to make him look bad.

David interrupted his thoughts by asking, "Should we deal with that reporter?"

"No. Our resources are better spent dealing with the Brits. Public opinion isn't a concern until we put an end to British rule of Scotland. Then, we'll let the Scots see who we really are."

"That reporter better be glad it wasn't my wife; I'd have his balls hung on my wall."

"Just not worth the time." Angus told him firmly.

"Fine, fine. Do you have any ideas to add to our current planning?"

"No. I heard the Brits started a blockade on Edinburgh and Glasgow."

David gave a nod as he said, "Yes. They must not know about our Chinese friends and Rosehearty since our supplies are still coming in."

"And our friends who want to help directly?"

"They're already here and have set up several small mobile garrisons throughout the Lowlands. We've given them any supplies they've asked for, and they've already helped with a few of the strikes. I've kept their existence between a few key men, and even their arrival was masked late at night when the docks in Rosehearty were empty." David told him.

"Excellent. They understand that both parties will disavow them, so hopefully they can cause a lot of disruption with the Brits."

"I also informed them not to fuck around with the civilians. We've gotta try and limit Scottish civilian casualties as much as possible."

"Thank you. We're already dealing with non-stop propaganda everywhere, acting as though we're the second coming of a mix of Hitler and Genghis Khan."

David laughed for a bit before declaring, "Bah, according to those fools, everyone they don't like is Hitler."

"Sometimes I wonder if anyone even knows what Hitler really did. It's insane to think that anyone honestly thinks a bunch of Scots fighting Brits over Scotland is anything like a Nazi."

"They know, but they don't give a fuck. It's all propaganda."

Angus said, "We've been tracking the Scottish media, and they've been much better since my little warning. I guess the threat of catching a bullet has kept them in line. It's all been unvarnished truth."

"I was impressed when I saw that. I thought for sure you were going to kill that one journalist."

Chuckling, Angus replied, "He pissed his drawers, that's enough. I just want our people to know the truth and judge it for themselves. We've also had men going to each school in Scotland to remove any far-left horse-shite as they find it. No LGBT crap, no communism, no Islam, and any other degenerate tripe. Imagine what will happen if we can win this thing. We'll force Scots to stop being soy-filled pussies and be the men they should be."

"That and we'll be free of outside interference. I'm only worried about the Chinese."

"I've balanced that scale." Angus stated firmly.

Raising his eyebrow, David asked, "How did you manage that?"

"They were impressed with how we knocked out the Brits' satellites, so I gave them the program I used. It made them quite happy."

David laughed before declaring, "That'll really mess up someone if they can pull it off."

Shrugging, Angus stated, "That'll be someone else's problem, not ours."

"True. You should probably head off to see your wife before tomorrow. I'll let you know if any important updates that you need to know about when they happen."

"Sounds good." Angus responded as he reached out and shook David's hand.

# Chapter 36

The sun was almost in the middle of the sky when Angus finally got back to Edinburgh. The meeting with the reporter for his interview was not for another hour, so he had time to clean up before sitting down with her. He was looking forward to the interview, although he fully expected to be pilloried by the Western media no matter what he did. The van rolled up to the flat that he was going to stay in for the night. He went in and quickly showered before dressing. Normally, he would wear something subtle just in case he was accidentally engaged in battle, which he thought could happen at any time, but today he decided to go with a nice suit to give a more professional appearance for the role he technically held. Once he was ready, he strode out of the flat and into his van. The drive to the Parliament building was short. He had the interview set in the same conference room he used for most meetings that he held. It was somewhere that he was used to and felt the most comfortable. Once he stepped out of the van, he was met by Michael.

Reaching out a hand, Michael stated, "Mr. President, your guest is here. I don't know why you chose an American, but we'll see how badly they mangle your words."

Shaking his hand, Angus chuckled before replying, "I'm convinced that Fox News is probably one of the few news outlets that is at least partially conservative. I figured it was them or Sky TV from Australia. Is our own recording equipment set up?"

"Of course. I told her that we'll let her run the interview first and we'll only play the full recording if they play any games."

"Outstanding. Let's go."

Angus strode confidently through the Parliament doors and then headed off to the conference room. As he entered, he saw the competing film crews. The large table with chairs had been removed, and in the centre of the room were two chairs. Sitting in one of them was an attractive blonde. Angus chuckled. He was certain that whoever hired these reporters at Fox News loved blondes. Every time he ever saw a video from them, it was also some blonde reporter. This one was wearing a sharp light blue business suit. She rose to her feet when he entered fully. He spotted the camera that his men were running had already begun recording.

Once he approached, she extended her hand and said, "Mr. Bruce, it's a pleasure to meet you."

Taking her offered hand, he responded, "President."

"Yes, sorry. Mr. President. Please have a seat."

Angus sat down in the chair opposite her. They were recording this interview about 3 feet apart from each other and slightly turned towards each other but set so their faces were both fully visible to the Fox News cameras.

Once he was fully seated, the woman introduced herself, "My name is Emma Wiśniewski."

"It's nice to meet you."

"Thank you. I was told that you didn't have any areas that you wouldn't object to me discussing with you."

"That's right."

"First, could you tell our viewers who you are?"

Giving a nod at her, Angus answered, "My name is Angus Edward Bruce. I'm 29 years old. I'm married to my sweet wife, Isla Grace Bruce, and we're close to having our fourth child. I'm a practising Catholic man with a degree in software engineering from the University of Scotland. I'm the current President of Scotland after leading a coup to remove our corrupt government. I own a ranch near Stirling, and I had one sister."

"Had?"

"Yes. My twin sister Annis was murdered by Asian men 7 years ago in Edinburgh while working at a refugee centre."

"Is that why you're doing all of this?"

Angus chuckled before stating, "It was my eye-opening moment. I was mad. The police claimed that they couldn't find them, but the reality is, they didn't try. Most likely, they feared being called Islamophobic, racist, or some other nonsense."

"So, you reject the claims that your movement is racist?"

"I don't care about such claims. Every race on God's green earth deserves the right to maintain and live in peace in their homelands. Do you claim the Nigerians are racist for wanting Nigeria to maintain itself? How about the UAE? Or India? Or Uruguay? Of course not. Each people deserve to keep their own nation and their own culture. Scotland should be for the Scots."

"Others claim you're a transphobe or a homophobe."

"I'm a Scot. I don't care what others claim. Transgenderism is a mental illness, and we're done pretending it's anything else. You can't sit here and claim that you're a chair and demand that I sit right down and pretend you're a chair because you're objectively not a chair. Men can't be women and women can't be men. In Scotland, we'll no longer pretend as such, and we'll no longer push that lie on our children. As far as homosexuality goes, it's a sin, and we'll not push that behaviour as anything else. In Scotland, we follow God's laws. If two men wish to lie in bed together, then they'll have to do so privately. In Scotland, we won't chase down homosexuals, but we won't raise them as anything more than the sinners that they are."

"So, there will be a law against it?"

"No. Scots have more important things to worry about than what two men do in their private time. God will settle that out later. Scotland will just not support things like homosexual marriage or allowing public homosexual events. Those will be illegal."

"Many will claim that you're a homophobe or a dictator because of those kinds of laws."

"I don't care. The West is constantly moralising its detestable views on other nations. They prance about as though they're our betters, but the reality is, the West is melting all around us. People are unhappy, the leaders are corrupt and liars, we have massive economic powers who use money to break down Christian societies, and we have spiritually weak religious leaders with the spine of a snail. Western nations like the United States, Germany, Australia, and more are not morally superior to anyone."

"I disagree. In our nations, we don't shoot unwanted political leaders in the head."

Angus laughed before stating, "Maybe you should. You Americans talk about being some sort of moral democracy that everyone should look up to, and yet your own President was a thief who used, as he put it, 'the largest election fraud system in history', to ensure his fake election. He used mail-in ballots, ballot stuffing, and glitched computers through his lackeys in key states to ensure a win. Yet… you cowardly Americans simply roll over and watch as the fraud in your White House quickly crashes the entire world's economy through cutting off your own oil supply while mass overprinting the American Dollar. You've got governors in states like Arizona who clearly and openly cheat in an election, and you fucking Americans do nothing."

"No proof of election fraud was ever shown."

"Bull-shite. It was everywhere. I've seen videos of your counters openly recounting ballots repeatedly. Why the hell are ballot counters kicking people out during the count and putting up barriers to prevent people from watching? The American elections are a fraud. You might as well just let your puppet masters in charge select whoever the hell they want because you're not the ones picking."

"We're not going to agree on this subject, Mr. President." She huffily told him.

"I know. What's your next question?"

"How do you expect to defeat the United Kingdom military?"

"I believe they already know, so you don't need to ask for them, but we're doing hit and run attacks to slowly drain them of resources. Eventually, they'll gain a foothold in Edinburgh and Glasgow, then we'll begin terror attacks on them there and elsewhere to drain support for their cause."

"Terror attacks?" she asked in a shocked tone.

"They're invaders in our lands, and we're going to do anything to repel them."

She must have decided to change the subject when she asked, "What do you think of the Chinese Communist Party formally recognising your government?"

"You mean China. This is the American arrogance that people tire of. The Chinese Communist Party is only a political party within China. It would be like me asking what I thought of the Republican Party as though it were the single force within the United States. But to answer your question, the people of Scotland greatly appreciate the people of China standing up for the rights of people in any nation to have the right to represent themselves freely."

If the woman was put off by him correcting her, she did not show it.

She pressed, "What of the rumours that the Chinese have been providing military and financial support to your movement?"

While he was not a fan of lying, Angus knew that the help that the Chinese gave must remain a secret for as long as possible, so he coolly answered, "Those aren't true. While we appreciate the Chinese recognising us, we're an independent movement wanting freedom from the United Kingdom."

She then said, "I want to go back to the racism claims by talking about two specific areas the world is concerned about."

"Okay."

"First, is the expulsion of Scottish people who were naturalised or born here, who are not white."

He interrupted, "Also known as people who are not Scottish. We don't recognise the British importation of people from all over the world as Scottish people. Unfortunately, we had to ask them to leave Scotland, but until we can remove British rule and install a free Scotland, we can't allow non-Scottish people access to Scotland."

"So once this is resolved, you plan to let them live in Scotland?"

"No. We'll only allow non-Scots the right to be within our borders for tourism or business. Non-Scots won't have citizenship rights, ever. Scotland is only for the Scots."

"Don't you see how outrageous this is? These people were born in Scotland and have a right to live there."

"No, they don't. Do you cry for people to come live in Mongolia while altering the nature of being a Mongolian? No. It's only in Western and Christian nations that these demands are made to force people from other nations into those nations. We reject this entirely."

"The world won't allow that."

He firmly replied, "I don't give a shite what the world wants. Scotland is for the Scots. However, I suspect that if the West wishes to push Scotland away, we'll find others who would be willing to trade and be friends with Scotland."

"The Chinese?"

"And likely others. Much of the world is, frankly, sick of the Yank's shite. Americans moralise over and over while they funnel billions to interfere with the free will of other nations. Libya, Syria, every damned nation in South America, Ukraine, and many more. The American government uses its military and economic might to force the world to its will. We'd love to be friends with the Americans, but we can't let some corrupt pile of goat shite sitting in Washington D.C., tell us how to live our lives. Look at Ukraine. In 2014, the American CIA removed a Russian-friendly President to replace him with their own lackey. They've pressured and economically attacked the Russians constantly and then act upset when the Russians finally decide they've had enough."

"There is no evidence to support your claim."

He laughed heartily before finally saying, "Of course not. The Russians just go around invading everyone for fun. So, what was your second question, going back to racism?"

She did not appear pleased with his obvious mocking of her statement.

"Yes, what right do you have to justify the banning of Islam in Scotland and the removal of the mosques?"

"Scotland is a Christian nation. We don't have to tolerate aggressive and unfriendly cults within our borders. We've also banned Scientology, but I notice you didn't seem overly concerned about that."

"Islam is not equivalent to Scientology."

He chuckled.

Rolling his eyes, he then stated, "I apologise to Scientologists. Islam is much more violent. It's better to have your money stolen and your family cast you out than to be forcibly converted or killed. Islam is a cult, and it'll be permanently banned in Scotland."

"Do you hate Muslims?"

"Nope. I just want them to worship their shite in their own countries and leave us alone in Scotland to worship God, like proper Christians."

"And you don't see this as a problem while claiming to demand freedom?"

"Nope. Scotland is free for Scots. The difference that you can't seem to understand is that we're not demanding the people of Saudi Arabia worship our God. We just want them to understand that in Scotland, we believe that Jesus Christ is King."

One of the men in the back area whispered out loud enough for Angus to hear, "Amen."

He turned back towards the man and grinned.
Giving the man a little wink, he looked back at the reporter and continued, "We'll expect that Muslims throughout the world won't be overly happy with my opinion on their religion, but that's fine because I expect they don't agree with my religion. The key difference is that we'd love to trade and be friends with every Islamic nation in the world. When our footie teams show up in their nations, we'll follow all their customs and courtesies while respecting their nation for what it is, as they want it to be. We'd expect them to honour us the same. We won't demand or even

suggest that they should change their ways for us. Something I think you Americans could learn from."

He figured that she had no response because she then went to the next question, "There were inquiries about what you would do if you did win."

"Well… We intend to sit down and write out an American-style Constitution with many more protections than you Yanks have. It'll include many laws set forth to protect Scotland for the Scots. I still don't understand why you continually let your government put the needs or interests of other people ahead of your own. The needs and interests of the Scottish people will be forthright in all that we do once the British finally acknowledge our right to sovereignty."

"You mentioned the American Constitution. Will this include the freedom of speech?"

"Yes." He answered.

"And what about people who disagree with you?"

"We've had students in Glasgow and Edinburgh protesting daily, and outside of the one group getting rough with the police, we've let them protest."

She looked slightly puzzled before she finally asked, "What do you think about other Scots disagreeing with the majority of your platform?"

"They're wrong. We've got millions of Scots who've been brainwashed by our own media and educational systems into believing the lies of people who attack their own nation daily. They'll see the light eventually."

"And if they don't?"

"It won't matter. Scotland is gonna be free, even if I've got to personally drag it there kicking and screaming. We're working to remove all the brainwashing."

"Brainwashing?"

"Yes. There was an interview done in 1985 with an ex-KGB agent named Yuri Bezmenov, where he describes how a whole generation can be subverted to believe Marxist lies to the point that the generation is purely lost. It's sad to see a lost generation of Scots, but if it means they dislike what we're doing here in Scotland so much that they leave, so be it. We're going forward, with or without them."

"And free press?" She then asked.

"The press has already been freed. If they report the actual truth and only the actual truth without their dumb opinions, my government has no quibble with them. Unlike Americans who let their President Obama allow propaganda, we're banning it outright."

She nodded lightly, clearly; he touched on something that she agreed with.

"What about the other Amendments?" She then asked.

"I like many of them. We intend for the Scots to have full gun rights, and things like the government not being able to search or seise a Scot's property are important."

"Didn't your government just seise a lot of land?"

"Only land that was owned by foreigners. No foreign government or non-Scot will have land rights in Scotland. As I've stated, Scotland will be for the Scots."

She continued by asking, "And what will your role be? Will you continue as President?"

"I intend to resign once the British acquiesce to our demands and then return home to my wife and children."

"Why don't you plan to continue leading?"

"I'm not a politician. I'm just the right guy at the right time, trying to do my best to save Scotland from the ruin being forced on it."

"What about the European Union? Will Scotland apply to join?"

"No. The EU is at the heart of many of the problems within Europe, and frankly, it should be dissolved."

"Why do you say that?"

"All of the issues I've told you Scotland has were caused by an unaccountable European Union making up rules as they saw fit, with no care about how it impacts the people they rule over. Let me ask you a question, Emma."

"Okay."

"Why in the world would a nation import hundreds of thousands to millions of people who detest that nation and its way of life?"

The reporter paused for a moment, attempting to come up with an answer.

Angus interrupted her thought process, "There isn't a good reason, and we Scots won't have it anymore."

"Is there any way you'd change your mind?" She asked.

"No. Scotland must be for the Scots. We've been enslaved by the British for centuries, and it's about time we finally are the free men that we should've been all along. Each man who stands with me is willing to die for that. As am I."

"Mr. President. This interview has been enlightening. I was wondering if you had something that you'd wish to share with the world before we close."

"Yes, thank you. I just want the world to know that we know that we're in the right. Scotland has the right to live how it chooses to live. Not how the West wants us to live. We've chosen our own path. We ask that you speak for us. Insist that the British remove themselves from Scotland and let us live freely."

"Thank you, Mr. President." The reporter stated as she offered a hand.

Angus shook her hand before saying, "Thank you for giving us a voice."

# Chapter 37

5 May 2023

Angus was quite pleased with the response from his friends and allies over the interview. While the Western nations continued to demean his claims, other nations like Iran, Cuba, and Russia openly cheered him. The General Secretary of China himself personally called Angus to congratulate him for showing himself to be the leader of Scotland that they needed. He stated that he was excited about the close friendship between China and Scotland. He also stated that once Scotland won its freedom, he would personally push to have Scotland added as a member of BRICS. It was an economic movement pushing away from the American dollar. Angus told him that he would be more than happy to have Scotland join. It was obvious at this point that the Americans, the EU, and the Brits were not going to ally with Scotland, so he would have to find strong allies elsewhere. He sat in the hotel with Isla Grace, enjoying a nice breakfast. It would be a wonderful day when he would be able to retire back to his home with her. As they sat there eating, there was a knock on the door.

Opening the door, he asked, "Yes?"

"Sir," One of the security men, as part of his team, was at the door speaking as he paused and then continued, "You've been summoned to the Edinburgh Command Centre."

"I'll be right out so we can go."

"Yes sir." The man responded before turning away to head to the vans.

Closing the door, he told Isla Grace, "I've got to go."

She hugged him tightly as she responded, "I understand. I must admit that I anticipate our victory."

Chuckling, he responded, "Me too."

Angus doubted that a victory was going to come anytime soon, but he sure hoped it would come. It was finally time for Scottish Independence. He bent over and gave Isla Grace a passionate kiss before heading out. It was a bit of a drive, and he had given instructions not to disturb him unless it was urgent, so whatever was going on must have been important. As he climbed into the waiting van, he waved to Isla Grace and his children. They all waved back at him. He sighed heavily. Part of him deeply regretted doing all of this. He could have easily stayed in his safe little home with his family. It was wonderful, and with as much money as he had, he would never have had to worry about anything for himself or his children. It was all for his nation and his kids. He always had to remind himself every time that he thought about Isla Grace and the little ones. The drive back to Edinburgh was not too bad, as he noted an unusually heavy traffic heading out of the city. It took him a moment to realise that it was probably wealthier people making their way far away from what was likely going to become a war zone. Typical of the wealthy to cut and run when things get tough. Angus planned to avoid heavy warfare in Edinburgh and would use selective terror strikes on British targets while hoping to avoid hurting his fellow Scots. He knew some would die, but he insisted they try their best to avoid it as much as possible. The van stopped and the passenger door opened.

"This way Mr. President." One of the bodyguards said.

Angus slid out of the van and saw immediately that they were at one of the many small hidden garrisons throughout Edinburgh. The Brits had reset their forces and were likely to attack again. Edinburgh was the jewel of Scotland, and Angus knew that the Brits wanted to capture it quite badly. No doubt Glasgow, which was the largest city in Scotland, was the second-best goal for the Brits. As Angus entered the flat, he spotted a few guards and the computer set up for him. One of the guards had a device to scan the room and another guard was using a device to scan the computer. He was told that one was for electronic listening devices and the other was for explosives. Both were provided by David, and he had to wait for both men to finish before he could get to work. Sitting down, he started the computer and then logged in to the system they used to communicate. He saw David's feed was up.

"Good morning Mr. President." David said on the computer.

"Hey Michael. How are things?"

"We've got Brits coming up A1 and A68 in full force to Edinburgh and A74 to Glasgow in full force."

"How far along are they?" Angus asked.

"Just started."

"Do we have any surprises waiting for them?"

David grinned at him through the camera before answering, "Of course. We're starting with anti-aircraft fire to limit or chase the helicopters, then anti-tank weapons for the vehicles, and as they get close to both the cities, we're hitting them with IEDs."

"All hit and run?" Angus asked while being concerned about his own men.

"Of course. We've got to limit our own casualties while doing as much damage to the Brits' military as possible."

Rubbing his chin, Angus asked, "How are our supplies from our benefactors holding out?"

"We're doing fine on that front. The Brits still aren't blockading Rosehearty. Likely because their satellites aren't up yet. I'm hoping we can conclude this whole mess before they get their satellites back up."

"I'm amazed the Americans aren't helping."

David laughed heartily before commenting, "The people in charge over there are fuckin' incompetent. I doubt they've got anyone trying to track what we're doing."

Chuckling in response, Angus stated, "I was kind of sad when Trump got cheated but having that doddering old man running things only helps us."

"He's just a puppet anyway. Half the time I bet he doesn't even know where the hell he is, let alone that he's supposed to be in charge."

Taking a moment to think on it, Angus stated, "I bet Trump would've probably tried to push the Brits into letting us go."

"Probably, but let's worry about what hand we've been dealt now."

"True. Looks like the Brits have started moving. No press this time."

Angus nodded as he looked at the dozen live feed videos waiting to see the Brits' movement. It was a good thirty minutes before he finally saw some movement. It was a large group of armoured vehicles packed with several dozen helicopters. Several rockets were launched from a variety of locations around the Brits, and while most of them missed, a few struck some of the helicopters. It continued from different spots, since David used two-man teams sprinkled all along the road. They would launch a Chinese rocket at a target and then run away so they do not get fired on or captured. The barrage continued to be spaced out as the Brits moved, eliminating another seven helicopters and chasing off the rest. Angus chuckled as the Brits attempted to return fire into empty spots since his men left immediately. Sadly, he did get a report message that either did not move fast enough or was not caught quickly. That meant at least four of his men were likely dead. Angus watched intently as the British vehicles continued to move forward along the roads.

David interrupted his thoughts as Angus watched, "I told the men to give 'em a little breather before we hit them again. This time it'll be much more spaced out to let the Brits get a nice think as they move north."

"Sounds like a plan." Angus commented.

"Well, we plan to mix things up and be unpredictable. We're hoping to push them back, but then next time we'll let them go right through to Edinburgh."

Angus frowned. It did not seem wise to simply give the Brits Edinburgh.

David chuckled as he must have seen Angus' facial expression before he stated, "Unpredictability is key. We're going to start our terror campaign once they get to Edinburgh, and then once the bulk of their forces are in Scotland, I want to heavily damage every single road that leads into Scotland all the way down to any dirt paths."

"Trap them?"

"Yes. A lot of fights need to be psychological. Have you ever seen a film called Watchmen?"

"Yep. It was a long time ago."

"Excellent. You have an assignment tonight. You're to watch the prison scene when the crazy redhead says that the prisoners are trapped in there with him. I want you to try and do that speech like a madman in an interview about why we took out all the roads."

Angus was not much of an actor, but he had to admit that the idea of turning him into an unhinged madman who would shoot people for no reason was an interesting way to make it seem like the Brits could take advantage of his instability, especially since Angus had been the only face of the movement. All his men's names have been hidden by pretending that Angus was an iron-fisted dictator.

David interrupted his thoughts again, "They're about to approach our first wave. More small man team hit and run strikes."

Angus nodded and continued watching the screen. The British vehicles plugged along, and out of nowhere, several rockets were launched into them. Many of them hit the target, with a few taking out a vehicle, but some did not do a lot of damage. He could only guess that the Chinese rockets were not as effective on the British vehicles as they were on the helicopters. The Brits pushed through and were now well past halfway to their goal of Edinburgh. Angus was surprised when an explosion hit one of the lead vehicles. It was much more violent than the rockets his men were using a bit ago.

His reaction must have been obvious because David commented. "IED. The men started setting them up when the Brits got past our anti-aircraft rockets."

The IED must have been highly effective because the Brits stopped moving. They were just outside of a smaller town called Lauder on A68, and the much bigger group along A1 got to Innerwick. The force heading to Glasgow made it to Douglas. Since it had been several hours of moving with the Scots hammering them from a distance, Angus suspected they had enough for the day and were setting up a rough base.

David commented, "More forces are moving across the border. Probably going to reinforce their three newly established garrisons before they continue to push into the big cities."

Angus stated, "We softened them up nicely."

"Yes, but Yanks and Krauts have been dumping money and supplies to reinforce the Brits. We're going to have to keep hammering them, even while they camp at night, to try and break their will."

"This might take a long time, won't it?" Angus asked.

"Probably."

He grimly looked at the screen. It was going to be a long, tough fight to get the Brits to give up Scotland.

# Chapter 38

6 May 2023

Angus was up early and, on his computer, watched the video feeds intently. He also had the BBC up and their reporters were talking about the casualties and the current position of the British forces. He really appreciated the idiot reporters talking openly about information that really should be secret. No one knew the strength, location, or plans of his men except the Scottish leadership. David's camera invitation popped up, so Angus clicked on it to accept.

"Good morning Mr. President." David said.

"Morning, David. What's the plan for today?"

"Well… We've set up a host of about ten thousand men to meet the Brits when their force gets to Haddington. It's going to be our first real engagement, and the plan is to let the Brits have it, so they'll be shaken."

"Any news on their numbers?" Angus asked.

"Well… It appears they've called up all their reserves and have recalled as many men overseas as they could. There are rumours they're even planning to mass recruit and seek help from outside the United Kingdom."

"Going all in, eh?"

"They're going to outnumber us, but the good news is that the Americans have nothing outside of satellites to offer because they've been dumping so much cash into Ukraine. Maybe they'll send some troops to help, but so far, the senile old man in D.C. has said no."

Chuckling, Angus replied, "This ain't Ukraine, so the Yanks can't funnel money back into their own pockets with the Brits or us, so why would they give a shite about us? How about the EU?"

"The Krauts and their puppets? Oh, they've given lip service but nothing else. It's just gonna be us versus the Brits." David answered.

Angus nodded. The whole Ukraine war, which was clearly caused by a mixture of American aggression towards the Russians and the incompetence of their current leadership. That stupid old man was clearly just a puppet; the man was incoherent, and honestly, Angus saw his presidency as an extension of the Obama presidency. It was also straight-up elderly abuse. He was hoping that in 2024, Trump would win again, so Scotland could look for either American neutrality or even outright forcing the Brits to give up on Scotland. For now, the focus would be on their upcoming terror plan against the Brits. He had little doubt that eventually Edinburgh would fall to the Brits. Glasgow would likely be next after that, and then his people would be forced into the terror campaign. Angus was still very concerned about spreading it into England, but he was starting to think that it might be the only way to go since the Scots had won every engagement and yet the Brits kept coming. It might take extreme outrage to force their hand.

David interrupted his thoughts by saying, "The Brits are forming up to push through to Edinburgh. We've also got a strong force of Brits heading up to Glasgow. We have some hit-and-run forces to slow them down, but Edinburgh is our primary defensive plan."

"Once they take Glasgow what is the plan there?"

"We've got volunteers who we trained on the IED-style attacks and using light artillery to harass the Brits once they get settled in Glasgow."

"Risks to civilians?"

David chuckled before replying, "Higher than normal, but we've given instructions to focus on the Brits."

Angus nodded to no one in particular. The main camera they had watching the Brits was showing them approaching Haddington up the A1. The secondary force of Brits was moving up the A68 but were way behind due to Angus' men shelling them and hundreds of IEDs along the highway. Pretty much everything south of Edinburgh had been shut down because of the fight.

David commented, "They're getting close to Haddington. I'm getting messages stating that the Brits are amassing more forces in northern England."

"Any idea on numbers?" Angus asked.

"It's huge. Likely to be their main force."

"Do we have men to take out the roads into England after they pass?"

"Yep." David then gestured towards something before saying, "The Brits are almost to our men. It's about to get ugly."

Angus nodded as he watched the camera panning over the British military moving up A1. It was a pretty large group of armoured vehicles. He had spotted helicopters earlier. Without the satellites, at least the British airpower was unable to be implemented with a strong effect. With the Russians at war with Ukraine, the American satellite system was distracted somewhat, but he heard rumours from their Chinese friends that the Brits were still getting some help. The anti-aircraft weapons that his men had stolen from British garrisons were destroyed. Angus knew it would happen, so he had his men leave it all unmanned. The camera split into a multi-camera system as the Brits got closer to Haddington.

"Check up on my brother-in-law, Liam. I need him to move out of Edinburgh. My wife will be upset if something happens to him."

"Of course. I'll have him moved to Stirling; he's going to have to fight just like the rest of us."

Angus nodded, but he felt there was no need to rush it. As he watched intently, the battle was engaged by his men. The Brits must have expected it because they immediately returned fire. He was shocked when, in a matter of minutes, several jets flew overhead and launched bombs into the Scottish lines. It was not going well at all. As Angus watched, it was clear that if his men stayed firing their weapons at the Brits, they would get wiped out by the jets flying overhead.

Right as he thought that, he heard David order, "Tell the men to withdraw."

Speaking aloud, Angus stated, "If they're gonna use bombers, then we'll use IEDs in their lands. Bombs aren't targeted, and I guarantee they've killed innocent Scots."

David replied, "Let me finish having our men withdraw. The Brits are going to take Edinburgh today. I need you to pack up right now and head off to Stirling."

"I'm heading out." Angus firmly stated before he quickly shut down his laptop and packed it.

Looking at the guards around him, Angus said, "Please take me to our first base in Stirling."

"Yes sir." Lieutenant Napier said before he gestured for his men to move out.

Angus followed closely behind the Lieutenant as they marched out of the living room, where he was sitting, and then got into the van designated for him. They immediately rolled out, driving north. It was about an hour away, and Angus imagined it was going to be a long hour. His phone rang.

Answering his cell phone, he said, “Yes?”

David’s voice came through, “We’ve pulled our men back, and I’ve already started to execute our hit and run attacks both along the road to Edinburgh, but also attacks within Edinburgh. We’re gonna make ‘em pay for taking it.”

“Good. And my request?”

“I’ve put out the order. The question is, do we strike at military targets or is anything game?”

Angus sat thoughtfully, thinking about it. He did not want to kill children or innocent women, but they needed to send a strong message.

Deciding to be the bold leader, he stated, “Military and government only.”

“I’ll put out the order.” David responded before announcing, “For Scotland.”

“For Scotland.” Angus replied before hanging up the phone.

Angus then called Michael.

“Hello, Mr. President.”

“Michael. I want you to release a statement.”

After a brief pause, Michael asked, “What do you want it to say?”

“Decry the British attack and taking of Edinburgh. Announce that we will use any tactics needed to defend ourselves. State that this attack will be responded to in measure on British targets within England itself.”

“So, the war begins in earnest?”

“Yes.”

“I’ll take care of it. Keep yourself safe.”

“Thank you. I’ll keep in touch.”

Angus hung up and looked out onto the highway. The road was quite busy, and it was clear that many of the people around Edinburgh decided to flee the upcoming war zone that was going to be the city. He was sad thinking about all his fellow Scots who were about to die in the battle for their freedom. All the polling and media about Angus’ movement were generally negative. He suspected that plenty of Scots in the city would help the Brits. It was something that greatly disappointed Angus, but he expected it since the Scots have been under decades of Marxist brainwashing in their media. It would take a while for the Scots to be free of it and embrace their God-given right to be free men. His mind continued to wander, thinking about the upcoming fight, when his phone buzzed. He got a text message. It was Isla Grace asking him if he was safe. He replied that he was fine, and she expressed her relief. Once their communication ended, they finally made it to the safe house in Stirling. Angus followed closely behind his men and into the small single-family home that was just outside Stirling in a wooded area. It allowed a good amount of much-needed privacy since the last thing that he needed was someone telling the Brits where he was. Once he got inside, he set up his laptop again. He could hear the guards rustling around in the house, and before long, they brought him some food. It was just a heated meal, but Angus was glad for anything. He was so busy today that he barely had a chance to eat anything. Once he finished, he logged back on with David.

David spoke immediately, "The Brits are almost to Edinburgh, but we've really slowed them down. Soon they'll be in the capital. They took Glasgow easily, but they're in for a big surprise because we purposely wanted them to feel safe."

"What's the plan there?" Angus asked.

"I had the men stockpile a lot of the Chinese explosives in a few safehouses in Edinburgh. We'll be using them to hammer the Brits hard in Glasgow." David answered.

"And in Edinburgh?"

"Something different. More hit and run strikes, sniper hits, and the occasional IED."

"The other thing?"

David's facial expression went serious before he answered, "We've got men moving into position. I want to hit London with the first ones and then shift north to other major cities."

"What do you think the response will be?"

Giving a nod, David answered, "At first, they'll be mad at us, likely even more willing to fight."

Angus interjected, "Well, I think maybe if we keep at it, that'll break the spirit of the Brits so we can get our freedom."

"That's the plan. Do you need anything else?"

"No. Message me if you need something." Angus replied.

"I will." David stated before disconnecting.

Wanting to know what the response was to the battle, Angus looked online. There were a lot of happy responses to seeing the Brits take both Glasgow and Edinburgh. He imagined they would not be so happy once the Scottish attacks started in earnest. He was quite surprised to find out that a small handful of "progressive" types in America were rooting for the Scottish. More nonsense about colonialism and white supremacy from the British. It made Angus chuckle because he felt these people, who were mostly blacks and Hispanics in America, would not be so happy once Angus' men won. The rules the Scots planned to execute could only be described as far right, so much so that it would turn Scotland into the first real far-right nation in a long time. The wacko liberals in Europe had dominated for so long that liberal nonsense was the norm throughout Europe and other major Western nations. Angus was ambivalent to it all until his sister died. Since then, he has been aggressively moving further and further right. With nothing much else to do, Angus sent out messages to Isla Grace to let her know how things were going. It was going to be a long slog from here out.

# Chapter 39

9 May 2023

The BBC news report Angus was watching made him grimace slightly. His men had succeeded in bombing Westminster, London City Hall, and the Lancaster House. The Westminster bombing was very minor, but his men decimated the Lancaster House entirely. Angus made sure to give instructions to everyone involved that they had to hit and run while targeting government buildings only, especially on slow days, to limit casualties. He wanted damage more than death. Even with this plan, the Lancaster House casualties were significant. From the news report, it sounds as though about ninety people died. Angus had to harden himself; this was going to be a messy war. David sent a message that all their men had made it out of London and were headed north. The goal was to get these men north across the border through the wilderness between the two nations. The Brits had locked up every road between them, so there was no way his men could get across normally. It made things a little tricky, but at least it tied up a lot of British troops because there were so many roads between the two countries that the Brits needed thousands of troops to manage the border. Angus was still in Stirling and hiding in the same house he was in a few days ago. Tomorrow, they will move to another place a bit further out of town to keep their location mobile and a secret. His phone buzzed. Looking at his phone, Angus saw it was Michael calling him.

As soon as he answered, Michael said, “That’s going to be hard to justify.”

Giving a nod to no one, Angus replied, “We warned them that invading Scotland had repercussions.”

“That’s a lot of non-combatants that we just killed.”

“And? Three days ago, when they bombed our men in Haddington, they killed thirty civilians. It's war, and they declared it by invading Scotland.”

“I understand.”

"Also remember, we haven't signed the Geneva Convention, so we don't have to follow up their made-up rules."

There was a brief pause before Michael asked, "Do you plan on using chemicals or one of those British nukes you stole?"

"No. I'm not going to purposely attack civilian targets."

"Angus, would you like to tell them yourself? I could arrange an interview for you if you want."

Thinking for a moment, Angus decided to go for it, so he answered, "Yes. Pick Sky News this time."

"I'll let you know in the next hour, I'm sure they'd leap at a chance to interview you."

"Alright." Angus said before hanging up his phone.

He looked back at the news report on the BBC. Suddenly, there was a break in the story with a report about a bombing in Birmingham. Angus grinned. The goal of these attacks was to soften the will of the British people so that the government was forced to let the Scots free. It was a bit over an hour before his computer beeped. It was the TEAMS software letting Angus know that he had a call. It was likely the Sky News people for his interview. The security procedures Angus had gone through on his computer to mask his location were strong. Masking his IP while making it bounce around the world was all part of the trick. If someone were to successfully track him, it would show that he was in a small, abandoned house outside Dalwhinnie, up north of him.

He answered the call and said, "Hello."

The person on the other end of the call was a woman with dark brown hair wearing a light brown business suit. Behind her, he could not see much else. Likely, the whole call would be him looking at whoever was interviewing him while he responded. Angus planned to keep the call short and directly state the reasons his men attacked England.

In an Australian accent, she responded, "Good morning Mr. Bruce."

Angus corrected her, "President."

"Yes, sorry Mr. President. Please wait a little bit, and we'll have you on with Mr. Kenny."

Angus nodded. He purposely chose Chris Kenny because the man seemed to be more even in his approach and was clearly conservative. Granted, Australian conservatives were very liberal compared to Angus, but they would work for this. His camera view shifted to a front-facing view of Chris Kenny. The man interviewing

Angus was probably in his late 40's with a balding head and a white beard. He was wearing glasses and a nicely fitted blue suit. There was no exchange of pleasantries as he was talking clearly to his audience, as he briefly described the history of the conflict between Scotland and the Brits since Angus and his men took down the SNP. After that, the man introduced Angus before turning slightly to look directly at the camera that was facing Angus.

"Good morning Mr. President. The people of the world have a lot of questions, starting with the recent terror attacks that happened in London and Birmingham."

"Good morning, Chris. Go ahead and ask away."

"Why did your men commit terror attacks? The death toll is over eighty people who were non-combatants." He asked.

"I'd like to start by stating that the British are the ones who initiated the fight with us after we declared our independence. Everything we've done has been a response, and I was very clear that we would do anything that we had to do to defend ourselves, to include these attacks."

"What about all the innocent people killed in your attacks?

Angus replied, "What about the innocent Scots killed during an air raid bombing three days ago. I don't hear anyone crying for them."

The man did not say anything, so Angus continued, "All of this could end tomorrow if the Brits simply acknowledge our independence and withdraw from Scottish lands."

"I doubt they will. Do you regret the civilian casualties, and will these types of attacks continue?"

"It's unfortunate, but sadly, I've got no choice but to continue using any method available to me. The sooner the British leave Scotland, the sooner all of this will be over."

"It seems outrageous to me that you'd willingly and openly act as a terrorist."

Angus chuckled before stating, "A terrorist is someone who uses unlawful violence for a political aim. As the President of Scotland, I am fully authorised to use violence in defence of the nation. As the right of any world leader to defend their nation. Thus, it is not unlawful. I will not sit here and claim striking government or military buildings in England is ideal, but we've got to do what we must to repel the British invaders."

Chris replied to Angus, "It's a violation of the Geneva Convention."

Angus laughed heartily. This was a comment he expected and was hoping it would be brought up. He thought long and hard about how to answer it.

Once he stopped laughing, Angus smartly replied, "It sure is convenient to have these made-up rules of war that favour the mechanizations of massive and horribly corrupt governments. These rules also conveniently ensure that the powers in charge stay in charge. The Scottish people never signed any agreement and reject it as some sort of rule we must follow."

Angus' response clearly stunned the anchor because he paused in place for an unusually long moment before finally asking, "And what about innocent people or historical buildings?"

"Like anyone gives a shit about historical buildings or innocent people. On January 27th, the St. Mark's church in north-west London burned down, and we all know the Muslim invaders brought in by our so-called leaders did it. Thousands of British women and girls are violated, and people are murdered and assaulted. All because of so called immigrants brought in by UK leaders. So don't 'what about' me when it comes to innocents or historical buildings. The British don't give a shite about anything but control. We Scots will continue to fight back in whatever way I see fit to get the Brits to finally leave Scotland to the Scots."

"And what of the proposal to have you declared a war criminal?"

Once again, Angus laughed. The media were anything but predictable.

"Again, it sure is convenient to label anyone fighting against a major world power as a war criminal. Am I really as bad as Barack Obama of the United States, who killed about 3,800 people with drone attacks? How many of those people were innocent? What about Anwar Al-Aulai? A teenage American citizen was murdered by a drone for no reason whatsoever. What about George W. Bush of the United States, who murdered hundreds of thousands of innocent Iraqis, plus over four thousand of his own men killed fighting a fraudulent war over weapons of mass destruction that never existed? A war, I'll point out, that the British government supported. The moral grandstanding of the world powers while they constantly violate their own made-up laws when it's convenient for them is sickening and hypocritical. The rest of the world is tired of the shite. It is my right as the leader of Scotland, an established area of land with its own distinct people for at least six thousand years, to reject the dominance of another nation and rule ourselves."

His long, thought-out diatribe was more effective than he expected, as once he finished, the Australian broadcaster had nothing to say.

Angus took a moment to ask, "Do you have anything else to ask me?"

The man recovered and immediately answered, "Yes. I know that you have denied it before, but I need to ask if you have received any assistance from the Chinese."

Angus had gotten used to puking out this lie, so he quickly responded, "Outside of their kindness in recognizing the Scottish nation, we have not received any assistance. I suspect they're quite pleased just watching the British government struggle to deal with us, which might just be enough for them. I also would suspect that they're right now taking a significant amount of glee hearing me having a go at the Americans a few moments ago."

The reporter must have fully recovered because he continued by asking, "What about the rumours of Chinese forces in Scotland fighting against the British right now?"

It was another question Angus had prepared for, so he answered smoothly, "Sadly, we don't have control of our borders due to an invasion of a foreign force, so if there were Chinese forces in Scotland, I'd have no ability to prove or disprove their existence. I personally don't know of any nor have I seen any Chinese within our borders since I ordered the expulsion of all non-Scots from Scotland."

The reporter nodded at Angus before looking down at his notes and then asking, "There have been some questions about some of the laws you're proposing for Scotland if you win."

"Such as?"

"Everything around homosexuality and transgenderism, for example."

Angus gave his beard a gentle tug before he responded, "I've been clear on both. Homosexuality won't be banned for any reason; it just will be banned as something to be publicly supported. No more idiotic pride parades or pushing it in schools. People can mess about with who they want in private. As far as transgenderism, we reject it outright as anything but a mental illness. We'll make it a health priority to find a mental health solution for it that doesn't include people cutting off body parts. A man can't be a woman through any means any more than he can be a rabbit. It's a mental illness."

"Much of the world rejects that."

"Scotsmen don't base their beliefs on the public opinions of leftist twats in France, Australia, or anywhere else in the world."

The reporter in front of Angus chuckled lightly. He must have appreciated Angus' firm rejection of leftist beliefs.

The reporter then asked, "How long will you and your men fight the U.K.?"

Giving the most serious look that Angus could muster, he replied, "Until every last one of us is dead."

There was a minor pause before Angus saw in the corner of his eyes one of his guards gesturing at him, a sign that he was being called for something more important.

Angus turned back to the reporter and stated, "I'm afraid I must go. The defence of Scotland calls. Thank you for your time."

The man replied, "Thank you for your time, Mr. President."

Angus nodded at him and then ended the call. The guard apologised to him and pointed at Angus' cell phone. It was a call from Isla Grace. He had not told her about the interview but the opportunity to speak with her was so limited that he was happy to speak to her about boring household things.

# Chapter 40

16 July 2023

Angus paced in his small room while the speakers blared out reports about the action in the field. It took the Brits several months to finally settle their control over Edinburgh and Glasgow. His men made them pay dearly with plenty of hit-and-run attacks on the Brits in those cities, but also with random but limited terror attacks in Britain. He was confident that the will of the British people was slowly beginning to sap. The modern Brit had been weakened spiritually by the leftist infection in the West. If this were the World War 2 Brit that Angus and his men were fighting, he doubted they would quit. Modern Brits were a sorry shell of what they once were. The only possible exception was probably the ones serving in the military that Angus and his men were fighting against. Angus would be happy to see Scotland restored and the modern Scot reinvigorated with Scottish pride. He was nervous as the Brits had finally decided to make their move northward. British troops had begun moving out of Edinburgh and Glasgow. It looked like a pincer manoeuvre by the Brits to capture the historically significant city of Falkirk. It was also a trap set by David. He had masked as though there was a large grouping of the Scottish forces located in Falkirk. A video call chimed on Angus' computer, so he bent over to answer it. The screen displayed David.

"Good morning Mr. President." David said through the screen.

"Morning. How are things going?" Angus replied.

David nodded at him before stating, "Right to business. We've got a large formation of units in Falkirk for the American satellites to capture. Once the British started moving, we shifted our forces to make it look like we're preparing to hold pat in Falkirk. Once they get close enough that they're committed to the attack, we're going to withdraw and then shift around them and hit the Glasgow forces alone."

“Wouldn’t that give the Brits coming from Edinburgh, Falkirk?”

“Yes, but only for a moment. Once the Brits coming from Glasgow withdraw, we’ll turn back around and hammer the other men. They split their forces to circle us, but I suspect they aren’t expecting us to just surrender Falkirk without a fight.”

“What if the Glasgow forces see you coming?”

“Well, by the time we shift, they’ll already be committed, but we’ve hidden a few companies in Bonnybridge along the highway they’ll have to travel along to hit them lightly from behind and cause chaos when our forces strike them from the front.”

“What’s our current force size?” Angus asked.

“A bit under 20,000. We lost a few thousand men, and maybe triple that are injured.”

“Recruiting?”

“It’s stagnated. We get small boosts when we win a battle and draw flat when we lose.”

Angus nodded. It would take something huge to get the average Scotsman to finally act.

“I’ve also prepared a secondary attack on the border. The Brits have several control points located on the M6, A1, A7, and A68. They control everything going in and out of Scotland there. We’re going to have small strike forces hit them any moment now.”

Angus nodded. Sowing a little discord in the Brit ranks.

He then asked, “And how is the support from our benefactors?”

David chuckled before answering, “We’ve had to use submarines to sneak supplies now that the Brits have finally encircled the entire country to blockade us in. Thankfully, we had a huge supply beforehand, and I’ve tried to ration our supplies to ensure we don’t run out. Plus, we have all the gear we acquired from the British bases in Scotland.”

“Sounds good. I need to call Michael; I’ll call you back in a bit.”

“Understood.” David replied before Angus ended the call.

Angus selected Michael’s number and dialled it. It rang for a few moments before Michael’s face appeared.

“Good morning Mr. President.”

“Good morning. I was wondering if we’ve had contact with any other nations about possible assistance.”

"I must be honest with you Mr. President. We've mostly had only contact with the most unsavoury of nations. Russia, Belarus, Cuba, and North Korea aren't exactly the sorts we really want to associate with."

"I understand Michael. Sadly, the whole of the West has been captured by evil. They're rejecting us outright, so we need to find any allies we can, anywhere we can."

Michael nodded with a very grim look on his face before stating, "I understand."

There was an awkward moment of silence before Michael chuckled and then commented, "The Irish contacted us."

Angus was stunned, and it took him a moment before he responded, "The Irish?"

"They hate the fucking Brits so much they haven't committed to anything, but they're hinting that they might be willing to recognise us if we can do something big."

"Like this battle?"

"Possibly, but no guarantees."

Nodding at his computer screen, Angus stated, "Makes sense. We're about to hopefully succeed in a big way. I must go catch up on that. Thank you for the call."

"Of course, Mr. President. Hopefully, we can win the day... for Scotland."

"For Scotland." Angus replied as he disconnected the call.

Angus finally felt his nerves calm enough to sit down. He sat down in his chair and scanned the various cameras hidden to keep an eye on the roads. The Brits were still just barely leaving Edinburgh. The ones in Glasgow had clearly left some time ago. Centred on his program is an electronic map of Scotland with dots showing the positions of the military forces. After taking a moment, he rang up David. It was a matter of moments before David responded.

"One moment Mr. President." He said, gesturing towards as though he was on another call.

Angus sat quietly as he listened to David communicate with several groups on the ground. He did not want to say anything or distract David at this key moment. Angus felt his stomach drop like he was due to take a test or something crazy. It was very frustrating at times being in his position because most of what he did was tell others what to do, and then he had to rely on them to do it. Sitting and waiting around, unable to do anything, was very irritating. He understood that while he was the leader of their movement, he was now an important figurehead for it as well. It did not make him feel better to sit around watching a screen most of the time.

After a bit of a wait, David finally returned, "Our men have engaged the border points with a quick strike. Hopefully, that will make the Brits hesitate or even question their current attack."

Angus nodded. He was quite surprised when the Edinburgh forces that finally left for Falkirk seemed to pause after barely making it out of the city. Angus shifted his eyes to the map to see that the dots representing the Brits who left Glasgow did not stop.

David commented, "Its looking perfect. It's nice that luck has finally shifted in our favour. We've taken quite a hit in public with the Brits taking both Edinburgh and Glasgow."

Angus nodded. He could see the men in Falkirk had begun to move. They were on the side roads heading to Bonneybridge. Unlike the Brits, who had proper military vehicles, Angus' men had to use normal cars, lorries, and vans to transport their men. They used it to mask their forces as well. David had them split up, taking the M876 and several other smaller roads to meet up in Bonneybridge.

While watching the map, Angus asked, "What about the Chinese?"

"Some of them are hitting the Brits at the border on A7, and the rest are already in position outside Dennyloanhead. They're going to help hit the Brits coming from Glasgow with an attack from behind."

Angus simply nodded as he watched the dots on the map slowly move. The dots representing his men stopped just a bit north of Bonney Bridge in what he guessed was a car park. It meant that they were setting up the attack. It was going to be the first time the Scots were going to fight in a more traditional style of combat. The Brits were in Cumbernald moving north along the M80. Angus had little doubt that the Brits probably would realise his men were waiting for them in Bonneybridge soon enough. David shifted away from the view of the camera.

David called out, clearly not talking to Angus but his commanders in the field, "The Brits are scrambling some fighters and bombers. Prep anti-aircraft weapons we've got set up."

A voice that Angus did not know responded, "Yes sir."

It was a long, dreadful wait as Angus just sat there. He could not help, and he sure as hell did not want to hinder David's work, so he said nothing.

David yelled out, "Engage!"

Angus watched the dots as the British finally made their way through Bonneybridge and met the main Scottish force. Angus turned on one of the cameras they had placed on some of the signs around Bonneybridge. It was a mess with a lot of smoke and noise. He could not tell one side from the other. Activating more cameras, Angus got bits and pieces of the battle. He spotted British planes flying overhead being shot at by rockets. It was the weapons that the Chinese had smuggled in for them. Angus realised that without the Chinese, this battle would never have happened.

David then said, "Send men on the right flank, the Brits are making their way through the line and onto A803. We can't have them making it to Falkirk."

The dots on the map did not move at all. Angus suspected that they were just a general location identifier and not their exact spot. Angus' view went to the images of the battle on his screen. Some of the cameras had gone dead, likely from damage in the battle. From the working ones, it was still the same mess. He could see his men firing at the Brits, and in the others, he could see some with the Brits fighting back. The Brits were a notoriously well-controlled and strong force, but they must not have expected this attack. Likely since the Scots have never stood and fought since the very first battle between them. Even in the mess that was the videos, Angus could see that his men were winning. Even with the bombing runs, the Scots were winning the fight. He could feel nervousness continuing to wrack through him as the fight continued.

David spoke, finally speaking to Angus, "Mr. President, things are going well. I think we've won the day. The Brits have started to withdraw."

"Congratulations." Angus stated.

"Sorry Mr. President, but our day is not complete. One moment."

Angus paused as he listened to David continue, "Withdraw back to Stirling. We've got to hold there in case the Brits from Edinburgh push through."

Looking back at the map, he saw the dots representing the Brits from Glasgow withdrawing back to the city. On the camera, he saw his men begin loading up in their vehicles and started driving rapidly north. The dots of the Brits that came from Edinburgh suddenly stopped. Angus nervously watched and waited to see if the Brits would decide to try and take Stirling with half their forces or withdraw. It seemed like forever, but finally the dot began to move back towards Edinburgh. Through the computer, Angus could hear the people around David cheer out. Relief washed over Angus.

In a firm voice, Angus heard David state, "Send some men back to Bonneybridge to recover our injured or dead."

"Yes sir." Another voice, someone Angus could not see, replied.

David's face reappeared with a large grin on his face as he stated, "Mr. President, we won."

# Chapter 41

24 July 2023

With the British pulling back to Edinburgh and Glasgow, Angus and his men got a real nice win. It was very relieving to hear that his brother-in-law, Liam, was involved in the battle and came through unscathed. There would be no doubt if something bad happened to Liam; Angus would never hear the end of it. It also would have been heartbreaking. Angus wanted to put him further north and safer, but Liam did not have any of that. He was saddened to hear that there seemed to be no boost in recruiting. Angus was hopeful that maybe a big win would help, but David had informed him in the last week that the numbers had not really moved at all.

Angus sat down in a chair at a conference meeting room in a hotel as he said, "Hello men."

The various men at the meeting responded in kind with various greetings. Angus took a moment to examine the crowd. He saw Michael and probably 5 or 6 of the men in his cabinet.

Once Angus was settled down, Michael spoke, "Mr. President, things are going well, even with the lost ground, but I think that we need to find some way to rally the people. Our recruiting numbers aren't where we need them to be, and unless something major happens, we're gonna run out of men eventually. I'm surprised how much the Brits are willing to put their own men into the grinder."

Angus commented, "A point of pride, no doubt that bloody fool of a King pushing for it."

The men around him nodded. Sure, technically, the King was not in charge, but he was when he needed to be, with his massive influence in the United Kingdom. It must have really burned his chaps to have the Scots rebel.

Michael nodded at him and added, "Very likely. We asked you here because we think that you should have a rally in Stirling to try and rouse our fellow Scots into joining us."

Giving a nod, Angus thought for a moment about it. If they were really struggling with recruiting it might be a good idea to try and burn the coals of the Scottish heart into battle. Michael was right that they had to try something.

As Angus continued to ponder what he would say, Michael interrupted his thoughts, "We had some of our best writers come up with a speech for you. It's not very long but should stir the hearts of our fellow Scots."

Michael slid a few sheets of paper for Angus to review. Picking up the papers, Angus began reading. The speech was neatly written and seemed to try to invoke the previous attempts at independence by the Scots from the Brits. It cited the many times Scots have tried to gain their freedom and really focused on their one-time success. Deciding to change a few words here or there in the written speech, Angus nodded at Micheal. Anything to help the cause for Scotland.

"When and where will we be doing it?"

"Tomorrow evening, after most people get off work." Michael answered.

"Security?" Angus asked.

"We'll have a lot of security on buildings all around the place, including all around you. Only people in this room will know we're going to be there until right before we move in."

Angus nodded. It seemed like a bunch of pretty solid precautions.

"You won't mind if I alter your speech a little bit?" Angus asked.

Michael chuckled, "I'd be surprised if you didn't."

Angus nodded before asking, "Was there anything else?"

"We've got a few little issues here and there, but honestly, it seems like most people in Scotland are just sitting and waiting to see what happens."

"People are a little too soft and timid. Even with their own society rotting around them." Angus stated firmly.

The men around him nodded at Angus. He felt they were all brave men for taking this stance, especially since there was a good chance it could fail.

"For Scotland." Angus said as he stood up.

"For Scotland!" They replied to him.

Turning on his heel, Angus strode out of the room. He was going to head to the rental he was staying at for today. There, he would get his brief from David. There had been little movement on the part of the British over the last few days, and it was quite suspicious. The ride to his temporary lodging was smooth in the daily traffic through Stirling. Angus really wished that he could go home and see his family. He knew that it would put them all at risk, so he could not do it. There was little doubt that the Brits kept a razor-sharp eye on Isla Grace and would use some type of drone or rocket to take him out if they could, even with his wife and kids there. Angus knew all their bluster about being good was all lies; they would murder a whole school filled with children just to get at one person. He shrugged it off as he started up his laptop and listened to David's report. It was clear the Brits were probably planning another push soon, but until they made a move, Angus' men could not really do much. It was sort of calm before the storm. Angus then gave Isla Grace a call, and after talking for a few minutes, he called it a night, after all, tomorrow was going to be a big day.

*****

Angus strolled along confidently through the hallway, heading to Forthbank Performance Sport Centre. There was going to be a game at the Forthbank Stadium, so a crowd was already there to see their teams play some footie. Angus was going to speak to them before the event in the hope of firing up the Scottish people to join their cause. Things were going well overall, but the number of fighting men he had to fight the Brits was starting to wane a lot more than David was comfortable with. If things continued at their current pace, the Scottish Republicans would lose in a year.

A security man approached Angus and instructed, "Wait here Mr. President. We are preparing things for your arrival."

Stopping in place, Angus nodded at the man. A lot of what he did as President was sitting around waiting for things. Nerves hit him a little bit. He memorised the heck out of the speech he was handed, but even still, he was not the best public speaker out there. Angus took a few deep breaths before the security man came back and waved for him to follow. Giving the man a nod, Angus began walking. He remembered holding his shoulders up proudly to try to give an impression of extreme confidence. Back in college, he took a public speaking class, and they went on and on about different tips and tricks. None of them are coming to mind at his moment of need.

The only other time he gave a public speech was at the start of the revolution. His nerves of the moment carried him through it. The man Angus was following led him to a larger group of security. They circled Angus, and the whole group walked through the building and out onto the field of Forthbank Stadium.

One of the security men told him, "Mr. President, there is a microphone in the middle of the field on the small stand for you to speak to the crowd. Please try to keep it short and sweet; we couldn't search everyone in the audience. Thankfully, the Brits chased most of the guns out of the public's hands, so it shouldn't be a problem."

Angus nodded. One of the many platforms he planned to add if they won was to give the people the right to own firearms. Some in his own party were against it, but Angus knew that a monocultural society was a much more peaceful one, especially in Western cultures, before the globalist nonsense, things would be just fine. A fine example of course being Switzerland. It would take a generation or so to get Scots to realise Angus was right, but he knew that saving his homeland from globalism was worth it. As Angus entered the field, there was a very mild cheer at best. He knew that he was not the most popular man in Scotland right now, so he was mildly surprised he was not booed.

Picking up the microphone, Angus cleared his voice and started speaking, "My fellow Scots."

There was a loud noise coming from the sideline where the players were waiting to start their game. Angus was shocked to see about three men burst out of the group of players, and before he could react, all three men began firing handguns at him. His security men began to react, but as Angus shifted to move away, he felt something stab him on his left shoulder, by his neck. It caused Angus to stumble and slightly spin away from the force with which he was hit.

Someone from his security team yelled, "He's been hit!"

Before Angus could say anything, his security team around him buried him with their bodies to protect him. The others formed a circle around him. Angus felt something warm running down the front of his shirt under his bulletproof vest. Somehow, he had dropped the microphone that he was holding, so he took his now free right hand and reached up to touch his shoulder. It felt horrible, and the second his hand touched his shoulder, it dawned on him that one of the shots that had fired at him had struck him next to his neck and shoulder. Angus frowned because it was still bleeding. He pushed his hand against himself to try to stifle the bleeding somewhat.

There were several shots fired, and after a bit of a pause, he heard one of the security men order loudly, "Get the President up and let's get him to safety."

Angus just followed the instructions of his security team as they guided him out of the stadium and quickly through the building before making it to a van. Angus carefully climbed in, and as the door closed, the van sped off. His phone rang. Since he did not want to risk losing too much blood, Angus decided to ignore it. Looking around for a bit, he found one of the many jumpers he would wear sometimes. Releasing his wound for a moment, Angus grabbed the jumper and pushed it as hard as he could into his shoulder. It hurt immensely. As the van raced down the street, he thought back to the whole thing. Normally, Scots did not have access to handguns. Those men were clearly plants, which meant that someone in his own cadre of men had betrayed them. This caused Angus to frown. He was probably lucky that he was only injured. Taking a moment to look out the window, he realised they were taking him to the Stirling Community Hospital. It was probably the closest hospital to the stadium. The van stopped in the ambulance bay, and the door opened.

"Mr. President, follow me. We've got only a short time to get you patched up before we must leave."

Giving the man a nod, Angus got out of the van and followed his security team. His shoulder had gone from intense pain to a throbbing numbness. As they walked in, Angus could see the surprise of the medical staff and the other patients.

One of the security men commanded, "We need a doctor now."

The young woman running the front desk of the Minor Injuries Centre responded, "We've got a list of people who need to be seen."

"This isn't an option miss. The President has been shot in the shoulder and needs care."

Before Angus could say anything, a doctor approached and instructed, "Bring him back, I'll take care of him."

He was happy that the young woman was willing to help. The last thing that Angus needed was a conflict. Angus followed behind the young woman. Two of the security men went with them while the rest seemed to be busy securing the building. The female doctor who took Angus back to get looked at was probably in her mid-forties. She had light brown hair with a few tinges of silver streaked in it. She was wearing a light green blouse, a pair of tan trousers, and, of course, a white jacket.

"Have a seat." She said while pointing at one of the flat beds in a waiting room.

Angus took a seat without saying a word.

She then ordered, "Take that vest off and then your shirt so I can see what I'm dealing with."

Moving slowly, Angus slowly unbuckled the vest he was wearing. It was then he realised that he was also hit in the chest. The vest had saved his life as a slug was still embedded in the front of his vest, right over his heart. The slug fell out as Angus moved to set down the vest. His shoulder was screaming out in pain as he stripped off the long-sleeved black shirt he had been wearing.

The doctor saw the slug fall to the earth and commented, "I guess that answers why you're here."

He nodded at her before finally getting the chance to look at where he was hit. There was a nasty tear as a chunk of his trap was now a bloody mess. The bullet that hit his shoulder ripped through him.

The doctor took a moment to examine his injury before saying, "I need to get some supplies. I'll be right back."

"Okay."

Once she had left, Angus took a moment to realise just how lucky he was. He should be dead, but somehow, he was only slightly injured. He took another look at the slug on the ground. That bullet should have killed him. Angus slid off the bed he was sitting on and took a knee in prayer. He decided to thank God for protecting him, so he began the prayer of thanks. He did not see the doctor re-enter the room, but he heard her midway through his prayer.

He continued praying, and once he was done, he softly said, "Amen."

Standing back up, Angus took another seat on the bed. The doctor examined his wound again before she began cleaning it and finally attempted to stitch it up.

Once she was done, she handed him a packet filled with some pills before saying, "Here are some antibiotics. Take one a day for a few days, and you should be fine."

"God bless you." He told her.

The security man who was with him said, "Mr. President, we need to leave."

# Chapter 42

It was not until he got out into the main lobby of the Minor Care Centre that Angus realised why the security team was so on edge. Outside the building, there was thick smoke that was clearly from a smoke grenade of some kind because it was a very clean white colour.

"Out the back door." One security man ordered.

Angus followed him as they hurriedly moved through the building, trying to find somewhere to go to escape. The damned Brits clearly planned this whole thing out. He could hear some shots being fired, likely the remainder of his security team fighting off the Brits. This was a very unfortunate place for combat to take place, and ironically, proved Angus right. The Brits would kill innocents in a hospital to kill an already injured man they tried to assassinate. They made their way through the building but found the other exit already blocked off.

The security man frowned before saying, "I guess we're surrounded. Might as well head back and fight."

Angus nodded grimly. It was not good, and maybe his end was finally coming. Hopefully, the movement would continue without him if this were the case.

He looked at the security man and asked, "Got an extra weapon? I left mine in the car."

The man pulled out a smaller handgun and passed it to Angus. Taking a moment to examine the handgun, Angus noted it was a 9-millimetre Browning. Not his favourite, but it would work. The two security men and Angus jogged quickly back through the building and into the medical entrance area. He could still hear weapons fire outside, but it seemed like it was a lot less than it had been before.

"Wait here Mr. President, we'll try to clear a way to the car."

The two men hefted their rifles and led the way. Angus was supposed to wait, but at this point, he felt it was probably pointless, so he paused for a moment before following the men out. The heavy smoke was still there, but it was much thinner. He scurried to the front of his van and took a moment to examine what was going on. Several vans were part of his convoy, lined up with dozens of bullet holes. One had even somehow caught fire. Most of his security team was dead, but he spotted plenty of heavily armed and dead British soldiers lying on the earth. The two men who were with him had moved to the corner of the building and were firing their weapons. Angus decided to flank around the cars and try to provide extra fire. He slid to the side of his car and opened the door. His personal handgun, which he named after his sister, was sitting holstered, so he grabbed the shoulder-worn holster and slipped it on. It had a few extra magazines just in case Angus needed them. He decided to use the Browning first before trading over to his own weapon. His security men were still firing their weapons around the corner of the building. Angus spotted a few homes across the road from where he was. He was thankful that they were behind a huge, tall brick wall that protected the homes. It was time to move, so he jetted around the car and then sprinted towards the next van in line. Down the spot meant for ambulances, he was able to spot the vehicles of the Brits who had attacked them. They were using armoured vehicles of some kind. His flanking strategy might work if he could slip around the vans and along the tall brick wall. As he moved, he raised the Browning and fired it towards the Brits. It was still so smoky that he could not see if he even came close to hitting something. Angus dashed along the wall. He was thankful for the Brits using so much smoke, as he was well hidden as he ran.

The voices of one of his security men yelled out, “I’m hit.”

“I’ve got you.” The other man yelled out.

A few more rounds were fired between the two sides. Whatever happened, it was clear that the numbers on both sides had been severely cut down. Angus stopped running as he finally made it to the back of the group of British vehicles. The smoke was still there, but it continued to thin out. He could now easily see that the Brits were all dead. He could no longer see his own men.

Since they had won the fight and he would hate to have them shoot him, Angus yelled out, “Thistle!”

Thistle was the code word meant to let their side know to cease fire. Stopping with his weapon raised, Angus moved from vehicle to vehicle, looking for anyone still fighting. There was no more shooting. As he moved, he heard an unusually low moan. Someone nearby was alive and in pain. Started looking at the bodies of the Brits until he came to the man who was still alive. He was slumped sideways initially with his back facing Angus. Raising his weapon, Angus slowly turned the man over; he was clenching both of his hands to his abdomen.

"Don't shoot me." The man called out in a panic before continuing, "I'm already dying."

Angus examined the man's hands, and he had been shot in the stomach and was bleeding. He was wearing the full battle gear of a British soldier, so all Angus could see was his face. His skin was very pale, like due to shock. He had green eyes and several days' worth of blonde stubble poking out through the chinstrap of his helmet.

The man looked briefly stunned as he looked at Angus before saying, "Its you."

"Yes. You were sent here to kill me." Angus told the man angrily as he raised his Browning at the man.

"Please don't kill me. I'm sorry. I was just following orders." The man stammered out.

Angus was about to get angrier, but the man continued, "Please. I've got two small children. I just wanna go home to them. Help me, please."

Realising that he was not a cold-blooded killer, Angus sighed and then tossed aside the weapon before kneeling to look at the man's injuries. It was still bleeding, and Angus had no idea what to do.

The man must have realised it because he instructed Angus, "Go to that man over, and you'll see a pouch with a red cross on it. In that, look for something called 'Celox' and bring it over here."

Angus moved quickly to the pouch in question, and after a bit of searching, he saw a green plastic pouch with yellow writing that said the name in question. He brought it over to the injured man.

"That's it. Help me get this crap off and then pour it on the wound."

Angus nodded before setting the pouch down and stripping open the front of the man's vest and shirt. He brought the pouch over to the open wound and ripped it open as he began pouring the powder on the man's injury. It started to bubble and fizzle loudly. The man grunted heavily in pain. After the fizzling stopped, the wound looked nasty, but it was not bleeding anymore.

The man stated, "I've lost a lot of blood, I don't think I can stand."

Angus grunted. It made sense to try to drag this man to the hospital entrance; maybe someone there will be able to help. He clenched his teeth and hooked the back of the man's vest, which was still on him, and started dragging. Since his shoulder was hurt, he was forced to use only his right hand, which made things a bit harder. Slowly but surely, Angus dragged the man single-handedly to the entrance. As he finally made it around the corner, he was quite surprised to be met by a squad of his own men, being led by Liam!

Liam excitedly called out, "Angus! Christ, man, we were so worried about you."

Running up to him, Liam gave Angus a big hug. Angus let go of the Brit he was dragging and hugged Liam back. He had not seen his brother-in-law in some time, so he was happy to see him.

While still hugging him, Liam asked, "What the hell happened to you? I heard you got shot. Bastards tried to assassinate you."

"Was about to give a speech, and a few Brits ambushed me at Forthbank and then again here. I'm fine, the docs here bandaged me up."

"Why are you dragging this cunt?" Liam asked when he let Angus go.

"I found him injured and brought him here to get medical aid."

"Fuck this cunt, I should put a bullet into him here and now."

The British soldier shifted weakly away and put his hands up to try to protect himself.

"No Liam. I didn't save his life just for you to kill him. Take him to get medical care and then have someone take him back to the border."

Liam frowned before asking, "What's gonna keep this cunt from recovering and then coming back for more?"

The man called out, "I swear, I'm done with Scotland. I'll never return. I just want to go see my children."

Scoffing loudly, Liam commented, "The bastard probably doesn't even have children."

"I do." The man interjected before continuing, "I've got a girl named Leslie who is four and a boy named Paul who is almost two."

"Its fine." Angus interrupted their mild argument before saying, "Liam, I'm ordering you to take him to get medical care and shipped back to the Brits. Also, have the lads check up on our men and clean up this mess. Call for someone to take me to the hideout."

Liam's face shifted to the direct order before saying, "Yes Mr. President."

The Brit then said softly, "Thank you."

Angus nodded at him.

Liam started barking orders before another group of vans arrived, holding a new team of men to take Angus to the next hideout, this time a little further north in Dunblane. Angus pulled out his phone to finally make a few calls once he sat down in the van, only to discover that his phone was damaged in the fight somehow. He sighed heavily since he would have to wait for a new phone once he got to Dunblane. Isla Grace was not going to be happy to hear about all that happened.

# Chapter 43

9 August 2023

It had been a fortnight after he was shot, and Angus had to deal with Isla Grace on the phone regularly, making sure he was not doing anything unwise or unsafe. He tried his best to explain to her that sometimes risks were involved in this, but she was not having it. Once Angus finished another of his very lengthy calls with Isla Grace, he started to call David for an update. Right as he started the call, he got a notification for communication from David online.

As soon as he answered the call, David started speaking by asking, “How’s the shoulder?”

“It’s fine.”

Angus’ shoulder still hurts quite a bit. It was now bandaged and wrapped tightly with a strap to hold his arm in place. It was very uncomfortable to deal with, but he was happy to just have a sore shoulder that the doctors said he would recover from, instead of being in a much worse condition.

Angus chuckled before asking, “Status update?”

Sighing heavily, David responded, “The Brits clearly knew what was going to happen because they did a quick movement before we could prepare from Edinburgh to Stirling.”

Frowning, Angus asked, “So we lost Stirling?”

“Yes. I’ve already put together a plan to take back Stirling tomorrow. I figure they might not expect a large counter-offensive.”

“Sounds good.”

“We assume if we hit them real early and quickly, we might be able to surprise them instead of waiting to build up a force to hit them.”

Angus asked, “Do we have enough men to do that?”

David answered, “Yes, we do, but our recruiting has stagnated, so we can’t get involved with too many big conflicts.”

“Why retake Stirling?”

“The idea is that we need a big win, and we need to keep the Brits on their toes. It’s been a while since the last time we fought them directly. Also, it makes sense to hit them occasionally, so they don't get too comfortable."

Angus nodded. It made sense. He was getting tired of sitting around doing nothing, so he planned to go and see this battle up close and personal. Knowing that David would try to stop him, Angus decided not to say anything about his newly formed plans.

"About what time were you planning this attack?"

Shrugging, David answered, "Not sure yet, but it has to be unconventional. Militaries expect an early morning or late-night attack, so I'm thinking mid-day, maybe right before lunch."

Without giving anything away, Angus just nodded. He pulled up the information on their secured serve and identified where the command station would be for the attack.

Before Angus could say anything, David told him, "Thankfully, without their satellites, they've been forced to be much more reactionary to anything significant we do. Most of all our heavy equipment that we stole from the Brits, we've had to hide to be able to use it for this next fight. I suspect we likely have a lot of British spies within our own borders keeping an eye on as much as they can."

"After the battle, where will we put them?"

"We've got random warehouses sprinkled throughout Scotland, up north, but not too far north of Stirling. We mix them into normal traffic, when possible, to hide their movement."

Angus nodded. Even without the satellites, the British still had a major advantage because of their air superiority.

David interrupted his thoughts, "We've got something else interesting that you might want to see."

"Which is?"

A link appeared in their chat to a Twitter video as David answered, "Someone from your past posted a video. The Brits tried to hide it quickly, but since Elon Musk bought Twitter and renamed it to fucking X, the Brits lost a lot of control over the online narrative."

"What is it?"

"Just watch it."

Angus clicked the link, and he saw an image of a blonde-haired man close up, but clearly not wearing a shirt. His abdomen was covered in thick bandaging. Angus took a moment to look at the man, trying to remember who he was. After a few moments, he realised who the man was. It was the British soldier he saved a few weeks ago. Curiosity got the better of him, so he clicked play on the video.

It sat for a moment before the man began to speak, "My name is Benjamin Taylor. I am posted with the 22 SAS Regiment. A fortnight ago, I was assigned to a special mission in Stirling. We were to watch a hospital nearest to a sporting event where others were performing a targeted removal. We were there in case the target was injured and went to the hospital. It was a smart decision because our target, Angus Bruce, is a hard-to-find target. After the attempt, Bruce survived but was injured and made his way to our hospital."

Benjamin's facial expression shifted as he paused for a moment. He looked very stern.

He continued speaking, "We waited until he went into the hospital with the bulk of his security team before we struck. The firefight was rough, with the Scots eventually overwhelming us with surprise numbers. I was one of the last ones shot from our side. We took out their whole side as well, excluding the target. I was shot through my gut and was going to die. I'd accepted my fate when Angus Bruce appeared out of nowhere next to me."

He paused again, waving towards someone behind the camera. Two small children came into view. The man put his arms around each one. The older one of the two was a little girl who looked to be around four years old, and the younger one was a little boy who looked to be around two. They both had blonde hair and looked very much like the man.

The man looked into the camera as he said, "Mr. Bruce, this is my daughter Leslie and my son Paul."

Angus felt a little emotion well up, and his eyes teared a tiny bit. He could have taken away these two small children's father, and one random decision was the hair between that choice and what was in front of him now.

"Go to mum." The man stated before continuing, "Now I come to the point of my video where I'm probably going to get in trouble."

He paused again before his face shifted to a very serious look, "We need to stop. These are our brothers and sisters that we're killing over something that the United Kingdom has done before. India, Fiji, Canada, New Zealand, Australia, and more. All nations that the U.K. let go peacefully. We let Scotland even vote on independence before, but now that they demand it, we fight them?

It's all about pride and ego. We must let Scotland go. I know I will get in trouble for this, but someone has to say it. We need to stop the fighting and just let them go peacefully."

Benjamin paused once again before declaring firmly, "God save the King."

The video ended. Angus pondered it all. He was right about the Scots fighting the English. It was unnecessary on the part of the Brits. They had offered to let the Scots vote for freedom, but now it was different. Angus knew it was the globalists who would never let a truly free country exist outside of their control. He knew that even with Benjamin's inspiring words, he could not stop; Scotland must have its freedom, and he was the one who would have to keep fighting for it.

David's voice cut through the speakers, "It has you in deep thought, eh?"

Angus had forgotten that he was still on the call with David, but he shook Angus out of his own thoughts as he replied, "Yes."

"What shall we do?"

Shaking his head in response, Angus stated, "Keep fighting. The Brits cannot regain Scotland. This isn't about my life or your life but about the freedom of Scotland."

"Agreed. I've got planning to do, I'll talk to you tomorrow."

"Okay." Angus replied.

Once David disconnected, Angus was inspired to record his own video. He pulled out his phone and set it up so he could record while sitting in front of it. He reached out and hit record before setting back into his chair.

"People of Scotland and Britain. I just finished watching the video of Benjamin Taylor and his call for a peaceful settlement. I ask the British leadership to seriously consider his words. We can peacefully end the fighting here and now if the British would just let Scotland be free. I'm afraid that we must continue fighting for our freedom, but we would very much like to stop. I ask not only for myself, or Benjamin, but for all the Leslies and Pauls out there who have lost their fathers or have their fathers at risk. Please reach out to my people and let Scotland go."

Angus paused as Benjamin did before firmly stating, "For Scotland."

# Chapter 44

10 August 2023

Angus was riding along on another caravan headed somewhat south and east to Stirling. He had been staying in various locations further north in cities like Dundee and Perth to avoid the Brits. Today, he was going to join the planned fight in Stirling, the plan being to win a battle and keep the Brits on their toes. After the fight, he knew that he would have to go farther up north to lead the nation, or what was left of it, that they had controlled. Likely, it would be Rosehearthy where he would hunker down for a long period in the future. The Brits had taken control of Edinburgh, Glasgow, and Stirling. At this point, Isla Grace and his children were forced out of their home when the Brits took Stirling. They were now living far up north in Inverness. He did not doubt that they would push further north to Aberdeen and beyond. His phone rang, and Angus looked at his phone to see that it was David calling.

"Hello?" Angus said as he answered the call.

"We're about to start our assault in Stirling." David stated.

"Excellent. What's the plan?

David answered, "We're hitting them from the south with hit and run strikes before striking from the northwest with the bulk of our forces. I've had scouts all over Stirling getting me all their positions. We've limited our small previous attacks from the northeast to give a false impression of our strength."

"Very smart. I'm going to be moving positions, so just text me updates."

"Will do."

Angus hung up the phone. It was a lovely autumn day. Scotland was one of the most beautiful places in the world. It was green and hilly as he looked out the window. He was about an hour or so north of Stirling, so he would arrive right before the attack started. The drive to the location where the headquarters was pleasant. Technically based on control of land, the Scots were losing, but he was pleased with the very heavy toll they were inflicting on the Brits. Just last week, there was a bombing that took out a whole section of British tanks. It was probably a billion or more pounds worth of military equipment. They were going to bleed the Brits until the Brits begged to end this nonsense.

"Mr. President, we're arriving at the security point."

The van began to slow down before coming to a stop. As the van stopped, the driver rolled down the window, facing Angus as one of the guards approached.

He immediately recognised Angus and saluted before saying, "Apologies Mr. President."

The guard waved towards someone to let Angus and his caravan move forward. The window rolled up as Angus returned the salute, and the van began to move. It was only a few minutes before they arrived at their military headquarters. It was on a hill to the northwest of Stirling and across the M9 near the River Forth. Somehow, they managed to hide the headquarters tents in a nicely wooded area. Angus guessed that likely scouts were all around them to give warning if this point was attacked. Once the van stopped, Angus stepped out to several men saluting him.

An officer quickly ran up to him and said, "Mr. President, apologies, we were not told that you would be coming."

"I wanted to see how it was going myself."

"Yes Mr. President, let me take you to Lieutenant General Keith."

Angus nodded as he followed the officer into the largest tent located in the middle of the hidden camp. As soon as Angus stepped into the tent, he was greeted with a huge array of desks with a pair of men on the phone. In the centre of the tent was a large table with a monitor lying flat on it. As he approached it, he could see it was a digital map of Stirling with various light red dots on it. He did not recognise any of the men in the tent except one, Markus Keith.

The officer who brought Angus in announced with a salute, "Sir, President Bruce has come to visit us."

Markus returned the man's salute before saying, "Thank you, Captain."

He dropped the salute and turned to Angus while extending his hand to shake. Angus took his hand.

"Mr. President, we're surprised to see you here, but welcome."

“Thank you, Markus. I wanted to get a closer look at what was going on.”

Markus nodded before he began to brief Angus, “We’ve got our men ready to go, and so far, no one has noticed.”

He reached out and pointed along the northwest edges of Stirling as he continued, “We have men queued up here as our primary force.”

Moving his finger along the east and northeast, he said, “We’ll have men doing light strikes and a few surprises to act as a distraction for the main attack.”

Angus asked, “How long until that starts?”

Markus looked over at one of the officers before nodding at him and then turning back to say, “Now.”

Reaching out with his finger, Markus tapped the screen on a red button before tapping several locations on the map. The monitor flickered briefly before the points Markus clicked opened into camera views. Somehow, Markus was able to get into the camera systems in Stirling and was using them to monitor the fight. In one camera, he spotted some of his men beginning the attack. Sounds of explosions in the distance could be heard from outside their tent.

They stood silently watching for a few moments before Markus pointed towards one of the cameras and stated, “This one’s a problem.”

Angus asked, “What’s wrong?”

“The Brits are holding the point, and if we can’t push them back, it will cause a hole in our line.”

Markus turned to gesture to one of his men and asked, “Major, do we have any reserves or other men available?”

The Major frowned and shook his head, which Markus grunted in response to. Angus looked at the spot where the camera was covering. It was the nearest point of Stirling close to where they were, right south of Stirling Castle by the King’s Knot.

Giving out another grunt, Markus turned to another man and asked him, “Ideas?”

“All we can do is hope the men there hold out while we deal with the rest of the Brits in Stirling.”

“Well, shit, this isn’t good.”

Angus decided immediately that he had the number of men on his security team that would be able to push the battle in their favour, so he turned to Markus and firmly ordered, "I'm bringing my security team to help, let them know we're coming."

Before Markus could respond, Angus' head of security stated firmly, "Mr. President, I was instructed to keep you far away from combat."

Looking at the man, Angus said firmly, "I'm going to help with or without you."

The security man frowned because he knew that Angus was in charge. He just nodded.

Markus finally spoke up, "Mr. President, this is a really bad idea."

"Talk to me again after I'm back." Angus announced firmly before heading out.

He knew this was probably a bad idea, but he knew that they had to win this fight. His men needed a real combat win after all the recent losses. Hit and run strikes are not the same as proper combat. Angus headed out to the vans and hopped in. He could hear his men quickly loading up, and it was not long before they headed off. His head of security must have known where to go. Angus drags out his protective vest and straps it on. He checks Anise and then makes sure he has plenty of ammo.

As soon as they stopped at the location, the head of Angus' security came up and instructed, "Stay close to us and let us lead. I know you've been in a fight before, but we're experts."

Angus just nodded and followed as the man began to bellow out instructions. As they moved forward, Angus pulled Anise out. Almost instantly, they were involved in the fight. Each of Angus' men moved forward, firing as they advanced. After a moment of just following them, Angus decided to start joining the fight. He shifted upwards and peered over a car he had moved behind. In the distance, he spotted several men shooting towards Angus and his men. Angus aimed Annis at them and started firing.

His head of security yelled, "Push forward!"

Angus continued firing Annis as he moved with the security team around him. The Brits must not have expected an additional group attacking because they began to withdraw, with a few of them falling from being hit. Angus was not sure if he was hitting anything, but he was trying. They continued firing more as they moved, but it became clear that the Brits decided to withdraw. Overall, they probably spend only 3 hours working their way into

Stirling on foot, fighting the Brits before the withdrawal. His men had won the day.

# Chapter 45

Angus confidently strolled back with his security and got into the vans they came in. He waited until the whole team loaded and they drove back to the nearby temporary headquarters. Then he entered the main tent where Markus was waiting for him.

Markus extended a hand and then said, “Fine work Mr. President.”

Angus took his hand before nodding.

While they shook hands, Markus continued, “The Brits appear to have withdrawn as far as our scouts can see.”

Giving a grin, Angus told him, “Excellent work, General.”

“We couldn’t have done it without you and your men.”

Angus shrugged, “We didn’t do much. It was your plan and the men. Now that we’ve succeeded here, I’m heading off. Let’s keep my participation a secret?”

Giving a nod, Markus replied, “Yes sir.”

After returning the salute from Markus, Angus headed out of the tent and back into his van. His phone buzzed. It was a message from David, and it said, ‘We took Stirling’. Angus replied with a congratulatory message. Angus sat back and relaxed for a bit, enjoying the lovely weather of a nice autumn evening.

* * * * *

Angus woke the next morning to a swarm of messages and a request for a meeting with Michael. Without Michael, Angus still had no idea how he would have done anything when it came to running their struggling nation. Angus could not wait to finally step down from leadership and go back to his ranch. Once he finished a toilet break, Angus sat down at his laptop and fired up a meeting with Michael. As soon as they connected, Michael began laughing heartily. Deciding to patiently wait and see what was so funny, Angus sat quietly.

After a few more minutes of laughing, Michael finally said, “Things are turning in our favour.”

Rubbing his chin, Angus wondered what he meant. Sure, the win in Stirling was nice, but honestly, he expected the Brits to turn around almost immediately and push back into Stirling.

Michael must have seen his look of confusion because he announced, "The Russians, Poles, Hungarians, and Cubans have all announced a formal recognition of us as the rightful leaders of an independent Scotland."

Giving a large grin, Angus stated, "Wonderful news!"

"Indeed. Once we get a few nations on our side, the numbers will grow."

"Just need to hold out and win more fights."

Giving a slight nod, Michael replied, "Well, the Stirling win was quite a blow since it shows we can win fights and won't simply be rolled over by the Brits."

"Especially since we haven't won much since the start of all this." Angus stated.

"Right. If we can keep pushing them and reach out to more nations for recognition, maybe we'll end up having international pressure put on the Brits."

Giving another pause and a long scratch on his bearded chin, something that was becoming very common for Angus, he finally replied, "I want you to reach out first to the Russians to see if they can give us some aid and then start contacting as many as you can foreign governments as you can to see who else might be willing to recognise our independence."

"Yes Mr. President." Michael replied before pausing and then saying, "For Scotland."

"For Scotland." Angus replied before disconnecting.

A security man entered and announced, "Mr. President, it is time to move out."

Shuffling some paperwork and then turning to the man, Angus stated, "One moment and we'll head out."

After collecting everything they would need, Angus loaded into one of the vans, and they headed north. Last night they stayed in Perth, but tonight the plan was to go much further north for heavier security. It was an order brought on by David, which led Angus to think that he might have heard about the adventure that Angus had in Stirling. Keep him as far away from the front as they could. Tonight, he would be staying at Portlethen, and then he would move to Inverness, where his family was located. It was a pleasant drive along the coast, and before long, they were in Portlethen.

The moment he reconnected his laptop, he received several messages from David that clearly expressed irritation with his actions in Stirling. One message linked several videos from Twitter that showed Angus actively fighting the Brit in Stirling. He had not remembered doing it, but in one of the videos, he directly shot and killed a man who was aiming a rifle at him. Shrugging, Angus figured the mind has odd ways of sometimes suppressing bad things. It was unfortunate that he did it, but Scotland needed him to do whatever it took to gain independence from both the British and the globalists trying to ruin the entire Western society. Finally caving in, Angus replied to the latest message from David with a 'my bad'. David immediately called him through TEAMS.

"Hello." Angus answered coolly.

"I wanna be mad at you, but your stunt in Stirling was apparently critical to our success and now there are dozens of videos of you charging madly into the Brits with your security team."

"I couldn't think of anything else to do when Markus said they were in trouble and had no one else to help reinforce that point."

David announced, "Well, I can't do anything again. From now on, you stay away from the front lines. We can't afford to lose our symbol."

He was probably easily replaceable at this point, so he scoffed.

"Angus, promise me you'll stay the hell away from Edinburgh."

Giving a slight pause, Angus said, "I'll do my best."

Letting out a deep sigh, David responded, "Well, I suppose that's the best I can get. Back to business. With the Brits pulling back, we've decided not to rest on our laurels, and we're pushing hit-and-run attacks in Edinburgh."

"Keep them on their feet."

"Yes. Also, I've gotten word from Michael to expect more aid from the Chinese, and maybe even the Russians might be willing to send a little something, although most of their efforts are still in that Ukrainian mess that they got themselves in."

"It's probably a good thing too, the Americans are spending so much money with the Ukrainians that they are barely lifting a finger to help the Brits. If the Chinese can keep helping, we can probably hold out for a long time." Angus said.

Michael waited for a moment while looking at something before saying, "I must run. We're about to strike Edinburgh. Check in once you make it to Inverness."

"Will do." Angus replied before disconnecting.

After getting up and searching for some food to eat, Angus called Isla Grace and let her know that he would be arriving in Inverness tonight. He was very excited to see his family again. He had not seen her in a while. Angus climbed into his usual van that was in the middle of their caravan, heading north. The drive north was a little over 3 hours. The place that they kept Isla Grace at was not really in Inverness but in a village south of the city called Essich. It was one of those tourist villages around Loch Ness. Angus chuckled. Hiding in a tourist hot spot was a bit of an unusual idea, but it probably would work since no one would expect it. His children dashed excitedly into his arms as he approached the rented cottage where his family was hidden away.

Angus chuckled as Robert excitedly screamed out, "Daddy!"

He grabbed Robert up with his uninjured arm and gave him a spin, which caused Robert to squeal in joy.

After he put Robert down, Isla Grace strolled up and neutrally said, "It is pleasing to see you."

"I missed you too." Angus said sarcastically to her.

Right as he hugged her tightly, his phone buzzed. Angus took a moment to read it before laughing uproariously.

"What is so funny?" She asked.

Saying with a chuckle, Angus answered, "The Irish just recognised our government."

# Chapter 46

14 August 2023

Angus was enjoying the extra time with his family. It had been a few days, and he knew that he would likely have to leave them to go back into hiding, so he could not be easily found. The plan was to take a visit to Rosehearty and then bounce around northern Scotland, far from trouble. For now, he wanted to catch up with Michael and David to see where things were. With two-year old Elizabeth sitting on his lap, he called up Michael first.

Once Michael saw Elizabeth sitting on his lap, he chuckled before saying, "Glad you got some time to catch up with your family."

"Thanks. I really needed it."

"I bet."

"Any updates on contacting other nations?"
Michael's face shifted slightly in what looked like slight disappointment before he stated, "Sadly, the Russians said that they could not offer us anything but recognition. They did, however, convince all their close allies in Belarus, Venezuela, Armenia, and Azerbaijan to recognise us."

"A real who's who of not exactly the best." Angus stated with a sarcastic grin.

"Yes, but we'll take who we can get."

"Tell me about the Irish." Angus asked.

"I contacted them, and the Taoiseach seemed eager to put one over on the Brits."

"Isn't Varadkar a globalist too?"

Michael chuckled, "Maybe. Even the Irish globalists still don't like the Brits."

"What about the Americans?"

Michael shook his head before stating, "They don't even have a leader, just that muppet old man. All attempts to ask for them to insist on our independence have fallen on deaf ears."

There was a bit of a pause between them before Michael announced, "I have a call with the Japanese."

"Japanese?" Angus asked.

"Yes. They've insisted on secrecy, but they want to look into investing in Scotland if we can get our freedom."

Angus grinned evilly. Globalists might have a lot of control over many people, but things like the Irish desire to stick it to the damned Brits and the Japanese always wanting to take advantage of financial opportunities that arise.

"Alright, I'll let you go. Good luck with them." Angus stated as he nodded and then ended the call.

Angus had a few other calls with various issues that needed to be dealt with before David finally called.

"Good morning Mr. President."

"Morning David. How are things going?"

"Unfortunately, we were not able to make much of a dent on the Brits in Edinburgh, and the rumour mill is that they are looking to push forward through Stirling and then up the coast to Aberdeen."

"Anything we can do to slow them down?"

"Well, we've started planning a few surprises, but honestly, we can't risk too many direct conflicts."

Elizabeth rolled off his lap and ran off. He could hear his children making a lot of noise as they played just outside the cabin he was in.

"I'll let you go manage that then. Anything else I should know about?" Angus asked.

"Nothing Mr. President."

"For Scotland." Angus stated before ending the call.

He sat alone, staring at the screen, pondering what his next step should be. The idea that there must be some sort of way to end this war more quickly, without a bunch of people dying, was something he really wished to see. Shrugging because he could not see a way to do that, he stood up. He was probably going to have to leave in a few hours, so he thought that he should spend as much time with Isla Grace and his kids.

He headed out right away, and as soon as he stepped outside, Richard yelled, "Daddy, play tag with us!"

Angus chuckled and started chasing Richard. He did not want to run him down right away, so he let Richard run for a bit before catching him and then turning to run away as his son started to chase him. They played for some time before a very plain-looking Kia pulled up. His security team became very alert as several men approached the car. The car stopped, and the driver's door opened, revealing the man, who was not Deng Li, but it was the only name he knew the Chinese man by. He was the Chinese spy who helped his movement.

Speaking firmly, Angus said, "Let him through."

Deng Li grinned as he passed through his security team and walked up to him.

As he reached his hand out to greet Angus, Deng Li said, "It has been some time, and things are plodding along, aren't they?"

"Plodding is one way to put it."

Deng Li chuckled before commenting, "Well, we've seen some ups and downs, but you're making progress."

Angus nodded before realising that the only times he had ever seen Deng Li were when he had some important information to share with Angus.

"Yes, I have something important to share."

He wondered if his face was that easy to read. Deciding to be patient, he just nodded.

"I'm sure that you heard that the British plan to retaliate for your recent victory in Stirling."

Angus just gave a slight nod.

"It's much worse than you realise. The British have been building an overwhelming force in Glasgow since your men have not been fighting much there."

Reaching up to scratch his chin, Angus frowned. They had not been fighting much along the western parts of Scotland due to manpower issues.

"They will be leaving both Glasgow and Edinburgh tomorrow, with the bulk of their forces in Glasgow. We're talking about the bulk of everything, reserves included. They plan to meet in Stirling and then steamroll north."

Thoughts about the potential response to this news rolled through his head. Angus had some serious concerns because this push could end their movement a lot earlier than they had hoped.

"I'll leave you with your thoughts." Deng Li stated before he gave Angus another handshake and left.

"That is not good news." Isla Grace said with her normal monotone voice.

"Yes, but I think we might be able to do something with it."

"What did you have in mind?"

"Not sure yet, but we need to take a look at a map."

Turning away, Angus jogged back into the cabin and pulled up Google Maps. He examined Glasgow to see what possibilities there were. Glasgow was only about 40 minutes from Stirling. The only real way up from Glasgow to Stirling was through the M80 because of the size of the military vehicles the Brits would be moving. Edinburgh had a few options, and he suspected that if the Brits wanted to take Stirling, they would approach from both the south and the east, which would bring the Brits north from Edinburgh on M90 and then east on A91. As he looked at Stirling, he saw a name that made him smile and gave him an idea to finally put this whole damned war to an end. Bannockburn.

# Chapter 47

15 August 2023

Angus eagerly logged off his computer after sharing the news with both David and Michael. He had come up with his own plan, and both were very upset with it. Angus wanted to finally end this war and do it without hurting anyone. He ordered both men to put out the word. They were going to bring everyone willing to meet him to the fields of Bannockburn. It was time to finally force the Brits to withdraw, and if his plan worked how he thought it would, this would do the trick.

As soon as Angus stood up, Isla Grace announced, "We are going too."

He frowned. It was one thing to risk himself, but he had no intention of risking his family, too.

"I don't think that is smart."

"Either we all participate, or it will fail."

While generally Isla Grace would follow whatever Angus wanted, he could sense that this would be one of the cases where her stubborn Scottish pride would not let her bend in this case.

He knew that the whole thing he had planned was a big risk, but he doubted he could talk her out of it, so he just gave a big sigh.

Isla Grace gave a slight nod before declaring, "We had better get going, it is a long drive to Stirling."

* * * * *

16 August 2023

Nerves built up deep in Angus' soul like they had not likely done since the first day of this fight. It was one thing to initially stand up and shoot Sturgeon but now instead of just himself it was also his family and what so far had been around one hundred thousand unarmed Scots who had joined them just south of

Bannockburn House where M80 merged into the M9 and it would be the spot where the Brits coming from Glasgow would have to go through to move into Stirling. When they arrived late last night, he was surprised by the raw numbers of Scots who showed up and, in the morning, the number kept growing. If they had weapons, it would have been an overwhelming force, but most of the people present were not fighting men but women, the elderly and children who joined as well. Isla Grace was sitting in one of the chairs that they had brought, and his children were nearby so she could manage them. Not far from her, he spotted his parents, her parents, her siblings, and Liam with his own family. The amount of faith they all had in him was quite touching. He heard footsteps coming up to him, and as he turned, he spotted Markus Keith.

As Markus extended his hand to shake Angus' hand, he asked, "Are you really sure about this plan?"

Giving a nod, Angus answered, "Yes. The bloodshed must end so we can gain our freedom."

Markus nodded as he responded to the statement Angus made, "I'm with you."

Chuckling, Angus stated, "Well, if it doesn't work out at least, we'll have several live recordings."

"True. Scouts have said that the Brits coming towards us from Glasgow have just passed through Denny. They'll be here soon."

Motioning with a nod, Angus grabbed his portable mic and announced loudly, "Everyone in place. The Brits will be here soon."

People around him began to scurry about. Angus strolled to a table and a pair of chairs that had been placed directly in the middle of M80. He took his planned seat, which was facing directly down the road in the direction that the Brits would come from. A few dozen men took their places in front of him. All around them there was a large crowd of various Scots. Men, women, children, the elderly, and even some people's pets were there. It was a unification of the Scottish people. What he was told was that his actions in Stirling, where videos of him fighting and getting injured had inspired his people to join him. It was exactly like he said when he was interviewed after they began the coup: the Scots respected strength. He knew, however, that this was only partially true, the Scots respected bravery much more. A man of his word who bled for his people was a Scot. A low rumbling noise suddenly started south of where he was sitting.

"Here they come." A voice behind him said.

Angus said nothing as he waited. The noise became louder and louder as time passed until he could finally see the caravan of British vehicles. He could also hear noise coming from the air, and when he looked around, he spotted helicopters in the air. Finally, the British vehicles were so close that Angus could see the men in the lead vehicle as it came to a stop. Angus knew that they would never just run over a bunch of people in the road. One of the two men he could see clearly reached down and then brought something to his head and was speaking into it. Likely, it was a phone of some kind. After a few moments, a group of British soldiers approached the front of the crowd.

"Hey!" One of them yelled and then continued in a loud voice, "You people need to clear out."

Angus stood so they could see them. They must have recognised him right away because they levelled their weapons at him.

"Angus Bruce, come out and surrender." The obvious leader of the group yelled.

A wicked grin spread across his face as he replied, "No, but I might be willing to if you send your general out to come and have some tea with me."

The man looked very confused by the statement before he turned away and disappeared for a moment.

Once he returned, he announced, "Major General Ackerly stated he does not trust you."

Calling out loudly, Angus retorted, "He's got a massive military advantage over our large, unarmed group, but to offer assurance, I'd like to point out to you that my wife and children are sitting right over there."

He pointed at Isla Grace before continuing, "You've got my assurance as a Scotsman that your General won't be harmed nor taken against his will."

The man nodded before leaving again.

It was another long moment before the man came back and stated, "He agreed and will be here soon with his security team."

The wait for the General was not too long before Angus spotted a man who appeared to be in his early 50's. He had a slightly bushy peppered grey moustache. He was wearing British military fatigues with the usual military gear they would wear in a battle. Angus was impressed with his aura of leadership as he confidently strolled towards the table. The Scots between Angus and the General parted to allow him to come to the table. Angus stood as the man approached the table.

The General then said, "I was not expecting this."

"Me either, but I think you and I need to have a conversation before you continue to Stirling." Angus commented.

While it was normally not his policy to shake hands with representatives from the British side, he felt that showing the General respect was wisest, so he extended his hand out. The man shook his hand.

Gesturing to the chair next to the General, Angus said, "Have a seat, please."

Angus took the lead and took a seat. The General slowly removed his helmet, revealing his neatly trimmed peppered grey hair, and handed it to a nearby member of his team before taking a seat. The expression on his face was one of curiosity. Angus waved off to his left. Someone brought a kettle with hot tea. Another brought some plates, and then a plate of scones with clotted cream and jam was set on the table.

Taking the initiative, Angus said, "Apologies for the simple set-up. It is hard to bring proper teatime to the middle of a motorway."

"The effort is appreciated." The General said before continuing, "I propose we skip the usual pleasantries, and we move right to the matter at hand."

He had always appreciated directness, something few members of the British elite would deal in.

"Yes, of course. It is time to end this war and the bloodshed between our two sides."

"So, you wish to surrender?" The General asked.

"No," Angus answered, and after a pause, he then stated, "I'm requesting you to surrender to me."

A face of humour crossed the General's face before he stated, "We've got the military advantage right now. Why would I do that?"

Reaching out to grab his chin and give his fingers a run through his beard, Angus gave a slight smile before asking, "Do you?"

The General looked briefly and responded, "You promised me no harm."

"Oh, of course, but I think you misunderstand. Of course, you have way more weapons than we do. Every Scot you see, me included, is unarmed."

Angus pointed at his empty holster. He left Annis back in the boot of his car.

Confusion crossed the General's face before he finally asked, "I don't understand what your ploy is."

"The moment your vehicles stopped, over one hundred thousand unarmed Scots surrounded your convoy. Not just fighting men, but women, children, and the elderly have completely encircled you. A question for you… Do you know where we are?"

The General once again glanced around before looking at his men.

One of his men answered the question, "Bannockburn sir."

A look of realisation crossed the man's face. It was these same fields where the Scots had won their last battle of independence in 1314.

"And you plan this to be your last fight for your independence?"

"Not quite. You see, currently we've got about one hundred thousand Scots around us, and many more are coming here from all over Scotland to surround your military force permanently."

The General asked, "And what will that accomplish?

"It gives you two choices." Angus answered.

"Which are?"

"Either you can surrender your entire force to me, which will guarantee safety for you and your men back into England once your government finally acquiesce to our demands for freedom. Which they will have no choice due to the massive size of your force and the significant loss in their total fighting power."

"Or?"

"You can become the Butcher of Bannockburn."

The implication was crystal clear. The British would have no choice but to slaughter the hundred thousand or more unarmed Scots surrounding them if they wished to continue fighting. As the man glanced around him, Angus pointed towards one of his men holding a video camera. A clue to the General that whatever happens next was going to be recorded.

Turning back to face Angus, the General stated, "You've got us both in quite a bind."

"Yes. Either you surrender, and Scotland gains its much-deserved and frequently offered freedom or…"

Someone from the crowd, a female voice, called out, "Or you'll have to gun down a bunch of unarmed women and children."

The General looked very uncomfortable. Angus suspected this was not a decision that he expected or likely ever wanted to make. It grew extremely quiet as the General sat there looking at him. Angus did not flinch and stared right into the man's eyes. They must have stared at each other for several minutes before the General gestured to a nearby man. As the man leant close, the General began whispering to him. The man nodded and ran off. The General turned back and looked sternly at Angus. After a few moments, the man who was sent off returned with something long wrapped in a heavy green cloth.

The General took the item from him and then turned back to Angus before stating, "This day I'll choose to be known as the man who surrendered rather than a butcher."

The tension was thick as Angus realised his gambit was about to pay off. He struggled to hold back a smile. The General slowly unwrapped the item and revealed it was a military sword of some kind.

The General took the sword in both hands, and as he reached across the table towards Angus, he stated, "My name is Major-General Willem Ackerly, and I offer up my sabre. I expect you to honour your word and treat me and my men as required according to the Geneva Convention."

Reaching out, while trying to control his hands from shaking, Angus took the sabre with both hands before stating firmly, "You and your men will be treated with honour, Major-General."

The General nodded grimly. Angus slowly rose from his chair, and with both of his hands firmly gripping the sabre, he raised it into the air over his head. The crowd around him cheered raucously. Pride, joy, and a sense of relief flooded through Angus. With this military force captured, the British would no longer have enough men and equipment to continue fighting. The war was over. Angus grinned madly as he turned to look at Isla Grace. Her face was still mostly stoic, but he could see that tiny little grin form once they caught eyes. Suddenly, he could hear a light chanting from the Scots around him.

"Angus." Was called out first.

Others responded, "The Bruce."

The chant became louder and louder while growing in strength... Angus, the Bruce. Over and over they chanted.

# Epilogue

25 January 2025

Angus fidgeted with his light blue tie as he sat looking at himself in the mirror. He still had no idea how he got himself in this mess. His original plan to resign his post as President was completely ruined after overwhelming demand by the Scottish people that forced him to accept the first formal term as the official President of Scotland. Today was the inauguration, and he sat in a small nearby dressing room finishing his final preparations for the swearing-in ceremony. The ceremony was going to take place just outside the Parliament building. Due to the time he and his fellow Scottish Republicans spent pre-writing their goals for a new constitution, the framework was easy to assemble. The little details took a bit longer, but they eventually came to an agreement on a constitution very similar to the American one. The Scottish one had many more protections to ensure its stability and defense of the Scottish people, as they had wanted. Along with protections to prevent corruption of that Constitution. And this constitution was based on the principles of Christianity, with Christianity acknowledged as the only formal religion of the state. As he was lost in his thoughts, thinking about how quickly the Brits folded once the surrender in Bannockburn happened, Isla Grace approached to wrap her arms around his shoulders.

"You look magnificent, Mr. President." She stated in her usual flat tone.

"As do you, my First Lady." He told her.

"I'm happy you decided to trim that scruffy beard down to a respectable length."

Angus laughed heartily before stating, "Well, I figured a world leader needed to represent his country with dignity in appearance."

She just nodded. There was a knock on the door.

"Yes?" He asked.

Michael's head appeared as he entered before stating, "It's time, Mr. President.

# About the Author

Born in Muskegon, MI and raised in Concord, CA, S.W. Gunn used his early experience as a role-playing geek to expand upon his imagination. Unable to purchase the proper Dungeon and Dragons manuals at a young age, he developed his own roleplaying paper and pen game for himself and his friends to play. While living in Hawaii, he completed his bachelor's in art degree in History at Chaminade University of Honolulu. He is married to his lovely wife Parneeta, and they have three wonderful children, Shawn (2nd), Spencer, and Astir. They live in Phoenix, AZ.

# Thank you

I would like to take time to thank God for my time here on Earth and gifting humans this wonderful talent to write and read all sorts of fictional works. I would like to thank my beautiful wife Parneeta for being my anchor to help me push in writing. To my three kids, Shawn II, Spencer, and Astir. I love each of you for your unique personalities. To my family and friends for being as such, even if you did not want to be. Lastly, I would like to thank my readers like you. Without you, this is all pointless. This work is very risky in that many might find it offensive, but I felt as though it was important to release this work as a warning of what could be if leaders of the world don't change what they're doing.

# Other works by this Author:

The Heima Series:
Heima: The Ninth Kostir
Heima: Challenge to the Crown
Heima: Neinn

The Legenda Series:
Smuggler's Luck
Gift of Flight

Paladin Series:
The Thrill of Battle

Acciaccato
The Almighty Paw
The Priestess Princess
Angels of Evernal
Medusa
First Contact
Orange
Skybound

Non-fiction Works:
Historical Journey through a Master's Degree
American Federalism: A Changing Political Philosophy
100 Reasons to Keep Undocumented Migrants in the USA

www.ingramcontent.com/pod-product-compliance
Lightning Source LLC
LaVergne TN
LVHW010603100826
845148LV00014B/2823

* 9 7 9 8 9 8 8 2 5 1 1 1 8 *